TRADITIONAL GREEK HUSBANDS

Notorious Greek tycoons seek brides!

Childhood friends Neo and Zephyr worked
themselves up from the slums of Athens
and made their fortunes on Wall Street!

They fought hard for their freedom
and their fortunes. Now, like brothers,
they rely only on one another.

Together they hold on to their Greek traditions…
and the time has come for them
to claim their brides!

This month Neo's story:
The Shy Bride

Next month meet Zephyr in…
The Greek's Pregnant Lover

All about the author...
Lucy Monroe

Award-winning and bestselling author
LUCY MONROE sold her first book in September
of 2002 to the Harlequin® Presents line. That book
represented a dream that had been burning in her
heart for years...the dream to share her stories with
readers who love romance as much as she does.
Since then she has sold more than thirty books to
three publishers and hit national bestsellers lists
in the U.S. and England. But what has touched her
most deeply, since selling that first book, are the
reader letters she receives. Her most important
goal with every book is to touch a reader's heart
and when she hears she's done that, it makes every
night spent writing into the wee hours of morning
worth it.

She started reading Harlequin Presents very young
and discovered a heroic type of man between the
covers of those books—an honorable man, capable
of faithfulness and sacrifice for the people he
loves. Now married to what she terms her "alpha
male at the end of a book," Lucy believes there is
a lot more reality to the fantasy stories she writes
than most people give credit for. She believes in
happy endings that are really marvelous beginnings
and that's why she writes them. She hopes her
books help readers to believe a little too...just like
romance did for her so many years ago.

She really does love to hear from readers and
responds to every e-mail. You can reach her by
e-mailing lucymonroe@lucymonroe.com.

Lucy Monroe

THE SHY BRIDE

TRADITIONAL
GREEK HUSBANDS

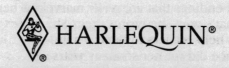

HARLEQUIN®

TORONTO • NEW YORK • LONDON
AMSTERDAM • PARIS • SYDNEY • HAMBURG
STOCKHOLM • ATHENS • TOKYO • MILAN • MADRID
PRAGUE • WARSAW • BUDAPEST • AUCKLAND

Recycling programs
for this product may
not exist in your area.

ISBN-13: 978-0-373-12929-4

THE SHY BRIDE

First North American Publication 2010.

Copyright © 2010 by Lucy Monroe.

Printed in U.S.A.

THE SHY BRIDE

For Robin Hart,
a wonderful friend and hypnotherapist
who has helped me tremendously
through a very difficult time. Thank you!

PROLOGUE

THE port of Seattle didn't look so different from some of the hundreds of other ports Neo Stamos had been in since joining the crew of the cargo ship *Hera* at the age of fourteen. And yet it was unique from all the others because this is where his life changed. This is where he would walk off the *Hera* and never walk back onto it.

He and his friend Zephyr Nikos had had to lie about their ages to join the *Hera*'s crew six years ago, but that had been a small price to pay in order to leave behind the life they'd known in Greece. Neo and Zephyr had been Athens street thugs that found a common desire—that of making something more of their lives than rising to the top ranks in their gang.

And they were going to do it, twenty-year-old Neo vowed as the sun broke the eastern horizon.

"You ready for the next step?" Zephyr asked in English.

Neo nodded, his gaze set on the port growing closer by the minute. "No more living in the streets."

"We haven't lived in the streets for six years."

"True. Though some would not consider our bunks here on the *Hera* much of an improvement."

"They are."

Neo agreed, though he didn't say so. Zephyr knew and shared his feelings. Anything was better than scavenging to eke out an existence that still required living by someone else's rules. "But what is to come will be even better."

"Yes. It may have taken six years, but we have the money to take the next step in our new lives."

Six years of a hell of a lot of hard work and sacrifice. They had saved every drachma possible of their earnings. For two men who had grown up in an orphanage and then the streets when they ran away, that had been a lot. They knew how to come by clothes, books and other necessities through interesting if not necessarily legal methods. Not unless one considered underage gambling a stumbling block to legality.

When they were not working, or gambling to augment their meager salaries, they had been reading everything they could get their hands on about business and real estate development. Each had become an expert in a different aspect of the field, combining their superior brainpower rather than duplicating effort.

They now had a detailed plan to increase their assets through initially flipping houses and, eventually, full-scale, high-end real estate developments.

"Next it will be business tycoons Zephyr Nikos and Neo Stamos," Zephyr said with conviction.

A slow, extremely rare smile curved Neo's lips. "Before we are thirty."

"Before we are thirty." Zephyr's voice was filled with the same determination Neo felt deep in his gut.

They would succeed.

Failure was not an option.

CHAPTER ONE

"THIS is a joke, right?" Neo Stamos stared at the fancy certificate with the logo of a local charity fund-raiser on it.

His oldest and only real friend, not to mention business partner, Zephyr Nikos had to be kidding. *He had to be*. No way could the certificate be meant for Neo. He had to have gotten it for someone else and was using it to pull Neo's chain before giving it to them.

"No joke. Happy thirty-fifth birthday, *filos mou*." Unlike in the early years of their friendship when they had tried to speak only English to one another to improve their grasp of the language, they now spoke in Greek so they would not forget their native tongue.

"A *friend* would know better than to give me such a gift."

"On the contrary, only a friend would know how appropriate, how needed this little present is."

"Piano lessons?" A year's worth. No damn way. "I don't think so."

Zephyr leaned against the edge of Neo's handcrafted

mahogany desk that had cost more than he had earned his first year of gainful employment. "Oh, I do think so. You lost the bet."

Neo glared, knowing anything he said in repudiation would sound like whining rather than the rational argument it would be. As they had so often reminded each other over the years, a bet was a bet. And he should have known better than to make one with his shark of a friend.

Zephyr's gaze reflected his knowledge of Neo's quandary. "Think of it as a prescription."

"Prescription for what? A way to waste an hour a week? I don't have thirty minutes to waste, much less a full hour." Neo shook his head. There was a reason all of his designer suits were purchased and tailored by an exclusive men's dressing service, and it wasn't because he liked to shout his billionaire status to the world.

It was because Neo Stamos did not have time to shop for himself.

"Unless you know about something I do not…" Like the cancellation of one of their property development projects going on worldwide. "There is no place in my schedule for piano lessons."

Bet or no bet.

"There is definitely something going on you don't know about, Neo. It's called life and it's going on all around you, but you're so busy with our company, it's passing you by."

"Stamos and Nikos Enterprises *is* my life."

Zephyr gave Neo a look of pity, as if the other man hadn't worked just as hard to leave their shared history behind. "The company was supposed to be our way to a new life, not the only thing you lived for. Don't you remember, Neo? We were going to be tycoons by thirty."

"And we made it." They'd made their first million within three years of stepping onto American soil. They'd been multimillionaires a few years later, and held assets in excess of a billion dollars by the time Neo was thirty. Now he and Zephyr were the primary shareholders in a multibillion-dollar company. Stamos & Nikos Enterprises didn't simply bear his name; it consumed his waking and sleeping hours.

And he was just fine with that.

"You wanted to buy a big house, start a family, remember?" Zephyr asked in chiding tone.

"Things change." Some dreams were mere childhood fancy and needed to be left behind. "I like my penthouse."

Zephyr rolled his eyes. "That's not the point, Neo."

"What is the point? *You think I need piano lessons*?"

"As a matter of fact, yes. Even if your GP had not issued you a warning at your latest physical, I would know something has to give in your life. Considering the stress you live under, it doesn't take a doctor to know you are a heart attack waiting to happen."

"I work out six days a week. My meals are planned by a top nutritionist. My housekeeper prepares them to exact specifications and I eat on a schedule more regular than you keep. My body is in top physical condition."

"You sleep less than six hours a night and you do nothing that works as a pressure valve for the stress in your life."

"What do you consider my workouts?"

"Another outlet for your highly competitive nature. You are always pushing yourself to do more."

Zephyr should know. He was right there competing with Neo. So, the other man had started leaving the office closer to six than eight a couple of years ago. And maybe he'd taken up a hobby unrelated to real estate development or investments, but that didn't mean his life was better than Neo's. It was just a little different.

"There is nothing wrong with striving to achieve."

"That is true." Zephyr frowned. "When you have some measure of balance to your life. You, my friend, do not have a life."

"I have a life."

"You have more drive than any man I have ever met, but you do not balance it with the things that give life meaning."

As if Zephyr had any room to talk.

"You think piano lessons will give my life meaning?" Maybe Zephyr was the one who needed a break. He was losing his grip on reality.

"No. I think they will give you a place to be Neo Stamos for one hour a week, not the Greek tycoon who could buy and sell most companies many times over, not to mention people."

"I do not buy and sell people."

"No, we buy property, develop it and sell it. And we are damn good at making a profit at it. Your insistence on diversifying our investments early on paid off, too, but when will it be enough?"

"I am satisfied with my life."

"But you are never satisfied with your success."

"And you are any different?"

Zephyr shrugged, his own tailored Italian suit jacket moving over his shoulders flawlessly. "We are talking about you." He crossed his arms and stared Neo down. "When was the last time you made love to a woman, Neo?"

"We're past the age of scoring and sharing, Zee."

Zephyr cracked a smile. "I don't want to hear about your

conquests. And even if I did, you couldn't tell me about this one because you've never done it."

"What the hell? I have sex as often as I want it."

"Sex, yes. But you have never made love."

"What difference does it make?"

"You are afraid of intimacy."

"How the blue bloody hell did we get from piano lessons to psychobabble? And when did you start spouting that garbage at all?"

Zephyr had the nerve to look offended. "I am simply pointing out that your life is too narrow in its scope. You need to broaden your horizons."

"Now you sound like a travel commercial." And a damn hypocritical one at that.

"I sound like a friend who doesn't want you to die from a stress-related illness before your fortieth birthday, Neo."

"Where is all this coming from?"

"Your GP didn't just warn you at your physical? Gregor took me aside last month during our golf game and warned me that you are going to work yourself into an early grave."

"I'll have his license."

"No, you won't. He's our friend."

"He's your friend. He's my doctor."

"That's what I'm talking about, Neo. You've got no balance in your life. It's all business with you."

"What about you? If relationships are so necessary to a well-rounded life, why aren't you in one?"

"I date, Neo. And before you claim you do, too, let us both acknowledge that taking a woman out for the express purpose of having sex with her, and no intention of seeing her again, is not a date. That is a hookup."

"What century are you living in?"

"Believe me, I'm living in this one. And so are you, my friend. So, stop being an ass and accept my gift."

"Just like that?"

"Would you rather welch on our bet?"

There was no answer for that question Neo wanted to give. "I don't want to take piano lessons."

"You used to."

"What used to? When?"

"When we were boys together on the streets of Athens."

"I had many dreams as a boy that I learned to let go of." Accumulating the kind of wealth currently at his disposal required constant, intense sacrifice and he'd gladly made each and every one.

In the process, he'd made something of himself. Something completely different from the deadbeat father who had taken off before Neo was two and the mother who preferred booze to babysitting.

"Says the man who worked his way off the Athens streets and onto Wall Street."

"I live in Seattle."

Zephyr shrugged. "The stock market is on Wall Street and we lay claim to a significant chunk of it."

Neo could feel himself giving in, if for no other reason than not to disappoint the only person in the world he cared enough about to compromise for. "I will try it for two weeks."

"Six months."

"One month."

"Five."

"Two and that is my final offer."

"I bought a full year's worth, you'll note."

"And if I find benefit, I will use the lot." Though he had absolutely no doubts about that happening.

"Done."

Cassandra Baker smoothed the skirt of her Liz Claiborne A-line dress in navy blue and white oversized checks for the second time in less than a minute. Just because she lived like a hermit in a cave sometimes, that didn't mean she had to dress like one. Or so she told herself when ordering her new spring wardrobe online from her favorite department store.

Wearing stylish clothing, even if said outfits were rarely seen anywhere but her own home, was one of the small things she did to try to make herself feel normal.

It didn't always work. But she tried.

She was supposed to be playing the piano. It relaxed her. Or so everyone insisted, and she even sometimes believed it. Only her slim fingers were motionless on the keyboard of her Fazioli grand piano.

Neo Stamos was due for his lessons in less than five minutes.

When she had offered the year's worth of piano lessons to the charity fund-raising auction, as she did every year, she assumed she would get another student in her craft. A rising star seeking to work with an acknowledged if reclusive master pianist and New Age composer.

Cass unclipped, smoothed and then reclipped her long brown hair at the nape of her neck. Her hands dropped naturally back to the keyboard, but her fingers did not press down and no sound emitted from the beautiful instrument. She had been sure that just like in years past, the auction winner would be someone who shared her love of music. Hadn't doubted that her next student might not share Cass's adoration for the piano.

She'd had no reason to even speculate that a complete musical novice—a tycoon billionaire, no less—would be her student for the next year. It was worse than unbelievable; it was a personal nightmare for a woman who found it difficult enough to open her door to strangers.

Trying to circumvent that feeling, she'd spent an inordinate amount of time reading articles about him and studying publicity photos as well as the few candid shots of him she'd discovered on the Internet. None of that had helped.

If anything, her worry at the prospect of meeting him had increased. His publicity photos showed a man who looked like he rarely, if ever, listened to any sort of music at all. Why in the world would a man like that want to take piano lessons?

Apparently, he did, though. Because when the bids were well into the tens of thousands, Zephyr Nikos swooped in with an offer of *one hundred thousand dollars*. It boggled her mind—one hundred thousand dollars for one hour a week of Cass's time. Even though the lessons lasted a year, the bid had been beyond extravagant.

The organizer of the fund-raiser had been ecstatic, keeping Cass on the phone long past her usual chat time with people she barely knew. The older woman had waxed poetic about how wonderful it was Mr. Nikos had bought the lessons for his lifelong friend and business partner, Neo Stamos.

And indeed it had been Mr. Stamos's very efficient, and rather aloof, personal assistant who had called Cass to schedule the lesson. Cass had been tolerant because her own practice schedule was flexible and she had almost no social life to speak of.

Regardless, the 10:00 a.m. Tuesday morning classes were hardly a challenge to her schedule. Though Mr. Stamos's PA made it sound like he would be sacrificing something akin to his firstborn child to be there.

Having no idea why a fabulously wealthy, far too good-looking, clearly driven and supremely busy businessman would want the lessons, Cass was even more nervous than usual at the thought of meeting a new student for the first time. In fact, Cass hadn't felt this level of anxiety since the last time she had performed publicly.

She'd been telling herself all morning, she was being ridiculous. It hadn't helped.

The doorbell rang, startling her into immobility, even though she'd been expecting it. Her heart beat a rapid tattoo in her chest, her lungs panting little, short breaths. She turned on the bench, but did not stand to her rather average height of five feet six inches.

She needed to. She needed to answer the door. To meet her new student.

The bell pealed a second time, the impatient summons thankfully breaking her paralysis. She jumped to her feet and hurried to answer it even as worried questions that had been plaguing her since discovering the identity of her new student once again raced through her mind.

Would Neo Stamos himself be standing there, or his PA? Or maybe a bodyguard, or chauffeur? Did billionaires talk to their piano teachers, or keep underlings around to do that for them? Would she be expected to teach with others in the room? If he had them, where would his bodyguards and chauffeur wait during the lesson? Or his PA?

The thought of several people she did not know converging on her home made Cass feel like hyperventilating. She was proud of herself for continuing down the narrow hall to the front door of her modest house.

Maybe he was alone. If he'd driven himself, that opened another host of worries. Would he feel comfortable parking his expensive car in her all too normal neighborhood in west Seattle? Should she offer the use of her empty garage?

The bell rang a third time just as she swung the door open. Mr. Stamos, who looked even more imposing than he did in his publicity photos, did not appear in the least embarrassed to be caught impatiently ringing it again.

"Miss Cassandra Baker?" Green eyes, the rich color of summer leaves, set in a face almost overwhelmingly attractive in person, stared at her expectantly.

She tilted her head back to meet the dark-haired tycoon's gaze. "Yes." Then she forced herself to make the offer she would have to any other student. "You may call me Cass."

"You look like a Cassandra, not a Cass." His voice was deep, thrumming through her like a perfectly struck chord.

"Cass is what my protégés call me." Although referring to this man as a protégé struck her as decidedly off.

As if he found the term as incongruous as she, his perfectly formed lips quirked at one side. Though it could not be called a true smile by any stretch. "I will call you Cassandra."

She stared at him, uncertain how to take his arrogance. He didn't appear to mean anything by it. His expression said he believed it was simply his prerogative to call her by the name he felt suited her, rather than the one she used with the few people she had regular, ongoing communications.

"I believe it will be easier to start the lesson if you let me inside." His voice was tinged with impatience, but he did not frown.

Nevertheless, he made her feel gauche and lacking in manners. "Of course, I...did you want to park your car in the garage?"

He didn't even bother to glance over his Armani-clad shoulder at the sleek Mercedes resting in her driveway before shaking his head, a single economical movement to each side. "That won't be necessary."

"Okay, then. Let's go inside." She turned and led the way to the piano room.

It had been the back parlor when the house was first built in the late nineteenth century. Now it served beautifully to house her Fazioli and practically nothing else. There was a single oversized Queen Anne-style armchair for the use of her rare guests, with a tiny round side table, but no other furniture cluttered the room.

She indicated the wide, smooth piano bench, the same exact finish as the Fazioli. "Have a seat."

He did as she suggested, looking much more relaxed in front of the piano than *she* would have in his high-rise office.

A few inches over six feet, he was tall for the bench, and yet he did not look awkward there.

His body did not have the lithe grace or, conversely, the extra weight around the middle of most male pianists she knew, but was well-honed and very muscular. His hands were strong, with long but squared fingers bearing the wrong calluses for a pianist or a billionaire, if she were to guess it. His suit was more appropriate for a boardroom than her music room, and yet he did not look ill at ease in the least.

Perhaps the sable-haired, superrich Adonis simply did not have the awkward gene like normal people.

"Can I get you anything to drink before we begin?"

"We have already spent several minutes of the hour

allotted for this lesson, perhaps you would find it more efficient to dispense with the pleasantries."

"I do not mind going a few minutes over so you get your full lesson," she said, feeling guilty but equally certain she had nothing to be guilty for.

"I do."

"I see." Strangely enough, his abrupt manner was easing some of her anxiety.

Or was that simply because he had not brought the entourage she had feared? Regardless, she was finding the new situation much less excruciating than she had anticipated. Her gratitude over that fact made her want to be accommodating.

So, no pleasantries then. "Perhaps next week, you should forego ringing the bell and simply come inside," she offered.

His far too compelling green gaze narrowed. "You do not lock your door?" He didn't wait for her to answer before informing her, "I flipped the dead bolt when I closed it."

No doubt a man in his position would find it second nature to double-lock a door behind him. "I'm surprised you don't have bodyguards that have vetted the house."

Really, really surprised.

"I do have security but I do not live a sitcom cop show. You were thoroughly vetted before my PA called to schedule the lessons." He gave her slight frame a cursory perusal. "And you hardly pose a personal threat to me."

"I see." Vague discomfort at the fact she had been investigated settled in her stomach.

"It was not personal."

"Just necessary." As had been her research of him on the Internet.

Although, she suspected the background check done on

her had been far more invasive. No doubt, he knew her history. He was aware of what her manager termed her *idiosyncrasies*. And yet, he did not treat her like a freak.

"Exactly." He looked pointedly at his watch. Not a Rolex.

She found that interesting, but didn't comment on it. He'd made it very clear he was there for a piano lesson, not conversation. Again, his brusque approach was unexpectedly comforting.

The remainder of the hour went by surprisingly quickly.

Despite an entirely different sort of tension the tycoon elicited in Cass.

Neo did not understand the sense of anticipation he felt Tuesday morning when he woke and realized his second piano lesson would be today.

Cassandra Baker was exactly as the background check on her had implied she would be. Rather quiet, clearly uncomfortable with strangers and yet something about her charmed him. There were far more important events on his agenda, but his second meeting with the world-renowned pianist who refused to perform publicly was the first one that came to his mind.

Neo could not believe how much he had enjoyed his time with Cassandra Baker.

She was no beauty with her mousy brown hair, light freckles and slight build, and she was not the usual type of woman he found entertaining. More the average "girl next door" and he would readily admit he met few of those in his current lifestyle. And he would not have met her without Zephyr's intervention.

Zee was also the person to introduce Neo to Cassandra's music. His partner had given him her CDs for his birthday and Christmas. Neo started out listening to them when working out on the weight machines, then he would play them sometimes when he was working on the computer. Eventually, it got to where he had Cassandra's music playing pretty much anytime he was home.

He didn't concentrate on who the artist was, just played the music off his MP3 player. He hadn't even recognized her name on the gift certificate for his lessons. Not until the preliminary background report on her came in. That was the first time he realized she composed most of the music he found so pleasing as well.

And he wasn't the only one—Cassandra Baker was a top-selling New Age artist. He would not have expected such a popular musician to be so unassuming. Yet she made no effort to allude to her undeniable talent or fame, further cementing her girl-next-door qualities.

Although undeniably average, her amber eyes were somewhat stunning though, their open and honest expression captivated him and the color was undeniably unique in a way the colored contacts so popular among the artificial beauties he "hooked up" with—Zephyr even had Neo thinking in those terms now—could never be.

Although she wasn't a beauty, Cassandra was intriguing and vulnerable. There was just something about the reclusive pianist he liked. Perhaps it was simply knowing that she made the music that he enjoyed so much.

Whatever the reason, he looked forward to getting to know her better. And when was the last time he had allowed himself the luxury of something so personal not related to sex?

When he arrived at her house, four hours later, he discovered her door on the latch just as she had said it would be. The evidence of her lax security bothered him, but even more worrisome was the sound of music floating down the hall. She couldn't possibly know that he had come inside.

He was frowning when he entered the room she had led him to the week before.

She looked up from the piano, her fingers going still above the keys. "Good morning, Neo."

"Your door was unlocked."

"I told you it would be."

"That is not safe."

"I thought you would appreciate the expediency of getting right to your lesson."

Without waiting for her to offer, he took a seat beside her on the piano bench. "You could not hear me arrive."

"I did not need to. You knew where to come."

"That is not the point."

"Isn't it?" She looked at him as if she truly did not understand his problem.

"No."

"All right. Shall we start where we left off last week?"

Neo was not accustomed to being dismissed, in any form. Yet, rather than get angry, he couldn't help admiring the fact the shy woman had so adroitly shifted focus to the reason he was there.

Which was *not* to lecture her about her habit of leaving the door on the latch, he reminded himself.

He enjoyed Cassandra's soft voice as she guided him through the day's lesson. Her passion for her craft was apparent in every word she spoke and the very way she touched the piano they played. A man would give a great deal to be touched by a lover with such intense dedication.

And his thinking no doubt explained the inexplicable arousal he experienced during something as innocent as piano lessons.

CHAPTER TWO

CASSANDRA covered her mouth as she yawned for the third time in ten minutes. She hadn't slept well the night before each one of Neo's lessons since the first one five weeks ago. In the beginning, it had been her usual anxiety from inviting someone new into her life, even if it was only for an hour a week.

But anxiety had slowly and strangely morphed into anticipation. And she didn't know why. It wasn't as if Neo went out of his way to be friendly. He could not be mistaken for anything but a driven businessman, but she found herself truly enjoying his company. He took his lessons seriously, though it was obvious he did not practice between times.

His manner could best be described as abrupt, often arrogant. Strangely enough, she discovered a peace in his presence she did not experience with anyone else. She tried to analyze it, but couldn't come up with a reason for finding his company so pleasurable.

He'd become less adamant about what she had at first considered the "no pleasantries" rule. He did not complain when she went off on a tangent, discussing her favorite thing—music. He even asked intelligent questions that exhibited both a surprising interest and understanding.

So, she didn't feel too worried bringing up something that had been nagging at her since first meeting him. "You drive a Mercedes."

"Yes." It was clearly an invitation to continue as he played the chords she had just shown him.

"Well, you aren't wearing a Rolex, but you *are* wearing a custom-tailored designer suit."

"You are observant," he said with that little twitch of his lips she'd come to crave in some strange way.

"I suppose."

"But I do not see the point." He gave her a questioning look as his hands stilled on the keys.

"I would have expected you to drive a Ferrari, or something."

"Ah, I see." He smiled.

Really smiled.

And everything inside Cass flipped.

Like *kapow* to her midsection. This was not good. She'd never had a reaction like this to a student, or to anyone for that matter. But, seriously? His smile should come with a warning label. Something like: One glimpse is fatal!

"Few people are open enough to admit when they notice what they consider the inconsistencies of the wealthy man."

"I don't do subterfuge well." She hated social situations to begin with, adding deception to the mix only complicated things to the point of horror for her.

The smile turned into a full-out grin. "That is good to know."

"Is it?" If she'd thought she'd been in danger before, now was absolute Armageddon.

"Yes. Back to your question. It was a question, was it not?" He spoke with a slight Greek accent she found entirely too delicious.

She needed to get out more. Yeah. Right. That was so going to happen. She bit back a sigh. Not. Not going to happen and no matter how lovely she found his accent, it hardly mattered, did it?

It had surprised her at first, but then she'd decided it was to be expected. The information she had found about him online indicated he had left Greece as a young man. However, one article she read said that he spoke Greek with his business partner and had done several property developments in his country of origin over the years.

"Probably a nosy question, but yes," she finally answered.

"I do not mind your kind of nosy. The paparazzi demanding to know the name and measurements for my latest girlfriend is another thing entirely."

Heat suffused her neck and cheeks. "Yes, well, I can guarantee you I won't be asking those sorts of questions."

"No, your curiosity is much more innocent." Which seemed to please him. Odd.

She certainly didn't find her own innocence all that pleasing.

"To answer it, a man does not amass great wealth in a single lifetime by spending his money frivolously. My clothing is necessary to present a certain façade for our investors and buyers. My watch is rated as technically accurate and as sound as a Rolex, but only cost a few hundred rather than several thousand. My car is expensive enough to impress, but not ridiculously so for something that amounts to nothing more than a piece of equipment to get me from Point A to Point B."

"Unlike many men, your car is not one of your toys."

"I stopped playing with toys years before I left the orphanage I never called home."

She'd read that he had lived in an orphanage before leaving Athens. For all that his publicity people allowed the world to know, there was a cloak of mystery around his growing-up years.

Which was something she could understand. While her official biography for publicity purposes revealed that both her parents were dead, it said nothing about her mother's protracted illness. Nor did it mention years spent in a house shrouded in silence and steeped in fear of losing the person both she and her father had loved above all others.

Her father's death as the result of an unexpected, massive heart attack had made the headlines at the time. Mostly because it had heralded the end of rising star Cassandra Baker's public performances. Her withdrawal into seclusion had garnered more press than a good, if sometimes misguided, man's death.

"Some men try to make up for losing their childhood by having a second one."

"I am too busy."

"Yes, you are."

"You did not have a childhood, either." He said it so matter-of-factly.

Like it didn't really matter. And hadn't she decided a long time ago, that it didn't? The past could not be changed.

"Why piano lessons?" she asked Neo, wanting to talk about anything but her dismal formative years.

"I lost a bet."

"To your business partner?" That made more sense than anything she had been able to come up with on her own.

His brows quirked at her description of Zephyr Nikos. "Yes."

"If what you say is true, I wonder how he is rated as being as wealthy as you?"

"Meaning?"

"He spent one hundred thousand dollars on piano lessons you don't want. That sounds very frivolous to me."

"I do want the lessons." Neo looked as if he'd shocked himself with the assertion.

"That's surprising."

"When I was a youth, I wanted to learn piano. There was no chance then. Now, my time is in even shorter supply than money was to my younger self."

"And yet you make the time for these lessons." She could not imagine her own childhood without her piano to take away some of the pain.

"Zephyr does not consider the investment frivolous. He believes I need something besides work to occupy my time."

"For at least one hour a week." Though sixty out of the ten thousand and eighty minutes found in a week didn't sound like much of a relaxing distraction to Cass.

"Precisely."

"Still, he could have gotten you lessons with someone who teaches for a living at a much reduced rate."

"Zephyr and I believe in hiring the best people for the job. You are a master pianist."

"So I have been told." Many, many times since she was discovered as a child musical prodigy at the age of three.

"It is your turn to answer a question for me."

"If you like." And if she could. She braced herself for the question most people asked, and the one for which she did not have an answer anyone had found satisfying thus far.

"Why do you give lessons to the charity auction every year when you are a career composer and pianist, not actually a teacher?"

For a moment, she was so stunned he had not asked what everyone else did—why she had stopped performing publicly—that she was stumped for an answer. Finally, her brain caught up with his curiosity and she said, "Many up-and-coming pianists want to study with me. This is the one chance they have to do so."

"Why present the opportunity at all?"

"Because as much as I prefer a quiet life, one without any new people in it at all can get lonely. And I don't want to be that person. The woman who lives her life as a hermit." Even though in many ways that was exactly what she did.

"Were you disappointed to discover your lessons had been bought by a novice?"

"No, more nervous. Terrified really." She gave him a self-deprecating smile. "I was so dismayed, I begged my manager to get me out of it."

"He did not approach Zephyr, or myself to cancel the lessons."

"No."

Neo's eyes narrowed, but she wasn't sure what was making him look less than pleased. "Why were you so frightened? Even with your condition, you had done this before."

"Not for a successful billionaire."

"I am just like any other man."

It was her turn to frown, unhappy with his false assertion. "For a man who appreciates a lack of deception in others, that lie slid off your tongue rather easily. No way do you believe you are like every other man."

That almost smile touched his features again. "You are more observant than even I gave you credit for being."

"You aren't self-delusional and you aren't like any other man, therefore you could not believe it."

He shrugged. "Few men have the single-minded determination to achieve what Zephyr and I have done."

"And now Zephyr is worried you're too single-minded?"

"I made the mistake of sharing some concerns my doctor voiced on my last physical. Gregor, who is Zephyr's friend as well as my doctor, reiterated those concerns to him."

"The concerns shocked you, didn't they?" she asked, certain she knew the answer and a little surprised at herself for being willing to banter like this.

"How do you know that?"

"You strike me as a man who keeps himself in optimum physical condition as part of maintaining your position at the zenith of personal success. It would astound you that there was some element you had not accounted for."

"I thought you were a pianist, not a psychiatrist."

This, at least, she could explain. "It is easier to watch other people than to interact with them. It naturally follows that someone with my curiosity would try to figure out what makes them tick."

"You are uncannily accurate."

"Thank you for admitting it. I like honesty, too."

"That is something important we have in common."

She shifted beside him on the piano bench, trying to ignore the instant and growing reaction she'd had to his nearness since the first lesson.

"Yes. The other thing is that we both want you to learn piano. Let's get back to it."

Cass had no frame of reference for her response to Neo.

Which was probably why, at twenty-nine she had absolutely no experience in the bedroom. She'd had no time for dating when she was doing concert tours and she'd been doing them since childhood. After stopping public performance, she did not put herself in situations she might meet potential dates. All of which left her in the unenviable situation of being twenty-nine years old and never having been kissed with romantic intent.

And certainly she had never—not once before meeting Neo Stamos—felt this constriction deep in her belly. She'd read about arousal, but never experienced it. Which she knew made her a freak in the eyes of most of the world. But she wasn't just a virgin, she was wholly innocent and unsure how or if she ever wanted to risk changing that state.

When her nipples tightened into almost painful points, she had to bite her lip to keep a gasp from slipping past her lips. And this happened each and every time she sat beside Neo on the piano bench. Sometimes, even without him being there. The memory of their one hour together a week was enough to bring forth her first taste of physical passion.

Alien excitement thrummed through her now, making her thighs quiver and her heart rate increase beyond what even anxiety at meeting a new person produced.

This would never do. She had to get hold of her reactions before she made an absolute fool of herself, but so far telling herself that truth did nothing to diminish this… this…this *ardor* she felt for her student.

She tried to do what she had always done when life got too uncomfortable—concentrate on her music. It didn't always work. Nevertheless, fitting her fingers over the keys, she forced herself to show Neo the newest pattern she wanted him to learn.

"The sound of you playing on this instrument is phenomenal." Neo's deep, approving tones exacerbated each one of the reactions sparking through her.

Cass suppressed a telling shiver. "You should hear it really played."

"One day, perhaps I will."

"Perhaps." Though an invitation to sit in the only chair in the room and listen to her play was one she offered so rarely, even her pushy manager had stopped asking her to make exceptions. "Now you try it."

He stumbled at first, until she laid her fingers over his and led him through it. Which was disastrous for her equilibrium, but pretty efficient in terms of teaching him finger position. By the time his watch alarm went off, he was doing a passable job and she was a quivering mass of nerves hiding beneath her master pianist exterior.

Not so very different from the days when she performed live.

"There are exercises you can do to make your fingers more limber," she told him without looking up. "I suppose suggesting you practice between lessons would be a waste of my breath."

He shrugged. "I am enjoying myself more than I expected to."

"I'm glad." She smiled. "Music is a balm for your soul."

"It can be."

They shared a moment of silent agreement.

He got up from the bench and took a quick glance at his watch with one efficient move of his wrist. "I make no promises about how much practicing I will do, but I will have a piano delivered to my penthouse. My personal assistant will call you for a recommendation."

Neo's personal assistant called, but it wasn't to ask for a purchasing recommendation. It was to cancel Neo's next lesson. He would be out of Seattle the following week.

"Please do not mention this to anyone. Mr. Stamos's whereabouts could cause speculation that might adversely affect his current business negotiations." The woman's tone made it clear that if it had been left up to her, she would have cancelled the meeting without giving an explanation.

Apparently, Neo had felt otherwise. That knowledge made Cass smile, though she promised to be circumspect in perfectly somber tones.

Unfortunately for her, the fact that Neo was out of the city had not made it to the attention of the media, but his weekly visits to her home had.

She woke up Tuesday morning to the sound of car doors slamming and people talking in strident tones outside her home. She rushed to the bedroom that overlooked the street and peeked out through the privacy curtain.

Three media vans and a couple of cars were parked in front of her home. Someone rang the doorbell even as her eyes took in the spectacle before her.

The doorbell continued to ring as she rushed back to her

bedroom to dress. She would just ignore them. She didn't have to answer. She wasn't a public person any longer. The media had no call on her time or her person.

Nevertheless, she skipped her morning shower and pulled her clothes on with haste. Someone banged on the French doors to her bedroom and Cass screamed. Her brain told her it was nothing more than an enterprising reporter who had climbed up to the deck off her bedroom, but familiar panic threatened to immobilize her.

She grabbed the phone off her nightstand and dialed her manager. When she told Bob in short staccato bursts what was going on, he told her to calm down. That this kind of media attention was good for CD sales.

Cass didn't bother to argue. She was trying too hard not to heave from the stress. She hung up and dialed Neo's office, each insistent pound on the glass doors leading to her bedroom making her body flinch.

Her call went to voice mail and she couldn't remember what she said in the message, just that she left one.

She went into the bathroom, shut the door, locked it and prayed for the media to leave.

She was still there, curled up in a ball between the old-fashioned clawfoot tub and the wall, when someone knocked on the bathroom door itself. "Cassandra! Are you in there? Open the door, *pethi mou*. It is Neo."

Neo was out of the city. His personal assistant had said so. She shook her head at the door, another layer of perspiration coming over her already clammy skin.

The knob rattled. "Cassandra, open the door."

The voice sounded like Neo, but she could not accept that he was there. She hated being like this. Didn't want anyone else to know how bad it got, but the rational part of her mind told her to open the door.

The next knock was almost gentle and so was Neo's tone. "Please, little one, open the door."

She forced cramped muscles to work and stood. "I'm…I'm coming," she croaked.

He said something forceful in Greek and then, "Good. Thank you. Open the door."

She reached out and unlocked the door, then pulled it open.

The man standing there did not look like Neo's usual imperturbable self. He wasn't wearing his suit jacket and his expression was nothing less than grim.

She wiped at her face with the back of her hand. "I…they…someone leaked your Tuesday lessons to the media."

"Yes."

"I thought they might come inside."

"It is a good thing they did not."

She nodded, in total agreement.

"You look like you could use a hot shower. I will make you some tea."

"I…yes, that's a good idea." She looked around herself at the bathroom, at Neo, and her gaze skimmed the mirror then went screeching back to it.

She looked like a wreck. She hadn't brushed her hair since waking, her eyes looked haunted, her skin was pale and there were perspiration stains on her shirt. She needed more than a shower. She needed a complete transformation.

But she would have to settle for copious amounts of hot water and the promise of tea.

"Are you all right to be left alone?" Neo asked.

"Yes." Absolutely mortified by her own behavior, she wouldn't have asked him to stay even if it meant losing her piano.

She didn't wonder how he'd gotten into the house until after a twenty-minute shower under very hot water. Mulling the question over, she dried her hair as best she could with a towel. She wasn't going to get an answer until she went downstairs, so she donned fresh clothes and made her way to the kitchen.

Neo was waiting for her in the otherwise empty room. He indicated a mug of still steaming tea on the table. "Drink up."

She sat down and took a sip, almost choking on the sweetness. "How much sugar did you use?"

"Enough."

"For a sugaraholic maybe."

"Sweet tea is good for shock."

"You say that like you know."

"I called my PA, had her look it up."

Cass laughed. She couldn't help it. "I bet she enjoyed that."

Neo shrugged.

"How did you get in the house?" she asked.

"Bob let me in."

"He has a key."

"Apparently."

"I remember him coming," she admitted. She'd refused to answer when Bob knocked on the bathroom door, sure her manager would try to talk her into giving interviews.

"Only one media van remained when I arrived."

"What are you doing here?"

"You left a message on my voice mail."

"I thought you were out of the city."

"I was."

He'd come back. To help her? She had a hard time believing that, but she was glad he was there anyway. She glanced at the clock on the microwave and realized it was already early evening.

She'd spent more than eight hours in her bathroom. No wonder she'd been so cramped when she'd finally stood up. "I feel like an idiot."

"No."

"No?"

"You are no idiot."

She made a sound of disagreement and took another sip of the overly sweet tea.

He sat down across from her. "You have debilitating anxiety related to performing in public."

"Yes, but no one was asking me to perform today."

"Weren't they? Isn't that what the paparazzi do every time they insert themselves into our lives? They demand we perform for them and their audience with a prurient interest in the latest gossip."

"Do you think Bob leaked word of your lessons to the media?" Although she couldn't imagine the furor of this morning caused by piano lessons.

Neo grabbed a tabloid from the counter behind him and placed it in front of her on the table. It had a picture taken through a telephoto lens of Neo entering her house. "They think you're something far more interesting than my piano teacher. They believe you are my latest lover."

She shuddered, not at the thought of being his lover, but at the prospect of being hounded by the media because of the mistaken impression.

"The fact that I kept our relationship secret has given rise to wild speculation and the discovery of your identity only intensified interest."

"I guess it's a good thing you cancelled your lesson for today, or you might have walked right into it all."

He shook his head. "I apologize for what happened. My press manager has released details of the lessons, but I'm afraid at this point there has already been so much conjecture, interest may take some time to wane."

"It's all right. I overreacted."

"Most people would be overwhelmed by a pack of paparazzi on their front step."

"And my back deck."

"What do you mean?"

"Someone climbed the deck and tried to get me to open the French doors to my bedroom."

Fury suffused Neo's features. "That is unacceptable."

"I agree. It was really frightening." But the worst part was that she no longer knew what was normal fear, and what was the result of her abnormal phobia of crowds and public performance.

"That is understandable."

"I don't suppose you want a lesson as long as you are here."

He smiled. "Perhaps, after you have eaten."

Her stomach growled, right then, reminding her that she had not put anything in it since last night. "I'll just have some toast."

But that was unacceptable. He insisted on having one of his bodyguards deliver take-out. When the meal arrived, she surprised herself by being able to eat.

"Your manager wanted to stay and talk to you, but I insisted he leave," Neo said as they were finishing up.

"Thank you. He probably wanted me to do an interview."

"I got that impression." And Neo did not appear impressed by it.

"He told me the publicity would help CD sales."

"When?"

"I called him, before calling your office." She took a sip of the wine that had arrived with the meal. "I'm not sure why I called your office, now that I think about it. I wasn't exactly thinking rationally."

"I am glad you did. Clearly I am the reason for the problem. I should effect the solution."

"I think, Neo Stamos, that you are a good man."

He looked absolutely stunned by her words, but quickly masked his shock. "I take that as a compliment."

"I meant it as one."

They didn't end up having a lesson that evening, but Neo stayed until nine, when the wine and the release of adrenaline caught up with Cass and she began yawning every other minute.

"You need your rest."

"I do." She laughed softly. "I'm exhausted, though I shouldn't be."

"Of course you should. Sleep."

"I will."

She thought he was going to kiss her when she let him out the front door, but he only squeezed her shoulder and told her again to get some rest.

She shook her head at her own foolishness. Why would a man like Neo Stamos want to kiss her? Cass wasn't in his league in any shape or form. And then there were her "issues."

She wasn't housebound. She could buy food on her own without getting overly stressed as long as she went to the local grocer she'd been going to since she was a child. Although she did most of her other shopping online, she could go to familiar department stores, if she really needed to. She had overcome most of her anxiety related to recording at the studio, so long as the technicians and music producer did not change. And her manager didn't bring anyone in to watch her record.

Bob had stopped doing that after the last time she'd simply refused to play and gone home.

But today proved that she wasn't approaching normal, either. Her agoraphobia was mostly limited to performing, but the prospect of having strangers in her home, her sanctuary, always engendered deep anxiety in her. The barrage of media outside her home had brought back debilitating memories.

She had no idea how long she would have remained in her en suite bathroom if Neo had not shown up. Certainly, knowing Bob was there earlier had only increased her stress levels, knowing as she did how he would want to capitalize on the situation.

She really didn't understand why Neo's presence had made such a difference, but she was unutterably grateful it had.

CHAPTER THREE

THE following morning, Cass was working on a piece she planned to cut onto her next CD when the doorbell rang. She ignored it. There had been no media vans outside her home this morning and Neo had released a statement that should set most wagging tongues at rest. But that didn't mean an enterprising reporter would not come back looking for a quote from "the recluse pianist."

Even after learning the truth, there would be some who insisted on believing the billionaire and Cass had some sort of relationship. After all, that made better news copy than the fact he was taking piano lessons.

Besides, it wasn't completely out of the norm for her to get the occasional door-to-door salesman, despite her No Solicitors sign right above the doorbell.

She felt no compunction about ignoring *visitors* who paid no attention to her clearly stated wishes. And she definitely did not want to talk to a reporter, no matter how much her manager Bob, might wish otherwise. She was feeling a lot calmer today than she might have expected, but Neo's company the night before had helped settle her in a way even her father had been unable to do after a performance.

She'd felt safe when he was there and had trusted him to do his best to right the media mess.

The doorbell rang again, but her friends and business acquaintances knew to call first, so she continued to pay it no heed.

Then the phone rang.

She sighed with frustration, but got up. This piece was never going to gel with this kind of interruption. She grabbed the phone and answered it. "Hello?"

"Miss Baker?"

"Yes." What was Neo's PA doing calling her? Oh, right. "You're calling for the piano recommendation."

"Actually, no."

"No?" Disappointment filled her. "Does Mr. Stamos need to cancel his lesson for next week as well?" she asked.

Had he decided to stop them all together? She wouldn't blame him after yesterday.

"No."

"Oh." Maybe she should just wait until the other woman came to the point. Guessing games got annoying when they didn't bear immediate fruit. And she didn't like the answers her own brain was supplying so far.

So, Cass waited in silence for the PA to do just that.

The other woman cleared her throat. "Mr. Stamos asked me to schedule a locksmith to come out and fix the handle on your front door and add an additional lock to a set of French doors on your upper floor. The locksmith is there, but apparently your doorbell is not working properly."

"It's working just fine."

"The locksmith rang it. Twice."

"I do not answer my door when I am not expecting company." Cass did not make any further explanation. She'd learned a long time ago that trying to explain her idiosyncrasies only made matters worse.

Particularly with people like the cold-fish personal assistant employed by Neo Stamos.

"If you do not answer your door, the locksmith cannot fix the door handle problem."

"What problem is that exactly?" She hadn't noticed any trouble with her door handle sticking, though she was willing to entertain the possibility Neo had spotted something she missed when he had been there.

"Mr. Stamos left instructions for it to be replaced by a self-locking model."

"Mr. Stamos left instructions with you about my door?" she asked, stunned. "Without informing me?"

She knew he didn't like her practice of leaving the door on the latch when she was expecting company. It was part of her mental preparation for visitors—reminding herself she needed to be open to other people, at least in some limited capacity.

He complained about it every week, but did he really expect her to replace the handle because of it? Surely he realized she wasn't going to leave the door unlocked right now. Not with the paparazzi entirely too interested in her and Neo's association.

"I really can't speak to whether or not he informed you. I only know my instructions."

"You expect me to allow a perfect stranger into my home to replace my door handle, on your boss's say-so. When I did not request, much less authorize this *upgrade*?"

She used the word for lack of something better, though Cass wasn't convinced it was any such thing.

The personal assistant's silence said that was exactly what she expected.

She'd thought Neo understood. At least a little. Apparently she'd been wrong. "No."

"No? But Mr. Stamos—"

Cass felt no compunction in interrupting the officious woman. "Please call your locksmith and cancel the order. Right now."

"I can't possibly. Mr. Stamos—"

"Does not own this property. And, I, *the owner*," she added, her anxiety creeping through, "have no intention of replacing my perfectly functioning door handle."

"Mr. Stamos will not be happy about this," the PA warned ominously.

"I'm sure Mr. Stamos has many other things of much more importance for him to concern himself with."

"No doubt, but he left instructions."

One thing that could be said for Neo, he engendered loyalty and commitment to follow through from his employees.

"He should have run those instructions by me," Cass said with little sympathy. *She* wasn't one of Neo's employees. And if he had done so, she could have assured him she wouldn't be leaving the door unlocked for the foreseeable future.

"Mr. Stamos is not in the habit of asking the opinions of others."

"Really? I never would have guessed," Cass replied just a tad sarcastically. Then she winced at her own behavior. She knew Neo was just trying to make things better. He'd simply gone about it the wrong way. Because no matter how she might wish otherwise, he did not understand. "Cancel the locksmith."

An unmistakable huff of annoyance sounded over the line. "I will inform the locksmith his services are not required at present. Mr. Stamos will be made aware the delay is at your demand." The frigid tones of the personal assistant should have frozen the phone lines.

"You do that. You can further inform your boss that if my practice session is interrupted by the locksmith, or any of his other employees, he will spend *his* next lesson listening to me prepare my own music rather than teaching him his."

The silence that met her words actually brought half a smile to Cass's face. It was an empty threat, but it had felt good saying it. Would Neo see the humor in it, or would he lack understanding of that, too?

"I shall pass on your message verbatim," the other woman finally said.

"Thank you."

Neo was furious with himself. He should have called Cassandra and warned her about the locksmith, even gotten that annoying manager of hers to be there to supervise the changing of the locks. Instead, he'd left instructions with his PA as he always did and this was the result.

He had to smile at Cassandra's threat however. Getting a private concert from the superbly talented pianist would hardly be a hardship. Regardless, he felt badly. Which was a completely uncommon reaction for him. So was the acknowledgement that he had messed up. Both of which were the reasons he was calling Cassandra on his personal cell phone, in the middle of a corporate conference call with the project team in Hong Kong.

He muted his headset and listened with one ear while dialing Cassandra's number and then listening to the line ring.

"Hello?" she answered on the third ring, sounding downright cranky.

And why he should find that charming rather than annoying he could not have said.

"You sent my locksmith away."

"Actually, your personal assistant sent him away. I did not answer the door."

"Why?"

"I thought he was another reporter."

Neo had to stifle a groan at his own idiocy. He should have expected that. "I meant why did you send him away?"

"Why didn't you ask me if I wanted my door lock changed?"

"It needs to be done. You can't remember to keep your door locked."

"I don't forget; I just choose to leave it unlocked when I know someone is coming."

"That's not much of an improvement."

"I don't plan on leaving it unlocked anytime soon, if that makes you feel any better. I don't want reporters walking in on me unannounced."

"Some would, regardless of trespassing laws."

"Yes, the person who climbed onto my deck certainly wasn't worried about trespassing."

"For all your unwillingness to entertain strangers, you are much too lax when it comes to your personal safety. The locksmith was only a stopgap measure anyway. You need a full spectrum security consult."

"Not going to happen." There was not the slightest uncertainty in her voice.

Neo had gone against tougher negotiators than the renowned pianist. "Consider it a gift for opening your home to me."

"Are you saying this is for *your* safety?"

"Would it help you accept it if I did?"

"For an honest man, you're awfully adept at manipulation."

"Thank you."

"I am not letting a stranger into my home."

"I was a stranger when you allowed me inside for my lesson." But he could see now that he'd made a grave miscalculation in sending over an unknown locksmith.

Zee warned Neo that his impatience could cause problems and this wasn't the first time his friend had been right.

"Not entirely. One, I had prepared myself for taking on a new student. Two, I did my research, learning all I could about you before you came. And three, my manager told me if I didn't do the lessons he would quit."

"You got past being overwhelmed by me—you can deal with the security consultant."

"No."

"Cassandra, you are not being reasonable."

She laughed, the sound both exasperated and amused. "*I* am unreasonable?"

"Yes. It will only take thirty minutes, an hour at the most."

"It's not just about the time, but that is a consideration."

"The security expert can work around your schedule."

"I don't want to meet him." She sounded very definite.

"Cassandra, be sensible."

The quality of the silence at the other end of the line

bothered him. "If you are that concerned," she finally said, "we could probably arrange to have your lessons at my recording studio." She was silent again, this time clearly considering her own proposal. "Yes, that would work."

"I do not want my lessons at the studio."

"I do not want to entertain a stranger in my home." The growing agitation in her voice bothered him.

He did not like to think of his shy teaching aficionado getting upset.

"If I were there for the security consult, would you be all right then?" Neo absolutely stunned himself by asking.

From the expression on his PA's face she was similarly flummoxed.

But Cassandra had come out of her self-imposed prison of the bathroom yesterday for him when she had refused for her manager. Neo was used to being relied on by his employees and associates. It shouldn't make him feel special that Cassandra naturally did as others before her, but somehow it did.

"What? You be here? No. You're too busy. That's not necessary." Cassandra took an audible breath. "Look, I'll…I'll ask my manager. He'll come meet with the security consultant. He thinks these lessons are good for my career, though I really didn't understand why until the whole media fiasco yesterday. Bob will do it."

Unfamiliar amusement welled up, along with a highly out-of-character tolerance. He'd broken her brain. He must have broken his own as well because he didn't want Bob to be the one helping her deal with this, even though that had been his own idea not fifteen minutes ago.

"You don't want to be there for the consult at all? As you reminded my personal assistant, it is *your* home."

"Yes, well… Are you sure you don't want to meet in the studio?" she asked, sounding entirely too hopeful for a woman who spent so much of her time in her home.

Ignoring the repeated offer, he brought his schedule up on his phone. He marked two items for his PA to move and said, "I'll be there with the consultant tomorrow morning at ten."

"You don't have to. I said—"

"If your manager was capable of convincing you to implement better security, he already would have done so."

"I didn't have a billionaire student before."

"Nevertheless, the man is clearly incompetent when it comes to assuring your ongoing personal safety."

"I'm sure that you have a big need for personal security, but I'm a moderately successful musician. I don't even tour."

"You are a brilliant musician with a large fan base, despite your unwillingness to do live performances. You should have implemented additional home security long ago."

"I can see your point of view, but it's skewed by your lifestyle." She sounded just a tad desperate, though he couldn't begin to understand why. "You've got to be able to see that."

"I prefer not to waste time in useless argument."

"Good."

"I'll see you tomorrow morning."

She was still spluttering when he disconnected the line.

Cass glared at the phone, and then picked it up and dialed the number that showed up on her caller ID.

He picked up on the first ring. "Further argument will only serve to annoy me."

"How interesting." Neo really must get an unhealthy dose of arrogance with his morning coffee. "It is customary to say goodbye when hanging up. Please remember that in future."

"Duly noted. Goodbye."

"Goodbye."

She distinctly heard a chuckle as he once again ended the call.

Smiling for no reason she could fathom, especially considering what she had just agreed to, Cass went back to practicing her piece. When a certain set of green eyes kept interrupting her flow of thoughts and she found her fingers moving in a Vivaldi concerto segment she found particularly passionate, Cass knew she was in trouble.

True to his word, Neo arrived at exactly 10:00 a.m. the following morning. Her hair in a smooth French twist and wearing a bright pink Jackie-O style dress with matching jacket for courage, Cass was waiting for him in the music room, but she heard the low purr of his Mercedes as he pulled into her driveway.

She couldn't even pretend to play to settle her nerves. Neo was bringing a stranger who was going to make changes to her home. Changes that she would still be getting used to when his year's worth of lessons were over.

He rang the bell, but tried the handle as she had suspected he would. She heard the latch give and then footsteps. The door shut. More footsteps, Neo's distinctive purposeful tread and a quieter walk, though no less confident.

A few seconds later, Neo led a shorter, blond-haired man into her music room.

"Cassandra." The tycoon gave her a chiding look. "You left the door unlocked. You said you wouldn't."

"I only unlocked it a few minutes ago. I knew you would be on time."

Frowning, he shook his head. "What if traffic had prevented our timely arrival?"

"It wouldn't dare."

He didn't ask why she hadn't simply waited to let them in when they arrived and she was grateful. She had needed this one small coping mechanism this morning.

Having the security consultant over was such a simple thing, one that would not bother normal people, but Cass wasn't normal. She'd figured that out long before she understood what her idiosyncrasies would mean in her life.

Taking a firm grip on her irrational sense of dread, she turned to face the blond man. "I'm Cassandra Baker. Welcome to my home."

The security consultant put his hand out, "Cole Geary. It's an honor to meet you, Miss Baker. I'm a huge fan. I've got all your CDs."

She shook the man's hand and gave him her smile for public consumption. "Mr. Geary, it's a pleasure to meet you. I'm glad you like my music. It's the joy of my life."

"You can tell, the way you play, I mean."

Neo cleared his throat, giving them both his look that was probably supposed to mean, "Wasting time here, people."

Cole's expression went from open admiration to professional in a single blink. "Mr. Stamos has expressed some concern over your security here. Would it be all right if we took a look at the premises before I make any preliminary suggestions?"

The proper response would have been, "Of course not." Only she didn't want Cole Geary in her home. No matter how big a fan, or how nice he seemed.

"I don't want bars on my windows," she blurted out rather than answer his request. She lived with enough limitations caused by her own nearly debilitating shyness.

"As I said—"

"It will be all right," Neo said, interrupting his consultant. He laid his hand against the small of Cass's back. "Let's show Cole the rest of the house."

She looked up at him, begging him to understand the emotions roiling inside her, feelings that had both plagued and shamed her since childhood. The one and only therapist she had seen at her father's insistence had done little to help Cass overcome her anxiety. Though the man had helped her learn some necessary coping mechanisms.

He had once explained that her experiences growing up in the house of an invalid, combined with the pressure to perform at a young age, had severely exacerbated what had probably been a simple case of being a more timid personality type. That was his theory anyway.

All she knew was that she currently suffered a mild form of agoraphobia fed by sociophobia, though how mild she often wondered. Especially when she felt so completely out of her depth doing something as simple as meeting a security consultant and showing him her home.

"I should have had Bob meet you," she said so quietly she wasn't sure he would hear her.

"Trust me, Cassandra." Neo focused one-hundred percent of his attention on her, totally ignoring the other man for the moment. "You and I will do this together."

"I'm being ridiculous." She hated putting herself down like that, no matter how true she knew the words to be.

She just got tired of admitting such unpalatable truths about her reactions, particularly when she felt powerless to change them. It was one of the reasons she hesitated making friends. New relationships required fresh acknowledgement of the limitations she and the people in her life had learned to live with.

Neo shook his head decisively. "It is the world you live in. If you will but trust me, you will see there is nothing to worry you."

"My father used to say the same thing." Right before forcing her onto a stage where she had to lose herself in the music or lose her sanity, or so it felt to her.

She could remember the sea of faces that would confront her at each sold-out concert for the child prodigy pianist. And that memory still had the power to send a cold sweat down her spine. For as far back as she could remember, her music had always been a deeply personal thing for Cass. She used it to hide from the reality of her mother's illness and her father's often angry helplessness in the face of it.

How Cass had hated sharing her music with crowds of strangers, too many of whom wanted to meet the young pianist, after what had always been for her a soul-exhausting concert.

Something moved in Neo's green eyes. "You will tell me about that later, but realize I am not your father."

"No." The feelings she experienced in Neo's presence were far from familial. And he was not cajoling her to perform in a packed auditorium. She took a deep breath and let it out. "Okay. We can show him the house."

"Let's do this," Neo said to Cole.

The security consultant simply nodded, without giving Cass any of the strange looks she was used to receiving when her limitations got in the way of normal social interaction.

Gratitude washed over her and she gave him a genuine, if small, smile.

Then, despite the fact the man had gone past the music room and the hall only once before and that was yesterday, Neo led them on a flawless tour of *her* house. It was uncanny. He never once opened a closet door expecting a room, or missed a door that led to the outside. Although her house was small, there were four doors of that nature— the front door, the kitchen door, and French doors in both the master bedroom and dining room. Those in her room led out to a raised deck and the ones in the dining room opened onto the patio below that deck.

"Ideally, we would replace these doors with ones made of reinforced metal and shatterproof glass," Cole said, eyeing the bedroom's French doors with disfavor.

Cass gripped Neo's suit jacket without thought. "Neo," she pleaded. "Is that really necessary?"

"You will spend the day with me when the renovations are being done."

That was not what she had asked, nor should it have made her feel any better. After all, *Neo* was really just a student, not a friend or a protector, but he made her feel safer than she had in years. Maybe ever.

And wasn't that thought just a tad overwhelming. Neo would walk out of her life without a backward glance in less than a year's time. His lessons would be over and he would move on, but Cass did not think he would leave her unchanged.

And maybe that was okay.

It had been too long since she let anyone inside, but even if it led to pain and loss down the road, it might well be worth it.

"I'm sure your personal assistant will love that. She doesn't like me," she said to cover her nearly overwhelming relief at his offer.

Cass could not imagine spending the day trailing after the high-energy billionaire. But for the first time in years, just because she couldn't imagine it, did not mean she refused to try it.

"Miss Park? She is a very efficient personal assistant. I do not pay her to like or dislike people."

"Just because you don't pay for it, doesn't mean you don't get it." Did the man really think people worked that way?

"I have acted somewhat out of character in my dealings with you. No doubt that surprises her."

"Really?" Cass let go of his jacket and smoothed the expensive fabric. "I guess that *doesn't* surprise me. Even I realized you offering to come this morning was not the norm."

"No, but here I am."

"Why is that?" she asked. Was it possible he felt the same almost primal connection she did? And what would she do if he did?

No way would a dynamic man like Neo Stamos tolerate the cramp in his style a relationship with her would cause.

"I believe I am making a new friend for the first time in more years than I care to count."

"Oh." Of course he hadn't felt the same amazing attraction. Neo was surrounded by gorgeous, fully socially functional women. Cass wouldn't even register a blip on his female companionship radar, but friendship wasn't something to dismiss lightly. Not for her anyway. She didn't have so many she could or would want to dismiss his offer. "I think I'm honored."

"As am I, by your trust."

"I do trust you."

"I noticed."

Cole cleared his throat. "I've seen enough to write my preliminary report."

Neo's face twitched just enough to let her know that like her, he'd forgotten the other man was there.

"Good. I'll expect it on my desk by afternoon."

"For the rates you're paying, I can make that happen." Cole smiled as if he didn't mind rich clients throwing money at a problem they expected him to fix.

It was a good attitude to take, she was sure. If you wanted to keep working for said rich clients.

"I'd like to see the report as well," she said.

Cole's smile warmed up a couple of degrees as he turned it on her. "No problem."

"Naturally," Neo said at the same time.

And then like the whirlwind he was, Neo Stamos was gone, his security consultant along with him.

CHAPTER FOUR

CASS read the security report, her heart sinking further with each recommendation.

No way was all of this going to be done in one day, or even two. Despite most of the security upgrades being offered with options that made them as unobtrusive to her current lifestyle as possible, they were far too extensive for a single-day implementation. Looking at the report, she had visions of workmen coming and going, invading each and every room of her sanctuary, for a week at the least.

She appreciated Cole's efforts to keep the changes in the background, she really did. Just as she was grateful he had brought the report personally, instead of sending a messenger as he told her he had done for Neo.

However, no amount of understanding on the part of the security expert could alter the fact that he was recommending several anxiety-producing modifications to her home. Not least of which was a state-of-the-art alarm system that governed every window and door in her house.

Should she accidentally set the alarm off, a hundred-plus decibel noise would assault her ears and those of her neighbors. Not only that, but the system would be hooked into his private security company for twenty-four-hour monitoring. Someone there would have access to duplicate keys to all her outdoor locks. Even though Cole called the system typical in its implementation for residential security, Cass felt like it was all too cloak-and-dagger for words.

Cole had also recommended replacing all of her doors and windows with more secure models. He wanted to install biometric locks as well. She knew biometric referred to locks opened with retinal or fingerprint scanners, which almost sounded intriguing, if a little redolent of science fiction. She might actually like that upgrade.

But by far, the worst elements to the proposal, and the ones given the least explanation, were those recommended for the outside of her home. Cole wanted to cut back the lilac bushes her mother had planted the year Cass's parents had moved into the house. And that was only the beginning of the landscape changes he wanted to make outside.

There was nothing for it. If Neo's privacy and safety were the reasons for the upgrades, Neo would simply have to have his lessons in the studio. Which is what she told him when she called him a few moments later.

"We have already discussed that option and I do not find it acceptable."

"Then we'll have the lessons at your penthouse." Why hadn't she thought of that before? "You're planning to get a piano anyway. It would be beneficial to have your lessons on the instrument you use for practice."

"What is the problem here?" he asked without a sign of impatience, which rather surprised her. "I have looked at the report and I thought Cole Geary did a fair job of minimizing the impact of the improved safety measures."

She rolled her eyes, though of course he couldn't see. "For someone like you maybe."

"Someone like me would require an armed guard on the premises at all times."

"Sucks to be you." The words just slipped out, but she meant them. With every fiber of her being. She could not imagine spending her days under constant observation.

A surprised bark of laughter sounded. "I've got to admit that is the very first time in my adult life that particular phrase has been directed at me. What is even more astonishing is that I can tell you mean it."

"The life of a high-profile businessman is not for me," she said, amusement making the first tiny cracks in the wall of anxiety that had been building since she had agreed to have the security consultant come over yesterday.

"It's a good thing you are just my friend, not my business partner." He sounded like he was smiling, if not laughing outright.

"I'm sure Zephyr Nikos is grateful for that as well," she said dryly.

"I don't know. I can push too hard at times, but then so can he."

It amazed her how humble the tycoon could sound after all that he had accomplished in his thirty-five years. She couldn't afford to get sidetracked by admiration though. "I, on the other hand, may not be pushy, but I am also not a pushover."

"I never thought you were. It takes determination to refuse the lucrative life of a concert performer."

"My manager calls it bullheaded stubbornness."

"Naturally, the more money you make, the more he does."

"That's one way to look at life."

"Are you saying you don't think he does?"

"Honestly? I don't know. When my father died, I clung to Bob because he was someone familiar. I assumed he had my best interests at heart, and mostly, I think he does."

"But he is motivated by a desire for financial success like so many of us."

"Oh, I don't think it's mere money that motivates you. I get the feeling you like being a rich man, but you enjoy being a powerful one even more."

"You think so?"

"I do. You wear the mantle of control with complete comfort."

"This is true, but what makes you say so?" His tone couldn't be mistaken for anything but genuine curiosity, no defensiveness there.

She laughed. She couldn't help herself. And then she laughed some more. When she finally got her mirth under control, she was met by silence at the other end of the phone.

"Are you still there?"

"Yes. Are you finished laughing?"

"Um…I think so."

"It is another first for me."

"What?"

"Being laughed at. Even Zephyr would not dare."

"Oh, come on. You trip and fall and your best friend would not laugh?"

"I would never trip and fall."

"I suppose you never spill sauce on your shirt at a restaurant, either."

"No."

"Hmm…you never mistake someone's identity in an embarrassing and amusing-to-your-friends way?"

"I do not make mistakes."

"You sound like you mean that."

"I also do not say things I do not mean."

Wow, such arrogance.

"Even when you are negotiating a real estate deal?"

"I never bluff."

"Oh." For some reason that was just a little nerve-wracking to know.

"Should I apologize for finding you funny?" she wondered out loud.

"Not necessary, but I would appreciate you sharing the joke."

"You."

"I am the joke?" he asked in an odd voice.

"Um…yes."

"Explain."

"Neo, you have done nothing but boss me around since the moment I met you. Your control issues are hardly a deeply-seated psychological secret."

"I do not have issues with control," he replied with clear affront.

She almost laughed again, but she managed to stop herself with a judicious bite to her lower lip. It hurt, but it was effective. "No, you just insist on being the one who has it."

"I cede control when necessary."

"Which I'm sure isn't often."

"True, but there is nothing wrong with that." His tone was almost defensive this time.

She couldn't quite stifle the grin that caused, but she tried very hard not to let it show in her voice. "If you can handle the stress of so much responsibility, maybe not, but your insistence on changing my home to suit your whim *is* taking it a bit far. If you don't mind my saying so."

"We have discussed this. Concern for your safety is hardly a whim."

"I thought we were implementing these changes for *your* safety."

"Yesterday was disturbing for both of us. And I have bodyguards."

"I see." She'd thought as much, but when he had been so insistent, she'd been unable to comprehend him being that way for her sake rather than his own. "I don't want to change my house *for me*."

She didn't want to change it at all, but particularly if the reason for doing so was some spurious need to increase her personal safety. She had lived her whole life in that house and was doing just fine. Even alone, like she had been since her father's death.

"Consider, if the ruthlessly forward reporter that climbed your back deck had broken one of the glass panes on the French doors to your bedroom. Which he could have done all too easily. He could have gotten inside. Even if his intention was not to harm you, such an action would cause you grave distress."

"There's no reason to believe there will be a repeat of yesterday anytime soon, if ever."

"You are a celebrity. You may be a shy one that does not court the spotlight, but with the increase in sales on each new album, you build a wider and wider fan base. An incident just like yesterday's could indeed happen again, and *soon*."

She shivered, feeling slightly nauseated at the prospect. Still, she had stopped being a public performer years ago.

"Even though I have reasonable success with my music, I'm hardly at risk like a pop star."

"But you are at risk."

"Why are you so insistent?" she asked almost plaintively.

"It is what is best for you. I am used to doing what is best for the people who rely on me."

"I am not one of your employees."

"It does not matter." He sighed, as if exasperated. "I have already arranged for payment if that is what concerns you."

"You know it's not."

"Cassandra—"

"I'll see you next week. Let me know if you wish to meet at the studio or your penthouse."

He said her name again, but she simply said, "Goodbye," at the same time.

She hung the phone up without another word.

Cass wished she was surprised when the doorbell rang the next morning before she'd even had her first cup of coffee, but she wasn't. She was even less surprised to look out the window in the bedroom that overlooked the drive and see Neo's Mercedes parked there.

He was not the type of man to let someone else set terms. Besides, no matter what she thought, he was convinced she needed to upgrade her house's security.

She was less than halfway down the stairs when the doorbell rang. Impatient and quick, Neo didn't linger on the doorstop dithering about whether or not to bother her so early in the morning as she would have done. She didn't even consider trying to ignore the bell, or the man ringing it.

Neo would not be deterred by a mere refusal to answer the door. Besides, as much as she hated confrontation, she did not hide from it when necessary. And it was necessary to make Neo understand she wasn't transforming her home on his whim.

All words along that vein and any others dried up when she swung the door wide to be confronted by the man in person. He was so darn gorgeous in today's business suit, each dark hair perfectly in place, his green gaze locked on her with laserlike intensity.

She went hot all over and stopped breathing. For just a few seconds, but it was enough to remind her how out of control she felt in his presence.

Why did he affect her this way?

It was like the anxiety she felt at being in a crowd of strangers, only not. Because as unsettling as this feeling was, she liked it. She liked him.

Even when he was trying to boss her around.

He'd opened his mouth to speak, but shut it when he saw her. "What are you wearing?" he demanded after several seconds of silence.

Not sure what had him so confused, she looked down at herself. Yes, she *had* remembered to don her robe. The teal blue silk covered her from neck to ankle in more than adequate modesty. Her feet were bare, but she was in her own home, surely that wasn't a crime?

She lifted her head and met his bright blue gaze, which was fixed on her with far too much intensity for this early in the morning.

"It's not polite to stare." Especially when the look felt so much like a physical touch. It just wasn't right. "I haven't even had my morning caffeine yet," she grumbled.

He seemed less than impressed. "I have been up for two hours."

"Good for you." So, he'd gotten up at five-thirty? What a masochist. "Only, normal people wait to visit others, *especially when they neglect to call ahead*, until after eight, sometimes even nine."

His brow quirked in that sexy way he had. "We have already established I am no average man."

"Being extraordinary in no way gives you leave to be rude." But she had to admit that this man would probably get away with a lot more than she would allow anyone else in her life.

And that did not bode well for the outcome of the discussion coming.

"This from the woman who hung up on me yesterday."

"I said goodbye."

"You refused to discuss Cole's proposal in any way resembling a rational manner."

"Maybe I'm not rational, but then I live alone with no personal obligation to anyone. I can insist on keeping my home as it is for no other reason than because I want to."

"Are you going to offer me coffee?" It was a clear tactic to change the subject, but she was not fooled.

Neo wasn't convinced. Not by a long shot. The man didn't know what it meant to give up. His nature wouldn't allow it.

Foreboding skittered along her nerves as she spun on her heel without a word. He could follow her to the kitchen, or not. His choice.

He followed. The sound of his confident tread behind her further emphasized her certainty that he expected to get his way.

She poured two mugs of coffee from the pot that she had set up on the timer the night before. "Cream or sugar?" she asked.

"No."

She handed him his mug and then doctored her own with a liberal dollop of half-and-half and two teaspoons of sugar.

He was frowning at her when she looked up.

"What? I have no need to prove my masculinity by drinking black coffee."

"That is good, since you are entirely feminine." His frown deepened. "Do you often answer the door wearing nothing but a silky robe that clings to your every curve?"

She stared at him in shock for a full minute before gathering her thoughts enough to answer. "One, I am wearing pajamas under my robe."

He snorted.

"I am," she insisted. And then undid the robe that had reminded her of the beautiful blue-green depths of the ocean off Hawaii's shores to prove it. "See?"

She'd bought the pajama-and-robe set when she'd realized she probably would never see the warm waters in person again. Who would she go with? She didn't like traveling alone. And she was no longer traveling for her music.

His green eyes narrowed dangerously as she revealed the matching camisole and shorts she slept in. She didn't know what that was all about, but she was on a roll and not about to stop now.

She recinched the robe and glared up at him. "Two, I don't have enough curves to speak of to worry about such a thing." That at least should be obvious to him. "Three, I only answered the door *after* looking out the window upstairs and recognizing your car in the drive."

"News flash, Cassandra, I am a man."

"That's hardly a secret." She didn't know what was bugging him, but honestly right now, she couldn't expend the energy or brainpower to figure it out. She was too busy trying to hide her reaction to his presence…. "The point is, I never answer the door to strangers, in my robe or otherwise."

"Do you answer your door to your manager in your robe?"

Where were these questions coming from? "Of course not. Bob always warns me ahead of coming over and I am therefore not caught unawares before my caffeine or morning ablutions."

"Good."

She barely suppressed the urge to roll her eyes. "I'm glad you approve. Now drink your coffee quietly for a few minutes and let me wake up sufficiently to argue with you."

"Are we going to argue?"

"Are you going to insist on changing my home?"

"Yes."

At least he was honest.

She headed for the door. "As you are obviously not going to let me drink my coffee in peace. I'm going upstairs to shower and change. I will be back down when I feel more able to deal with you."

"Get there fast. We leave for my office in less than thirty minutes."

"You can leave whenever you like, but I have no intention of rushing my shower, or any other part of my morning regimen."

"I am not sitting down here and cooling my jets for three hours while you make yourself presentable."

"Do the women in your life really take that long to get ready in the morning?" No wonder the man got a little cranky. She'd be annoyed by that kind of time-wasting, too.

"Are you saying you do not?"

"I own exactly two types of makeup, mascara and tinted

lip balms, what do you think?" She liked stylish clothing, but it didn't take any longer to put on than jeans and a T-shirt. And if she was in a hurry, she pulled her hair back in a French plait, even if it was still wet.

"I think you now have five minutes less than you did to get ready."

"I'm not going to your office, Neo." That was so not going to happen.

"The installers will be here at eight-thirty. You can stay and supervise them, or you can come with me."

She stomped up to where he leaned negligently against her countertop and poked him in the chest, looking way too edible for a man she wanted to strangle. Only figuratively speaking, of course…mostly.

"Contractors are not tearing my house apart, Neo. It is not going to happen. If one of them so much as tries to trim the lilac bushes, I will call the police." And then her manager and fire him for getting her into this mess.

After he came over and got rid of the strangers from her home. She was never giving piano lessons away to the charity auction again.

She might have muttered that under her breath because Neo gave her an amused, if increasingly exasperated, look.

"We are going to discuss this rationally." Neo caught her hand with his, sending the rational thought he was so sure she wasn't capable of right out the window. "After."

"After what?"

"After you shower and dress." He should be angry.

She was.

But he looked perfectly calm, even somewhat tolerant, and more than a little amused.

She should be berating him for his assumption, but her

throat had gone dry and her mouth didn't want to form words. It wanted kisses. His kisses. The thought caught her up short. What was the matter with her?

Asking herself didn't miraculously present her with answers or renew her fading grasp on reality. She really wanted to be kissed by him and that was so astonishing, she wasn't sure how to handle it. She didn't know where the urge came from, but it was there. And it was strong.

He was so close. She wanted him closer. Mere inches separated their lips. How many?

"Ten inches," she guessed aloud.

"What?"

"How far," she said before she thought and would have bitten her own tongue in reprimand, but she was too busy simply trying to keep it still.

"How far what?" he asked, looking both confused and yet like he might have a glimmer what she was thinking.

"Never mind." She wanted to look away, but couldn't make herself do so.

She'd lamented the fact of her loneliness, the fact she would probably never have a family of her own. But never having been plagued with desires to kiss or touch another man, she'd also come to terms with her lack of sensuality.

Now she had to wonder, if she simply had never met the right man. She had never met Neo.

"What is ten inches?" he asked in silky demand.

And somehow she could not help telling him. "The distance between our mouths."

He didn't ask why that mattered, or laugh, or look at her like she was deranged. He didn't do any of those things. He simply lowered his head, closing those ten inches in slow-motion intensity, and then his lips were covering hers.

Shock coursed through Cass, seizing her to immobility. Neo Stamos was kissing her. And it was wonderful. More than wonderful, it was amazing, fabulous, stupendous.

Her first kiss.

Pure, unadulterated pleasure washed over her in one tropical warm wave after another. Neo's lips were firm and all male as they moved confidently against her own.

She could smell his aftershave, an expensive musk that made her knees turn to water. Or was that the feel of his tongue teasing at the seam of her lips, requesting, maybe even *demanding* entrance?

She moaned, loving the alien feeling of his tongue on her lips. The sound of his jacket rasping against his shirt as he put his arms around her sent a shiver of alien need shimmering through her. It was not a sound she had heard very often in her life, never in this context, and certainly she had not expected to hear it with him. It brought home the reality of their circumstance as his lips on hers did not.

They were too delicious. Too tingle-producing. Too amazing. Too outside her realm of catalogued experiences.

But the sound of the fabrics moving against each other was more mundane, easier to comprehend and proof positive she was indeed being held by him. Neo Stamos. The most utterly gorgeous man she had ever met, or seen even. The feel of his suit trousers against her silk-covered legs was something else altogether.

His hands roamed over her, caressing her back and hips through the thin, slippery fabric of her robe. When his large, strong hands cupped her backside, she whimpered against his mouth, her lips finally parting of their own volition to let him inside.

He deepened the kiss immediately, his mouth laying

claim to hers with both the skill and strength of a seasoned campaigner. If this was how he kissed all his women, no wonder he had a different one on his arm each night.

Even the thought of the revolving door in his bedroom could not dampen her ardor. She'd never known anything like the passion escalating inside her. She wanted to devour him. She wanted to be devoured by him. She wanted everything she had never had and so much she had never even thought about before.

What she got was a skilled mouth taking her to heights of pleasure while sure, steady hands kneaded her backside, dipping between her legs to barely caress the apex of her thighs. She cried out into his mouth at the slight touch. Naked. Yes. Naked would be good.

Only she couldn't make herself break the kiss long enough to say so. And the tiny, still-functioning part of her brain was grateful.

No part of her was happy when he tore his lips from hers though.

"No. Don't stop," she pleaded.

He set her away from him, his expression so intense, she shivered from it.

CHAPTER FIVE

HE FROWNED, not appearing in the least bit happy. "I should not have done that."

"Why?" She'd liked it, but maybe he hadn't? No, he'd been enjoying himself, or doing a wonderful job of faking it.

From everything she'd read, that wasn't the man's job. To fake it. Of course, women weren't supposed to do that, either, but some did. She wouldn't have to. If they made love. She was certain of it, regardless of the fact that she'd never actually had any practical experience in that regard.

She recognized a master when she met one and this man was a master at the art of touch. And kissing.

He blew out a long breath. "We are friends."

"Friends don't kiss?" she asked, not entirely conscious of the words coming out of her mouth, but truly confused nonetheless.

"I do not know. I have never had a female friend."

"That makes two of us."

"You have never had another woman as a friend?" His tone said he didn't think she was telling the truth.

"I've never had a billionaire tycoon friend. We are even." Well, maybe not entirely.

Female friends, or not, the man knew *a lot* more about women than she knew about men and what made them tick, billionaire tycoons or otherwise.

"So, friends can't kiss?" she asked again, going back to the part of the conversation that most interested her.

"No."

"Why not?"

"Women I have sex with rarely last more than a night, a few at the most, in my life. I would like our friendship to be more long-standing." He actually managed to sound almost vulnerable.

"We were kissing, not having sex. Weren't we?" Maybe she hadn't recognized foreplay when she felt it? She certainly wouldn't have said no if he'd asked for more and she had wanted them naked, hadn't she?

Oh, goodness, gracious, *she had wanted them naked*.

"You are so innocent."

"And you aren't. That sounds like a good combination to me."

"Only in your ingenious mind."

"Now you're just being condescending."

"I am being realistic."

"I think I might like you spontaneous better."

"Good." The look in his eyes said anything but.

"Good?"

"What could be more spontaneous than spending the day together?"

"We're back to that, are we?"

His smile said they were indeed. "You need to take a shower. I will prepare your breakfast while you dress."

"You can cook?"

"I did not start out life a rich man."

"Granted." But she hadn't considered what that might mean practicality-wise about how he lived earlier in his life.

"Do you prefer a hot or cold breakfast?" he asked, managing not to sound like a waiter taking an order so much as a superconfident Greek man trying to sound like one.

"A toasted bagel with peanut butter would be fine." She'd grab an apple on the way out the door and round out the meal nicely.

Which meant she was considering leaving with him. More than considering it, resigned to it. Maybe not even resigned, but actually looking forward to it. After a single kiss. She was in so much trouble.

Maybe his no-kissing rule for them was a good idea, after all.

"If they cut so much as a leaf off of my bushes, I will never forgive you," she said as she walked out of the room and hoped he realized she was very serious about that one.

Neo felt like someone had kicked him in the chest.

Kissing Cassandra had been better than anything he had felt in a long time. Maybe ever. He had not wanted to stop, had felt helpless to do so. That shocking realization, more than anything—more than the knowledge that Geary's team would be arriving soon, more than Neo's own pressing schedule—had given him the impetus he needed to break the kiss.

Neo was never helpless. Had not once in his entire life considered that word applicable to himself. And he was not about to begin now. Almost as alarming, he could not remember the last time he had lost control sexually or any other way, much less so quickly.

When he'd touched her lips, he'd been close to climaxing and that had *never* happened, not even in his youth. *From a kiss.* He hadn't even touched Cassandra's small but tempting breasts, or gotten to naked skin at all. But he'd wanted to. More than he'd wanted to be on time for his morning meeting. Damn it.

She hadn't touched him, either, except to respond to his kiss with her lips. That response had been untutored— innocently sensual, but incredibly, sweetly passionate. If his instincts were right, and they usually were, she was a virgin.

Which was one very good reason to steer clear of sexual intimacy with her. It had nothing to do with the fact she engendered such a surprising reaction in him. Neo was not afraid of anything, but he only slept with women who understood the expectations going in, experienced women who would not mistake physical desire for more ephemeral emotions.

His sex partners usually shared his jaded view of sex, but not much more. Women he would never consider spending an entire day with, not even in bed. Damn, he sounded like a chauvinist, even in his own mind.

But he could not help that he had never developed friendships with the fairer sex. He didn't usually make friends at all. As Zephyr had pointed out with such relish.

Neo couldn't say what drew him to Cassandra. All he knew was that the last few weeks, he had looked forward to his piano lessons and seeing her more than he ever would have expected. There was no denying he liked her as a person. With all her quirks, she was charming.

He liked how she seemed to identify with him on a level

only Zephyr ever had before. She knew what it was to have a childhood in name only. She understood loss and fear and hunger, even if it had been for love rather than food.

Her friendship was all too important. He wasn't about to jeopardize it for something as fleeting as sexual attraction. No matter how overwhelming.

He found the bagel she'd requested and started it toasting. He called Cole's cell phone while he waited for it.

"Geary Security," the other man answered on the first ring.

"She agreed to the substantive changes to the structure of the house, but doesn't want the foliage touched."

"That doesn't surprise me."

"It doesn't?" It sure as hell had stunned Neo. If it had been him, he would have had the opposite reaction.

"I researched her house's history after dropping off the proposals. Her parents bought that house before she was born," Cole said. "From the size of most of the bushes, I'd say someone planted them soon after her parents moved into the house. If I had to guess, I would suggest it was her mother."

"So, it is a sentimental thing?" Not something Neo had much experience with, for with all the luxury now at his disposal, sentimentality was still something he could ill afford.

"That's what I'm guessing, but they really do provide too much cover for burglars or stalkers."

An image of Cassandra's expression before she'd swept out of the kitchen played in Neo's mind's eye. "She's not going to let that sway her."

"You persuaded her to go for the doors and windows. You can convince her about the foliage. I'll reschedule the gardener when you do."

Neo wished he was as confident, but for the first time in years, he considered the possibility he'd met someone as stubborn as he was. In fact, the last time he remembered doing so, he'd befriended the man and ended up eventually making him his business partner.

There was only one word to describe Cassandra when she came downstairs, dressed for the day in a navy blue pantsuit.

Cranky.

She sat down to eat her bagel with a grudging thank-you tossed in his direction, the hapless bagel getting a glare before she took a resounding bite.

"You look nice," he complimented. "I like the bright pink accents." Most women he knew preened under directed praise.

And he did like the pink scarf and shoes she'd added to the more basic white blouse and dark pantsuit. Her oversized pink-and-white earrings were a nice, if unexpected touch, too.

Cassandra didn't so much as smile, though he received yet another perfunctory, "Thanks."

"I am surprised you wear so many bright colors."

He got her full attention with that comment. She glared at him. "Why?"

"I would think you wouldn't want to draw attention to yourself." "Debilitatingly shy" did not equal "vibrant dress style" in his mind, but then he was no psychologist.

"What, you think I should dress only in shades of gray and wear my hair in a bun, or something?"

"No." But he wouldn't have been surprised if she had, knowing what he knew about her hermitlike ways.

"I'm not fond of talking to strangers."

That was one way of putting it. Agoraphobic was another, but he didn't say a word.

"That doesn't mean I want to dress like a piece of cheap office furniture," she huffed and then grimaced. "It's important to me not be a caricature. I don't like to perform, but I *can* leave the house. I'm uncomfortable meeting strangers, but I don't need to dress like a hermit with no fashion sense. My life has enough limitations, I take pleasure where I find it and I happen to like bright colors."

"I'll remember that."

"I can't imagine why you'd need to."

Come to that, he couldn't, either. She wasn't one of his pillow-mates that he bought gifts for in lieu of giving anything of himself. Hell, who was he kidding? He planned to give more of himself to Cassandra today than he had to anyone in a long time. He intended to give her his time.

Still. "Now, you're just being argumentative for the sake of it."

"You think so?" she asked in a tone so subtly snarky he couldn't help but be impressed.

And amused, though he was far too intelligent to let that show. He *should be* irritated. He'd cancelled all but his most pressing meetings and cleared his schedule in a way he hadn't done in years. He would still work some, but he planned to entertain Cassandra. After all, it was his fault she was being evicted from her house for the day.

When he told her so, her frown grew slightly less dark, but it was still in the black range on the color spectrum. "I suppose you expect me to be grateful."

"Is that likely to be on the menu anytime soon?"

"No."

She was so refreshingly honest. Once she'd got past

seeing him as a stranger, he didn't intimidate her like he did almost everyone else. Again, he had an unexpected urge to smile, but he smothered it. "I'd settle for you being happy."

"Why on earth do you care if I'm happy, or not?"

"I don't know, but I do. Chalk it up to friendship."

She sighed and looked more frustrated than annoyed. "The thing is, I have obligations, too, Neo. The music for my next album isn't going to write itself. Only I can't work on it while strangers are tearing apart my house."

"So, we both take an unexpected break. What is one day?" He ignored the fact that him saying such a thing would be considered anathema by any and all who knew him.

She opened her mouth to speak and then closed it, looking at him contemplatively. "When was the last time *you* took a break?"

That was easy. "My first piano lesson."

"Before that?" she asked with a degree of consideration that made him nervous. Though he didn't know why.

"I don't take breaks."

Now she would use that truth as an excuse and say she didn't need time off, either.

She surprised him by asking very seriously, "Ever?"

"Ever."

"You *do* need a break."

So Zephyr and Gregor insisted. "If the number of compositions you have created in the past years is any indication, so do you."

That seemed to startle her. "Music is my life."

"According to both my doctor and business partner, that attitude is not a healthy one."

"I exercise."

He remembered seeing her home gym when showing Cole Geary around her house. "So do I."

"I eat right."

"So do I."

"Then why are they so concerned for you?"

Neo shrugged. "Got me, but if it's bad for me to be so obsessed by Stamos and Nikos Enterprises, then it stands to reason your single-minded pursuit of music needs tempering."

"I don't want to spend the day being dissected by strangers."

"Not going to happen."

"Why?"

"They'll be too busy watching me in wonder."

She laughed at that as he'd meant her to do. "It makes me cranky to think of my house getting torn up."

"It won't be torn up. Cole gave me his word that you'll barely be able to tell they were even here."

"How is that possible? I saw the list. They can never get it all done in one day."

"In fact, they can."

"Money talks?"

"In even more languages than I do."

A smile played at the edges of her lips. "I'm fluent in Mandarin, Italian and German."

"You are accomplished." He himself spoke Greek and English, of course, but Japanese and Spanish as well. "I understand the Italian and German, considering your passion for piano composition, but why Mandarin?"

"I like the way it's written."

"You are fluent in the Kanji?"

"Yes, though I'm still studying. I have a pen pal from

the Hunan province and he tutors me. He's a scholar and something of a recluse."

"What do you write to him about?"

"Music, what else? He plays and composes on the *guzheng*. It's kind of like a Chinese zither. Unlike the older and more traditional *guqin*, which only has seven strings and no bridges, it has sixteen to twenty-five strings with movable bridges. He can create complicated and very beautiful compositions on it."

She was babbling. She was still nervous about leaving with him and letting the security company do their job. But she was going to do it. He was proud of her.

"How do you share your music?"

"We both have Web cams." She laughed, but it didn't sound like she found that funny. "It's kind of pathetic, but I see more of him and my other online friends via the Internet than I do anyone else."

It was unfortunate, not pathetic. One day, he would help her make that distinction. "Have you ever wanted to visit him in person?"

"Yes."

"Naturally, you have not gone."

"I would. Though not easily, I *can* travel anonymously, but I have no one to travel with."

"So, it is not simply leaving your house that bothers you?"

She lifted her shoulders in a half shrug before turning back to her breakfast without answering.

He wasn't done with the subject however. "You don't like being recognized as Cassandra Baker, the renowned pianist and New Age composer."

"Something like that."

"But you wouldn't answer your door to the locksmith."

"No."

"Why?"

"My father used to say I was debilitatingly shy."

From her tone, Neo guessed the other man had considered that a liability, most likely to his brilliantly talented daughter's career plans.

"Were you always shy?"

"My mother said I was an outgoing toddler. That's how they learned I was a musical prodigy. I was always trying to entertain them and discovered the piano at the age of three. I played music I had heard from memory."

"That's amazing."

"That's what my teachers said."

"They started you with a teacher at age three?" He could not help the appalled shock in his tone.

"Mom came down sick and I guess my parents saw the lessons as a way to divert my attention from her so I would not demand too much of her time."

"That would imply you spent significant time each day playing piano."

"I did."

"How much time are we talking here?"

"I don't remember exactly." Though something in her expression belied that claim.

"Take a guess."

"A couple of hours every morning and evening before bedtime."

"Impossible."

"Entirely possible. And that does not count the time I spent practicing on my own."

"You must be mistaken." Children often miscalculated the length of time spent doing something, or so he had heard.

"I used to think I might have been, too. However, I found the records of my lessons in a box of papers after my father's death and there it was in black and white."

"What?"

"Proof my parents did not want me around."

"That is a harsh assessment."

"How did you end up in an orphanage?" she asked challengingly.

"My parents both wanted something different from life than being a parent."

"Harsh assessment, or reality?"

"Touché."

"I have often wished I hadn't found those records. I preferred the gentler fantasy that I mistook the number of hours I spent working on my music before I was old enough to go to school." She bit her lip and looked away, old sadness sitting on her like a mantle. "Cleaning out the house of my parents' personal possessions was supposed to be cathartic."

"Who told you so?"

"My manager."

"And was it?"

She laughed, another less than amused sound. "Define cathartic. It forced me to face my loss, to accept that they were gone and never coming back. Which was good, I suppose." She met his gaze again, remembered pain stark in her amber eyes. "But it hurt. Horribly."

"I am sorry."

"Thank you."

"Enhancing your security will not make them any more gone," he felt compelled to point out.

"I know."

"But making the changes is bringing back those traumatic feelings, is it not?"

She nodded, but clearly forced herself to brighten. "You're pretty perceptive for a business tycoon."

"Figuring out what makes people tick is half the battle in business."

"And I bet you are good at it."

"Stellar."

She laughed, this time sounding much happier. "Egotistical?"

He smiled in response. He liked making her laugh. "Honest in my self-assessment. Like right now, I know I'll get damn short if I'm late for my teleconference."

"Can you call in from your cell phone in the car?"

"Yes, but until I have my computer in front of me with the information I need, I won't feel good about my input."

"I bet you have most of it memorized." But she got up from the table, gathering her dishes.

"I don't like making mistakes."

"I'd lay another bet that is an understatement." She put the dishes in the sink. "Just to show I respect your schedule, I'll leave these for later."

He ignored the jibe. He respected her schedule, he just wanted to route it for the day. "I gave up betting when a careless wager led to me taking piano lessons."

"Should I be offended?" she asked.

"No. I don't regret being forced to accept my gift. It brought me a new friend."

She shook her head, but her lips were curved in a small smile. "Some birthday pressie."

"I think he did mean the lessons to be something special for my thirty-fifth."

"He really thought you wanted piano lessons?"

"I wanted to learn to play when we were younger, but I hadn't thought of that pipe dream in years."

"Not such a pipe dream anymore."

"No, but even more than that, I'm a huge fan of yours. Though I didn't know it."

"You didn't know it? This I've got to hear, but not while it will make you late."

An hour later, still reeling from the knowledge Neo was a closet fan *and* now considered her a friend, Cass listened to her latest self-recording on her MP3 player and took notes on what was lacking in the composition. She hadn't been exaggerating when she told Neo she had work to do, too, but her implication she could only do it at home might have been stretching the reality of the situation.

She didn't want to spend all day, every day, at her piano bench, so she had started working on self-recordings early on. She loved the flexibility her tiny MP3 player gave her. She could listen to it while exercising, cooking or practicing her Kanji writing. Or sitting at a table in an empty conference room in the Stamos & Nikos Enterprises building in downtown Seattle.

She'd bought her first one on the recommendation of another musician she knew online and had upgraded with each new technological advancement.

A tap on her shoulder alerted Cass to someone else's presence.

She pulled one of the speaker buds from her ear and looked up. "Yes?"

"Mr. Stamos wanted me to make sure you have everything you need to make you comfortable." Miss Parks,

Neo's personal assistant, lived up to her voice and attitude over the phone.

Blonde, in her forties, she wore her pale hair in a sleek chignon and dressed in a female power suit by Chanel, but it had to be from a previous year's collection. Because this year the designer had gone whimsical, adding ruffles and lace that would look out of place on the businesswoman. Just as the polite query sounded out of character on her tongue.

Miss Parks clearly felt offering refreshments to her employer's piano teacher was beneath her.

However the woman had absolutely nothing on Cass in the "annoyed nearly beyond endurance" stakes. While Cass sat in a strange conference room, in a huge office building filled with strangers, even more strangers were tearing *her* house apart.

She didn't even attempt to hide her bad temper when she gave the blonde a curt, "Water would be nice."

Never mind tea. That might soothe her and she didn't feel like being soothed.

Without another word to the snarky PA, Cass put her speaker bud back in her ear and returned to work. A bottle of water and a glass with a slice of lemon showed up at her elbow a few minutes later.

Bad mood or not, Cass remembered her manners and looked up to give the deliverer a polite thank-you, only to clash eyes with a man every bit as overwhelming presence-wise as Neo.

Even if she hadn't recognized him from publicity photos, she would have known he couldn't be anyone but Neo's business partner, Zephyr Nikos.

CHAPTER SIX

THE clearly charismatic Greek smiled. "No problem."

She yanked her headphones out of her ears. "Um…"

"I'm glad to get the chance to meet you in person." Zephyr's smile would have been lethal if she hadn't been inoculated that morning with a kiss from Neo Stamos. "Neo isn't your only fan around here."

She put her hand out. "Thank you for buying the piano lessons, Mr. Nikos, and I'm glad you enjoy my music."

"Zephyr, please. And don't thank me yet, you've only given Neo a few lessons." He leaned against the dark solid wood conference table. "The jury's still out on what kind of student he'll make, but my gut tells me that if he sticks with it for the full year, you'll earn every one of the hundred thousand dollars I donated to charity on his behalf."

Cass let her lips tip in a wry half smile. "I'm sitting here working from my MP3 player instead of my piano because he's got a team of construction workers and security personnel tearing apart my home. I'm under no illusions he'll be an easy student to have." Or friend for that matter.

"They're replacing a few doors and windows, that is hardly tearing the place apart," Neo said from behind Cass, his tone chiding.

She pushed her chair back and looked at him over her shoulder. "Are you done with your meeting?"

"I am." He raised a single dark brow at Zephyr. "I thought you had a full schedule this morning, Zee."

The other gorgeous Greek shrugged his broad shoulders. "I had a minute and I decided to meet the reclusive Cassandra Baker."

"It's hardly a public appearance," Neo said, sounding borderline irritated. "She graciously agreed to spend the day with me while they do necessary security work on her home. She is not here for your entertainment."

She hadn't exactly been gracious, but she appreciated Neo's minor prevarication on her behalf.

"Don't worry, I didn't have a baby grand moved into Conference Room B for an impromptu concert," Zephyr mocked, clearly amused by Neo's protective stance.

"If you had, I might have gotten more done," Cassandra joked. "There are limits to what I can do working off my recordings."

"You can afford to take some time off work," Neo said with a perfectly straight face.

Zephyr laughed in clear amazement, his expression one of disbelief. "Coming from you, that's standup comedian material."

"I cancelled several events on my calendar today."

"I know." Zephyr gave Cass a strange look. "It's one of the reasons I wanted to meet this wonderfully talented lady. I knew she was a master pianist, I didn't know she was a miracle worker."

"More like a whiner," Cass said self-deprecatingly. "Neo would never have gotten me out of my house and those workmen in if he hadn't dragged me himself."

She didn't mention his form of persuasion had included a kiss that had about melted her brain.

"You are not a whiner." Neo had come to stand by Zephyr and his expression was more than a little stern. "You have agoraphobic issues that have to be addressed with the seriousness and caution they deserve."

"That sounds like something you'd read in a textbook on the subject," she said. And then realization dawned. "You've researched my condition."

"I had one of my top people do it for me."

"Wow. You take being my student way more seriously than anyone else has in the past."

Neo shrugged, but Zephyr appeared anything but nonchalant at the admission. He was once again staring at his business partner with blatant incredulity.

Then his expression morphed and he turned a look of almost pity on Cass. "Watch out. When he gets the bit between his teeth, Neo has a tendency to take over."

"You think I haven't noticed this trait?" she asked with no little amusement.

Neo crossed his arms and frowned at Zephyr. "I think you've got better things to do than stand around gossiping, *partner*."

"Are you going to try and deny you've already got a recovery plan in the works for Miss Baker and her agoraphobia?" he asked instead of taking the hint.

"My research has not reached that point yet."

Cass's heart pounded in her chest. That "yet" was *ominous*. "Just because you talked me into upgrading the security on my home, do not for one minute think you are going to convince me to go through one of those antiphobia seminars. It's not going to happen."

She'd been there, done that and had the scars to prove it.

"You've tried such a thing?" Neo asked perceptively.

She nodded shortly.

"And it did not go well?" he added.

"I still refuse to answer the door to strangers, don't I?"

"That's just intelligent caution," Zephyr said approvingly.

She smiled gratefully at him. Very few people had ever tried to make her feel more normal. The people in her life were mostly vested in getting her back on the stage and that meant making sure she understood just how different she was. *Different* being one of the kindest terms they used. *Broken*, *foolish*, *weak*, and *irresponsible* were some others.

"I'll want details from the attempts you have made to overcome this challenge in the past."

"You're kidding."

"I assure you, I am not."

"Neo doesn't have much of a sense of humor." Zephyr shook his head like he pitied the other man.

Which she noticed made Neo's jaw clench and he turned a less-than-pleased look on his friend.

Zephyr put his hands out in the universal *What, me?* gesture. "I'm only speaking the truth."

Neo did not appear mollified. "I'm going to show you just how little a sense of humor I have in a minute."

Zephyr pushed away from the table and headed to the door. "Ah, reduced to threats. My job here is done." He looked back at Cass. "Nice to meet you, Miss Baker."

"Cass, please."

He grinned. "Nice to meet you, *Cass*."

"It was a pleasure to meet you, too."

"Have fun on your day off." Zephyr winked at Neo.

Neo flipped him a rude hand gesture.

Cass gasped and started laughing as the conference room door closed behind the departing tycoon.

"I apologize. I shouldn't have done that in front of you."

Cass was still smiling when she shook her head at Neo. "If you can't tell, I'm amused, not offended. I liked watching the interplay between you."

"Why?"

"It shows a side to you I don't think you exhibit elsewhere."

"What if it does?"

"Tit for tat. You want to know and have already made efforts to discover stuff about me I don't usually share with strangers, or anyone for that matter."

"So, you think you should know similarly personal things about me?"

"Exactly."

"You drive a hard bargain, Cassandra."

"I must. I got you to take time off work, even if that wasn't my intention."

"Yes. And speaking of, the rest of my morning is clear."

"You plan to entertain me?"

"I do."

"That's not necessary. I do have my MP3 player and a pad to take notes on," she admitted with some shame for her crankiness with him earlier. "And this room is nice and quiet, no distractions…well, except your business partner."

"He bought me my first CD of your music. In fact, he

bought all of them for me over time. I am embarrassed to admit I never checked for the artist so I could buy them myself, though I listen to your music daily."

"That explains how you could be a fan without knowing it."

"Yes."

She shook her head. "I love music, as you know. I can't imagine not trying to find out who created and played music I enjoy."

He shrugged, but it was obvious he meant it when he said he was embarrassed by his oversight.

She reached out and squeezed his forearm. "Hey, I don't have a clue who designed and built my house, but I bet you know."

"It was part of the security consult report."

"I skimmed that bit."

"Are you trying to make me feel less idiotic?"

"Definitely, because you aren't even sort of stupid. Is it working?"

"Yes."

"So, you took the morning off." That still boggled her mind, but she'd decided that morning he needed the break he was so determined she take.

She wasn't going to backslide and let her fear of being in the way stop her from encouraging him to leave work behind for a little while.

He nodded. "I thought I might take advantage of your undivided attention and that we could go shopping for my piano? Since both are available."

"I see." She bit her lip, considering whether or not she could psyche herself into going shopping with the man.

If she wanted to get him out of the office, she'd have to.

It didn't promise to be a pleasant morning for her, but if they stayed out of crowded malls, she should be able to manage her anxiety levels.

And he made her feel safe, like being with him she could do things that normally were beyond her comfort zone.

"Online."

"What?"

"We can retire to my penthouse and do the shopping online," he explained.

"Really? You don't mind? But honestly? You should always test out a piano before buying it."

"Do you think if I had an employee buy the instrument that I would have gone to test it out before purchase?"

"Um, no? But since you have put yourself under the aegis of my expertise, I will have to insist on it. However, we can narrow down our external shopping trip through visiting Web sites and making a few phone calls."

He looked pleased with her for some reason. "That sounds good."

She stood up. "Lead the way."

Before he had a chance to open the door, it swung inward and his PA stood there. "Mr. Stamos, I have Julian from Paris on the line in your office."

"Handle it."

"But, Mr. Stamos—"

"I told you, I am taking the morning off."

That caused the blonde to give Cass a frown that turned into a death glare when she noticed the untouched bottle of water on the table.

Cass grabbed the bottle. "I'll just take this with me."

"I have water in my penthouse," Neo said, sounding bemused.

"There's no sense wasting it." Miss Parks had been annoyed enough at having fetched it for Cass in the first place.

Though Zephyr had delivered it, Cass didn't want any more black marks in the other woman's book than she already had.

Neo put his hand out, indicating Cass should go ahead of him. "Whatever makes you happy."

The PA's already stony expression went positively sour. "Do not keep Julian waiting, Miss Park."

The older woman nodded and left without another word.

"You call your personal assistant Miss Park?" Cass asked.

"That is her name."

"It surprises me that you use surnames with each other."

"She's worked for me for six years and that's always been the way she's preferred it." Neo didn't sound like he cared one way or another.

"Do all of your employees call you Mr. Stamos?"

Neo frowned. "Yes, I suppose. Why?"

"Does Zephyr's personal assistant call him Mr. Nikos?"

"No. Again, why?"

"You keep people at a distance more than he does."

"Just because Zephyr doesn't think I make friends, doesn't mean I don't. I made friends with you, didn't I?"

If he considered steamrolling her into making substantive changes on her house as making friends. But that wasn't really being fair to him, either. "Yes."

"You sound uncertain. I thought we'd already established we are becoming friends."

"We are."

"But?"

"You're a pretty forceful kind of guy, aren't you?"

Get 2 Books FREE!

Harlequin® Books,
publisher of women's fiction,
presents

GET 2 BOOKS

We'd like to send you two *Harlequin Presents*® novels absolutely free. Accepting them puts you under no obligation to purchase any more books.

HOW TO GET YOUR 2 FREE BOOKS AND 2 FREE GIFTS

1. Return the reply card today, and we'll send you two *Harlequin Presents* novels, absolutely free! We'll even pay the postage!

2. Accepting free books places you under no obligation to buy anything, ever. Whatever you decide, the free books and gifts are yours to keep, free!

3. We hope that after receiving your free books you'll want to remain a subscriber, but the choice is yours—to continue or cancel, any time at all!

EXTRA BONUS

You'll also get two free mystery gifts! (worth about $10)

FREE!

**Return this card promptly to get
2 FREE BOOKS and 2 FREE GIFTS!**

HARLEQUIN®

Presents

YES! Please send me 2 FREE *Harlequin Presents®*
novels, and 2 free mystery gifts as well. I understand
I am under no obligation to purchase anything, as
explained on the back of this insert.

*About how many NEW paperback fiction books have
you purchased in the past 3 months?*

☐ 0-2
EZK3

☐ 3-6
EZLF

☐ 7 or more
EZLR

☐ I prefer the regular-print edition
106/306 HDL

☐ I prefer the larger-print edition
176/376 HDL

FIRST NAME	LAST NAME

ADDRESS

APT.#	CITY

Visit us at:
www.ReaderService.com

STATE/PROV.	ZIP/POSTAL CODE

◄ DETACH AND MAIL CARD TODAY! ▼

(H-P-07/10)

Offer limited to one per household and not valid to current subscribers of Harlequin Presents books. Please
allow 4 to 6 weeks for delivery. Offer valid while quantities last. All orders subject to approval. **Your Privacy—**
Harlequin Books is committed to protecting your privacy. Our Privacy Policy is available online at
www.ReaderService.com or upon request from the Reader Service. From time to time we make our lists of customers available to reputable third parties who may have a product or service of interest to you. If you would
prefer for us not to share your name and address, please check here ☐. **Help us get it right—**We strive for
accurate, respectful and relevant communications. To clarify or modify your communication preferences, visit us at
www.ReaderService.com/consumerchoice.

"You do not get to where I am being a pushover."

"No, I don't imagine that you do."

"That does not mean I always have to have things my own way. I'm taking piano lessons, aren't I?"

"Yes." And he'd taken the morning off when he *never* took time off so that she would be comfortable. Steamroller, or not, Neo had the makings of a *good* friend. "Where is your penthouse?"

"At the top of this building. Zephyr and I share the top floor for our living quarters."

"Considering the size of this building, your apartments must be huge."

"Part of the penthouse floor is taken up with the pool and workout facility."

"You have a pool?"

"Zephyr and I share it."

"Wow. I've thought about having one installed in my backyard, but then I wouldn't have much yard left and I'd only get to use it a few months out of the year."

"Seattle's climate isn't conducive to year-round outdoor living," he agreed.

"Not like Greece."

"Living here has its compensations."

"I'm glad you like it here."

"Yes?"

"Yes, I wouldn't have a new friend otherwise."

He grinned, his expression nothing short of pleased. "Just so."

"Still, I envy you the pool."

He laughed warmly. "Finally, something my billionaire status makes you want to have."

"You've got enough people wishing they were you."

"Are you saying I don't need another fan?"

"Oh, I'm a fan all right." Especially of his kisses, but she was nowhere near outrageous enough to say so.

"I am sure."

"I mean it. You're a great guy."

That startled another laugh from him, though she couldn't imagine why. "You cannot know what a refreshing attitude yours is for me."

"Thank you. I think?"

"Definitely. As for the pool, you are welcome to come use ours anytime you like. I will make sure you get a keycard for our top floor."

He couldn't know how tempting that offer was. She loved to swim, but public pools were more than mildly daunting for her. Or perhaps he did, considering the research he'd done on her condition.

Regardless, it was more than generous and not a gift she would dismiss on any level. "Thank you."

"Not at all. What are friends for?"

She was smiling as she followed him to the private elevator that serviced his and Zephyr's offices and penthouse floor.

Finding the piano turned out easier than Cass expected. She hit it lucky with her first phone call. She'd called her own supplier with little hope they'd have something in stock locally, but they had just taken a Steinway baby grand in as trade on a new, bigger Irmler parlor grand for another professional pianist who lived on Bainbridge Island.

"It's something of an extravagance, but the price and immediate availability are very tempting," she told him after the initial phone call. "And you've got the space in your sitting room."

Neo's apartment was huge and although it had obviously been furnished by a professional, it was pretty minimalistic—almost sparse.

"An upright would be considerably less expensive."

"Yes, but not equivalent in tone or performance. That is your standard by which you judge a monetary outlay, right?"

"More or less. Yes."

"If you're serious about learning the piano, you may as well practice on an instrument of true quality."

"You are seduced by this piano's pedigree."

"Maybe a little. A Steinway isn't to be sneezed at and it really is a bargain."

"You're very animated. I like seeing you like this."

She felt herself blushing.

He shook his head, but smiled. "Is it available to test out like you want?"

"We can go by their showroom and try the piano out today anytime."

He looked at his watch. "Where are they located?"

She told him the address in west Seattle, which was admittedly closer to her home than his building downtown.

He nodded. "If we go now, we can make it back in time."

"I thought you took most of the day off?"

"I did, though I still have a meeting later this afternoon."

"It won't take that long."

"I did not think it would."

"Then what do we have to be back in time for?" she asked in confusion.

"Lunch. It will be ready at eleven-thirty."

"Isn't that early?"

"I eat breakfast at six-thirty and you ate only an hour later."

"I'm surprised your nutritionist doesn't have you snacking midmorning with a later lunch."

"Normally, you would be right, but today is special."

Because he was taking it off?

"How did you know I use a nutritionist?" he asked. "I don't remember mentioning that."

She shrugged, tucking her cell phone back into her purse. "Lucky guess. Keeping yourself fit would be top priority and what you don't have time to do yourself, you would pay for."

"You can't do business from a sick bed."

"Oh, I'm sure you can. Furthermore, I'm sure you have."

"Not as effectively. And Zephyr goes all Greek patriarch on me when he finds out about it."

"I bet you do the same to him."

"Naturally. I can take care of whatever needs seeing to, but Zee stubbornly refuses to see that and get proper rest."

"And he feels the same when you are ill."

Neo just shrugged.

Cass grinned. "You're two peas in a pod."

"We just know who we can rely on."

"Each other."

"Yes."

"No one else?"

Neo didn't answer, but she didn't need him to. It was obvious. They were two men who had learned early not to give their trust easily. Which made the fact Neo saw himself as her friend and had offered her a key to the top floor of his building even more amazing.

She could not remember feeling so accepted, not even with her parents. Maybe especially with her parents.

Neo had never been in a store like the one Cass took him to.

It was located in a converted Victorian house. The entire

ground floor had been remodeled into a showroom for the wind instruments and pianos the company sold. The interior designer had done an outstanding job of creating an environment that showed off each instrument to its best advantage. And the acoustics had been enhanced with subtly engineered ceiling panels to maximize the splendor of sound the instruments made.

He was given a sample of the result when Cass picked up a flute, and after wiping the mouthpiece with a cloth provided by the salesman, played a mesmerizing melody that froze Neo in place.

When she was done and put the flute down, he cleared his throat. "I thought you didn't like to perform."

She blushed, looking around at the almost empty store. "That wasn't a performance. It's only the flute."

"It was beautiful."

"Thank you, but I was just messing around."

Interesting. "I thought you only played the piano."

"I dabble on the flute, is all. I wanted to learn the guitar, too, but my parents discouraged it." She brushed her hand over the flute. "They thought I should keep my focus."

"If that's dabbling, I wonder what you would have achieved with a little less focus on the piano."

Cass's smile was nothing short of beautiful. "Thank you. I love the sounds a flute can make."

"I think under your hands, any instrument would sound amazing."

She shook her head. "Flatterer."

"Not at all."

"I love music."

"It shows in your compositions."

"You really listen to my CDs?"

"All of them. Don't ask me to pick a favorite though because no matter how many times I listen, that changes almost daily."

She blushed and turned away, toward the glassed-in, soundproofed room that held the piano they had come in to see.

He followed her. "Surely you are used to such compliments."

"Actually, no. One of the side effects of my not performing is that I don't hear from many of my fans. And when I did perform, my father and manager made sure I spoke to the big money music aficionados, but not normal people who listened to my music just to make their day a little brighter."

"We have already established I do not define normal."

"But you are nothing like the *patrons* I was told to cultivate, either."

"No, none of them became your friend."

She shook her head. "A Greek tycoon for a friend. Who would have thought it?"

"It only matters that I did."

"Too true." She grinned.

"You get letters though," he surmised, going back to the original topic as they stepped up onto the platform where the baby grand piano rested.

Cassandra slid onto the piano bench, her hands caressing the piano as if it was a dear friend she was meeting for the first time. If that made any sense. "Some. Fans only have my CD label's address to send them to. Someone there answers fan mail and passes the letters along to me a couple of times a year."

"I suppose the demand for your music speaks for itself."

"That's what I tell myself."

"Do you miss it?"

She looked up at him, her amber gaze taking his breath away for a second. "What?"

He swallowed, forcing down a reaction that was not acceptable. She was his *friend*. "Performing."

"No." She shuddered, a look of true revulsion coming over her features.

"You didn't enjoy it at all?"

"I hated it. The only thing that kept me sane was the music itself."

"But—"

"I wanted to be home with my mother, not on the road with my father, or more often with a minder. I knew she was ill and I was terrified every time I left on a trip that I would not see her again."

"You knew she was dying? At such a young age?"

"Yes." There was a wealth of pain in that single word. "Like any child, I had my own sense of logic and it told me that if I was there, she could not die. I was wrong." Cassandra shook herself. "Performing for groups of strangers that were allowed to fawn over the child prodigy afterward, saying things they never would have said to an adult performer, I never forgot how much I hated it. Even after Mom died and my dad travelled with me to all my concerts, my earlier feelings colored the experience."

"He pushed you to keep performing."

"Even when Mom got very, very, *very* sick. Just as I'd always feared would happen, she died when I was on tour in Europe. I was seventeen. They didn't tell me until two days later—my father put me off when I tried to phone her.

She'd been so weak, I believed him when he said she was resting every time I called. I felt selfish asking her to call me, like it would tax her waning strength too much."

CHAPTER SEVEN

"THAT is monstrous!" Neo wanted to hit something, but there was nothing to hit and no one to yell at for the sins committed against this woman. "Why would they do such a thing?"

"They didn't want to spoil the last performances on the tour. My father and Bob said I owed *all* my fans the best I was capable of."

He cursed in Greek. Colorfully.

Cassandra's lips twisted in a near smile. "Exactly. My father channeled his grief into my career."

"Where did you channel yours?"

"Into the music."

"But you hated it."

"Not the music, just the concerts."

"So, when he died you stopped torturing yourself."

"That's how I saw it. My manager does not agree."

"Naturally not."

"Bob thinks I'm hiding from my parents' deaths by surrounding myself with their things."

"Isn't he the one who convinced you to get rid of their personal things?" And why the hell was the man still her manager?

"Yes, not that it made a bit of difference in my desire to go on tour."

"Not the catharsis he was expecting then."

"All I know is that the idea of getting on a stage in a packed concert hall makes me want to throw up."

"Do not worry. I will not ever ask you to play for me and I will ensure Zephyr does not, either."

Her mood changed with a flash and nothing but pleasure glowed in her lovely amber gaze. "I wouldn't mind playing for you."

His knees wanted to give, whether it was from the shock of her offer or the effect her clear happiness at the thought had on him, he did not know. Hiding the momentary weakness, Neo slid next to her on the bench at the Steinway. "You would play for me?"

"What are friends for?" she asked, tossing his own words back at him and making him smile.

"I would like that very much."

"Then consider it done." She grinned, all shadows gone from her features for the moment. She tipped her head down and looked at him shyly through her lashes. "I didn't know if I would want to, but I do. In fact, I look forward to it. I used to really enjoy playing for my parents."

But no one else, or so her words implied. "I am honored. It is something I will look forward to with great anticipation."

Smiling, Cassandra concentrated on the instrument in front of her. She looked to check that the door was shut on the soundproof room and then played a short piece, not any music he recognized, just a series of chords. Her head was cocked as if listening for something he couldn't begin to hear.

It sounded fine to him. More than fine.

"Well?" he asked, when she sat in silence for several seconds after the keys fell silent.

"Try your scales on it."

He played the keys as she'd taught him at the first lesson.

"Now, try a few of the chords you've learned."

He did.

"What do *you* think?" she asked.

"It's good?" he asked in uncharacteristic hesitation.

"Did the keys feel natural, not clunky?"

He considered and then nodded. "They felt fine."

"A baby grand really does have better key play than an upright, but nothing can compare to a concert grand like I have. I'm spoiled, but this is a nice instrument." She patted the top of the Steinway.

"What you are saying is that it is not as nice as yours though."

"Buying a Fazioli for a beginner would be an excessive extravagance and you told me you don't squander money indiscriminately. Besides, their waiting list is a long one."

"A Steinway isn't an extravagance?" he asked with a quirk of his lips.

"Not at the price they're offering it."

"So, we *are* getting a deal?" he asked, making no effort to hide his relish at the thought.

"I told you we were. A very good one." She told him how much they would be saving and even he was impressed.

"I knew bringing you with me would be a benefit."

She laughed and shook her head before playing a simple

children's tune as if her fingers could not stay still that close to a well-tuned instrument.

He caught the salesman's eye through the glass and waved the man over.

Neo handed the salesman a black American Express card when he entered the soundproof room. "We'll take it. You can arrange delivery with my personal assistant. Here is my business card. Call this number and it will go directly to her line."

"Very good, Mr. Stamos. We'll arrange a piano tuner to accompany the movers so it is ready for use directly after delivery."

Cassandra nodded her approval and Neo said, "Fine."

The salesman left with Neo's American Express and business cards, but neither Neo nor Cassandra moved to get up from the piano bench.

She brushed her fingertips along the keys. "It's been a few years since I bought a new instrument."

"Getting the urge?"

"To replace my Fazioli? Never. But I might be persuaded to buy some new music for my flute."

"So, you decided you could afford to play a second instrument."

"I dabble, like I said, but sure, why not? If I can learn foreign languages and make time for Tai Chi, why not play a second instrument as a hobby?"

"Zephyr says I have no hobbies."

"Don't worry." She patted his back consolingly. "You have one now. Playing the piano."

"Yes."

"Let's work on some chords."

"Here?"

She looked around the soundproof room and the mostly empty showroom beyond. "Why not?"

"Isn't that like performing?"

"No one can hear us in here."

"You're addicted. That's what this is about, isn't it? You miss your piano?"

"I'll make a deal with you. You learn two chords and I'll play a short piece from my newest score for you."

"Here?" he asked again, inelegantly.

"Where else? It's soundproof in here and we can close the drape over the window for extra privacy. And we can't exactly go back to my house."

"We could, but I'd prefer you not return to the scene of the crime until the last bit of sawdust has been vacuumed up."

"Scene of the crime is right."

"Stop whining and show me a chord."

He couldn't believe how much he enjoyed learning the chords she wanted to teach him. No one bothered them. Not even the salesman, who came in quietly only to leave the receipt and paperwork for Neo's purchase on top of the piano, and then left just as quietly.

"Okay, I think I've got it," he said after playing the chords successfully several times. "Now, it's your turn to keep your part of the bargain."

"You got it." She got up and closed the drape on the window then tugged on the door to make sure it was shut.

She returned to the piano bench. She didn't ask him to leave it and he was curiously hesitant to do so. So, he stayed.

She started to play a piece he recognized from one of her early albums. It was a particular favorite of his and he sat quietly while she played it *just for him*. It wasn't a long, or complicated piece, so it was over all too soon, but he would cherish the memory of that impromptu entertainment for years to come.

She looked sideways at him. "That was just a warm-up."

She really was going to play a new piece. Again *just for him*. Her fingers danced across the keys, coaxing gorgeous sounds from the Steinway and he knew this new CD would be one of her best yet.

When she finished she looked up at him and smiled. "It's nice, isn't it?"

He didn't know if she meant the piano or the piece, but he said, "Yes," to both. "Thank you." He looked down at her, hard pressed to refrain from following his gratitude with a kiss.

She tilted her head back and met his gaze, her amber eyes glowing with joy from the music and something he could not define. "You are welcome. That was the first time I've ever played in a public place and enjoyed it."

The showroom wasn't exactly a concert hall, but he was proud of her for keeping her end of the bargain all the same. "Glad to be of service."

"You make me feel safe."

He was lost for words.

She blushed and ducked her head. "Isn't it about time we got back for lunch?"

"I'm sure it is." He tipped her face up so their eyes met. The moment was too profound to ignore. "Thank you."

"I…"

"I have rarely in my life been as honored as I am by your trust in me." His head tilted forward of its own volition.

She let out a soft puff of air. "Are you going to kiss me again?"

"Not a good idea."

"Why?"

"We are friends."

"And friends cannot kiss." She smiled and pulled her chin from his hand, clearly trying to lighten the atmosphere between them.

He would do his part. "I have never kissed Zephyr."

"Liar."

That made him reel back. "I have never kissed a man."

"That whole kissing on the cheek thing you Greek guys do? What's that?"

"Oh." Heat climbed the cheeks she mentioned. "That is not the same." At all.

"No, but it's still a kiss."

"You are walking a dangerous path, *pethi mou.*"

"Pethi mou?"

"Little one." His little one, but he didn't need to tell her that bit.

"I'm not that little."

"Compared to me?"

"You're just oversized."

"I thought that was my ego."

"O-ho, so you have perturbed a girlfriend, or two."

"I've never had a girlfriend, but yes, more than one pillow-mate has remarked that I have a rather healthy ego."

"I'll bet."

"I will tell you what I tell them—it is deserved."

"And do they agree?"

"Naturally."

She bit her lip, looking away from him, that adorable expression he could easily become addicted to on her features. He liked Cassandra Baker shy. He wondered if he should tell her.

Not everyone thought she had to perform publicly to be valuable.

"I've never had a boyfriend, either," she whispered, breaking in to his thoughts.

"Never?" That should not have shocked him, but it did. He had guessed she was a virgin, but to be wholly innocent of male-female games? He could not imagine it.

"Um…no."

"How old are you?"

"Twenty-nine. I'm a real freak, aren't I?"

"What?" He grabbed her shoulders and made her meet his eyes by sheer force of will. When her amber gaze was looking into his, he said, "You are precious, but are you saying this morning was your first kiss?"

"Well, actually, um…yes."

Oh, hell, didn't his libido just love that? "I wish I'd known."

"Why?"

"I would have made it special."

"It felt pretty special to me."

"It could have been better."

"How?"

"It's not something I can explain with words."

"Novelists do."

"I'm a businessman, not a writer. I'll have to show you."

"Here?" she squeaked.

"Yes." He covered her lips with his before she could get another query out.

Gently. More carefully than he had ever kissed another woman. Even his first time. But damn. The knowledge no other man had done this battered at his vaunted self-control. However, he would not give in to the mouth-ravaging his own desires demanded.

Her lips tasted every bit as good as they had that morning, but the knowledge they were his and no one else's added a sweetness he had never once thought to experience. A sweetness so real, he could taste it as certainly as he did the unique flavor of Cassandra's delicious mouth.

Of their own volition, his arms slid around her, pulling her so close their body heat mixed. She felt right in his arms. Too right. Like she fit exactly as if she had been made to be held exactly as he held her.

He refused to dwell on that sensation of rightness, choosing instead to enjoy this anomalous moment in time. His tongue swept through her mouth, claiming her as only he had ever done.

His body demanded he claim her in other ways. Thankfully they were in a semipublic setting, or he might not have had the strength to deny himself.

This being friends with a woman was harder than he had ever expected it to be.

Her slender fingers tunneled into his hair, short-circuiting rational thought. Cassandra kissed him back with an unfettered sensuality he knew would be a joy between the sheets.

She had never kissed another man, but she knew exactly how to tease his tongue into her mouth. Her feminine instincts were rock solid as she dueled with his tongue while making whimpering sounds of need that drove his libido through the roof and beyond.

Damn. Damn. Damn.

He was seriously considering pulling her under the piano and away from prying eyes when the sound of a near tortured squawk had him yanking his head back.

He reared up and looked around only to see that the door to their soundproof room stood open. The salesman must have thought to speak to them only to get an eyeful when he opened the door.

Through the doorway, Neo could see a young boy blowing determinedly into a clarinet. The source of the awful noise. The child's mother was staring at Neo and Cassandra with a sappy expression that had Neo jumping off the piano bench.

That woman's look screamed, "Romance...isn't that sweet?" He didn't do romance. Not even for Cassandra.

He put his hand out. "Come. We'll be late for lunch."

"Don't forget your paperwork," she said, though her eyes indicated she wanted to say something entirely different.

Lunch was a banquet of Mediterranean cuisine. It had started with *fasolada*, the bean soup Cass had always associated with Greece. Then there had been a small salad made up of leafy greens, pine nuts and crumbled feta with a dressing unlike anything she'd tasted before.

"This is amazing," Cass said as she scooped a bite of the main dish, spinach *spanakopita*, onto her fork. "There's no way you eat like this every meal."

"Naturally not. But today I have a guest. My housekeeper was thrilled I told her not to worry about the nutritionist's directives and to prepare a traditional Greek meal for you. She is from the Old Country and she does not approve of my nutritionist's directives, to say the least."

And far from bothering him, Neo seemed to enjoy the Greek woman's attitude. Cass would bet her new flute music that his housekeeper was an older woman and that what she fed him wasn't the only thing she fussed about.

Neo had found a way to have a mother without the emotional baggage of a close relationship.

Cass waved toward the table with her fork. "This is a feast."

"I'm glad you are enjoying it."

"I fell in love with Greek food when I played in Athens."

"You played in Athens?"

"Yes. When I was twelve. It's a beautiful city."

"I agree, though I couldn't wait to see the back of it when I was younger."

"I'm sure it looks different to you now than it did to the orphan boy who left it behind."

"Very much so."

"Do you and Zephyr return often to Greece?"

"At least once a year, though always under the guise of business. We have never taken a vacation there."

That wasn't saying much. "You don't vacation at all," she chided gently.

"Neither does Zephyr."

"So, you are both workaholics."

"And you? Are you a composeraholic?"

"Making up words now?"

"Why not? Scientists do it all the time."

She couldn't help laughing. "Zephyr said you don't have a sense of humor, but I think he's wrong."

"That is only because his sense of what is amusing borders on the insane."

"You are lucky to have each other."

"He is the brother of my heart."

She stared at Neo for several seconds before saying, "I'm surprised to hear you say something like that."

"Why?"

"I don't know. It sounds so sentimental, I guess."

"Truth is not sentimentality," he said in a tone that left no doubt he was offended.

She stifled a smile. "Well, I'm glad you have that truth in your life."

"You do not, do you?"

"What do you mean?" But she knew. It wasn't something she liked to think about.

"You had parents, but they were taken from you long before their deaths by your mother's illness and your father's choices."

She couldn't deny his observation, but agreeing with it would hurt too much so Cass remained silent.

"And now, you have no one you would call family."

How true. Online friends could fill her free time, but not the heart's need for proximity relationships. And her agoraphobia prevented her from developing those. Oh, she made friends on occasion, certainly more frequently than Neo seemed to.

But eventually all those she would call friend got fed up with her limitations and either moved on, or turned into what she considered martyr friends. Those people that wouldn't dump her because of her issues, but who so obviously wished they were elsewhere when they were with her.

She was determined to enjoy every moment of her friendship with Neo.

But even with that resolve, the loneliness of her life rose up and slapped her emotions a stinging blow. However, she made herself shrug noncommittally. "I have friends."

"None that you trust as I trust Zephyr."

"I never trusted my parents as much as you trust him. And I wouldn't have trusted siblings that way, either." Maybe. It helped her to believe that right then.

"You cannot know that."

She should have known he would call her on it. "You're correct, of course. In fact, don't laugh, but my favorite daydream as a child was that I had brothers and sisters who loved me for me and not because I could play a piano the way I do."

"There is nothing in that to make me laugh." He reached across the table and cupped her cheek. "Know this—our friendship does not rely on your playing piano."

And even though she was his piano teacher and he was a fan of her music, she believed him. "Thank you."

"We have two hours until my next meeting, is there something particular you would like to do?"

"Do you watch movies?"

"It is one of my guilty pleasures."

She grinned, internally shaking off the negative thoughts their conversation had produced. "A movie then."

He showed her his collection and she discovered that Neo had another secret besides the stock that made up his portfolio. The man liked old movies. The classics. They watched a film starring Spencer Tracy and Katharine Hepburn, both laughing in all the same places.

When it was over, Neo had to return to his office for a meeting. "You can stay up here if you like."

"Thank you, I'd like that." She sighed. "I wish I'd known you had a pool. I would have brought my suit."

"Zephyr and I keep a selection of swimsuits in the changing room for our female guests. I'm sure you could find one to fit you."

"Are you serious?"

"Yes. They are replaced each spring with a selection of the season's new styles."

"I suppose for a couple of playboys like you, that's not a wasteful expenditure."

"It has come in handy a time or two," he admitted without a single blush.

"I bet." It took her a second to realize the emotion she was feeling was jealousy, but she refused to acknowledge it. She did not have that kind of a claim on Neo, even if he had kissed her. Twice.

"You can access the pool through that door. You'll have to prop it open with a chair because it locks automatically when it closes. I'll have a key made for you to access this floor, but it won't open my apartment, or Zephyr's."

So, his trust of her only extended so far. No surprise that. The only true shock was that he trusted her at all. She shook her head at him. "You've got a real thing about locked doors, don't you?"

"Safety first."

She cracked up.

Amusement still showed on his face when he left.

She found a burnt orange bikini that fit as if it had been made for her and changed into it. If the sexiness of the cut might tempt Neo to further kissing extravagances, who was she to argue? Who was she kidding? Neo wasn't about to be tempted by her not-so-curvy form.

She still liked the swimsuit. It made her feel sexy, even if maybe she wasn't exactly femme fatale material. And she found she felt perfectly comfortable at the thought of Neo seeing her in it. Even if it didn't tempt him to mind-melting kisses.

The pool was the perfect temperature and she swam several laps, enjoying the unlooked-for treat.

She was sitting on the side, dangling her feet in the wet and drinking water from a bottle she'd found in the pool bar's fridge when Neo returned.

He looked harried.

"Tough meeting?" she asked.

"I am regretting my choice in contractors."

"That's not a feeling you have often, I'm sure."

"You're right. I weigh my choices carefully and I thought I had this time, too."

"What happened?"

"He had done two smaller projects for me before, but despite his claims to the contrary, it is now obvious he does not have the resources for this much larger one."

"I'm sorry to hear that."

"He'll be far sorrier if I have to fly out there."

"Where is it?"

"Dubai."

"Really? I've always wanted to go."

"I'll make a deal with you—if I go, I'll take you."

She rolled her eyes. "Yeah. Thanks."

"Are you afraid of flying?"

"Flying? No. The crowds in the airport and on the plane are enough to give me nightmares." Though she could deal with them if she had to. Maybe.

"What about a private jet?"

"I've never flown on one."

"It is the only way I travel. For both expediency and security reasons."

Wow. She leaned back and smiled up at him. "Of course you have your own jet."

"Well?"

"Well what?" She thought she should know what he was asking, but it was escaping her.

"Would you like to go to Dubai with me on my private jet if the project ends up requiring my personal supervision?"

"I…" Was he serious? He certainly seemed so. "You…" The prospect was so tempting. She missed travelling so much and she could not imagine a better partner for doing it. She couldn't imagine anyone else making her feel comfortable enough to be so tempted. "I think so, yes."

"Fantastic." And he looked like he really meant it. Like he was proud of her.

She bit her lip, blinking back tears. He was an amazing man. And the trip sounded wonderful. But best of all, she would be with Neo. That was even more tempting than the travel. "I've never thought to try flying private."

She could have rented a private jet to fly her domestically at least, but the thought had never occurred to her, even when she used to jokingly lament about the lack of private railcars nowadays.

"We'll have to give it a test. Before Dubai. Go somewhere not too far away. Maybe a trip to Napa Valley."

"Are you kidding?"

"I don't have a sense of humor, remember?"

"I know that's not true."

"Well, I am not joking."

CHAPTER EIGHT

"BUT there's nothing in it for you." And wouldn't such a trip require him taking even more time off from work?

Her head was reeling and so was her heart.

"Helping my friend with her desire to travel is something."

"You're crazy."

"I do not think so."

She laughed, feeling happier than she had in years.

"Besides, I like California wines. I wouldn't mind a chance to visit some of the better vineyards and purchasing some of their selective stock."

"Hmm…"

"Do you like wine?"

"I don't drink."

"Religious reasons?"

"No. It's just…I'm a lightweight."

"How light?"

"I smell the cork and I'm tipsy."

"This I should like to see."

"And when I start making words up to go with my instrumental compositions? So not pretty."

"I would like to hear you sing."

"No, you wouldn't. Trust me. As talented as I am on the piano, I am conversely as horrible a singer."

"You only increase my desire to hear it."

"You're a masochist? I never would have thought it."

"And if you had, you would have been wrong, but I like the idea of hearing you be less than perfect."

Implying what? That he thought she was mostly perfect? Now that wasn't possible. With her problems, no one thought she was perfect. Or even close to it. "So you can laugh at me?" she teased.

"Laughing *with you* is surprisingly pleasurable."

She remembered the movie and nodded. "It is."

"So, you will sing for me?"

"If we go to Napa Valley and if you convince me to taste some of this selective wine you plan to buy, you just might get that treat."

"I'll hold you to that."

"There were a lot of ifs and maybes in there," she warned.

He shrugged as if the only words he knew or heard were *yes, can* and *do*. "Are you all swimmed out?"

"I could do a few more laps."

"Then, I will join you."

"Great." That's just what she needed. The most gorgeous man she'd ever met running around in a swimsuit.

After the two kisses today, her body was going through all sorts of palpitations and excitations. She wanted to grab him and throw him on the deck beside the pool and kiss him until both their lips were sore, but he said friends couldn't kiss. And he wanted to be her friend.

He'd already shown that meant something real to him. Friendship. He'd been there for her when she needed him and he'd never once chastised her for her weakness. He'd given her his time today and she knew that was something special.

Neo Stamos was a dream man. If only her limitations weren't so redolent of a nightmare.

She wasn't going to do anything to mess this relationship up before it ran the natural course all her other friendships had over her life.

Seeing him in his swimsuit was worse than she expected. Neo was clearly not ashamed of his body. Showing his European upbringing, he wore spandex swim trunks that showed off his stomach and thighs like no California board shorts could ever do. It wasn't a Speedo, having a little leg to it. But it was enough to make her whimper as feelings she had read about, but never personally experienced before meeting him, zinged through her body.

"Did you say something?"

She had to clear her throat. "Uh, nothing. Nice suit."

"It creates minimum drag when I am doing laps."

"Of course." She thought he'd just bought it to seduce unwary virgin pianists. Well, maybe not.

They swam several laps, even racing a couple, which he won.

"It's just because I wore myself out swimming before you came up." It didn't help that she had a hard time concentrating on her breast stroke when all she wanted to think about was what Neo would feel like pressed up against her as he had been at the piano showroom.

Only wearing nothing but swimwear. Not that she was about to admit that out loud. Still, she shivered in the heated water at the yummy picture her mind presented her yet again.

"Ah," he said sagely. "It's got nothing to do with the fact I'm more than a half a foot taller than you with more powerful leg muscles?"

"Let's leave your leg muscles out of it." She scrunched her face at him. "You'll give me a complex."

"Your bird legs are quite lovely."

"Bird legs?" she screeched. Had he seriously called her legs birdlike? "What is that? Scrawny and orange?" Oh, he was so going down. She shot under the water, diving for his ankles.

Whether it was surprise or simply good timing, she managed to get her arms around his ankles and yank, pulling him under the water. Not being an idiot, she let go immediately and bolted to the other side of the pool as fast as she could swim. She was half out when big hands clamped onto her waist and lifted.

She went sailing through the air to land with a splash in the center of the pool. She had the presence of mind to hold her breath as she went under, but still came up spluttering. *And* ready to get her own back only to find him waiting for her, a devilish smile on his too handsome face.

This was fun. Really, really fun. She hadn't played like this in, well…ever. In just five weeks, Neo had given her so much. Her heart was so full, she felt it might burst.

At the last second, she checked her instinct to grab him and try another dunking. She couldn't help noticing that Neo stood firm, his head and most of his shoulders above the pool line while she had to tread water to keep her face out of it.

"You think you've won?" she demanded breathlessly.

"I think we're even right this minute," he said with obvious concession.

She mock growled at his taunting, but said, "A smart woman would leave it at that, I suppose."

"A draw is better than defeat," he acknowledged.

She gave him a really good glare and sent a wave of water cascading toward him. "You're so sure I would lose?"

With hardly a blink at the deluge that broke over his head, he wiped the excess water droplets from his face and shrugged. Definitely his confidence was unquestionable. And totally justified. Unfortunately.

"You might be bigger, but maybe I'm more devious," she posited.

"Highly doubtful." He grinned. "I'm a real estate developer. I deal with devious every day."

"You've got me there." The music industry could be cutthroat, but she stayed out of the business side as much as possible.

"Can I sweeten the *draw* with an offer of refreshments?" he asked.

Why did the word *draw* sound so much like *defeat*? "What kind of refreshments?" she asked, tempted despite her newly awakened sense of competition.

"Macadamia nut cookies and baklava. My housekeeper was *very* happy to have her normal restrictions lifted."

Cass's mouth watered and any thoughts of futile attempts at a second dunking for the big man flew from her mind. "You've sold me."

"I'll meet you inside."

Only if she could get out of the pool after nearly drowning herself when she forgot to keep treading water while watching his muscular backside walking away from her toward one of the shower enclosures.

* * *

Neo heated the water for tea to go with their pastries and reminded himself of all the reasons he could not bed the sexy woman still drying her hair in his guest bathroom. Hell, he'd come close to making love to her in the pool. Then on the deck when she'd stepped out of the water.

He should never have looked back before closing the door on the shower room. She'd had a glazed look in her eye he associated with things not remotely related to swimming.

But damn did she look delectable in a swimsuit. Supermodels would kill for a body so well-toned. Cassandra wasn't anorexically thin like those women. Thank heaven. No protruding bones in places where at least a minimal layer of insulation should reside.

But the only things that jiggled were supposed to. Even if her curves were modest, they were mouth-wateringly succulent. Petite but perfect breasts and small round globes of a bottom that tempted his hands and mouth. He had wanted to leave a love bite on one flawless mound in the worst way.

She'd almost started something very different than what she'd intended with her dunking game. When he picked her up to toss her into the pool, he'd very nearly brought her body to his mouth instead of letting her go to splash in the water.

Oh, hell. What had he been thinking suggesting she use the pool?

That she'd wear one of the more modest one-pieces he knew could be found in the changing room. That's what. Absolutely not that she'd choose to swim laps in three tiny triangles that revealed more than they hid. The damn bottoms were almost a thong. And Cassandra had a perfect butt.

Luscious. Well-rounded, but clearly the result of time spent in her exercise room because…damn. Perfect. Yes, that was the only word that fit. And the lack of tan line indicated whatever sunbathing she did, she wore a suit of similar construction.

His heart could barely take the strain of thinking about that one. His virginal friend was too damn sexy for either of their sakes.

Hearing the continued sound of the hair dryer just made him want to go in there and offer his services helping her dry those glorious, silky tresses. What woman in today's age grew her hair to her waist like Cassandra had? Didn't she know it took too much work for a modern woman to maintain?

He nearly laughed at his own musings. Apparently, Cassandra had not gotten the memo.

He'd had no idea how long the soft brown curtain was until he'd seen her braid as she sat beside the pool. It hung down the middle of her back, the tail brushing enticingly against the top curve of her backside. He had immediately wanted to see what the brown silk would look like fanned out on his pillow, or hanging down around both their faces as she rode him to ecstasy.

His eyes slid shut, the pain of unabated arousal humming through him as he bit off a Greek word even he didn't say very often.

He grabbed his phone and dialed.

Zephyr picked up on the second ring. "What's up?" he asked in Greek.

"Remind me why it's a bad idea to have sex with your friends."

"Did I say that?" Was that amusement Neo heard in his partner's voice?

"No. I did, but I need reminding."

"What friend are we talking about? The new piano teacher?" That was definitely laughter lacing Zephyr's tone.

Neo growled, "Yes."

"I'm surprised."

"That I want to have sex with her?" He always thought Zephyr was more discerning than that.

"No, that you are calling her friend already."

"She's special."

"I see." All amusement was gone now.

Finally, the other man was taking this seriously. "Good, because I do not. Tell me to keep my hands to myself."

"When have you ever listened to me?"

"Damn it, Zee…"

"You really are in a quandary, aren't you?"

"I like being her friend. I don't want to ruin that."

"And having sex with her would do that?"

"Of course. Wouldn't it?"

"That depends."

"On what?"

"On what her expectations are going into the sex. When both people are on the same playing field, sex between friends can be more mind blowing than anything you'll experience with a mere hookup."

He wasn't sure he and Cassandra *could* be on level playing ground. "She's a virgin," he told his friend with simple honesty. "Totally innocent."

"At her age?"

"Yes, and another reason not to take her to my bed."

"Unless she's tired of being inexperienced. Are you sure her state is by choice?" he asked in a tone that implied Zephyr knew something about this sort of situation from his own experience.

"What do you mean?"

"Think about it. Cass has lived her whole life for her ailing mother and her music. I doubt her father let her date when she was younger and now she's got this agoraphobia thing going on. When is she going to meet a man she might enjoy making love to?"

"That's not the point."

"It's not?"

"No. *I* can't be that man." That was the point.

"Why not?"

"Because she'll end up hurt. She's not like my—"

"Other hookups? Maybe it's time you graduated beyond the one-night stand."

"I am not looking for a relationship. I don't have the time."

"Everyone has time for friends, Neo."

"No, they do not."

"Let me rephrase that. Everyone should make time for friends. What's the point of being at the top of your pyramid if there isn't anyone up there with you to enjoy it?"

"I have you."

"Your business partner and only friend. Hell, Neo, half the time you and I are in different countries dealing with our business."

"So?"

"So, you can't spend all your time working."

"This record is getting old, Zee."

"Is it? Or is it finally starting to sink in?"

"You know you are a hypocrite, don't you?"

"We aren't talking about me right now."

"Good thing for your sake."

"Right. Listen, does Cass want you?"

"I think so, yes." Hell, if he was wrong then somebody shoot him now, he'd lost his ability to read people.

"So, let her know the score and allow her to make her own choice."

"She might not make the one best for her."

"She's an adult, Neo. It is her call."

"You make it sound so damn simple."

"And you are letting it get way more complicated than it needs to be."

Neo didn't need Zephyr to tell him sex with Cassandra would be better than any hookup. His body had been yelling that very message at him since she'd opened her door to him the first time. In fact, he realized he didn't need Zee to tell him anything at all.

He already knew what he wanted and he damn well knew what he was going to do about it.

Maybe she wasn't his usual type, but she wasn't the Plain Jane he had first considered her. Cassandra was no supermodel.

Damn it, she was better.

She might love her bright designer fashions, but there wasn't a vain bone in her body. Her innocent sensuality was a thousand times more provocative than another woman's practiced seduction and he had the erection from hell to prove it.

Neo had never practiced self-denial when it came to sex. He met a woman he wanted, she wanted him, too, and they danced the horizontal mamba a few bars. Well, he wanted Cassandra, and he was damn sure she wanted him, too, but for the first time, that wasn't the only consideration at hand.

The blow dryer cut off. Neo's hands fisted at his sides

as he fought through an internal quagmire of conflicting thoughts. One thing shone through the rest—Cassandra Baker had spent twenty-nine years being denied aspects to life most people took for granted. First by the circumstances of her childhood and then by the limitations of the anxiety that plagued her.

He could give her a taste of passion—more than a taste, a whole buffet. Maybe friendship didn't have to preclude sex. Not if both people wanted it.

And Neo wanted it. So did Cassandra.

Cass walked into the kitchen expecting to find Neo making tea, which was such a domestic thing to do, it really endeared him to her.

What she did not expect was the feral gleam in his green eyes and the clear tension thrumming through his body.

"Are you all right, Neo?" she asked, wondering if she should have put her suit jacket back on and not sure why that particular thought was flitting through her brain.

Except for the way he was looking at her. Like her white silk blouse was transparent and the lacy bra she wore beneath it not much better.

"You left it down."

She looked to the right and then to the left, but neither the pristine counter nor the small bistro table set with goodies and tea things gave her a clue what he was going on about. "Um, okay. Did you want me to pour the tea?"

He didn't answer, his hands clenched as if he was trying to stop himself touching something.

"Uh, Neo? You're starting to worry me."

"Is it desire or lack of opportunity?" he demanded in a guttural voice.

"I don't think I know what you are talking about." In fact, she was sure of it.

"Your virginity?"

"My vir…" she squeaked, choking the word off midway. "What are you talking about?" And why were they talking about it? Being untouched at age twenty-nine was not exactly her favorite topic for contemplation.

He crossed the distance between them with two long strides. "Your innocence. Is it a condition you are pleased about?"

"Pleased?" Right. Because every woman wanted to stare thirty down without ever having had a boyfriend, much less a serious relationship. "Neo, you aren't making any sense!"

"It is a simple question, *pethi mou*."

"I'm sure it is, only I don't know what the question is." She was getting an inkling, though, and her face was flaming because of it.

"Zee said you might not be a virgin by choice, but rather by necessity."

"Necessity?"

"For lack of opportunity," he clarified.

"You talked to Zephyr about my sex life?" she asked in outrage as her brain finally caught up.

He ignored her. "Lack of sex life. If you had a sex life, my own would be so much easier."

"I don't see how."

He slid his hand under her hair to cup her nape, the gentle touch at odds with the feral gleam in his green gaze. "Don't you?"

The heat from his hand froze her vocal chords. No, that didn't make any sense. Shouldn't heat unfreeze them? But they felt frozen, unable to move. All she really knew was that she couldn't speak. She wasn't even sure why she was having the silent dialogue in her head, except that it was easier to think about that then what Neo was trying to discuss.

"I do not wish to take advantage of you." His thumb brushed her neck, up and down…up and down, sending tingles through her with each light sweep.

Her vocal chords finally unstuck. "Neo, you cannot go around discussing my private life with Zephyr." Really, really.

"I did not go anywhere. I called him from right here."

"You know what I mean."

"I know I want you."

"You do?" Okay, that bit of information was certainly enough to sidetrack her.

"Definitely."

"But what about the *no kissing friends* rule?"

"I am rethinking my stance on that one."

"Oh." Well, it was probably a good idea, considering the fact he kept breaking it.

"Hence the call to Zephyr." Where they talked about her virginity.

Oh, man. Her whole body flushed with embarrassment. "And he said…"

"That I should let you make your own choices. That you are an adult."

"He's right. I've been all grown up for years and as much as it seems to happen—or used to—I detest having others make important decisions for me. Only the problem here is that I'm not sure what I'm supposed to be choosing between."

"Sex with me."

Oh, heavens. Okay, she really got it now. "As opposed to friendship without sex?" she asked, just to be sure.

"Precisely."

"And after the sex?"

"The friendship remains."

Friendship never remained for her, sex, or no sex, but now probably wasn't the time to mention that salient little fact to him. "Friends with benefits."

"I guess." A sound of dark amusement came out of him. "Some benefit. As I told you, I have never had a female friend before."

"But you do now. And you want to make love, er, have sex with her."

A brilliant smile broke over his features. "Exactly."

"But you don't want anything else. Beyond friendship?"

The troubled expression returned. "It is not fair to you."

"Why? If it's fair to you and I do assume you think it is? Why wouldn't it be fair to me?" What made her so special?

"You are far less cynical than I. And I'm worried you will mistake our intimacy for…"

"Love?" she asked, clueing in to the fact that even in the abstract he wasn't comfortable saying the word. Never mind the obvious reality that he thought she wasn't just lacking in cynicism but was encumbered with a big dose of emotional naiveté.

"Right."

"It goes without saying you won't make the same mistake."

He shrugged one shoulder. "I have never fallen for any of the women I've taken to my bed."

"If you had, we wouldn't be having this conversation." And even the thought had the power to hurt her. Maybe she was more at risk here than she realized.

"The truth is, I don't think I'm a guy who does the softer emotions."

"Ah, you don't think you are capable of love?"

"I have never loved anyone, never been loved by anyone."

She knew that wasn't true. The affection he and Zephyr shared was love if she'd ever seen it. They loved like brothers. Like family. She hadn't experienced it but she knew what it looked like. Family love. Neo was clearly uncomfortable acknowledging the feeling but he'd been lucky to experience it.

The discussion was moot in regard to her anyway. She hadn't engendered unconditional love in her own parents, no way was it going to spring forth from Neo's manly chest in relation to her. She had never expected to be loved—longed for it, but never expected it. And it had been years since she allowed herself to even daydream about such a thing. She didn't feel as lonely when she didn't dwell on what she could not have.

And she wasn't going to let it stop her from having what she could.

"I'm not expecting love from you," she told him honestly.

CHAPTER NINE

"WHAT do you expect?"

"Nothing. I learned a long time ago that expectations lead to disappointment."

"What are you looking for, then?"

"I'm not sure I'm looking for anything. Your advent into my life was like a comet dropping from the sky, totally unanticipated and a little earthshaking, if you want the truth. Your friendship is a remarkable gift."

He took a deep breath and stepped back. "That's it then."

"But sex would be wonderful, too." Not that she thought *wonderful* even began to describe what she would feel sharing her body with this man.

"So it *is* a matter of opportunity."

"Not exactly." She hadn't dated. She'd never kissed, but she'd met men who wanted to bed her. Groupies that might be rich and snobby, but were groupies nonetheless and frankly, they'd scared her silly.

Almost as badly as getting on stage to play a concert.

Talk about performance anxiety. What would someone who almost deified her because of something she couldn't control—her talent—expect from her in bed?

"But you do want me now?"

"Right now?" she asked with an embarrassing hitch in her voice.

"Yes, right now."

"I always want you," she admitted quietly. "From the very beginning I've wanted you, even when I didn't recognize what that feeling was."

"But you recognize it now?"

"Yes." And how. It was a screaming ache inside her. And he was offering to assuage it. She could have cried with relief.

"And you are ready to act on those feelings?"

"Here? Now?" Her voice had gone high with nerves, though to be honest—yes, and *yes*.

"Do you have other plans?"

"Tea?"

He smiled, almost indulgently, though his demeanor was anything but. He looked like an ancient warrior contemplating his next conquering. "I think tea can wait."

She could do nothing but nod. Tea *could* wait. He could not. Her virginity would not. She maintained a façade of semicalm on the outside, but inside, she was shaking.

He must have sensed it because he bent down and picked her up, one arm under her legs and another behind her back. Just like always, she felt safe with him, even when faced with the unknown. He turned and headed down the hall that led to the bedrooms.

"I don't want to get naked in a bed tons of other women have gotten sweaty in." Not only did her heart—which wasn't supposed to be engaged in this—rebel, but so did her *ick* factor.

The last must be the only thing that registered with him because instead of getting all worried that she was getting emotionally carried away, he laughed. "I change the sheets or rather, my housekeeper does."

"I don't care. We can use a guest bed."

"Actually, we cannot."

She frowned up at him.

"When I bring them back to my penthouse, I don't take women to my bedroom, we go into the guest room."

"Okay, it's the master bedroom then."

"You do not mind *my* sweat?"

"We are friends."

"Ah." But he was still clearly laughing at her.

She didn't care. He could be as amused as he liked, but while she might not ever have his heart, she would demand every concession his friendship afforded.

Neo could not believe that he was carrying Cassandra into his bedroom with serious intent. The intent to share his bed and his body. His hold on her tightened as he inhaled her scent and reveled in the knowledge of what was to come.

His body rejoiced while his brain tried to wrap around the change in his circumstances. She wanted him and she understood the limitations of their relationship. Not only understood, but accepted.

Friends with benefits. He would have to discuss this concept with her. The idea she might decide to have benefits with another friend down the road did not sit well with him. Their case was a special one and she would need to understand that. Another man might not treat her generosity with the respect and appreciation it deserved.

But right now, Neo was going to give her exactly what he had promised. He was going to blow her mind with pleasure.

They entered the bedroom and he turned on the light with his elbow. The California king-size bed was in the center of the room and he headed directly for it. He leaned down to pull back the top sheet and duvet, then he laid her on his black Egyptian cotton sheet-covered mattress. Her beautiful brown hair fanned out on the pillows just as he had known it would.

Reaching out, he smoothed his fingers through it. "It's like silk."

"It flies everywhere when I don't keep it put up."

"And yet you left it down for me."

She looked at him with confusion for a second, but then she smiled and nodded. "Yes, I think I did."

"You knew I craved to see and feel it."

"I did notice you looking at my braid rather intently by the pool."

"I was looking at all of you intently."

"I wasn't sure if I wasn't imagining that."

"You were not."

"I'm glad." Her smile was sweet and, for all her innocence, full of womanly mystery.

"As am I."

"I wanted to feel our bodies pressed close together in just our swimwear."

"I will give you better than that. There will be nothing between us."

She shuddered, her eyelids going half-mast. "I might not survive it."

"You are good for my ego." And Zee had been so right. Even the bantering with her was different…he was himself, he wanted to talk.

"Does it need stroking?"

"No," he admitted with a smile. "But it feels good nonetheless."

"I get that."

"Do you?"

"Yes. I know I have uncommon talent with the piano, but it still feels really nice when others express their appreciation."

"You do get it." She got *him* like no one else. Not even Zephyr. The warm approval in her pretty amber eyes went straight to his groin. "Yep."

"Get this," he said as his hungry mouth pressed down over hers.

Her lips gave way under his almost immediately and he took instant advantage, sliding his tongue inside to taste sweetness that was rapidly becoming addictive. Her response was complete and unhesitating. She flicked her tongue against his while her sweet lips moved with unconscious sensuality.

His body knew what to do and without even thinking about it, he started stripping his clothing away as he kept her occupied with one devouring kiss after another. He wore only his briefs when he started on the buttons of her blouse.

Her hands slid down from his head and seemed to stutter when they encountered naked skin, but within seconds she was caressing everywhere she could reach, her slender fingers mapping his torso with passionate curiosity.

He slid her blouse back, revealing her lovely body. He wanted to see, but he didn't want to stop kissing her.

She made up his mind for him by dragging her mouth from his. "You won't be disappointed?"

He reared back and looked down at her, taking in the satin smooth skin of her stomach and the worried glint in her amber gaze at the same time. "How could I be disappointed? You are beautiful."

"I am not."

"Who determines the splendor of a piece of music?" he demanded.

"The person listening."

"And who decides what is beautiful in what they see?"

She hesitated for a moment, but then grudgingly said, "The person looking."

"So?"

"To you I am beautiful, but you're just saying that."

"No."

"But…"

"You must trust my words."

"Okay."

"Okay." He used the moment of trust to pull her blouse the rest of the way off and dispense with her bra in one well-practiced series of movements.

Instead of trying to cover up as he half suspected she might, she reached up. "Come closer, I want to feel your skin against mine."

"You are perfect for me," he told her heatedly. "I adore this passionate innocence of yours."

"Passionate innocence. That's me," she said with a self-deprecating laugh that choked off into a moan when he gave her what she craved and felt the trembling result in the feminine limbs wrapped around his shoulders.

How had such a sensual woman made it to twenty-nine without having sex? Even with her lifestyle and limitations?

"That's so good," she breathed into his ear while moving from side to side infinitesimally. "So good."

"Yes, it is."

"I want my slacks off, too."

"My pleasure." And it was, undoing the crisp navy trousers and pulling them down her legs.

He had to stop and look, soak in the sight of her sprawled out on his bed in nothing but her panties.

"Incredible," he said.

She shook her head. "Now, I know you are lying. You told me I had bird legs."

"I was teasing." With a shake of his head for her ignorance, he pressed his body down onto hers, reveling in the feel of naked flesh pressed against naked flesh. "I was picturing them wrapped around my torso while I pleasured you."

"You weren't."

"I was."

"Like this?" she asked in an innocent tone, completely belied by the mischievous sparkle in her eyes. Her legs wrapped around his hips, her calves hooking over his thighs.

"Exactly like that." He took a deep breath and held it while keeping his body rigid. "Careful, *pethi mou*. I am in grave danger of reaching the goal long before the game is over."

"A Casanova like you?" she teased. "I don't believe it."

"Believe." No matter how embarrassing he might find it, that was the truth.

"I like affecting you that strongly."

"I, too, like it." And to prove how much, he began to kiss

her again. This time, caressing her with his lips all over her face and down her neck.

Her legs' hold on his hips broke as he continued his oral caresses down over her satiny shoulders and lower to her breasts.

Her breathing, which had grown rapid and shallow, hitched. "Oh, oh…Neo…yes. I like that."

He would have laughed if he had any air to make the sound, but he didn't feel like laughing when his lips closed around one delicately pink peak and she cried out with shocked delight. He felt like giving the victory chant. She was so incredibly responsive. To him.

Every one of her reactions belonged to him and him alone. As did she.

No matter how temporary his possession, it pounded through him as a primitive, fierce drumbeat. She was his.

He nibbled, suckled and licked her nipple and the soft mound surrounding it, like she was a particularly tasty ice cream cone, until she was making incoherent sounds of need. And then he moved to her other petite breast and gave it just as much attention.

Her hands went from caressing him, to burying in his hair, to pulling his hair, as she bucked her hips in an ancient if unconscious plea.

No matter how much he wanted to give in to that silent demand, she wasn't ready. Not yet. But she would be.

He was going to drive his sensual little virgin out of her mind with carnal delight.

With that goal firmly entrenched in his mind, he moved down her torso, his lips and tongue caressing and tasting the salty smoothness of her skin. She writhed under his ministrations, making incoherent demands when he tongued her belly button. His hands were busy revisiting every spot his mouth had already been.

He played with her breasts, but it wasn't until he pinched and teased at her hard little nubs that she tried to arch up off the bed. He laughed in victory-filled pleasure against her smooth stomach and slid his mouth lower. When he reached her hot pink panties, he stopped with his teeth on her waistband.

Everything in Cassandra seemed to go still. She stared down at him. Their eyes locked as he made silent promises and she reeled from the message he knew she could read in his gaze. He was going to make this the best first time she could possibly have.

She deserved the most incredible experience he could give her. She wasn't just a one-night stand; she was his friend. And her innocence was not merely a powerful aphrodisiac, it was a great responsibility as well.

With a jerk of his head, he tugged the small scrap of lace down. Blatant desire tinged by virginal uncertainty washed over Cassandra's precious features. She canted her pelvis so that he could pull off her last piece of clothing over her hips.

In other circumstances, she might be shy, but in this, Cassandra was tantalizingly open.

Pretty brown curls were revealed to his hungry gaze now that her panties were on the floor with the rest of their clothes. The natural feminine mystique was a nice change from the waxed, shaved and tweezed nether regions he'd been exposed to over the past few years.

He ruffled the curls with his fingertips and she bit her lip on a moan.

He smiled. "Sensitive?"

"Yes, but…"

He brushed his hands down her legs, stopping with them clasped around her ankles. "There are so many things your body can feel that I look forward to showing you."

"And will you feel them, too?"

She was smart, his sweet little Cassandra. "Yes. Giving you pleasure will turn me on so much I won't be able to stop—"

"Pounding into me."

The earthy words coming from her prim mouth were almost enough to send him over the edge. "You are dangerous, *pethi mou.*"

"That's good to know." And indeed, she did look proud of herself. Then she dipped her head, looking up at him through her lashes in a gesture he was coming to recognize as her default in uncertainty. "You won't really pound. Not at first, will you?"

"Sweetheart, I will never hurt you. Not even accidentally. I will be so careful with you, you will beg me to hurry."

"That could be fun." Her words were all bravado, but the relief in her lovely features told its own story.

"Yes, I think it will be."

"You know what else would be fun?"

"Many things. What did you have in mind?" he asked, enjoying himself in a way he never had in bed with a woman.

"You. Naked."

"You are a delight."

"I can't tell you how pleased I am to hear that. Now, strip."

"I have already stripped, or hadn't you noticed?"

"Don't be smart. You know what I want."

"Ah, you wish equal disrobing?"

"Well, you've just got those small briefs left and they

don't look like they're very comfortable." She did her best to appear like his comfort was all that concerned her. Of course, the innocent hunger in her eyes sort of ruined that.

Nevertheless, he looked down at himself and had to agree with her assessment. His briefs did not look comfortable, not with the way his hardness was trying to press out of them. The fabric was stretched thin trying to cover the length of his rigid penis and he had to wonder how much longer they would be able to do so. Though he was not sure he wanted to remove them just yet.

Leaving them on was a mental boundary for him. The last barrier between him and the untouched channel between her legs.

Instead of answering, he stalled for time by running a hand up the inside of her thigh.

She shivered, letting her legs drift farther apart. "Everywhere you touch feels so amazing, like I've got electric currents running under my skin and your fingers are the conductors."

"I like making you feel electrified." He let his fingertip dip into the honeyed warmth of her passage and had to stifle a growl of pleasure. She was soft, silky and wet.

Everything he so desperately needed.

Neo's fingers breached Cass's vaginal entrance for the first time and her brain emptied in a red haze of desire.

Everything they had done so far was new for her, but this was in its own class. Having him touch her there made her feel like she belonged to him on a primal level. And although he was the one doing the touching, that didn't stop her from feeling like he belonged to her, too.

A wholly alien sense of possessiveness washed over

her even as she shifted again to give him better access to her most feminine place.

He touched her like he couldn't get enough and that was more stimulating than the caresses themselves. It made her feel wanted for something other than her talent at the piano. For the first time in her memory.

This was no friend having pity on the hopelessly innocent. Neo wanted her and every touch of his hand or mouth showed just how much.

As did the erection seriously tenting his briefs. She wanted to see his male member, she really did, but couldn't seem to remember how to make her mouth work to remind him of that fact. She couldn't take her eyes off his body.

He chuckled, a dark and sexy sound that only increased the arousal pulsing powerfully through her body.

"How does this feel?" He pressed one finger inside her. She wondered how anything bigger was ever going to fit because she felt stretched with that single entry.

"Full," she got out breathlessly.

"Do not worry. You will stretch to accommodate me."

"Maybe."

"Definitely."

"You're a lot bigger than your finger." But that finger felt so good.

"You'll be thankful for that later."

"I'll take your word for it," she gasped out between panting breaths as his finger caressed her interior.

He pushed a little farther inside and she felt a flash of pain. Making a noise of dissent, she tried to arch away.

"Shh…relax. This is your hymen and it must be breached for our intimacy to be achieved."

"I'm not a Victorian maiden. I know that, but it hurts."

It was unsettling the impact a little pain marring her pleasure could have on her. She would have to trust him to know what he was doing.

But she was acting on instinct, too.

"I want you inside me when the last barrier to my virginity is crossed."

"Are you certain?"

"Yes."

He smiled and nodded.

"As you wish." He got up. "I need to get condoms."

"Where are they?"

"In the guest room."

He really never had sex in here. For some inexplicable reason, Cass was really pleased about that fact. Sex in his bed was for her and her alone. The newly developed streak of possessiveness in her nature rejoiced.

He was gone less than a minute, returning with a small box that he tossed onto the bedside stand. He'd already taken one of the small, square foil packets out of it and was tearing it open.

"Watch me. Next time, I want you to do this."

"Has anyone ever told you that you're bossy?" she asked even as part of her thrilled at his instruction. It wasn't as if she wanted to look anywhere else.

"Demanding. Assertive. Pushy. Stubborn. Difficult. Perhaps bossy once or twice."

She huffed out a laugh. "I have a feeling I'll be using all those and more."

"No doubt." He pulled his hand away. "Now I make love to you, *yineka mou*." The Greek in his accent was thick and strong.

She didn't correct his semantics. She didn't want to.

Right now, for the first time, she needed to feel like they were making love. Even if it was just sex. Between friends.

And then, as impossible as it might seem, she realized in that moment it was because she *did* love him. She didn't know how it had happened so quickly, or even if the feeling was real, but she felt a depth of feeling for him she had not felt in any form since her parents' deaths.

And wasn't this exactly what he had warned her against? Mistaking sexual feelings for real emotion? Only it did not feel like a mistake. And she had to wonder if the sex could feel so good and right for her without some emotion attached.

She wasn't about to ask him, but it was a topic she would explore with some of her online friends. Ones who had more of a life than she did and might be able to give her the insight she needed.

For now, she just concentrated on how it felt to have Neo joining their bodies. It wasn't all joy and yet rather than making her irritable as she'd feared it would, the pain felt even more intimate than the pleasure.

An indelible marking on her soul that would connect her to him for the rest of her life.

Though he was slow and careful entering her, it still hurt and tears leaked down her temples. He leaned down to kiss them away and whisper soothing Greek in her ear. She didn't know what he was saying, but the tone comforted her and caressed the ragged edges of her spirit.

Once their pelvises touched, he stopped moving completely, giving her time…? She thought that must be it because the sweat beads formed on his forehead told their own story about the cost such patience had on him.

"I feel so connected to you," she whispered as their gazes joined as intimately as their bodies.

His eyes closed and he whispered what sounded like no.

"No?" she asked, unaccountably hurt.

"*Ne*. Yes," he hissed. "It is Greek."

"Oh." Good.

"You make me lose my English."

She thought that might be one of the nicest things any-one had ever said to her.

"Is it always like this?"

His eyelids lifted, revealing a gaze gone dark with passion. "No. It is never like this. Not for me."

She wanted to say something to that, but didn't know what. He was not declaring love or even an intent for some-thing long-term; he was simply acknowledging that this moment was special. For all she knew, she was his first virgin.

"Zephyr told me it would be phenomenal." Neo's voice was strained, like the toll from remaining still was getting heavier.

"Sex with a virgin?"

"Sex with a friend."

"Oh."

"Indeed."

"But I already knew it would be like this with you."

"You did?"

"Why do you think I wanted it so much?"

"Oh," she said again, not having any other words.

He pulled out slowly, abrading torn tissues, but causing a jolt of pleasure to go through her all the same.

"Okay?" he asked.

"Yes." Maybe more than.

And then he was moving, swiveling his hips and hitting a spot inside her that sent jolt after jolt of electric sensa-tion through her body.

"So good," she fairly groaned, though the soreness had not gone entirely. She felt a muted spiral of pleasure and she wanted more but wasn't sure how to make it happen.

He sat back and tugged at her wrist until he had her own hand placed palm down on her belly just below her belly button. He pulled until the tip of her middle finger just brushed her clitoris.

She cried out at the surge of sensation that tiny touch caused.

"Keep it there," he instructed and then he started moving again, faster this time. And with every body-jarring thrust, her fingertip caressed her center of pleasure.

That muted spiral became a tornado and she felt orgasm claim her in shattering convulsions.

Finally, she went limp from the quakes and aftershocks and only then did she feel him stiffen above her.

He yelled something in Greek as he climaxed, and then he looked down at her. "Amazing, *yineka mou.*"

She would have to ask him what *yineka mou* meant, but not right now. All she wanted to do in this moment was bask.

He quirked a brow at her, his face reflecting satiated pleasure.

"Mind-blowing."

His smile was as good as the kiss that came after it.

CHAPTER TEN

NEO lay next to Cassandra and watched her sleep. He had insisted she soak in a mineral bath after their lovemaking, and then had tucked her into bed, where he had served her a late supper instead of seducing her into round two as his body had urged him to do. Now she slept and he remained awake, shocked at his own behavior.

Since when did he pamper his sex partners, much less actually *sleep* with them?

He was not a selfish lover, but he shied away from any form of intimacy, spoiling with anything but extravagant gifts included. This friends-with-benefits situation was a dangerous thing, he realized.

Cassandra deserved a little coddling. No doubt about it. And perhaps that was all this urge to pamper, coddle and care for was about. He saw a dearth in his precious friend's life and was determined to fill it.

She'd received little enough of it in her life even though common sense might say she should have gotten more than her share. But no one in the brilliant musician's sphere had seen the price she paid for her music as anything other than what had to be done.

Her mother had been an invalid, and yet rather than giving the small child Cassandra had been extra love and attention to make up for that, she'd been thrown into a world of public performance that clearly terrified her. Worse, she'd been forced to stay there.

Neo might have grown up on the streets, with a short stint in an orphanage, but he knew that wasn't acceptable behavior for a family. He could not regret her father was dead, or Neo would be tempted to beat the man. Not that her manager was entirely safe. The temptation to destroy the man was strong, but Neo would rather focus his energies on helping Cassandra regain certain elements to her life.

Like travel.

She had seemed so excited at the prospect of going to Dubai, and even Napa Valley with him. He would never have thought she enjoyed travel so much, being as connected as it was to her public performing.

But apparently the incredibly talented pianist had found one thing to enjoy on her concert tours. Experiencing new places.

He was determined she would know that joy again.

He would look at his schedule in the morning to see when they might plan the trip to Napa Valley. It would have to be soon, because if he ended up going to Dubai, it would be in the next month. And chances were good on that trip. He wanted to take Cassandra. He wanted his new friend to experience all the delight life had to offer.

Including, but not limited to, devastating sex.

And maybe he would find her a new manager, one who

saw Cassandra as a person, not a meal ticket. Or at least was very good at pretending so.

Cass woke in a strange bed for the first time since her father died and she stopped travelling for her music. It was a comfortable bed with soft sheets and duvet of perfect weight. She could easily snuggle down and go back to sleep, a sense of warmth and safety enveloping her.

Until her brain supplied just whose bed she had woken in. Neo's!

She could still smell him on the sheets. That yummy aftershave he wore and a scent she would forever associate with sex. She reached out, but found the sheets beside her empty. They were still warm from another body, though. Neo had slept with her.

Memories of strong arms holding her, a tender kiss on her lips and a whispered "Good night, *yineka mou*" warmed her.

She could barely wrap her mind around the fact he had slept with her—all night long, much less her lascivious memories of the night before.

Sitting up in the Ralph Lauren white T-shirt Neo had lent her to sleep in, she felt only tiny twinges in muscles used so differently from her normal exercise regime. The mineral bath had helped. A lot.

She bit her lip on the smile Neo's insistence she soak in the enhanced hot water brought to her face. He'd been so sweet, but she intuited he would not thank her for saying so.

He'd taken such good care of her, but what had really surprised her was him carrying her to *his* bed after the bath. She'd assumed that if she was staying over, she would do so in the guest room. But that wasn't what happened.

He'd brought her to his bed. Without the slightest hesitation or discussion.

And though she'd never once slept in the same bed as another person, she had rested deeply, waking only once in the wee hours of the night. Rather than being bothered by the body wrapped so protectively around hers, she had reveled in the experience, knowing it might not ever happen again.

She didn't think Neo made a habit of sleeping with his mistresses. No doubt he'd made an exception for her because it had been her first time.

He really was a nice man.

"What's put that smile on your face?" the man himself asked from the doorway, dressed immaculately and obviously ready for work.

"You," she admitted.

His brows rose.

"Really. You're a very nice man, Neo Stamos, billionaire business mogul."

He shook his head. "Don't let my contractors hear you say that."

"I wouldn't dream of it."

"Dora has breakfast waiting for you when you are ready."

Cass looked around, but did not see a clock. "What time is it?"

Neo flicked a glance at his watch. "Seven-thirty."

"You look ready to go to work."

"I am. I woke late, but have a meeting I must attend."

"Can I return to my house today?" she asked, fearful of the answer. She couldn't help noticing, he had never mentioned Cole Geary calling the night before with the all clear.

"Yes, of course. Cole's team finished the installations before dinnertime yesterday."

"You didn't say anything."

He shrugged, but the skin over his sculpted cheekbones went a burnished hue. "I was enjoying your company."

"Ditto," she hastened to assure him. "I certainly don't mind, but it would be good to get back to work on my composition."

"Get done what needs doing by Friday."

"There goes that bossy gene again."

"A hazard of spending your time around business moguls."

"You think?"

"I know."

"Just so you don't expect to always get your way."

"Just so you don't expect me not to try."

She laughed, feeling more free than she had since her initial decision to stop performing. "What's happening on Friday?"

"We're flying to Napa Valley after dinner and staying for the weekend."

Shocked to her pink, bare toes, she jumped out of the bed. She hadn't let herself hope he meant it about travelling together, but hadn't he told her at least once he did not say things he didn't mean? "You're serious?"

"I've instructed my pilot to book both takeoff and landing slots and Miss Parks to rent a house for the weekend."

"All since waking up?"

"I texted them both last night, after you fell asleep."

"But it's such short notice."

"Money—"

"Talks and the rest of the world listens." She shook her head in disbelief. He gave her so much and didn't seem to even realize it. "You're amazing! Thank you!"

He accepted her enthusiastic hug without a glimmer of

hesitation, but kept his kiss swift. "I cannot afford to get sidetracked by your too-alluring lips this morning."

"You find my lips alluring?"

"Most definitely."

"Good to know." She was feeling positively giddy and it showed in her voice.

"You think?"

"Sure, knowledge is power," she said cheekily.

"So they say." His eyes travelled down her T-shirt-clad body, the heat factor increasing steadily until he gave her a look that singed her to her toes. "Know this, if I did not have to attend this meeting, I would be taking you back to bed and touching you until you screamed."

"Wow. Maybe we can try that scenario in California this weekend." Yes. Please.

"Consider it done." He took a deep breath. "I am leaving now. Do not be intimidated by Dora. She is my house-keeper, therefore not a stranger."

It said a lot about how much she trusted *him* and how comfortable she was in Neo's home that his words actually settled inside her with truth. "Got it. Not a stranger."

"Will you be okay with her driving you home?"

"Surely that's not in her job description?"

He shrugged. "I thought you would be more comfort-able with her than my usual driver."

"So, you do use one."

"When necessary, yes. I like driving though."

"And you like being on time. Go."

He shook his head and then grabbed her and placed a hard, lingering kiss on her lips. Then he spun on his heel and left the bedroom.

She put her fingers over her lips. "Wow." She spun in a circle. "Just wow."

Dora turned out to be a Greek woman in her mid-fifties with salt-and-pepper hair worn in a neat bun. She had a kind smile and the apparent desire to feed the nations. The breakfast she laid out for Cass was big enough to feed an army.

When she said so, the older woman grinned. "One day That One," she said, tilting her head toward the door as if Neo were still in the apartment, "will settle down and give me some *bebes* to cook for."

The image of little boys with green eyes and dark hair teasing a sister into eating her dinner so they could all leave the table to play flashed through Cass's mind. It filled her with a longing she thought she had long ago conquered. "He'll make a wonderful father."

"Not that he knows it." Dora rolled her eyes as she poured Cass a cup of aromatic coffee. "Men!"

Cass laughed. "I don't have much experience with the species, except my manager." And Bob was less a man in her mind than the nagging voice of business.

Neo's bossiness didn't really bother her, but when Bob got overly demanding, she felt borderline bullied. One thing was for sure, if he could have cajoled her into returning to the stage, he would have done it. Goodness knew he kept trying.

He'd played every guilt card in the deck. At least twice.

"You are the pianist. Mr. Neo told me. I enjoy your music."

"Thank you."

"You will have to slow down when you have children. Two CDs a year." She shook her head.

"I doubt I'll ever have children, but I would not mind cutting back on my composing for their sake if I did."

"Why should you not have children?"

"Some people never find that special person to spend their lives with. I wouldn't wish myself on a child as a single parent, either." Not with her limitations. It wouldn't be fair to the child.

"So, you're a little shy. I've read your biography. Not everybody likes to be the center of attention. You'll make a wonderful mother. You mark my words."

Cass just smiled, hiding how much she wished the other woman's words weren't just wise, but were prophetic. Only Cass knew how impossible such dreams were in her life. "Neo said you would drive me home this morning."

"Yes. He did not think you would like going with his driver, or so he said."

"That's right. Strangers can intimidate me."

"Yes, I'm sure. It has nothing to do with the fact his driver is a very attractive young man. No. Of course not."

Cass was startled into laughter. "I do not think Neo is the jealous type."

Dora made a noncommittal noise and then told Cass to eat her breakfast.

Cole Geary was waiting for Cass when she arrived at her house.

She was amused to discover that Dora had no intention of leaving Cass alone with a man. The older woman's traditional values were showing. Cass was only surprised Dora didn't seem to think less of her for so obviously spending the night with her employer.

Cole walked Cass through all the changes, which *were* pretty unobtrusive. Getting used to the alarm system was going to be the hardest part.

"Strange to look out through a window and realize the glass wouldn't shatter if a neighbor kid hit a ball at it."

"You get used to it," Cole said.

Dora nodded. "Mr. Neo's got a glass partition around his balcony that's supposed to stop bullets. It's got to be cleaned just like any window."

"It's top-quality shatterproof material." Cole sounded proud of that fact. "The same stuff they used during the president's acceptance speech."

"He takes his safety seriously," Cass remarked.

"He has to."

Cass felt an internal shudder at that reminder. "Sometimes, I forget he's such a successful tycoon."

Cole looked at her like she'd lost her mind, but Dora's smile was clearly approving.

Once they'd finished the tour of the new security measures and programmed her palm print into the biometric locks, Cass offered the other two coffee. Cole declined due to another appointment. Dora accepted, offering to make the coffee while Cass changed into fresh clothes for the day.

As Cass was dressing for the second time that morning, it occurred to her she may well have made a second friend.

The phone rang that night just as Cass was getting ready for bed. It was Neo.

"Dora said Cole walked you through the changes."

"Yes. They're better than I expected. They even painted all my window trims the same color they were. You can barely tell the difference."

"I told you."

"It's not nice to rub it in when you are right, Neo."

"You did not mind me being right about how good intimacy between us would be."

She choked out a laugh. "Jerk."

"Seriously? You just called the great Neo Stamos a jerk?"

"I was teasing, oh, Mr. Greatness."

His laughter was rich and warm.

"Were you late for your meeting this morning?"

"Naturally not." He paused. "But I did not have time to do my usual preparations."

"I'm sorry."

"You do not sound so."

"What do you expect? I impacted the great Neo Stamos's schedule. That's pretty impressive."

"Proud of yourself, are you?"

"Absolutely."

"I feel the same."

"You do?"

"You can ask that after the honor you did me last night?"

"Was it such an honor?"

"Very much so."

"So, um…you haven't had a lot of experience, with virgins I mean."

"No, but more importantly, I have never made love to a woman who touched me like you do."

"I don't know how to touch you," she wailed, admitting one of her fears. She'd spent the day reliving the night before and one thing had become glaringly obvious; she had been the recipient, not the giver. She was going to have to do some research.

"I was not talking about the physical, but trust me when I tell you there is nothing to fear there."

"I do trust you."

"I know. You are flying to Napa Valley with me."

"You sound like I'm doing you a favor and we both know the opposite is true." For the first time in years, Cass felt like she was truly living, not just existing through her music.

"Every time you give me your time it is something to appreciate."

"Your brain doesn't work like other men."

"You are just now realizing this?"

She laughed. "Don't be annoying."

"But I am good at it. Ask anyone."

"I don't believe it. Demanding. Commanding. Brilliant even. But not regularly annoying."

"Perhaps it is a talent that only comes out with you."

"It does that. I still can't believe you kidnapped me from my house yesterday."

"Do you regret it?"

"Not even a little."

"Good."

"Will you still be here for your piano lesson next week?" she asked.

"Yes."

"I promise not to waste time on pleasantries," she teased.

"I do not."

"No?"

"No. I find it very pleasant to kiss you."

"If you expect kisses and…other stuff…you had better schedule extra time because I expect you to learn more chords."

"You are a slave driver."

"I've heard that one before and I'll tell you what I've told my other students."

"That is?"

"You bought lessons to learn to play the piano, not sit and stare at it."

"Technically, I did not buy the lessons at all."

He had a point, but she wasn't foolish enough to acknowledge it. "Zephyr would not be happy to hear his lessons were being wasted."

Neo said something in Greek and she laughed.

"I get the feeling I don't want to know what you just said."

"Certainly I do not want to tell you."

"Embarrassing much?"

"Perhaps a bit. You can take the boy out of the streets, but not the streets out of the boy."

"I don't believe that. You've come too far from your origins to see yourself as a homeless urchin in any way."

"I do not forget my beginning. It drives me to achieve more in the present."

"Will it ever be enough? The success you've achieved?"

"Funny, Zee asked the same thing recently." The bantering humor had dissolved from his voice to be replaced by something that almost sounded like melancholy.

"What did you tell him?"

"That he was just like me."

"Which is not an answer at all."

"I do not know."

She knew Neo did not mean he didn't know what he had said, but rather that he did not know if his success would ever be enough.

"I'm sorry."

"Now, you sound like you mean it."

"You should be happy with what you have done with your life, proud of yourself, but you're still striving to prove something to yourself."

"It is not something I think about."

"Maybe you should."

"Perhaps, but right now, I am too busy thinking how I am going to schedule enough time to have both you *and* my lesson next week."

"Focus on clearing your schedule for the weekend. That comes first." And he'd probably get enough of her he wouldn't feel the need to do more than study piano the following Tuesday.

Neo called the next morning to remind her to turn off her alarm system before stepping outside. He called again after lunch to ask how her current composition was going. She told him if she got it done, she would play it for him over the weekend.

She wasn't at all surprised when the phone that never rang did for the third time as she started making preparations for a solitary meal.

"Hello, Neo."

"How did you know it was me?"

"No one else calls me, except my manager and people from my CD label. None of them ever calls after five p.m. I guess they don't keep your kind of hours."

"Speaking of work hours, my teleconference call for this evening got rescheduled. Would you like a dinner guest?"

"Hasn't your housekeeper already prepared your dinner?"

"Whatever Dora made will keep."

"Wouldn't you rather eat out?" she asked and then wanted to smack herself for the defeatist behavior. He was already aware of her shortcomings; she didn't need to outline them in stark relief.

"I would rather share this time with you."

Oh, darn. Could he get any more perfect? That feeling

of love she was so sure couldn't be real so soon only got stronger. "Then by all means, come over."

"I'll be there in thirty minutes."

"I'll see you then."

He was as good as his word, ringing the bell exactly twenty-nine minutes later.

"It smells good," he said appreciatively as he followed her into the kitchen.

"It's just pasta and chicken." She picked up the serving dish and headed to the dining room, but didn't stop at the table. "It's such a nice night; I thought we could eat on the back patio. There are no shatterproof clear barriers, but I think we'll survive one night."

He chuckled. "Don't let my bodyguards hear you say that."

"Heaven forefend."

"Just so."

"So, tell me about the project in Dubai," she said as they took turns serving each other.

She put pasta on his plate while he served her vegetables. It was all very smooth and domestic, as if they'd been sharing meals like this for years.

He told her about Dubai, enthralling her with his vision for the complex he and his investors were building. "It sounds amazing."

"That's the hope."

"You're a real visionary, aren't you?"

"You have to see what can be, not what is, if you want to reach the top." He made it sound like no big thing, but in fact, it was.

"You don't limit yourself by what others are doing." And she really, really liked that about him.

"Zephyr and I made a name for ourselves thinking outside the box, pulling together projects no one else would have considered."

"That's how I see music, as too dynamic to fit inside some preconceived set of parameters." Sometimes, that garnered her praise and others, harsh criticism.

"No doubt that is why I enjoy your music so much."

Now that was so worth any number of comments from petty critics. "Thank you."

"I don't imagine your father encouraged you to stray from playing the classics."

"No." He hadn't encouraged the composing, either. He believed it diluted her focus. If only he had understood; after a while, making the music was all that kept her going.

"So, how did you get into New Age composition?"

"I heard a George Winston CD when I was a young teen, I was hooked. His music had a lot in common with the classical composers, but he took it a new direction and I knew that was something I wanted to do." And no matter how many fights it had caused between her and her dad, she had refused to give that creativity up.

"And the rest of us benefitted."

She smiled, warmth suffusing her. "I only wish I had a voice like Enya to add to my piano."

"Your piano doesn't need it."

"You'd better watch yourself. I'm likely to get addicted to compliments like those."

"That is a problem?"

"Only for me," she admitted.

"It is no problem so long as I am around to supply them."

"Right." But how long could she reasonably expect that to be?

CHAPTER ELEVEN

AFTER dinner and another lavish compliment about her talents, this one directed at her cooking accompanied by a promise to return the favor, they migrated to the music room. Neo was the only billionaire tycoon she could imagine making a promise of dinner and meaning he intended to cook, not having it catered.

He ran his hand along the Fazioli's glossy top. "Play for me?" The request really pleased her, showing that he wasn't afraid of invading her personal space like he had invited her into his.

She slid onto the bench, letting her fingers play gently across the keys as she always did when she sat down at a piano. "With pleasure."

He turned to face her, his expression as serious as she'd ever seen it. "Is it?"

He couldn't know how much that question meant to her. "It is. I *want* to play for you."

"Do I have to sit in that chair over there?"

"Not if you don't want to," she said uncertainly. Did he want to stand?

Her unspoken question was answered when he joined her on the piano bench, filling her space in a way nothing had in her life except the music.

"Don't hold any mistakes against me. I find your nearness distracting," she admitted with a smile.

"Then we are even."

"I distract you?"

"Near, or far. Yes, you do." He sounded bemused by that fact.

She didn't reply to what was a pretty shocking revelation to her as well. Instead, she started to play. It was a 1940s big band piece that sounded romantic on the piano. At least she thought so.

He listened in silence with a faint smile on his face for a minute before saying, "I like this, but I don't recognize it."

"It was popular in the forties."

"Are you serious?"

"Yes."

"Maybe I should expand my musical horizons."

"I'm always for opening yourself to new styles of music, or new to you anyway."

"You do know that I wouldn't be aware of any mistakes you might make?"

She grinned up at him as her fingers moved over the keyboard in a well-memorized pattern. "Maybe that's why I played it."

"Maybe it's time I upped the stakes."

Before she could ask what he meant, his strong arm snaked around her waist and his thumb began to play a matching beat to the piano music against her stomach.

Her fingers fumbled on the keyboard like they hadn't done since she was a small child. "That's upping the stakes all right."

"Do you want me to stop?"

"Not at all." She could play her music in her sleep. His nearness wasn't going to get the best of her.

She concentrated on the song and tried to ignore the movements of his hand, but when a gentle kiss landed on her temple, she froze. "I thought you wanted me to play for you."

"So did I, but I have discovered there are other things I want even more."

"What things?"

"This." He tipped her head up and kissed her, his lips molding hers with definite intent.

"Oh," she breathed against his mouth.

That was all she got out before he deepened the kiss. They were upstairs and she was only marginally aware of how they'd gotten there. She had a vague sense that she'd been carried, but she was too busy touching him and reveling in his touches to think much about it.

"I wasn't going to do this," he said when he had her naked beneath him.

"Why not?"

"You need time to recover from last night."

"I feel fine." She had a few twinges of soreness, but not anything near enough to stop her from pursuing pleasure like she'd experienced the night before.

But the pleasure wasn't like it had been the night before, it was bigger. She screamed his name when she climaxed and again moments later when he drew a second orgasm from her oversensitized body as he found his own completion.

Then he held her, helping her to come down from feelings so intense her body shook uncontrollably in the aftermath.

"If you ever get tired of being a big-shot tycoon, you've got another career as a gigolo waiting for you."

He laughed, the sound large in her usually silent bedroom. "I'll stick with unpaid pleasure, thank you."

"I'm glad. I don't think I could afford you."

"You are a nut."

"So I've been told," she said more soberly than she meant to.

"That is not what I meant. I do not think you are crazy."

Not yet anyway, but it always came. Sooner or later. That lack of comprehension when she could not make herself do something "normal" people took for granted. Regardless of what the future might hold, she was grateful for his attitude in the present.

"Thank you."

"My pleasure."

She grinned and shook her head. "Oh, I think that particular commodity is entirely mutual."

"Yes."

"Seriously. If I had known sex was this wonderful, I would have taken up with one of the groupies that showed interest," she joked, only half-kidding.

"It would not have been like this."

"Because none of them were the great Neo Stamos?"

"Because no one has ever given me anything approaching the pleasure I find with you. What we have here, Cassandra, it is very special."

She could think of nothing to say in response to those words that would not reveal the depth of her feeling, so she remained mute, but placed a tender kiss filled with the love she could not give voice onto his shoulder.

He smiled and returned the kiss, on her mouth. "I should not spend the night."

"Why?"

He sighed. "I have to be at the office at six a.m. for a phone call."

"Why so early?"

"Time differences."

"I understand. You could leave early," she suggested tentatively, unsure if she was reading his desire to stay right, or not.

"If you don't mind me possibly waking you when I get up to go?"

"I don't mind." And if her agreement was offered with the speed of light, who could criticize?

"Then I can sleep here. Thank you."

She was just very happy he wanted to stay. She'd only spent one night in his arms, but knew it was fast becoming one of her favorite things. Maybe even a necessity. It was the first time anyone had ever stayed overnight, and rather than make her feel anxious it made her feel excited.

Neo didn't wake her getting out of bed. In fact, she barely woke when he kissed her goodbye and warned her he would be resetting the alarm.

He followed the pattern of the day before, calling her at random intervals to ask this or tell her that. At one point, she teased him, "Why don't you just admit you called to hear my voice?"

"And if I did?"

"I'd be even more melted than I already am."

"Then I had better not admit it."

Did that mean he really did just call to hear her talk? She knew she loved listening to his voice. Adored it, really.

The trip to Napa Valley was incredible. The rental house Miss Parks found for them was nicer than Cass's own house, with a truly decadent master suite complete with two-person Jacuzzi. The sunken living room was a romantic paradise and Neo took full advantage of the option for candlelight and low-heat gas fireplace.

Cass discovered that flying on a personal jet did not trigger any of her agoraphobic fears. She also discovered that lovemaking was as much fun in the living room as the bedroom and up against a wall as on the bed. She seduced Neo in the pool, but decided after nearly drowning that the Jacuzzi might be the better option.

She slept the entire flight home. Neo worked.

Over the following days, Neo showed no signs of getting bored with her, or frustrated by her limitations. He continued to call her randomly throughout the day and came over or cajoled her into coming to his penthouse almost nightly. She loved swimming in the pool, so she didn't mind at all. He requested that she use the suit she had the first time and kept it in his private changing room so no one else could. In the event Zephyr had guests. Neo wasn't seeing anyone else.

So, a couple of weeks later, when he suggested she try hypnotherapy as they lay in bed together after making love, she didn't automatically assume he was like everyone else. Trying to fix her because she was not good enough the way she was.

"Bob suggested that a couple of years ago, but I wasn't willing to consider it because I knew he just wanted me to get well enough to perform publicly."

"I do not care if you ever perform for an audience. If you wanted it, I would do all in my power to help you achieve it, but you don't. However, I know you feel the pain of the limits your fears put on your life."

"I would like to go out to a restaurant with you without breaking into a sweat over it, or hyperventilating if someone recognizes me." She'd done well at the wine-tasting in Napa Valley and they'd eaten out there as well, at a quiet, intimate restaurant where no one but the waitstaff would have considered speaking to her.

She knew she'd been able to enjoy those things because she'd been with Neo. Not only did his presence give her the courage to try new things, but he adroitly ran interference between her and others. And he never took her anywhere overly crowded, or that made her get that sick feeling she might not be able to get out.

He was so careful of her and with her. She felt cherished.

"I, too, would enjoy this." But he said it with his arms wrapped firmly around her and she didn't take that to mean he was getting sick of eating in with her.

"Did you have someone in mind?"

"Of course."

She laughed and traced a shape over his chest, only realizing it was a heart when she finished. He didn't seem to notice. "*Of course*. You never offer a suggestion without a full plan behind it."

"Her name is Lark Corazon and she has had marked success treating agoraphobia and other phobias."

"You've met her?"

He shrugged.

Cass leaned up to look down at him. "You did. You met with her. What was she like?"

"A normal person."

"No crystal balls or colorful silks hanging from the ceiling."

"I think you're confusing a hypnotherapist with a fortune teller."

"Maybe. I'm willing to meet her." But only because it was Neo making the suggestion. She trusted him like she had never trusted anyone.

He gave her that look of approval she'd become fully addicted to. "I knew you would be. We have an appointment with her tomorrow."

"We?"

"You do not think I would make you go alone, do you?"

She snuggled into him. "You're too good to me, Neo."

"What are friends for?"

"I don't know. I've never had one like you."

"Ditto."

"Hypnotism is…I don't know."

"Different?"

"Yes."

"And a little scary," he suggested.

"I'm afraid of enough in my life." She didn't want to be afraid of this, too.

"But the idea of being hypnotized is overwhelming."

"Yes."

"Do you want me to stay through the session?"

"Would you?"

"Yes."

And he did, sitting in the corner, a solid presence that made her feel safe enough to answer all the hypnotherapist's questions honestly and then relax as much as she was capable during the hypnotherapy.

* * *

A month later, Cass and Neo shared a table at the restaurant at the top of the Space Needle. She had always wanted to come, but had not been able to deal with the thought of the crowds, much less being trapped in a restaurant that could only be reached or exited via a very long elevator ride.

Happiness bubbled inside her like delicious French champagne. The real thing.

"Lark says there is so much trauma mixed in with my public performing, it could be months or years before it's completely redirected."

"That is all right. Performing is not something you ever have to do again."

Cass's joy just increased with Neo's words. It was official, she was hopelessly, irrevocably in love with the billionaire Greek tycoon. Her Chinese scholar pen pal agreed, as did several of her online friends. The only one who didn't know and probably wouldn't agree was Neo himself.

She didn't let that thought hamper her current pleasure. "I know, but I love being able to do *this*."

"It is a joy to see you so happy."

She laughed. "You convinced me that you would never have grown tired of our friendship regardless of my limitations. You don't know how special that is."

"What was to grow tired of? We went piano shopping. And to Napa Valley."

"Yes, we did." And he was taking her to Dubai for the grand opening of his complex. His contractor had come through and Neo had told Cass he wanted to wait to go until she could go with him…comfortably.

Was it any wonder hope that he might feel something

for her besides friendship sprang eternal in her heart. Some days, she was even convinced he would welcome her words of love, but she always chickened out at the last minute.

"And now you will accompany me to that charity event," he said.

"Tell me again why you are going to a five-hundred-dollar-a-plate dinner to raise money for pet neutering? You don't even have a dog."

"And I don't plan on getting one, but lots of business gets done at dinners like this."

"Just like the golf course."

"A tedious game, but one in which I am more than proficient."

She shook her head. "Anything for business, hmm?"

"Perhaps that is why your friendship is so special to me. It is for me and me alone. Not the business. Not the next deal."

His words warmed her even as they gave her heart a twinge.

She wanted so much more than friendship with benefits and sometimes she thought he did, too, but then he reiterated his stance on their relationship. And as wonderful as she found his friendship, it hurt to know one day he would fall for another woman and she would be relegated to the fringes of his life.

That night, she decided to expand her lovemaking repertoire and when her mouth first touched his hardness, his body jerked in shock.

"What are you doing?"

"I believe it is referred to as—"

His laughter was choked. "I know what it is, you imp," he interrupted. "I am surprised you have decided to offer this gift to me."

"Why?" She licked along the length of his shaft, thoroughly enjoying the flavor of his skin. "I've been wanting to for a while."

"Why wait?"

"I was afraid of messing it up."

"Trust me, there is no messing up."

"Oh, I'm pretty sure there is. I read up on it and I've got it on good authority that a lack of care with my teeth would be a bad, bad, bad thing."

"There is that." For once, he was the breathless one.

She took the flared head of his erection in her mouth and swirled her tongue around it. He tasted sweet and she liked it.

"You taste good."

She closed her mouth over his throbbing flesh and sucked hard.

He shouted, canting his hips upward.

She'd been prepared for this reaction, her hand wrapped firmly around his big erection. It stopped him from thrusting too far into her mouth, but she loved this proof of how much he enjoyed what she was doing.

He'd used his mouth on her many times sending her into spasms of pleasure that seemed to last forever. She wanted to do the same for him.

She'd read about not letting him climax right away and intensifying the effect, so that was what she did.

She was unprepared for him grabbing her and dragging her up his body even as he flipped them, and then thrust into her. He stopped a moment later and swore. "I forgot the condom."

"I've been on birth control for several weeks."

"You did not tell me."

"It isn't something you discuss over dinner."

"It is something you mention to your partner before he has a heart attack making love to you without protection."

"I did tell you."

He shook his head, but resumed moving, taking them both over the pinnacle more quickly than she would have thought possible.

Afterward, she curled up into his side like she always did and faded into sleep, a proud little smile curling her lips.

Neo sat with Zephyr on the side of the pool after swimming laps with his business partner. They hadn't used the pool at the same time in months.

"How are things between you and Cass?" Zephyr asked. "I noticed you're still taking piano lessons."

"Yes." Though he spent as many lessons in her bed as he did on the piano bench. He'd made it a personal competition to see how often he could sidetrack Teacher.

"Is it serious between you?"

"Serious? We are friends."

"Who sleep together almost every night."

"How do you know this?"

"Please, I'm not blind."

He shrugged and repeated, "She is my friend."

"Friends with benefits?"

"That's what she calls it."

"So, you wouldn't mind if she shared similar benefits with other friends."

"She does not have other friends she sees in person." But now that she was overcoming her agoraphobia, that would change, a voice taunted in his brain.

"You haven't hooked up with anyone else since you met her."

"I grew tired of the one-night stands."

"But you don't want anything more than friends with benefits with Cass?"

"What else is there?"

"Marriage. Babies."

"Have you lost your mind?" he asked his friend. "I do not have time for a wife and children. I barely have time for Cassandra. Besides, things are fine just the way they are."

"Are they?"

"I don't want anything else."

"You're sure about that?"

"Absolutely."

"That's good I guess."

That response shocked Neo. He'd been prepared for Lecture 101 on the benefits of married life and family. Not that Zephyr would ever succumb to the institution. "Why?"

"Because Cass apparently decided to go swimming and I think she overheard pretty much everything we just said. I can't be sure, but the way she rushed out of here looking stricken spoke for itself, I think."

Neo surged to his feet. "Why didn't you say anything?"

"I didn't know she was there until too late, but hey. It wasn't like you said anything she didn't already know, right?"

No, but that didn't matter. "You said she looked stricken."

"*Ohi*, I'm not sure the whole friends-with-benefits thing is still working for her."

"You were meddling," Neo accused.

Zephyr gave him an innocent look he didn't believe for a minute. "I was just talking to you."

"Poking and prodding things best left alone."

"Maybe Cass didn't want them left alone."

"Maybe you should have minded your own damn business."

"Maybe instead of yelling at me, you should go fix this."

"And how am I to do that?"

"Start by getting your head out of your ass and go from there."

Neo barely restrained from punching his best friend right in the face. But damn it, Zee wasn't the one he was angry at. It was himself.

He'd spent so many years eschewing love that when it found its way into his life, he'd done everything but stand on his head to pretend it wasn't there. He'd denied any deeper feelings, denied the resurfaced yearnings he'd hadn't allowed through time since he was too young to know better. Yearning for love. For a family. For what others had and he had never known.

Neither had Cassandra, not really. Her life had been almost as barren as his own and still, he had withheld his emotions from her. Why?

He was ashamed to admit it was because of fear. He, Neo Stamos, billionaire and all-around powerful guy, was terrified of not being worthy of his precious pianist's heart.

Just as he had somehow not been worthy of his parents' love. Only wasn't that the thinking of his bruised child's heart? Didn't he realize as an adult, a rational thinker, that surely it was his parents' deficiency—not his—that accounted for the lack of love in his life.

And didn't he owe Cassandra something more than the residue of a painful childhood he'd left behind him long ago?

Silent tears rushed down Cass's cheeks as she let herself into her house. She was furious with herself for crying, but couldn't stop the emotional onslaught.

She knew Neo didn't want her for anything but sex and friendship, only she hadn't been able to help herself from hoping. She'd gone floating along in this little bubble of fantasy that their circumstances did nothing to pop.

He spent his off time with her. All of it. He called her several times a day just to talk. He was still learning to play the piano, though goodness knew he spent as much lesson time teaching her pleasure as she did teaching him music. They made love and spent the night together almost every day.

But the reality was, for him that was just friendship. Nothing more.

The problem was, she loved him and that love was burning a hole in her heart from staying hidden.

She wanted to get married. She wanted to have his babies and work with Dora to feed him healthy meals, but remind him that food wasn't just fuel. It could be enjoyed.

Cass wanted so much she knew she could never have. As far as she'd come with her issues, she was no match for a billionaire tycoon that could have any woman he wanted. And should have one that could offer unrestrained ability to couple him to business dinners and parties, not be limited to an event or two every couple of weeks.

Even able to go in crowded public places, Cass was still horrifically shy and had a hard time putting herself out there for others to get to know. Neo acted like he didn't mind, but that was because they were just friends. Anything more would be unthinkable.

She shied away from the music room and her bedroom was not where she wanted to be right now, either.

She stood in the hall and looked around her and wondered for the first time what she was doing living in her parents' house. It wasn't as if the memories of them all living here together were so good for her.

And yet she clung to the house as a link to the only people who had loved her, if only a little.

Neo found Cassandra in her small study when he finally reached her house. Red-rimmed eyes testified to the tears she had shed and his heart caught.

But far more alarming was what was on her computer screen. "You are looking to move?"

"Why not? There is nothing holding me here."

Paralyzed by unexpected pain, for a moment Neo could not breathe. "I am here."

She gave him a measuring look. "For how long?"

"What do you mean?"

"You'll eventually tire of our benefits and start dating other women again."

No way in hell, but he wasn't ready to say that. He was still grappling with the feelings he'd forced himself to acknowledge. Like the debilitating fear the thought of losing her caused. "We would still be friends."

"No."

"No?" Sharp pain lanced through him.

"Maybe. I don't know. You've done so much for me. You're the best friend I've ever had. You've been better to me than anyone in my life, including my parents. I wouldn't just ditch your friendship, but I don't know if I could handle watching you with other women." The pain in her voice nearly brought him to his knees.

It was unthinkable. "I would not ask you to."

She just gave him a look.

"Do you want more?" he asked her, marshalling his thoughts and arguments so he did not lose the most important person in his life.

"What difference would it make if I did? You don't. You made that clear enough."

"Maybe I was wrong."

"The things I want need something a lot stronger than maybe."

"What is love?"

Cass stared at Neo in shock. "What do you mean? You know what love is."

"No, in fact, I do not."

"But…"

"I have never been in love and no one has ever loved me."

"Zephyr loves you like a brother."

"I have no desire to marry Zephyr."

"You don't want to marry me, either."

"I was wrong."

"What?"

"I do want to marry you. I want everything, but I did not feel I had the right to ask for it."

She started to cry again and swiped at her cheeks. "Why would you say that?"

"I understand business, but relationships are something else entirely."

"You have been so good to me I don't know how you could question your ability to maintain a relationship."

"Do you think I have been good to you?"

"Yes!"

"Good." He looked relieved. As if there could be any doubt. "That is good."

"Neo, even though we are just friends, you treat me like a princess. You would make an amazing husband and father."

"We are not just friends," he said in a voice like shattered glass.

"We aren't?" Oh, please, please convince her.

"No."

"What are we then?"

"Everything. You are my everything and that is what I wish to be to you."

"You already are." She walked forward and reached up to put both her hands on either side of his handsome face. "How could you not know that? Neo, you are everything I have ever wanted, or ever could want. I love you, with everything that I am."

He pulled her close, tilting his head until their eyes had no choice but to lock gazes. "I love you. I have never said that to another person, but I will never stop saying it to you. I was afraid."

"Afraid of what?"

"Not being worthy of your love."

She didn't ask him how he could think that. His formative years explained it all. "Your parents didn't deserve you, not the other way around."

"Intellectually, I know this."

"I'm going to make sure you realize it deep in your heart as well. I love you, Neo, so much."

"I adore you, *yineka mou*, and I always will."

"Even with the hypnotherapy, I'll probably always be shy. I won't ever be a big society hostess."

"It does not matter. I do not want a big society hostess. I want you. And I want a wife…a woman who will maybe one day help me make a family different than the ones either of us knew growing up."

Oh, yes. "I can't imagine anything better."

"Neither can I."

Then he kissed her, or she kissed him…she really wasn't sure how their lips met, but meet they did and it was the most profound kiss in the history of kisses. It spoke of true love, and deep need and hopes and dreams deferred and almost lost, but found again leading to joy unimaginable.

She was in his lap when their lips finally parted. "What is *yineka mou*?"

"My woman, my wife."

She pressed their foreheads together, her fears laid completely to rest. "Oh, Neo. There really was never any doubt, was there?" He'd been calling her his for a very long time.

"No, my very precious woman, there never was. I just had to face a truth that scared the hell out of me. There was someone in this world more important to me than my business, or anything or anyone else."

"It is the same for me."

"I know and I'm so glad."

"Me, too."

"Athens for our honeymoon?" he asked.

"Definitely. We can start working on some of those *bebes* Dora is so sure we are going to have."

"That is one scary smart woman." Neo's laughter filled Cass's world just like the rest of him.

Neither of them had much experience with love, but they would make up for lack of quantity with the quality of their love. They would never take it for granted as others might. They were truly everything to each other.

Coming Next Month

in **Harlequin Presents® EXTRA.** Available July 13, 2010.

#109 HIRED FOR THE BOSS'S BEDROOM
Cathy Williams
Her Irresistible Boss

#110 THE COUNT OF CASTELFINO
Christina Hollis
Her Irresistible Boss

#111 RULING SHEIKH, UNRULY MISTRESS
Susan Stephens
P.S. I'm Pregnant!

#112 MISTRESS: AT WHAT PRICE?
Anne Oliver
P.S. I'm Pregnant!

Coming Next Month

in **Harlequin Presents®.** Available July 27, 2010.

#2933 THE ITALIAN DUKE'S VIRGIN MISTRESS
Penny Jordan

#2934 MIA AND THE POWERFUL GREEK
Michelle Reid
The Balfour Brides

#2935 THE GREEK'S PREGNANT LOVER
Lucy Monroe
Traditional Greek Husbands

#2936 AN HEIR FOR THE MILLIONAIRE
Julia James and Carole Mortimer
2 in 1

#2937 COUNT TOUSSAINT'S BABY
Kate Hewitt

#2938 MASTER OF THE DESERT
Susan Stephens

LARGER-PRINT
BOOKS!

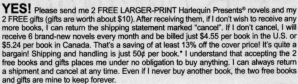

GET 2 FREE LARGER-PRINT
NOVELS PLUS 2 FREE GIFTS!

YES! Please send me 2 FREE LARGER-PRINT Harlequin Presents® novels and my 2 FREE gifts (gifts are worth about $10). After receiving them, if I don't wish to receive any more books, I can return the shipping statement marked "cancel". If I don't cancel, I will receive 6 brand-new novels every month and be billed just $4.55 per book in the U.S. or $5.24 per book in Canada. That's a saving of at least 13% off the cover price! It's quite a bargain! Shipping and handling is just 50¢ per book.* I understand that accepting the 2 free books and gifts places me under no obligation to buy anything. I can always return a shipment and cancel at any time. Even if I never buy another book, the two free books and gifts are mine to keep forever.

176/376 HDN E5NG

Name _____ (PLEASE PRINT) _____

Address _____ Apt. # _____

City _____ State/Prov. _____ Zip/Postal Code _____

Signature (if under 18, a parent or guardian must sign)

Mail to the **Harlequin Reader Service:**
IN U.S.A.: P.O. Box 1867, Buffalo, NY 14240-1867
IN CANADA: P.O. Box 609, Fort Erie, Ontario L2A 5X3

Not valid for current subscribers to Harlequin Presents Larger-Print books.

**Are you a subscriber to Harlequin Presents books
and want to receive the larger-print edition?
Call 1-800-873-8635 today!**

* Terms and prices subject to change without notice. Prices do not include applicable taxes. Sales tax applicable in N.Y. Canadian residents will be charged applicable provincial taxes and GST. Offer not valid in Quebec. This offer is limited to one order per household. All orders subject to approval. Credit or debit balances in a customer's account(s) may be offset by any other outstanding balance owed by or to the customer. Please allow 4 to 6 weeks for delivery. Offer available while quantities last.

Your Privacy: Harlequin Books is committed to protecting your privacy. Our Privacy Policy is available online at www.eHarlequin.com or upon request from the Reader Service. From time to time we make our lists of customers available to reputable third parties who have a product or service of interest to you. If you would prefer we not share your name and address, please check here. ☐

Help us get it right—We strive for accurate, respectful and relevant communications. To clarify or modify your communication preferences, visit us at www.ReaderService.com/consumerschoice.

HPLP10R

HARLEQUIN®

A Romance

FOR EVERY MOOD™

Spotlight on

Heart & Home

Heartwarming romances
where love can happen
right when you least expect it.

See the next page to enjoy a sneak peek
from Harlequin® American Romance®,
a Heart and Home series.

Five hunky Texas single fathers—five stories from Cathy Gillen Thacker's LONE STAR DADS *miniseries. Here's an excerpt from the latest,* THE MOMMY PROPOSAL *from Harlequin American Romance.*

"I hear you work miracles," Nate Hutchinson drawled. Brooke Mitchell had just stepped into his lavishly appointed office in downtown Fort Worth, Texas.

"Sometimes, I do." Brooke smiled and took the sexy financier's hand in hers, shook it briefly.

"Good." Nate looked her straight in the eye. "Because I'm in need of a home makeover—fast. The son of an old friend is coming to live with me."

She was still tingling from the feel of his warm palm. "Temporarily or permanently?"

"If all goes according to plan, I'll adopt Landry by summer's end."

Brooke had heard the founder of Nate Hutchinson Financial Services was eligible, wealthy and generous to a fault. She hadn't known he was in the market for a family, but she supposed she shouldn't be surprised. But Brooke had figured a man as successful and handsome as Nate would want one the old-fashioned way. *Not that this was any of her business...*

"So what's the child like?" she asked crisply, trying not to think how the marine-blue of Nate's dress shirt deepened the hue of his eyes.

"I don't know." Nate took a seat behind his massive antique mahogany desk. He relaxed against the smooth leather of the chair. "I've never met him."

"Yet you've invited this kid to live with you permanently?"

"It's complicated. But I'm sure it's going to be fine."

Obviously Nate Hutchinson knew as little about teenage

boys as he did about decorating. But that wasn't her problem. Finding a way to do the assignment without getting the least bit emotionally involved was.

Find out how a young boy brings Nate and Brooke together in THE MOMMY PROPOSAL, coming August 2010 from Harlequin American Romance.

HARLEQUIN Presents

The Balfour Brides

A powerful dynasty,
eight daughters in disgrace…

Absolute scandal has rocked the core of the infamous Balfour family. The glittering, gorgeous daughters are in disgrace.… Banished from the Balfour mansion, they're sent to the boldest, most magnificent men to be wedded, bedded…and tamed!

And so begins a scandalous saga of dazzling glamour and passionate surrender.

"I won't tell anyone that you kissed me."

Like she thought he was ashamed of his attraction to her? That wasn't true.

"You've got this all wrong, Courtney," Owen tried to tell her. But now she was shoving him back toward the door to the alley where he'd stood and watched her.

"Oh, no," she said. "I totally agree with you. This was a mistake. You coming here. You kissing me. It's a mistake we will never repeat."

"Well, that will be a damn shame," he said—because it had felt so incredible...

He couldn't remember a kiss ever being as sweet or sexy or...ever making him so desperate for more.

She shoved him again toward the door. "Get out!"

He sighed and relented. "Okay, I'm going."

He turned and pushed open the door. And as he stepped outside, a sudden chill passed through him. He'd forgotten his coat, but that wasn't why he was cold.

He had a strange feeling—like she must have had earlier—that someone was watching him.

Dear Reader,

I am very excited to bring you back to Northern Lakes, Michigan, for a new series featuring my Huron Hotshot firefighters. Hopefully, you've read the Harlequin Blaze books that started the series, *Red Hot*, *Hot Attraction*, *Hot Seduction* and *Hot Pursuit*, but if you haven't, you'll have no problem getting to know this elite team of hotshot firefighters. Stationed in Northern Lakes, Michigan, in the Huron National Forest, these US Forest Service firefighting specialists will travel wherever they're needed to fight wildfires. But the greatest danger hotshot/EMT Owen James faces is at home with someone trying to kill him. He doesn't know if Courtney Beaumont is seeking revenge on him for not saving her mom a few years ago or if someone else is out to get him. But he's determined to find out...even if he has to get very close to Courtney during his investigation. Courtney doesn't want to get close to Owen, though, because then she'll be in danger, too—of losing her heart to the hometown hero.

This series is very special to me because my husband inspired me to write it. On his summers off college, he worked with the US Forest Service's hotshot firefighting team. I'm thrilled to be able to give more of my Hotshot Heroes their own stories.

Happy reading!

Lisa Childs

HOTSHOT HERO
UNDER FIRE

———

Lisa Childs

HARLEQUIN
ROMANTIC
SUSPENSE

HARLEQUIN®
**ROMANTIC
SUSPENSE**™

Recycling programs
for this product may
not exist in your area.

ISBN-13: 978-1-335-75976-4

Hotshot Hero Under Fire

Copyright © 2022 by Lisa Childs

For questions and comments about the quality of this book,
please contact us at CustomerService@Harlequin.com.

Harlequin Enterprises ULC
22 Adelaide St. West, 41st Floor
Toronto, Ontario M5H 4E3, Canada
www.Harlequin.com

Printed in U.S.A.

Ever since **Lisa Childs** read her first romance novel (a Harlequin story, of course) at age eleven, all she wanted was to be a romance writer. With over seventy novels published with Harlequin, Lisa is living her dream. She is an award-winning, bestselling romance author. She loves to hear from readers, who can contact her on Facebook or through her website, lisachilds.com.

Books by Lisa Childs

Harlequin Romantic Suspense

Hotshot Heroes

Hotshot Hero Under Fire

Bachelor Bodyguards

His Christmas Assignment
Bodyguard Daddy
Bodyguard's Baby Surprise
Beauty and the Bodyguard
Nanny Bodyguard
Single Mom's Bodyguard
In the Bodyguard's Arms
Close Quarters with the Bodyguard
Bodyguard Under Siege

Colton 911: Chicago

Colton 911: Unlikely Alibi

The Coltons of Kansas

Colton Christmas Conspiracy

Visit the Author Profile page at
Harlequin.com for more titles.

With great appreciation and love to my husband, Andrew Ahearne, for inspiring this series and for inspiring and supporting me in every way!

Chapter 1

Some people became firefighters for the excitement. For the action. Especially the firefighters who joined the elite teams that traveled around the country to battle wildfires. Owen James was one of those elite firefighters with the US Forest Service—a Hotshot. But his tours as a Marine had cured him of whatever desire he'd had for excitement and action.

He lifted his fingers to the rigid line of flesh running along his cheek. Despite the coldness of the early-spring morning, the scar was warm from the sunshine streaking through the bare branches of the trees towering over him. Yeah, he'd had enough excitement and action as a Marine. The reason he was a firefighter was the same reason he was an EMT during the off-season: he wanted to help people.

Unfortunately, he wasn't able to help everyone—not

as a firefighter, nor as a paramedic. Most people understood that; they accepted that he did his best.

Except for one person.

Courtney Beaumont would never let him forget that he had failed. That he hadn't been able to save the person who'd mattered most to her. She reminded him every time he ran into her in town—hell, she'd even threatened to sue him for wrongful death and malpractice. She'd just recently returned to their hometown of Northern Lakes, Michigan, six months ago, which had shocked everybody because she'd always sworn that once she left after high school, she was never coming back. He didn't know if her determination to leave was because she'd always thought she was better than their small town or because of how some of the other kids had treated her for dressing and acting so differently. He felt a pang of regret that he hadn't stood up to the kids that had bullied her back then, that he had even laughed along with them. Now, coming back from his last deployment with his scar, he understood how she must have felt, to be stared at, to be ridiculed. And that pang of regret was a hollow ache.

Why had she returned? To reconnect with her sister, or to make his life miserable? While she'd stopped threatening to sue him, she still made snippy comments every time they ran into each other, which in a small town was often.

She didn't even have to say anything to him, just glare at him with those big dark eyes of hers, and his heart beat harder and faster. He needed to stop letting her get to him. But there was something about her… something that got under his skin and in his head and…

"Owen!"

The shout echoed throughout the woods, startling

birds into flying up from the branches of those towering trees. It startled Owen, too, and he rammed his elbow into the back of the truck he'd been leaning against. He stared down into the ravine where the shout had emanated from.

"Dirk," he called back. "What's wrong?"

"You," Dirk replied. "I need you to start working the winch if we're ever getting this beast up from the bottom of the ravine."

Owen chuckled. But he couldn't deny that the fallen tree was a beast. It had already damaged a couple of chain saws when they'd tried cutting it up. They needed to get the massive thing out of the way of where they needed to cut a firebreak through the national forest. A chain saw fired up in the distance—where the firebreak would begin, closer to town. They needed to protect Northern Lakes, especially after an arsonist had given the townspeople and firefighters uncomfortably close calls six months ago. That arsonist had set different areas of the national forest on fire several times, nearly killing a Boy Scout troop that had been camping. Then he'd burned down the firefighters' favorite restaurant and watering hole, the Filling Station, and Serena Beaumont's boardinghouse as well. The arsonist had been caught. He was a young local man who'd wanted to become a firefighter, but his application had been denied because of his juvenile record of arson. While there had been injuries, nobody had been killed, fortunately, but the fires he'd set had exposed the town's vulnerabilities…just like Courtney Beaumont's return had exposed Owen's.

Why the hell does she get to me?

"Owen!" Dirk shouted again.

"Sorry, sorry," he called back and drew in a deep

breath to clear thoughts of Courtney from his mind. He reached for the switch to the winch but hesitated a long moment.

So long that Dirk started trudging up the slope from the ravine. "What's the holdup?" the older Hotshot asked him.

"You checked this out, right?" Owen asked because when he breathed in, he'd noticed some acrid smell, like burning metal or maybe gears.

"Checked what out?" Dirk rubbed a hand over his bald head, which gleamed with sweat. He'd ditched his jacket, too, despite the coldness of the early-spring morning.

If he hadn't had a late call as a paramedic, Owen would have gotten there early enough that he would have done the hard work of wrangling the cable of the winch around the tree trunk. But Dirk had already been at it when he'd arrived. The guy must have gotten there at the crack of dawn.

Owen gestured at the rig, needing to confirm the equipment had had a standard safety check before proceeding. "Did you check the truck? The winch?"

"Yeah, yeah," Dirk called back. "Cody checked everything out this morning."

"I didn't think he was here yet," Owen said. He must have gotten there even earlier than Dirk had. "I didn't see his truck." Everybody else had parked their vehicles alongside the road.

"His fiancée and her sister picked up his truck," Dirk said. "They needed it to move something for that store the sister is opening in town."

Owen's pulse quickened. She'd been here…

Courtney Beaumont was the twin sister of Cody's fiancée, Serena. How could the women look so much alike but be so different? Serena didn't hold a grudge against him over their mother's death a year and a half ago. She was so sweet and nurturing.

Nothing like Courtney, with her sharp tongue and unforgiving nature. She was still ticked off at him over things that had happened back in high school, which seemed like a hundred years ago now after everything that had happened to him as a Marine and as a Hotshot. But as he thought back now, a pang of regret struck his heart again that he hadn't stopped the bullying.

"So can we do this?" Dirk asked, his voice sharp with frustration.

Owen focused on his friend. The guy had dark circles beneath his eyes, and although he was usually clean-shaven, he had more than a night's growth of stubble on his face. "Hey, you okay?" he asked.

Dirk jerked his head in a sharp nod. "Yeah. I'm not the one daydreaming on the job."

No. He wasn't.

"I'm sorry," Owen said.

Dirk shook his head again. "Don't worry about it."

But something in his tone—the weariness in it— worried Owen. "Are you sure you're okay?" he asked again.

Dirk turned away and headed back down the steep ravine. "I'm fine. Just want to get this beast up to the logging truck…"

Owen was curious, too, about what the hell was in the tree that it had chewed up a few chain saws. That had happened before, with other trees, but the fire department had been having a lot of little accidents lately. Stupid things, but they were starting to add up with costs.

Owen didn't have to worry about that, though. His

work as an EMT kept him busy. He would leave worrying about the budget to replace that equipment to
his boss, Superintendent Braden Zimmer. No, the only
thing worrying him right now was Courtney. But he
wasn't going to let her get to him anymore.

Before reaching for the winch, he called out to Dirk,
"You sure it's secure?"

"Sure," Dirk called back, and he sounded irritated
as well as frustrated now.

Owen couldn't blame him. His being so distracted
was probably annoying the crap out of his team member. He started the winch and the metal rope began
to wind back up, creaking and groaning in protest of
the weight of the tree it was dragging. Brush rustled,
crushed beneath the heavy weight of the trunk as it
scraped its way up the steep slope of the ravine. The
metal whined and whined as its protest grew.

Then the whine turned into a high-pitched metallic
scream as the winch snapped. The metal rope broke
apart, cables spiraling through the air, snarling like
whips.

Owen ducked and raised his arms to shield himself.
But his jacket was only fire-retardant. It would do little
to protect him from one of those razor-sharp cables. He
could get far worse than a scar if one of them struck
him. He could lose a limb or his life…

Courtney's body ached, from her neck and her shoulders down her spine to her lower back and hips. She
gritted her teeth, ignoring the pain, as she pushed the
end of the display case into position.

"Stop!" Serena shouted as she stepped into the store.
"I told you to wait until Cody gets off work."

"We don't need Cody," Courtney told her sister.

Serena smiled. "Speak for yourself. I do." From the twinkle in her dark eyes, it was clear she needed him for something other than moving furniture.

Courtney snorted disdainfully. She would never *need* a man.

"Jealous," Serena teased. She flipped her thick black braid over her shoulder and giggled.

Courtney was not at all jealous. She was thrilled that her sister was so happy. She just wished she'd found that happiness with someone other than a Hotshot firefighter.

Not that Cody didn't love her sister fiercely. He did. Courtney could attest to that. He still hadn't entirely forgiven her for how she'd hurt Serena when she'd tried to force her to sell the boardinghouse they'd inherited after their mother died. Courtney had been so scared that Serena would work herself to death running the place, just like their mother had, so she'd let herself get talked into suing her own sister six months ago.

Cody wasn't the only one who hadn't forgiven Courtney over that.

Guilt weighed heavily on her, bowing her shoulders. She hadn't forgiven herself either.

But Serena had. She had the biggest, warmest heart.

Although they had the same face, with their mother's delicate features and big dark eyes, they did not have the same heart.

Courtney was not warm and forgiving. Owen James knew that better than anyone. Since she'd moved back to Northern Lakes, she'd made it clear to him that she would never forgive him.

Not that he actually cared about what she thought or felt. He never had, or he wouldn't have treated her as cruelly as he had growing up. He was one of the reasons she'd left town and one of the reasons she hadn't wanted to ever return.

Serena's smile slid away, and she stepped closer and squeezed Courtney's arm. "I wish you would find someone, too."

Courtney shook her head. "The last thing I need right now is a man," she said, especially since she'd never had much luck with dating. Her most recent ex was a case in point. In that way, she was more like Mom than Serena was. "I'm too busy getting my store open."

"You need more than your store," Serena said.

Courtney looked around the space, and pride brightened her mood. The wainscoting had just been installed beneath the bright, paisley-patterned wallpaper she'd put up herself. She would also paint the wainscoting herself—a creamy ivory that she'd already picked out.

Courtney shook her head again. "No. This is all I need." The space was coming together so well. It was almost ready, which was good because her inventory would arrive soon.

"You're a hypocrite," Serena accused her.

Courtney widened her eyes in feigned confusion. She knew the accusation was valid but asked anyway. "What are you talking about?"

"You told me that I needed more than the boardinghouse in my life," Serena reminded her.

Courtney had done more than tell her; she'd tried to take the family business away from her. Not that she'd wanted it for herself. She just hadn't wanted Serena to have the crippling responsibility of it. She blamed the boardinghouse for their mother's death even more than she blamed Owen James. But if he'd shown up sooner, if he'd acted faster...

Their mother wouldn't have died. Courtney was

certain of it. Fit and only in her fifties, their mother should have survived the heart attack she'd had eighteen months ago.

"When I told you that you needed more than the boardinghouse, I didn't mean that you needed a man," Courtney clarified. "I meant that you needed to travel— experience life outside Northern Lakes."

"Like you did?" Serena asked.

Now she nodded.

"It doesn't seem to have made you happy," Serena observed. "Not like Cody makes me happy."

That was probably true.

"And you came back," her twin continued with a smile. "So you must have missed this place."

"I missed you," Courtney corrected her. "Not the town." She shuddered. She'd always hated her hometown. But staying away from it had made her sister think she hated her, too. That was why she'd come back—to make things right with her twin after the mistakes she'd made. Suing her to force her to sell the boardinghouse hadn't been the only one.

"You moved back for me," Serena said, and now she slung her arm around her sister's shoulders. "I appreciate that you did, and I just want you to be happy." Her smile grew. "Like Cody makes me."

Courtney wrapped her arm around her sister's tiny waist and squeezed. "I am happy."

Serena snorted now. "You don't look it." She touched a fingertip to what was probably a worry groove between Courtney's brows. "You look stressed."

"I am," she admitted. "I've been marketing for the grand opening in thirty days. But I'm stressed that the store won't be ready on time." And she was stressed about how the town would receive and accept it. She had designed all the clothes herself; they were her babies.

She didn't want anyone calling them ugly—like she'd been called ugly when she was younger. Maybe this had been a mistake…

Maybe she hadn't had to move back to Northern Lakes to repair her relationship with her twin. But being here had made it easier. With the boardinghouse gone, Serena seemed to enjoy helping her with the store.

And Courtney loved having her help and spending time getting to know her again. She'd never known her twin all that well. While they had grown up in the same house, they hadn't really grown up together. They'd been so different. Everybody had loved and accepted Serena, while Courtney had been the outsider, the reject, the freak…

And despite all the years she'd been gone, not much had changed. She and Serena still had little in common, and the town still considered her an outsider and a freak, especially after they'd learned she'd sued Serena. A twinge of regret struck her heart so sharply she flinched.

"Everything will be fine," Serena assured her. She was always so bright—so positive. And that wasn't just because she was in love. She had always been that way.

Courtney summoned a smile. "I will believe you," she said, "once we finish unloading Cody's truck." He'd let them borrow it to move the furniture she'd purchased for the store.

Serena chuckled. "Okay…although I think we should wait for Cody. He can recruit some of the other guys to help us, too."

Courtney jerked away from her sister and headed toward the back door. She didn't want Cody bringing any of his firefighting coworkers around—especially not Owen James—although it was unlikely that any of them would volunteer to help her anyway.

"We can get the rest of the stuff," she insisted as she pushed open the rear exit door to the alley.

Another truck had pulled in behind Cody's, blocking it into the narrow space between buildings. This other truck was black like Cody's and had the same insignia on the door for the US Forest Service.

Her stomach tightened with knots of apprehension. She hoped like hell it wasn't Owen. The man who stepped out of the truck had dark hair and eyes. Owen's hair was blond—albeit a darker shade than Cody's. And his eyes were blue. She breathed a sigh of relief.

"Where's Cody?" the man asked.

"Hey, Braden," Serena greeted him when she joined them in the alley.

Courtney recognized him now—by face and name. He was the superintendent of the Huron Hotshots— Cody's boss.

"Is Cody here?" His voice was gruff with impatience and something else…

Something that had goose bumps of apprehension rising up on Courtney's arms. Or maybe that was just a chill because she'd taken off her jacket and it was cold outside, especially in the shade of the buildings lining the alley.

"No," Serena replied. "We just borrowed his truck to move some stuff…" She gestured toward the furniture still in the bed of the truck. "I thought he was with you—at the site where you're starting work on the firebreak."

Braden shook his head. "I was at the firehouse. I put Cody in charge of that operation." He moved toward the open door of his truck.

But Serena rushed up before he could shut it and held it open. "What's going on, Braden?" she demanded to know. She must have noticed that *something else* in his voice, too.

Courtney stepped closer to her sister. But she was worried that she couldn't protect her from what they might learn.

"I got a call," Braden said. "There was an accident at the site."

Serena's body went still. "Cody?"

Braden shook his head but admitted, "I don't know. I can't get him on his phone."

Serena gasped, and all the color drained from her face. Courtney caught her just as she began to sway back on her feet. Wrapping her arms around her twin, she held on tightly. "Don't jump to conclusions," she warned her.

She'd done that too many times herself.

"You don't know that he's the one who's been hurt," Courtney reminded her. Then she focused on Braden, and the chill that had raised those goose bumps on her skin creeped into her voice as she asked him, "What do you know?"

The man met her gaze, and she saw the fear and concern in his eyes. He was just as scared as Serena was as she trembled in Courtney's embrace.

He was worried that he'd lost one of his men.

Tears stung Courtney's eyes, but she blinked them back. She had to be strong—for her sister. She hadn't been there before when Serena had needed her, so she would damn well be here now. "What do you know?" she repeated.

And why the hell was he here and not at the scene

of the accident with his men? She didn't ask that question, though.

But he answered it anyway. "They're already en route to the hospital. I'm on my way to meet the ambulance." And as he'd passed the alley, he must have noticed Cody's truck parked inside it. And he'd hoped...

What Courtney was hoping. That Cody was all right. He made her sister so happy. If she lost him...

But maybe—given the job he did—it wasn't a question of *if* she lost him but *when*.

Being a Hotshot was a dangerous job—one Courtney thought nobody in their right mind would want. But she wasn't thinking of Cody then. She was thinking instead of Owen James.

Could he be the firefighter who'd been hurt?

Or worse...

From the look of dread and horror on Braden Zimmer's face, it was clear that it was worse than hurt. Was the injured Hotshot already dead?

Was he dead? Had the plan worked? It must have. The ambulance had raced past the hiding spot just moments ago, sirens wailing. Of course, that meant only that someone had been hurt, not necessarily killed. An ambulance was called to deliver aid and move the victim to the hospital. It would have been more promising to see a hearse.

Or the coroner's van...

But the ambulance passed again, moments later, and this time the lights were off. They weren't rushing the victim to the hospital. The victim had to be beyond help.

He had to be dead.

Had he died as gruesomely as planned? Or had it

been quick and painless? And why did a flash of regret rise up at those thoughts?

A cell phone sat on the passenger seat. And the driver, who'd parked back from the road, hiding in a spot where nobody would see the vehicle, willed it to ring. Someone would call. They would have to deliver the news—about the accident.

About the death...

Had it been quick? Or had the Hotshot had time to figure out what was happening and who was responsible?

Had he figured it out and shared his suspicion with anyone else?

Chapter 2

Owen's hands twitched with the urge to take the wheel of the ambulance. He wanted to be in the driver's seat, wanted his foot pressing down hard on the accelerator, wanted to flip the switch for the lights and sirens.

But sitting in the back, beside the stretcher over which a sheet had been pulled, Owen knew there was no need for the lights and sirens. There was no hope of saving Dirk. The sheet was stained with blood, as were Owen's clothes.

"Let me check you over, Owen," the female EMT urged him again. Sandy worked for the ambulance company, not the fire department like Owen. But she and Owen often showed up at the same emergencies.

He shook his head. He wasn't physically hurt—much. The real hurt, which gripped his heart and pressed down heavily on his lungs, wasn't physical.

The incident flashed through his mind again, starting with the moment when the winch had snapped…

One of the broken tendrils of the cable lashed the sleeve of his heavy jacket, and he winced as a soft cry of pain slipped through his lips.

But a louder cry echoed his, one nearly as loud as the scream of the cable snapping.

Dirk.

Owen scrambled down the ravine, slipping on the dirt that the tree trunk had stripped bare of brush and topsoil—leaving only loose soil. His feet flew out from beneath him, and he slid down the rest of the way until he hit the trunk of the already fallen tree. The cable had chipped away some of its bark, leaving it stripped bare like the slope.

"Dirk?" he called out, his voice echoing with fear.

A groan answered him.

And he noticed the big black boots sticking out from beneath the tree. He hurried around to the other side, to where Dirk lay faceup on the ground, gasping for breath.

"You're going to be okay," Owen murmured reassuringly. But he had no way of knowing if he spoke the truth. He needed to assess Dirk's injuries. He had to move the massive tree off his friend. But he couldn't do that alone. And the winch was broken. He reached for his cell phone, but his pocket was empty. It must have fallen out when he fell.

A gloved hand gripped his arm. But the grasp was weak—like the man was now. He had to be hurt—badly. And he knew it; fear filled his dark eyes.

Owen focused on Dirk. "We're going to get this off you. We're going to get you help."

He could help—if he had his first-aid kit, if he had his EMT van…

"I'm going to get the rest of the team," he told Dirk. The entire team wasn't working the firebreak, but there were enough of them to lift the tree trunk from Dirk— enough to help carry him up to the street where the ambulance would be waiting once Owen called for it.

He needed his damn phone.

But Dirk held on to his sleeve, clutching at it.

And Owen met the man's tortured gaze. He was clearly in agony, his breaths just gurgles. Owen knew what that meant—that Dirk's lungs were filling with fluid, with blood. Owen needed to get the damn tree off him, so he could perform a thoracentesis. He had enough stuff in the first-aid kit in his truck that he could do it here—in the field as he'd treated soldiers during his deployments as a Marine medic. He had to release the fluid building up in Dirk's lungs.

"I'm going to get you—"

Dirk jerked at his sleeve now. And his gurgle for breath became a moan and then a name: "Lou… Lou…"

"Luke?" Owen guessed. Lucas Garrison was another team member—another Hotshot as well as one of Dirk's best friends. He had to be close; he was also working on the firebreak. "Luke!" he yelled.

But Dirk jerked his sleeve again and continued, "Louanne…"

And realization struck Owen. Louanne was Dirk's wife's name. "I'll send someone to get Louanne. She'll meet us at the hospital."

Dirk's fingers curled into his sleeve, pulling at it. "Louanne…"

Then his head turned toward the side and a bubble

of air and blood puffed out of his open mouth. His last breath…

"No!" Owen yelled.

He could save him yet. He just had to get the damn tree off. He started shoving at it—as he yelled for the others to come help.

He couldn't remember now when they had shown up. He could only remember the damage he'd seen once they'd rolled the log away from Dirk's broken body. It wasn't the tree that had killed their team member. It was the broken cable that had wrapped around him, that had nearly cut him in…

How the hell had Dirk found the strength to pull on Owen's sleeve? To murmur his wife's name…?

He should have died instantly. Hell, it would have been better for him—and infinitely more humane—if he had.

Owen flinched now and looked away from that blood-soaked sheet in the ambulance. Dirk had had no chance. There was nothing Owen could have done to save him.

He knew that.

But he still felt like he'd failed him. Like Courtney Beaumont thought he'd failed her mother because he hadn't been able to save her. To bring her back…

She'd already been dead when he'd arrived at the boardinghouse, where she'd collapsed. Maybe if he'd driven faster, maybe if he'd charged the defibrillator higher…

Maybe Courtney was right to hate him, because, at the moment, he hated himself. For Dirk's death and for her mother's and for all those young Marines he hadn't been able to save…

Dirk's wife was certain to hate him, too, when he

told her what had happened—that Dirk had been killed working with him.

And Owen hadn't managed to save him...

"I'm sure it's not Cody," Courtney said as Braden Zimmer backed his truck out of the alley. She was lying. She wasn't certain at all. She had no way of being certain. But she wanted to comfort her sister, who seemed about to fall apart at the thought of losing her fiancé.

Serena's fingers trembled as she fumbled with her cell phone. She pressed a button.

Courtney knew who she was calling. Cody.

"He's not picking up," Serena said, her voice shaking like her fingers now.

"Braden already said that," Courtney reminded her gently. But Cody might have been more inclined to pick up a call from his fiancée than his boss.

Unless he wasn't able to answer his phone...

"I—I can't lose him," Serena murmured.

"You won't," Courtney assured her. She wrapped her arm around her twin and led her toward the passenger side of Cody's pickup. "We'll follow Braden to the hospital, so you can see Cody—"

Serena gasped and clutched her arm. "You do think he's hurt!"

"No," Courtney lied again. She ignored the twinge of guilt she felt for not being honest. She had already hurt her sister enough. It was kinder to lie to her now than to tell her that she was afraid, too.

And if she was going to be completely honest with her twin, Courtney would have to admit that she thought Serena was crazy for ever dating a Hotshot firefighter, let alone falling for one. Every time he got sent out to a fire, his life was in danger.

"We will see Cody at the hospital because he'll be there to support the rest of his team." Courtney hadn't known her future brother-in-law long, but she knew how much he cared about his coworkers. They were the family that Cody Mallehan, a foster kid, had never really had.

Serena nodded as she expelled a shaky breath. "You're right. That's where he'll be."

Alive and well, Courtney hoped. She closed the passenger door on her sister and rushed around to the driver's side. Serena must not have been completely re-assured, though, because she was pressing Cody's contact on her phone again.

As Courtney climbed into the driver's seat, she felt a strange vibration. She shoved her hand between the seat and the back and pulled out Cody's cell phone. "That's why he hasn't been answering."

Serena expelled another shaky breath. "He lost his phone."

That didn't mean he would have been able to an-swer it even if it had been on him. That didn't mean he wasn't the one who was hurt. But Courtney held her silence and kept her worries in as she started the truck and headed toward the hospital.

Northern Lakes was a small town, so it wasn't long before she pulled the pickup into the parking lot of Northern Lakes Memorial Hospital. The lot was nearly full of other vehicles bearing the US Forest Service in-signia on their doors. Before she could put the trans-mission into Park, her sister opened the passenger door and jumped out.

Courtney quickly turned off the engine and rushed after Serena through the lobby doors of the emergency room. Like the parking lot, the waiting room was nearly full—with Hotshots. She saw Braden right away and one of his assistant superintendents, Wyatt Andrews. But no Cody...

And no Owen James.

Her pulse quickened, and something like dread gripped her. Could Owen be the one who was hurt?

But why would she care if something had happened to him? She'd never cared about him before—she certainly hadn't when they were kids.

And she wasn't like Serena, who cared about everyone she'd ever met. Hell, her twin didn't even have to meet someone to care about them. But Serena cared the most about Cody.

She was looking around the room, pushing through the people as she searched for one man: her fiancé. "Cody?" She uttered his name, but she wasn't calling out for him. She was asking where he was.

The others just shook their heads.

Did they not know?

Or did they not want to tell her?

Courtney caught up with Serena and grabbed her hand, pulling her to a stop. And just as she did, a doctor entered the waiting room through a door at the back.

Everyone turned to him.

"I'm sorry," he said. "But your friend passed away before he even arrived at the hospital. There was nothing we could do to revive him."

Serena gasped, and she swayed against Courtney. Had Cody died? Courtney trembled. Or had Owen?

But then Owen stepped through the same door the doctor had, and a sudden wave of relief eased the tightness Courtney hadn't even realized had been in her chest. He was okay. But why was she relieved? Over him?

It was ridiculous. Maybe she was more like her twin

than she'd given herself credit for—if she could actually care about a man who'd hurt her all those years ago, and then more recently when he hadn't helped her mother. She didn't hero-worship Owen James like the rest of the damn town always had. They'd worshipped him even before he'd been injured in the line of duty as a Marine medic—because he'd been a star athlete and had drawn the attention of every college recruiter in the country. But he hadn't been at college very long before leaving to join the Marines and then coming home with that scar.

"Cody?" Serena asked as she rushed toward Owen. "Was it Cody?"

"No." Owen shook his head. "It was Dirk." His voice was gruff with emotion. "Dirk Brown."

Serena pressed a hand to her mouth. "That's terrible…"

Owen nodded, and he looked physically sick. His face was so pale that his scar stood out even more than it usually did. And his clothes…

The yellow firefighter jacket and his brown pants were stained, not just with dirt but also something that looked like blood. Owen must have been there when it had happened, or he'd arrived shortly after and had tried to treat Dirk.

"Does Louanne know?" Serena asked.

Owen shook his head.

"I'll tell her," Braden said.

He must have walked up to them, but Courtney hadn't noticed. In fact, all the firefighters had gathered around, forming a circle of bodies around Owen, as if to protect him. He wasn't hurt, though. Was he? If any of that blood was his, he would still be in the emergency room—not in the waiting room. They must have been hovering protectively because of what he'd witnessed.

What the hell had happened? She wanted to ask. But before she could get the question out, Owen spoke again.

"I want to be the one to tell her," he said to his boss. "I was the one with him—" his voice cracked with emotion "—when it happened…"

And Courtney's suspicion was confirmed. He'd definitely seen what had happened. He'd witnessed a death. She couldn't imagine how awful that had been—no matter how many times he, as an EMT and Marine, might have done it.

"I need to do this," Owen said.

Braden hesitated a long moment before giving a slow nod. "I'll go with you—"

"No," Owen said. "I need to do this alone."

"No, you don't." But it was Serena who'd chimed in on the conversation. "I'll go with you. I know Louanne."

Courtney wasn't surprised. Her sister knew everyone in Northern Lakes, so of course she would know the spouses of her fiancé's coworkers.

"You don't have to do that," Courtney advised her twin in a soft whisper. Not when she was so shaken over worrying about her fiancé.

But Owen heard her and shook his head, as if disgusted with *her*.

"You don't know where Cody is yet," Courtney reminded her.

"He's back at the accident site," Owen said.

Braden tensed. "He is?"

Owen nodded.

"I better head over there," Braden said. But before he turned to leave, he grabbed Owen's shoulder. "I'm glad you're okay."

But was he okay?

He was so pale.

Braden turned then, but he didn't leave right away—not before he spoke to the rest of his crew gathered in the waiting room. "I know this tragedy has devastated all of us. Dirk was a good—" His voice cracked with emotion like Owen's had earlier. He cleared it and continued, "He was a good man. And his loss will be felt forever—by us and by his family. But we are family, too, and together we will all get through this."

Nobody else said anything, but some of the tension left the room, as if everyone had breathed a sigh of relief with his words. He'd comforted them.

She looked at Owen's face. The tension was still there, in the tightness of his jaw and in that horrifying look in his blue eyes. He was staring at her now—down at her since he was so much taller than she was.

Braden left, and the others began to file out after him. Maybe they intended to return to the accident site as well. She and Owen were almost alone when he murmured to her, "You probably think it's my fault that he died…"

She sucked in a breath that he would have suggested such a thing. But then, seeing that tortured look on his face, she wondered if he was the one who actually thought that. If he was blaming himself for the death of his friend.

She shrugged. "I don't know what happened…" But she could tell that he was hurting over it. There was such pain on his handsome face.

He snorted, as if he wasn't buying her reaction to his statement. "That hasn't stopped you before from blaming me…"

Even as sorry as she felt for him in the moment, she couldn't let go of her anger and resentment toward him for not saving her mother. "I'm sure you did everything you could to help *him*…"

Serena gasped now. Courtney hadn't even been aware that her twin was still there, unlike the others who'd slipped away. "Courtney—"

She waved off her sister's recrimination. "I know. I know…" It was a terrible thing to say, given her past with him, and especially given how upset he probably was.

She knew how badly it hurt to lose someone, but it was his fault that she knew that. She wasn't going to forgive him. No matter what he'd gone through in the Marines or as a firefighter.

So she was damn well not going to apologize to him or feel sorry for him. She just had to steel herself to resist the urge burning inside her to do both.

"We should go back to the store," she told Serena.

But her sister shook her head. "I'm going with Owen to talk to Louanne Brown."

"You don't need to do that," Courtney said.

And surprisingly, Owen nodded in agreement. "You don't."

"I don't need to," Serena agreed. "But I want to."

Courtney wasn't certain why—to comfort Dirk's widow? Or to comfort Owen?

"I'll go, too," she said. But she had no intention of making Owen feel better, and she didn't know the widow.

She just wanted to be there to support her sister. This death had to have hit Serena hard, too, with the realization that she could lose her fiancé just as easily as this woman had lost her husband.

Falling for a firefighter was way too risky.

It was easy to find the scene of the accident. Two state police SUVs, lights flashing, were parked among the few US Forest Service pickup trucks that remained along the shoulder of the road. The logging truck, with its big winch, was just a short distance from the side of the road, parked in a clearing they had earlier cut in the woods.

A few state troopers walked around it, taking notes, as Cody stood near it, his blond hair gleaming in the sunshine. Braden looked at the troopers again, hoping his old nemesis wasn't among them. He caught no glimpse of Martin Gingrich's bald head, though. It would have gleamed brighter than Cody's hair if he'd been here. Unless he was wearing a hat like a couple of the other troopers.

If he was here…Braden would demand that he leave. A man should not be able to investigate crimes for which he might be responsible. Not that Braden had any reason to think Dirk's death hadn't just been a tragic accident.

Yet.

But then Cody turned toward him, and from the look of anger and frustration on his face, Braden knew that what had happened here had been no accident. A member of his team had been murdered.

Chapter 3

As a paramedic, and before that as a Marine medic, Owen had had to deliver bad news many, many times. But this time…

His heart ached as Louanne Brown collapsed on her kitchen floor, her sobs echoing throughout the house she shared with her husband… *Had* shared with him.

Dirk would never come home again. Not to his wife.

At least he wasn't leaving behind any kids; they'd never had any. But maybe they would have been a comfort to Louanne, who seemed inconsolable. She'd always seemed so tough before; like one of the guys, she'd fished and hunted and played cards with them. Dirk had probably been her whole life. And now she'd lost that life.

"I'm sorry," Owen murmured. "I'm so sorry…"

He dropped to his knees beside her. But he didn't know what to do as she hunched over, as if trying to hold herself together. He lifted one of his arms to reach for her—to hold her. But then he noticed the blood on his jacket—all that blood. He damn well should have changed before he'd come here, but he hadn't wanted Louanne to hear the news from anyone else. And he'd been so distracted.

But that was no excuse. He had no excuse. Nothing to offer her but...

"I know nothing I say can make you feel any better," Owen said. "But I want you to know that at the very last he was thinking of you."

Louanne lifted her head from her hands and peered up at him. Her face was red like the hair that was tangled around her face. "How—how do you know?"

"He asked for you," Owen said.

She covered her face again as sobs racked her body. Serena dropped down next to her, and although she was smaller than Louanne, she wrapped her arms around the devastated woman, holding her close.

Serena could offer her the comfort that Owen couldn't. He felt too responsible for what had happened. All he could give Louanne right now was his guilt.

If only he'd been paying more attention...

If only he'd checked out that damn cable himself...

Guilt overwhelmed him now—so completely that it pressed on his lungs, stealing his breath away. He needed air. He jumped up from the cold tile floor and pushed open the sliding patio door.

Once on the deck, he gripped the railing, hanging on tightly as his head reeled. He had to be lacking oxygen because he was suddenly dizzy—so damn dizzy.

A small hand touched his back, and he felt the heat of it like an electrical shock. Startled, he jumped and whirled around to face...Courtney Beaumont.

Why the hell had she insisted on coming along with her sister?

He'd already found it so hard telling Louanne about Dirk, and her being there, silently judging him, had made it even harder. He felt so guilty already, and just seeing Courtney brought out so many feelings of guilt over the past, over her mom, even though he'd done all he could, all that anyone else could have done. He hadn't needed her here adding to the feeling so that it threatened to overwhelm him.

He was already too aware of her—always had been. And now that she'd touched him, his skin tingled. Why did she have to look like she did?

So incredibly beautiful…

He'd always thought Serena was pretty—in that sweet, wholesome way she had. But her twin…

There was nothing sweet or wholesome about Courtney. She'd always had such an edge to her, such a damn big chip on her slender shoulders. Even though they were twins, aside from coloring, they didn't look that much alike. At least, not to him…

While Serena's hair hung down her back in a long braid, Courtney's black hair was cut so short that it just skimmed her chin, framing her face and highlighting her perfect features. Features she no longer disguised like she had in high school, when she'd worn heavy black makeup on her eyes and her lips. She didn't need it. Her eyes were her most prominent feature, big and thickly lashed and so dark that a man could get lost in them. Owen felt himself slipping under her spell now.

"Go away," he implored her, his voice gruff with the emotions overwhelming him.

She tensed, then turned to walk back toward the patio doors leading into the kitchen. She wore jeans with so many holes he was surprised they didn't just fall off her. Her jacket was the same, like the ones she'd worn in high school held together with huge safety pins. But the denim she had on now was streaked with paint, so she must have been wearing it to work on her store—not as an advertisement for her designs.

When she reached for the door handle, a flash of both relief and regret shot through him. He couldn't be around her anymore—not when he was feeling like this, so raw and vulnerable. But he didn't want her to leave either—which was crazy.

If he was looking for comfort, she was the last one who would offer him any. Why had she joined him on the deck, anyway? To rub salt in his wounds?

To reprimand him again for letting her sister come along to make the death notification?

And even though he knew he should, he couldn't let her go. Not yet. Not until he knew why she'd sought him out.

Courtney hesitated, reluctant to leave Owen all by himself. She'd never seen anyone look as alone as he'd looked when he'd stepped onto the deck and gripped that railing like a lifeline. She had once felt that alone, so she knew what he was feeling.

He hadn't accepted her comfort, though. Hell, he hadn't even given her a chance to offer it. Instead he'd turned around and told her to go.

"Stop!" he called out, just as she touched the door handle, just as she'd been about to step back inside the kitchen.

Not that she wanted to go back in there. She could still hear the woman's high-pitched sobs. Louanne Brown seemed devastated. And Courtney wasn't good at soothing people, not like Serena was, so she shouldn't have bothered trying with Owen either.

But she'd felt that strange pull to follow him out, to make sure he wasn't alone. And for a moment—just a moment—she'd felt bad for blaming him for her loss.

According to Serena, Owen had tried hard, for a long time, to resuscitate their mother. But he'd failed her—just like he'd failed his friend. She figured, from how devastated he looked both here and at the hospital, that he hadn't had a choice with his friend. Maybe he hadn't had one with her mother either.

But Mom had been too young—far too young—for a heart attack to have taken her life, to have taken her from her daughters. There must have been something that could have been done to save her. If he'd gotten to the boardinghouse faster or administered something or brought her to the hospital sooner…instead of letting her die…

The loss ached inside Courtney, leaving her feeling hollow and empty. She'd thought moving back to Northern Lakes—finally getting close to her sister—would fill that emptiness. But it was still there—despite Serena, despite the store…

Maybe once Courtney's Couture was up and running, she would feel differently—about her loss, about Northern Lakes.

But she would never feel differently about Owen James. She pushed aside that brief flash of sympathy she'd felt for him and turned to face him. "What?"

"That's what I want to know," he said. "Why did you come out here?"

Despite the cool breeze blowing around the deck, heat rushed to her face. She was embarrassed now that she'd tried to comfort him, so she said nothing.

He prodded, "Did you want to kick me when I was down?"

She narrowed her eyes and glared at him. "Yes, that's what I wanted to do," she said. "Rub salt in the wound—all that. I'm the heartless one."

His lips curved into a faint smile. "That is what I've heard."

She tensed at the jab, but she didn't doubt that was what everyone in Northern Lakes believed. Serena was all heart, and she was none. She hadn't even come back for her mom's funeral, but it had been so hard to lose her. Even now, her heart ached with a hollow feeling. But, just like in high school, she wasn't going to let Owen James see that he'd affected her. She curved her lips into a faint smile, too.

He studied her smile, his blue eyes intense as he stared into hers. That intensity unsettled her, and a chill rushed over her now, chasing away the heat of embarrassment. She didn't like how he was looking at her—like he could see her.

Really see her...

Not the way he'd looked at her when he'd been a high school senior—the quarterback, the captain of the basketball team, the homecoming king...

Back then he'd looked at her, a lowly sophomore, like she was a freak. And when all his popular friends had called her that, he hadn't hesitated to laugh at her, too—in front of the entire school. The heat rushed over her again from embarrassment and anger.

"Now you stop," she told him.

"What?"

"Stop looking at me," she said.

He moved his broad shoulders in a slight shrug. "Why?" he asked. "Isn't that what you want? Isn't that why you've always dressed the way you have? For attention?"

She sucked in a breath. She'd been expressing herself—then and now. That was why she'd become a fashion designer. But she wasn't about to explain herself to him.

The outfit she was wearing now was conservative even by Northern Lakes standards.

"I never wanted your attention," she told him. But she wondered now if she spoke the truth—at least about the past. She didn't want his attention now. "And I shouldn't have followed you out here."

She turned away from him, but he reached out and locked his fingers around her wrist and whirled her back to face him. She gasped in surprise over his action and her reaction to it. A thrill raced through her, quickening her pulse.

"Go ahead," he said vehemently. "Kick me. I'm down. This is your chance."

She shook her head. "I don't want to…"

"Why not?" He sounded almost desperate. Like he wanted someone to blame him for what had happened… because he blamed himself?

She shrugged. "It's just no fun to kick you when you're already kicking yourself."

He expelled a ragged breath. "Are people wrong about you?" he asked. "Do you have a heart after all?"

She shook her head again, adding with mock seriousness, "Nope. No heart at all. It's just spite that pumps the blood through my body."

A hint of a smile appeared on his face, but then, as if he felt guilty for even that, his mouth pulled down again.

Surprising herself, she felt such sympathy for him in

that moment. She'd never seen anyone look as tortured as he did. "Why are you kicking yourself?"

He dropped his hand from her wrist and tunneled his fingers into his thick golden hair. Usually blond men's hair began to thin as they aged. But of course, that wouldn't be the case for Owen James. Even the scar on his face hadn't detracted from his good looks. In fact, it only made him better looking, adding a rugged air of danger to his former pretty-boy handsomeness.

She wanted to reach out and skim her fingertips over that scar, to see how it felt. But she knew she wouldn't stop at the scar. She might skim her fingers over his rigid-looking jaw or maybe over the sensual curve of his lips. His mouth was…

More dangerous-looking than that scar. She pulled her gaze from his lips and focused on his eyes. But they were no safer for her; they were such a deep blue and so full of anguish.

"What happened?" she asked.

She was surprised no one had questioned him at the hospital. But then, most of the people in the waiting room had probably been at the site of the accident, too, which was probably why they'd all looked so devastated as well.

But none of them had had as much blood on their clothes as Owen had. He was the one who'd tried the hardest to help his friend. He was the Hotshot hurting the most right now.

Owen shook his head, as if he was unable to answer her. But there was no doubt he had been there—that he knew. He just didn't want to share. With her? Or with anyone?

"Tell me," she implored him.

"You really want to know?"

No. She wasn't the type of person who slowed down to gawk at traffic accidents. She rarely even watched the news. But she could tell that he needed to talk, or he might explode with all the guilt and grief that radiated from him.

"Just tell me," she said, and she forced herself to sound impatient in order to compel him to start talking. "It's not like it's going to be kept a secret. There are no secrets in Northern Lakes."

He snorted, and a chuckle actually slipped through his lips. "Isn't that the truth…"

"So save me the trouble of hanging out at the coffee shop or the Filling Station until it comes out."

The Filling Station was a local bar that was still more popular than the new nightclub that had opened in town. Of course, the bar was technically newer than the club, since it had just been rebuilt after an arson fire totally destroyed it six months ago. The bar owner had made certain that it looked just as it had—casual and comfortable enough that customers just tossed their peanut shells on the floor.

"How did Dirk die?" she asked.

Strangely enough, his widow hadn't even asked that question when Owen had informed her of his death. But maybe the woman was just too overcome with grief to want to know the gory details. That wasn't what Courtney wanted to know either.

But Owen told her. His voice gruff with emotion, he shared how the cable on the back of a logging truck had suddenly snapped. His voice cracked when he detailed how he found his friend at the bottom of the ravine, under the log—how the guy was aspirating on his own blood…

She shuddered.

And then he told her what he'd seen when his co-workers arrived and they'd all worked together to lift the log from Dirk. And she shuddered again as horror and revulsion gripped her.

"There was nothing you could have done for him," she said—because that was clearly a fact. His injuries had been too severe.

But Owen shook his head in protest. "I should have been the one down there, the one under the log…"

"Why?" she asked. "Was that where you were supposed to be? Did you switch at the last minute?"

He shook his head again. "No. But Dirk got there before I did, so he was already getting the cable around the tree."

So was he blaming himself because he'd been late, just like she was always blaming him for being too late to help her mother? She should have felt vindicated, but she didn't.

"Did you know the cable was going to break?" she asked, even though she knew he hadn't. She just wanted him to see that it wasn't his fault.

"No," Owen said. "He told me that Cody checked the equipment that morning. If he'd thought it wasn't in proper working condition, he wouldn't have let us use it. The cable shouldn't have snapped."

"Then there was no way you could have known it would happen," she said. "And no way for you to have prevented what happened to Dirk."

He stared down at her then, a furrow between his dark blond brows as he studied her face. "Why are you trying to make me feel better?"

She shook her head. "That's not what I'm trying to do," she assured him. "I just can't blame you for this one." Feigning disappointment, she heaved a heavy sigh. "It's too bad that I can't, but…"

His lips curved into that slight smile and he shook his head. "I never would have believed you would be the one trying to make me feel better."

"Did it work?" she wondered aloud. But then she hastily added, "Not that that's what I was trying to do or anything…"

His grin widened. "Of course not…"

Her pulse quickened like it had when he'd touched her wrist and stopped her from leaving him. That grin of his had always affected her like that, even though it had never been directed her way…until now. She found a smile curving her own lips.

Even though she'd gotten a smile out of him, his body was so stiff and tense, his face still so pale. It had paled even more as he'd relived those awful moments. Maybe she shouldn't have made him talk about it. Maybe that hadn't been the right thing to do. However briefly he'd grinned, it was gone now.

He shook his head. "I can't help feeling like it should have been *me*."

A feeling of horror rushed over her, and she reached out and grabbed his forearms. She wanted to pull him to her, wanted to hang on to him so that he wouldn't slip away like the other firefighter had.

But he wasn't hers to hold on to. And he reminded her of that when he flinched, as if her touch—even through the thick sleeves of his firefighter coat—repulsed him.

That revulsion reminded her of high school, of how he'd looked at her and joined in the taunts. Some things apparently never changed.

"Sorry that the school *freak* dared to touch you. It certainly won't happen again," she said as she dropped her hands from his arms. Then she whirled away from him as the heat of embarrassment rushed over her. Apparently, no matter what she'd done and who she'd become, she would always be the outsider, and he would always be the golden boy.

"Courtney!" he called to her.

But she wasn't going to stop this time. She wasn't going to try to talk to him anymore. She was so angry with herself—for being stupid enough to try to comfort him in the first place.

"You're not getting any more sympathy out of me," she said. "Tell Serena that I'll be waiting in the truck." Instead of opening the slider, she walked down the steps to the sidewalk that wound around the back of the house to the driveway.

She couldn't believe that she'd wanted to comfort him. To make him feel better...

He'd never made her feel better. Not in high school when he'd laughed as his buddies picked on her and not after her mother died.

But then, nobody had been able to make her feel better about losing her mother. She shouldn't have tried to make Owen feel better about losing his friend.

They would never be close enough to help each other that way. She wouldn't make the mistake of letting her guard slip with him again.

Owen James should have died, too. But for some reason, except for some bloodstains on his clothes, he appeared completely unscathed. That wasn't all that had been on his clothes, though. There'd been some fibers from that cable...from where it had been torched...

The cable should have struck him, too. How hadn't that "accident" claimed his life as well as Dirk's?

Of course, it had been no accident.

And because of that, Owen James had to die now, before he realized what he might have heard or seen or smelled—before he put it all together and figured out what had really happened.

That that cable snapping hadn't been an accident at all. It had been murder.

The killer felt a rush of satisfaction that it had worked. Well, it had almost worked.

But there would be another "accident," and this one would take Owen James's life.

Chapter 4

When Braden called him to the firehouse, Owen had been relieved. He hadn't wanted to stay at Dirk's widow's house. He'd had nothing else to say to Louanne but sorry—over and over again. That regret tore at him, churning in his gut.

But now he wasn't just regretful about Dirk's death. He was regretful over that last encounter with Courtney. She'd actually been trying to be nice to him…until he'd flinched. Then she'd lashed out with so much anger and resentment.

School freak…

Guilt burned his face as he remembered calling her that with his friends when they'd teased him about how he always paid so much attention to her at school. Even with all the makeup and weird clothes, she'd been beautiful, and he'd admired her courage in daring to be so different from everyone else, in being herself no matter

how much she'd been ridiculed. His girlfriend had noticed his fascination with Courtney, too, and had been
furious with him. So, not wanting the head cheerleader
to dump him, or his friends to ridicule him, he'd joined
in their ridicule of Courtney and her clothes and her
makeup. His stomach churned with shame and regret
over what a jerk he'd been.

Trying to be so damn cool…

He touched the scar on his cheek. Eventually karma
had bitten him on the ass, and on the face, because now
he was the freak.

And Courtney was…

So beautiful and so angry.

He'd tried to stop her to explain why he'd flinched,
that it had had nothing to do with her, but she'd been
too mad to listen to him. He'd been right when he'd suspected that the grudge she harbored against him went
back further than her mother's death. It went back to
when they were kids. Stupid kids…

"Owen?" Braden nearly shouted his name, as if he'd
called it before and had been ignored.

Owen blinked and focused on his boss. Braden sat
behind the beat-up metal desk in his small windowless
office at the firehouse. The walls were cement block and
the bare floor was concrete. There was nothing warm
or inviting about the space. But it wasn't as if Braden
actually spent much time in it. He wasn't that kind of
boss. He was the kind who worked alongside his crew.
The kind of boss everybody respected.

How much longer would Braden be his boss, though?
Did he hold Owen responsible for Dirk's death? Owen
had felt responsible until Courtney—of all people—
had lessened his guilt. He couldn't believe she had even
tried, let alone been successful.

"I'm sorry," he said to Braden—because he hadn't been listening to him. Not because he thought he'd done something wrong.

Courtney was right. He hadn't caused the accident, and there was nothing he could have done to save Dirk—not with those injuries. He shuddered as he remembered the gruesome extent of them.

Braden's dark eyes were narrowed as he stared intently at Owen. "Are you really okay?"

He jerked his head in a quick nod.

"I went to inspect the scene," Braden said. "I know it had to have been…horrific…"

Owen closed his eyes, and that scene flashed through his head. He flinched. "It was…"

"I can't believe you weren't hurt, too," Braden said. He stood now and came around his desk to where Owen leaned against the doorjamb. "You're not hurt, are you?"

"I'm fine," he lied.

But Braden was astute. And he knew Owen too well. "This wasn't your fault."

Owen knew that he hadn't caused it, but maybe if he'd been more focused, he could have prevented it. Even though Dirk had insisted that Cody had checked it out, Owen should have insisted on inspecting the equipment himself. Especially after he'd noticed that strange acrid smell…

"Owen, it wasn't your fault," Braden reiterated.

He sighed and nodded. "I know. It was an accident."

They'd been having a lot of those lately, but until today, nobody had been seriously hurt. And because of those accidents, they'd been taking extra precautions. So Cody must have checked out the truck.

Braden remained silent—curiously so.

Owen stared at him now, wondering why his usually garrulous boss didn't comment further.

"That's what it was, right?" Owen asked. But that didn't quite make sense. "Dirk told me that Cody checked the equipment."

"He did," Braden said. "Early this morning."

"He didn't notice anything wrong with it?" Owen asked.

"Not then…"

"So what the hell went wrong?" he wondered aloud. It was more of a hypothetical question. He didn't expect Braden to know. Owen had actually been there, and he couldn't figure it out.

It had all happened so quickly, and after it had happened, he'd been focused on trying to save Dirk. He flinched again, and the ache wasn't just in his chest with his heart hurting over the loss of his friend. The ache was also in his forearm—where an end of a strand of that cable had lashed the sleeve of his heavy jacket.

"You *are* hurt," Braden said. He stepped away from his desk and grabbed Owen's arm. "I thought that blood was…"

Dirk's. And most of it was.

There had been so much blood.

But, unfortunately, some of it was Owen's. The cut wasn't deep—thanks to his coat. If only Dirk had been wearing his, too…

Maybe he wouldn't have been hurt as badly. Maybe Owen would have been able to save him.

"I'm fine," Owen said, but he had to say it through gritted teeth. The wound was throbbing now.

Braden cursed. "I'm taking you to the ER."

Owen shook his head and reminded his boss, "I'm a paramedic—"

"You can't treat yourself," Braden said.

"But I would know if I needed to be treated," he said. "And I don't. I'm fine." Or he would be...as long as he didn't lose his job. He drew in a deep breath and asked, "Why'd you call me here?"

To fire him?

Braden continued to intently study his face. "I just wanted to make sure you're really all right."

He wasn't really. Not after the day he'd had. But he had survived. Dirk had not been so lucky.

He uttered a ragged sigh. "I am," he assured his boss. Physically, anyway. Emotionally, he wasn't so sure. But he'd been through worse days than today.

Unfortunately...

"Is that the only reason you wanted to see me?" Owen asked.

Braden hesitated a long while again before replying, "Of course..."

"What happened today?" Owen asked.

"You know. You were there," Braden needlessly reminded him.

He would never be able to forget what had happened—no matter how hard he was going to try. "I guess I mean how...how the hell did it happen?" Owen wanted to know. "Especially after Cody checked the equipment..."

"I didn't unroll the entire cable," another voice chimed in—from the hall behind Owen.

He whirled around to his friend, and he could easily see that he wasn't the only one blaming himself for Dirk Brown's death. Cody looked like hell.

"I should have unwound the whole damn cable," Cody said, his voice gruff with emotion.

Owen reached out and clutched Cody's shoulder, squeezing it. "You didn't need to. If the cable was going bad, the whole thing would have shown wear—not just one part of it."

Unless…

He glanced from Cody to his boss and asked, "Do you think someone could have tampered with it?"

That was the only reason why an otherwise strong-looking cable might have snapped…if someone had damaged just one part of it.

But why?

Answering his own question, he shook his head. There was no reason for anyone to want to hurt one of them. Not since the arsonist who'd terrorized Northern Lakes had been caught…

They were no longer in any danger.

But then he remembered all those accidents his team had faced recently: the brakes that had gone out on the US Forest Service trucks, the chain saws and big equipment that had malfunctioned, and all the metal and stuff they'd found when cutting trees. A chill raced over his skin, making him shiver as he wondered aloud, "What the hell's going on?"

A look passed between Braden and Cody—a look that confirmed his suspicions that something sure as hell *was* going on.

"Tell me," he implored them.

Then there was that hesitation again—but it wasn't just Braden. Cody hesitated, too.

"Come on, guys," he said. "I could have been killed, too, today. I deserve to know what the hell's going on!"

"There's nothing to tell," Braden said. And he shot a quelling glance at Cody. He wasn't lying. There was nothing to tell—until they got some concrete evidence.

Owen's deep blue eyes narrowed with skepticism. He looked at Braden and then again at Cody.

"We do dangerous work," Braden reminded him. "There are bound to be fatalities."

"Fighting fires, maybe," Owen agreed. "But we were just making a break."

"Using heavy equipment," Braden said. "Wyatt's wife can quote you the mortality rates for operators of heavy equipment." His assistant superintendent was married to a life insurance salesperson.

Owen shook his head. He obviously wasn't buying his excuses. But Braden couldn't tell him—or anyone else—what was really going on. Not when he barely knew himself. Yet...

How could he sense when a fire was coming, but he had no clue when someone was about to go after one of his team?

He would figure it out. He had to—before anyone else got hurt. Or worse... Like Dirk Brown.

"Come on," Braden continued. "You're a paramedic. How many people have you treated in this town that were injured in accidents?"

Color flushed Owen's face. He sighed and admitted, "Most of them."

"It was an accident," Braden maintained. Until they could prove otherwise...

"Too bad you couldn't tell when one of those was about to happen..." Owen murmured. Then he pushed his hand through his hair and swayed slightly on his feet.

"You're exhausted," Braden said. "And I think you're hurt despite you claiming otherwise." There was so much blood on him. But it was dried. So even if all of it wasn't Dirk's, Owen was no longer bleeding. Maybe he didn't need to go to the ER. But he needed some rest. "Let Cody or me drive you home."

Owen shook his head again. "I can drive myself." He turned back to Cody. "Do you need a ride home? Serena and her sister have your truck."

Cody's eyes widened with surprise. "You know that?"

Owen nodded. "They went with me to inform Louanne…" His voice cracked. "About Dirk…"

Cody sighed. "Of course Serena would. But Courtney went along?"

"She was worried about her sister. Serena was pretty shaken up, worrying about you."

Cody's face flushed. "She didn't say anything when I called her from Luke's phone earlier today. I left mine in the damn truck." He sighed. "But Serena is…Serena." His lips curved into a smile. "She's always so strong. She's waiting for me outside."

And from the look of longing on his face, it was clear he wanted to be with her now. But Cody stayed even after Owen walked out.

As he watched the paramedic go, Braden felt a flash of panic.

Should he have warned Owen? What if that accident had been meant for him instead of Dirk?

But Braden wasn't sure if any of the accidents had been meant to hurt someone or were just intended to make their jobs more difficult. Cody was staring after Owen, too.

"Don't you think we should have told him the truth?" he asked, his voice full of concern.

"Not until we know what the hell that is," Braden said. But it was killing him not to come clean with his team. Then he remembered the note locked inside his desk.

Somebody on your team is not who you think they are...

When he'd received the note several months ago, he'd thought it had meant that the arsonist who'd been terrorizing Northern Lakes was on his team. He knew that wasn't true now since the guy had been caught. Matt Hamilton had admitted to setting the fires but had denied tampering with the brakes on the pickup trucks and sabotaging equipment. And since the incidents with the equipment had continued after his arrest, it was clear he'd been telling the truth. But who the hell *was* on Braden's team?

The person behind the accidents?

That person was now a killer.

He had no suspicions about Owen. But he only had proof that it wasn't either of his assistant superintendents, Wyatt and Dawson, and nor was it Cody. They'd been the ones who had nearly been hurt in previous incidents, and there was no way they'd sabotaged their own brakes or equipment. So those were the only members of his team he could trust right now...

"Don't keep Serena waiting," Braden said. "She must have had quite a scare today worrying about you. So make sure she knows you're safe."

"But I'm not," Cody said. "None of us is until we catch whoever the hell is behind these damn things happening."

"We'll catch him," Braden assured him.

"When?" Cody asked. "After we've lost another team member? We should have told Owen the truth. Hell, we should tell everyone what's going—"

"We can't!" Braden reminded him. "Or we might never figure out who's to blame."

And it was more important than ever that they catch

the person. Because now they would be catching a killer...

"Well, we've got to work fast now," Cody said. "Before anyone else gets hurt."

Braden nodded in agreement. "I've got a plan." One he should have put into motion a while ago, but he hadn't had an opening on his team then to bring in an outsider. Now, unfortunately, he did.

Because a man was dead...

He had to make sure nobody else died. Hell, maybe Cody was right. Maybe he should have warned Owen before he'd let him leave—because he did not want Owen to wind up dead like Dirk Brown.

A nervous energy pulsated inside Courtney, making her hands tremble slightly as she ran the sandpaper across the top of the display case she and Serena had carried into the store earlier that day.

What an incredibly long day it had proved to be...

Maybe she should have taken Serena's advice to take it easy the rest of the night. Once her twin had left, she could have gone upstairs to her apartment over the store. But she wouldn't have been able to relax, not even with a glass of wine, and not just because of all the work she had yet to do in the store.

The shop wasn't why she had all this nervous energy coursing through her. That was Owen James's fault.

She was so angry at him—for the way he'd reacted to her, for the way he'd made her feel...

Like that weird kid in high school who had never been able to fit in.

Not that she'd ever tried all that hard. She hadn't wanted to be like everybody else. She'd only wanted to be herself. An individual. Not just Serena's twin.

People hadn't just accepted Serena; they'd adored her. But Cody more than adored her twin; he loved her.

Courtney had ridden over to the firehouse with Serena earlier to drop off Cody's truck. Between a meeting with his boss, Cody had stepped outside to see his fiancée. Serena had run into his arms, and he hadn't flinched or pulled away. Instead he'd caught her and held her so close, it was as if the two of them had become one person. And the look on his face...

A pang of envy struck Courtney's heart. Nobody had ever looked at her the way Cody Mallehan looked at her sister. Not even the man who had proposed to her.

Serena deserved all of Cody's love and devotion. She was special. And, fortunately, she'd found a man who realized just how special she was.

But if Cody had died today... Maybe that was why Courtney was working on the display case tonight instead of her other project: Serena's wedding gown. She'd designed something so beautiful for her twin—something ethereal and delicate and totally Serena.

If anything had happened to him, Serena would have never been able to wear that dress. He was fine, though. And so was her sister. Since Cody had had to go back inside for that meeting, Serena had dropped her at the store and then returned to the firehouse to wait for him. Hopefully that wait would not be long.

And soon, Serena would walk down the aisle in her special gown, and Cody would stare at her with even more love and devotion. Courtney was happy for them— even if she was a little bit envious.

Sure, Bradford had proposed to her, but he had never looked at her with the depth of love she observed in the way Cody looked at Serena. She wasn't sure now what that look Bradford had given her had been: possession, obsession... She shivered as she remembered the guy she'd dated briefly who had become fixated on her. She hadn't been afraid of him. Just indifferent, like she'd been toward the other men she'd dated. Her career had meant more to her than any of them.

So it was probably her fault that nobody had truly fallen for her. Maybe she wasn't unlovable so much as incapable of falling in love herself.

She shivered again because of the wind blowing through the two open doors of the store. She needed the ventilation to dissipate the fumes of the stripper she'd used on the display case. The odor had already made her light-headed. But once the sun had gone down, the wind had gotten cold. She shivered again as the chill moved deeper inside her. She wasn't sure if it was the wind chilling her or the sudden sense she had that some-one was watching her.

She glanced toward the storefront, but the streetlamps illuminated the area around the door. Nobody stood out there. Then she glanced toward the back door. Usually a light glowed out there, in the alley. But she couldn't see it now for the shadow blocking it—the shadow of a man.

A big man...

Bradford had been tall. And he'd hated that he hadn't been able to convince her to accept his proposal and stay in New York with him.

Was he here?

She opened her mouth to let out the scream burning the back of her throat. But she knew it would be of no use to cry for help. Hers was the only building on this block that had an apartment above it. All the other businesses had closed for the night. Nobody was around to hear her scream.

Nobody could help her.

Chapter 5

Serena settled her head against Cody's broad shoulder and pressed her hand against his chest, which was slick with sweat.

Perspiration trickled down her back, but Cody brushed away the beads with a slightly shaking hand. "That was..." he murmured, his voice gruff, "...incredible."

"It was," she said with a wistful sigh. It always was, but tonight had been extra intense. She knew why. "I was so scared..." She shuddered as she remembered her fear when she hadn't been able to reach him, when she'd worried that he was the one injured—or worse—in the accident.

"I'm sorry," he said. "I'm so sorry. I didn't realize I'd left my phone in the truck. And there was so much going on that I didn't have a chance to call you until later." His arms tightened around her. "I'm so sorry."

She heard the regret in his voice and felt it in her

heart; it ached like she could feel his aching. And she knew he wasn't just sorry for having worried her. "What happened…it wasn't your fault," she assured him.

"I was in charge of checking the equipment," he said. "So yeah, it was my fault."

"You couldn't know that the cable would snap," she said.

He tensed. "How do you know what happened?"

They hadn't talked about it yet. Seeing how upset he was, Serena hadn't wanted to bring it up. She'd wanted to focus only on him. "Courtney told me."

He rolled her onto her back as he sat up. Then he stared down at her, his green eyes narrowed with suspicion. "How the hell did she know?"

"Owen told her."

He snorted. "Yeah, right, because they're such good buddies."

She sighed. From the comments and threats Courtney spewed to Owen every time they ran into each other in town, everyone knew about Courtney's grudge against the paramedic who hadn't been able to save their mother. For a while, Serena had felt as if Courtney had had a grudge against her, too. Her twin had actually filed a lawsuit against her, trying to force her to sell the boardinghouse they'd inherited from their mother. At the time, Serena had been devastated, but since then, Courtney had explained that she had only been trying to save Serena from the same fate that had befallen their mother and grandmother—from overworking herself into an early grave.

Courtney wasn't trying to save Owen from anything, especially not her anger and resentment toward him. She'd hated him for a long time—even before their mother had died—over how his friends had treated her in high school. Serena felt a pang of regret over that herself, over how hard it had been for Courtney to grow up in a small community like Northern Lakes.

"They talked today," Serena said.

"Did she bury the hatchet?" he asked. "Because I didn't notice it in his back when I saw him a while ago at the firehouse."

Serena fought the smile trying to curl her lips up. Cody was funny. It was one of the things she loved most about him. But her sister's hatred of Owen wasn't funny. She sighed. "No, she was even madder at him after they talked."

"So that cable nearly hitting him wasn't the most danger Owen was in today..." Cody murmured.

"Are you calling my sister a threat to his life?"

He chuckled but he didn't deny his concern.

And Serena couldn't deny that she was concerned, too. Her sister was still so hurt and angry, and when Courtney was hurt and angry, she had a tendency to lash out.

Owen James had already been through enough—even before today. But after today, he certainly didn't need to deal with Courtney.

Serena could only hope that from now on they stayed far away from each other.

For both their sakes...

Owen wrapped his arms around Courtney Beaumont's squirming body as her fists pummeled his chest and shoulders. "Let me go!" she yelled.

Just moments before, she'd screamed—which had sent him rushing into her store to see what had scared her. To protect her from whatever it was.

"What's the matter?" he asked. "What's wrong?"

She froze within his grasp, her body stiff and tense. But her hands relaxed from fists, so that now her palms rested against his chest. Even through the heavy material of his jacket and his shirt, it was as if he could feel her touch—as if her small hands had somehow branded him.

That was ridiculous. As ridiculous as his trying to protect her when his presence must have been what had frightened her.

"You!" she gasped between pants for breath.

"I know I'm hideous, but I thought living in the big city all these years had made you too street-smart tough to be scared of me," he chided her.

"I am too street-smart to keep my mouth shut when someone's creeping around in the alley," she replied.

Heat rushed to his face now. "I wasn't creeping," he said, but his denial was weak. When he'd found the door open, he should have knocked, should have made her aware of his presence. But he'd wanted to just watch her for a moment before she saw him, before she looked at him like she always looked at him—with such fury and resentment.

For a little while today, she had looked at him differently—almost sympathetically. But he'd ruined that somehow…like he always managed to ruin things with her.

"You were standing out there staring at me!" she accused him, and now she used her palms to shove him back—away from her.

So she had been aware of his presence.

He forced a grin and made it sound as if he was joking when he replied, "I was trying to work up the nerve to knock."

She snorted. "Like I make you nervous."

"You do," he said. And he was being completely honest now. She made him damn nervous. She had for years—even when they were kids. Hell, maybe especially when they were kids, because then he'd been afraid of stupid things, like losing face in front of his friends or being embarrassed. Now he knew those were the least of life's problems.

"You were a Marine and now you're a firefighter," she said. "I doubt there's much that makes you nervous."

He sighed. "Which shows you how stupid I can be…"

She snorted again. "You were your class valedictorian, a scholar, athlete…"

He tilted his head, surprised that she knew those things about him. She'd been a couple of years behind him in school and had seemed totally uninterested in him back then.

But had she been?

"Of course, there is a difference between book-smart and street-smart," she continued.

He grinned. "It's clear which you think is better."

Her lips curved into a slight smile, too. "You already called me street-smart."

He nodded. "Because I didn't think you'd be so easily frightened—not after all your years of living in the big city."

She sighed now. "There is so much crime and there are so many monsters in the big city," she said. "That's why I'm very careful now."

Implying that she hadn't always been. Had there been a monster or two in Courtney's life? He wanted to ask; he wanted to know more about her. Hell, he wanted to know everything about her.

But he doubted she would open up as easily to him as he had to her that afternoon. He couldn't believe how he'd talked to her. Military therapists had tried to get him to talk, about all those horrible things he'd seen as a Marine medic, but they hadn't been able to compel him to confide in them. Not like Courtney had when he'd told her all the gruesome details of Dirk's death. And about how guilty he felt...

"Am I a monster to you?" he asked.

She stared at him, but her gaze didn't focus on his scar, which was all most other people saw when they looked at him now. She was staring into his eyes, almost as if she was trying to see what he saw.

"You're the one who flinched when I touched you," she reminded him. Then she murmured, "I guess some people never grow up, no matter what they've been through."

Despite how much he wished he could, he couldn't go back and undo what an idiot he'd been in school. But he could go back to this afternoon and show her why he'd flinched. He shrugged off his jacket. Then he peeled back the sleeve of the sweatshirt he wore beneath it. The blood had dried, sticking to his wound. He cursed as he reopened it.

And she gasped and stumbled back.

Despite the pain of reopening the wound, he managed to chuckle at her reaction. "Now you understand why I pulled away..."

Courtney felt like screaming again, but not because of fear or disgust. She felt like screaming in frustration. "What the hell is wrong with you?"

"One of the pieces of the cable hit me," Owen said.

"I get that," she said. The deep gash in his forearm looked like someone had sliced through it with a meat cleaver. "What I don't understand is why you haven't had it treated."

He glanced down at his arm and shrugged. "It's not that bad."

"Bullshit." She didn't have a medical background like her sister, who'd been working toward a nursing degree before giving up college to help their mother with the boardinghouse, but Courtney had eyes. She could see how deep the wound was and how blood oozed from it. Little metal fibers were even embedded in it, the ends of them looking charred. "You need that cleaned up, and you need stitches."

He sighed. "It had stopped bleeding before I messed with it."

But it had hurt him when she'd touched him. That was why he'd flinched. Not because he'd been repulsed...

She pushed that thought aside to focus on him, though. He was clearly in pain. "What the hell is wrong with you?" she asked again. "Why won't you get that treated? It's going to get infected."

"I'm a paramedic," he said—as if she needed the reminder that he and Dawson Hess had been the first responders to her mother's heart attack. "I can take care of it myself."

"You're a lousy paramedic," she said.

He flinched now, as if she'd slapped him. He probably thought she was referring to his letting her mother die—because that was usually what she brought up with him. Every time they bumped into each other, she made some comment about his being late, not working hard enough or fast enough. But that wasn't what was bothering her now.

"You won't even help yourself," she said.

"I don't need help," he insisted—stubbornly.

She'd had no idea how stubborn he was. But then, she had never really known Owen personally—only what everyone else had always said about him. And none of those things had been negative, of course.

So maybe she knew him better than anyone else did since she now knew about this self-destructive obstinacy of his. She reached out for his forearm again, but he jerked back before she could touch his wound. And she shook her head. "You're an idiot. But even you have to realize you need to have that injury treated."

He smiled. "I am wounded," he admitted. "By your opinion of me."

She laughed. "Like you care…"

"I do," he said. "That's why I'm here."

"I have been wondering why you're here," she admitted. Especially when it was now clear he should be at the hospital instead.

"I wanted to show you this," he said, holding up his arm.

"You should be showing a doctor," she said. "Or Serena. She's the one with the nursing background."

He glanced around the store. "Aren't you something of a seamstress, being a fashion designer? Couldn't you stitch me up?"

"That's not why you came here," she said.

"You have to admit that you would enjoy sticking a needle in me."

Even as frustrated as she was with him, she didn't want to hurt him. And she didn't want him to be hurt. "You need a doctor," she said. "Not me."

He stepped closer to her. She tried to take a step back, but her butt bumped into the display case. She was trapped between it and his body—his big, muscular body. The heat of it penetrated her clothes, making her hot.

"I need you to understand," he said. "That this is why I pulled away from you earlier."

She shrugged. "You didn't have to come here," she said. In fact, she would have preferred that he hadn't. Not only had he scared her when she'd noticed him at the door, but he was also scaring her now...

With how he was making her feel. Her pulse was pounding so fast and hard. And her skin was hot and tingly.

She was damned if she'd let him know how he affected her, though. So she lifted her chin and lied, "I don't care..."

He narrowed his eyes and studied her face. "That's not how you acted earlier today," he said. "You brought up high school and the stupid name kids called you back then."

Heat climbed into her face, but along with humiliation, she felt a rush of anger. "You called me a freak back then, too," she reminded him.

"Like you said, I'm an idiot."

She also felt like an idiot, for bringing up the past. That was so long ago and so much had happened since then, like her mother dying, which had given her another reason to hate Owen. But she wasn't feeling hatred or even anger for him right now. She was feeling an attraction—an overwhelming attraction. Maybe that was why she didn't push him away when he leaned closer, when he lowered his head to hers.

A jolt shot through her when his lips brushed across hers. Then that tingling spread throughout her body. She'd never felt so much from just a kiss.

He deepened the kiss, parting her lips. And he kissed

her hungrily. But only his mouth touched hers. He didn't wrap his arms around her. He didn't pull her close.

She could have moved away from him at any time. But instead she leaned into him, needing his touch, needing to touch him back. She lifted her hands to his face, tracing the rigid line of his square jaw before her fingers skimmed higher, over the ridge of his scar.

He tensed and jerked back. Panting for breath, he stumbled a few steps away from her—like she'd shoved him.

But she'd only touched his face. His scar...

"Did I hurt you?" she asked—between draws for breath herself. Her lungs burned with the need for oxygen. And her head felt so light.

Maybe it was just the fumes from the furniture stripper. Maybe it had nothing to do with the kiss.

But she knew she was lying again—this time to herself. And she felt as scared as she'd been when she'd noticed the shadow blocking the light from the alley. Like then, she felt like she was in danger.

Real danger...

Chapter 6

The look on her face staggered Owen almost as much as the kiss had. She looked scared—even more scared than when she'd screamed earlier.

"I'm sorry," he said.

He shouldn't have kissed her. Hell, maybe he'd lost more blood than he'd thought, and it was making him woozy. Or maybe he'd just lost his damn mind.

Of course she hadn't wanted him to kiss her.

But she hadn't shoved him away. She hadn't said no.

In fact, she'd touched him.

She'd touched his scar.

And that touch had jolted Owen to his senses, had cleared the passion from his mind.

Had his disfigurement turned her off?

Since he'd been injured on that deployment, he'd dated only a few women who'd been able to get past it, to see beyond it, but that was because they'd idealized it and him. Courtney certainly didn't do that.

He wanted her.

But he'd never treated her like he should have—back in high school or even after she'd lost her mother. Afraid she was going to sue him like she had her sister, he'd always gotten defensive about her assertion that he could have saved her mother—had he just gotten there sooner and tried harder.

"I'm sorry," he said again. "That—that kiss was a mistake..." But it hadn't felt like a mistake. It had been the only good thing about his day.

A man had lost his life today. A wife had lost her husband, and Owen had lost a dear friend.

Then he had sought solace in the arms of the woman who hated his guts. He had definitely lost his mind. And he had probably only made Courtney hate him more—if that was even possible.

"I—I have to get out of here," he said. Before he did something even stupider, like kiss her again, like pull her against his body, which ached with tension that he suspected only she might be able to release.

He couldn't use her like that. He couldn't use her to get his mind off what had happened today. Off what else could have happened...

He could have died.

And after that meeting with his boss and Cody, he had a feeling that all the accidents they'd been having lately might not have been accidents at all.

"Don't worry," she said.

And he jumped, for a moment wondering if she'd read his mind.

But then she said, "I won't tell anyone that you kissed me."

Like she thought he was ashamed of his attraction to her? That was crazy.

"You've got this all wrong, Courtney," he tried to tell her.

But now she was shoving him back, toward the door to the alley where he'd stood and watched her sanding that piece of furniture. He'd been surprised to find her working on something like that. She was handier than he'd realized.

"Oh, no," she said. "I totally agree with you. This was a mistake. You coming here. You kissing me. It's a mistake we will never repeat."

"Well, that will be a damn shame," he said—because it had felt so good. So incredible...

He couldn't remember a kiss ever being as sweet or sexy or...ever making him so desperate for more. Kissing her hadn't been nearly enough.

She shoved him again toward the door. "Get out!"

He sighed and relented. "Okay, I'm going."

He turned and pushed open the door that had swung shut behind him when he'd rushed inside her store earlier. And as he stepped outside, a sudden chill passed through him. He'd forgotten his coat, but that wasn't why he was cold.

He had a strange feeling—like she must have had earlier—that someone was watching him. Maybe he'd just psyched himself out with his suspicions about the accidents.

Or maybe he was right, and someone was watching him. When he swung back toward the store, Courtney had already slammed the door shut behind him.

He thought about going back inside to warn her to lock her doors. She shouldn't have had them open earlier. Sure, Northern Lakes was a pretty safe town—at least, now that the arsonist was behind bars.

But what about those accidents?

What if they weren't accidents?

That would mean someone was deliberately causing them. And that someone had killed today. Which meant that, once again, there was a dangerous person on the loose in town.

Of course, that dangerous person might have been Courtney. Because she'd affected him so damn much with just the touch of her lips against his, of her fingers on his face...

He shivered and pulled open the door to his truck. It had been a long day. He needed to go home—to get some rest. But he knew that the moment he closed his eyes he would see Dirk, and maybe he would see the others, too. The ones he hadn't been able to help when he'd been a Marine medic.

Hell, he might even see Courtney's mother lying dead just outside her boardinghouse. She'd collapsed watering flowers. Nothing strenuous—especially for a woman seemingly as fit as she'd been. But he hadn't been able to save her.

Or all those others...

Rather than seeing them, he would rather see Courtney—in his bed, in his arms...

Yes, he'd lost his mind. He could only hope that he wouldn't lose his life, too.

Mistake...

It damn sure was a mistake. Courtney never should have let him kiss her. She should have slapped him, but touching him had had the same effect as slapping him. He'd jerked away from her. He'd come to his senses.

What the hell had happened to hers?

Her head was swimming, her lips tingling...

She wanted him to kiss her again. She wanted to kiss him—passionately. She wanted his arms to wrap around her, to hold her close to his big, muscular body. But that wasn't because she wanted *him*. She didn't even like him.

Maybe she was more jealous of what Serena and Cody had than she'd realized. And that jealousy had made her desperate enough that she'd even enjoyed kissing Owen James.

She shivered, but it wasn't with revulsion. A tingling sensation spread throughout her body again at just the memory of feeling his mouth pressing against hers. Her flesh heated. Despite the breeze blowing through the open front door, she was warm.

But she hurried through the store and slammed it shut anyway. Then she locked it. She still had that unsettling feeling of being watched.

Had she locked the back door? She'd slammed it shut behind Owen. But had she locked it?

As she started back through the store, she noticed his jacket lying on top of the display case. The bloodstains dulled the yellow color. Without it, he was probably cold. She grabbed it from the case and headed toward the back door. But when she pushed it open, she found the alley empty.

He'd already driven away, probably in a hurry to get away from her and the mistake he'd made. His truck had left behind a puddle of liquid on the asphalt. It must have come from his vehicle because she hadn't noticed it earlier, when she'd thrown out the rags from the stripper she'd used on the display case. She would have walked through the puddle on her way to the dumpster, so she couldn't have missed it.

What the hell had drained from his truck?

Water from the air conditioner?

She shivered as the wind chilled her. The weather was still too cool for anyone to need air-conditioning. And Owen had been wearing his jacket. That could have been his reason for turning it on, though—if he'd been warm in the jacket and hadn't wanted to take it off. He hadn't wanted anyone to know that he'd been injured, too.

So why had he shown her?

To explain why he'd flinched earlier? Did he actually care what she thought?

Damn it. Despite herself, she cared, too. She wanted to make sure that he got that arm treated. He definitely needed to have the wound cleaned up and some stitches—at least. Maybe a cast, too, if the bone was broken.

Instead of shoving him out the door, she should have driven him to the hospital. But when he'd called the kiss a mistake, she'd gotten so angry. It had reminded her of those times his friends had teased him about staring at her, and he'd shoot back some comment that it was just because she was such a freak.

Why did he affect her so much?

After that kiss, she knew now that anger wasn't the only strong emotion he drew from her. She'd never felt passion like that before either. Maybe that was because of the rage, though. Maybe it was because he brought out all the emotions she'd tried so hard to bury.

The humiliation and pain…

He had to be in pain now—over his wound and over losing his friend.

She cursed—because she knew she was going to have to do something. There was no way she would sleep until she knew that he'd gotten his wound treated.

And even then, she probably wouldn't sleep—because of that kiss. He was right. It had been a mistake. A mistake Courtney wanted badly to repeat.

Owen James was about to have an accident. And given the day he'd had, nobody would suspect that it was anything other than just an accident.

He was distraught.

He was distracted.

That would explain how the crash happened.

No one would notice the little hole in his brake line. No one would realize that he hadn't been able to stop— just as no one had realized that the cable on the logging truck had been tampered with. They would think that the cable had just been worn out and snapped...unless Owen had noticed that smell of burned metal the torch had left in the air.

Owen James might realize what had happened, and that it hadn't been an accident. That was the reason he had to die. He needed to get the hell out of the way.

Tonight.

Chapter 7

The doorbell dinged, but it didn't wake up Cody, who had been lying awake in bed next to his fiancée. He hadn't been sleeping. He'd been worrying...

About Serena.

About his team members.

He couldn't lose another one of them. And he didn't want to lose his own life either. He had everything to live for with his beautiful, loving fiancée.

She murmured in her sleep, and he leaned down to kiss her cheek. "I'll get it," he assured her as he slipped out of their tangled sheets. He pulled on his jeans and headed out of the bedroom.

Who could be at the door?

Had Stanley forgotten his key again?

Usually it wouldn't have mattered. Usually they didn't lock the doors. But after the fire had burned down the boardinghouse, after the accidents had continued...

Cody always made certain to lock up now, to keep his family safe. Even though they weren't married yet, Serena was family. And Stanley—whom Cody had met years ago when they'd both been in foster care—was family, too. Cody had been in his late teens while Stanley had been a little kid, so Stanley was like his little brother. The nineteen-year-old was sleeping, his snoring coming from beneath the bedroom door Cody passed on his way to the front of the house.

Or maybe it was Annie snoring. The overgrown sheepdog/mastiff puppy snored louder than her owner. But nobody cared. The firehouse mascot had saved too many lives for even Braden to begrudge her the occasional accidents she had in his office.

Cody waited for a bark or a rustling sound from within Stanley's bedroom. But Annie didn't stir. Usually she was a pretty sharp watchdog, but maybe she didn't consider someone ringing the doorbell a threat.

Cody wouldn't have either—if not for the incidents that surely had to be sabotage. And Dirk's death...

That wasn't just tragic. It was criminal. Someone had murdered the man. Maybe they hadn't meant to kill him. Maybe they'd just meant to cause trouble like the other stunts had. But now that a man had died, the threat had intensified—not just to the team but to the person responsible.

Since they were going to go down for murder once they were caught anyway, they no longer had anything to lose. Cody had a horrible feeling that it would be much easier now for this person to kill again.

And again...

He tensed as he neared the front door. The porch light hadn't come on, so he had no way of knowing who stood out there, waiting for him. He'd already had a few of those accidents himself that actually hadn't been accidents.

At first, they'd thought the arsonist had been responsible. But when they'd finally caught him, he had claimed no knowledge of those mishaps.

So who was it? Whoever stood at his door?

Had Cody been the intended target instead of poor Dirk? And had the killer come to remedy his mistake?

He patted his pocket, but his cell wasn't in it. He'd left it next to the bed. He didn't carry a gun, so he looked for another weapon, picking up the lamp from the foyer table. Holding it aloft, he unlocked the door and slowly pulled it open.

The person standing on the front porch was small and delicately built—like his fiancée. Almost exactly like Serena. He sighed with a bit of relief. But not much...

He was not a fan of Courtney's, not after how she'd treated the love of his life. "She's sleeping," he told her. And he was damn well not going to wake her up, not after the stressful day she'd had.

"I didn't come here to talk to Serena," Courtney said, but she didn't sound any happier to see him than he'd been to see her.

"Have you and Stanley become friends?" he asked. He wouldn't have been surprised. Stanley considered everyone he met a friend, a trait the arsonist had exploited. But Courtney was not as friendly as Stanley or even the arsonist had been.

Her brow furrowed. "Stanley? That kid that lives with you and Serena?"

Stanley was nineteen, but due to some developmental challenges, he seemed younger—which was why Cody had been concerned when he'd aged out of foster care a year ago. While the system considered eighteen old enough to live alone, it wasn't for everyone.

"Yes," he replied.

She shook her head.

So that left him or Annie.

Because he didn't want to wake up the dog, or anyone else in the house, he stepped onto the porch with her. And the cold wind chilled his bare skin. Maybe he should have grabbed a shirt as well as his jeans.

But then Courtney handed him a coat—a heavy yellow firefighter jacket. As he stared down at it, he noted the bloodstains, and he tensed with concern. "Where'd you get this?"

"It's Owen's," she said.

"I know. Where did you get it?"

"I didn't kill him and keep his jacket," she said, "if that's what you're worried about…"

"I am worried about him," Cody said.

She sighed. "I am, too. That's why I came here."

He narrowed his eyes to study her, and there must have been enough light on the porch for her to see his skepticism. But then, she hadn't made a secret of her resentment for the paramedic. She'd made some scenes at the Filling Station and the firehouse.

"I *am* worried," she insisted. "Some of that blood is his."

Cody tensed and stared down at the jacket again.

"And no, I am not the one who made him bleed," she replied before Cody could ask. "He got hit with that cable, too."

Cody cursed. "Why the hell didn't he say anything?"

She shrugged. "Because he's stubborn and stupid and—"

He held up a hand. "Okay, I know what you think of

him." So it surprised the hell out of him that she was here. And that she had Owen's jacket. He clutched it in his hand. "How'd you get this?"

"He—he left it at the store," she murmured, as if uncomfortable.

He couldn't see much of her face. The porch roof blocked the glow from the moon and the streetlamps.

"What the hell was he doing at your store?" he asked. Usually Owen went out of his way to avoid Courtney—not confront her.

She shrugged again. "I don't know. Maybe something other than his arm is wounded. Maybe he has a concussion or something, too."

Owen would have to have a head injury to think that Courtney would offer him any help—if that was what he'd been looking for. Yet she was here, and she was clearly concerned about him.

"You should call him," she urged. "Make sure he's gone to the hospital."

"You don't have his number?" he asked.

She shook her head. "We're not exactly texting buddies."

So why had Owen visited her?

Cody wished he could see her face better. "I left my phone in the bedroom," he said. "Do you have yours?"

She reached into her pocket and pulled out her cell. After unlocking it, she held it out to him. Her face was very pale in the light from the cell screen. She was worried.

And that worry caused Cody's anxiety to increase. He dialed Owen's number, but it went straight to voice mail. "He didn't pick up," he said, even though she had probably already realized as much.

"You should find him," she insisted.

Cody drew in a deep breath, trying to calm his own fears. "He might have just shut off his phone because he went to sleep," he said. "He was probably getting a lot of calls from people checking on him." Everyone had been concerned that he would blame himself for what had happened—since he'd been working with Dirk.

But Cody was the one who was responsible for checking the equipment. And he had. He hadn't noticed any sign of anyone tampering with the cable—until after the accident. Then he'd seen the torch marks where it had broken.

If only he would have rolled out the whole damn thing to inspect it...

"You should check on him," she said.

"Is his arm that bad?" Cody wondered. And why the hell hadn't Owen gotten it treated? He'd been at the hospital.

"It's not just his arm..." Courtney murmured, almost as if she was reluctant to share more.

What the hell had happened between them at the store? Whatever it was had shaken her. And maybe it had shaken Owen, too, so much that she was actually concerned about him now.

"What is it, Courtney?" he prodded her when she trailed off. "What's going on?"

She shrugged again.

And he cursed. "Come on. You didn't come over here just to give me his jacket."

"I don't know..." she murmured. "Maybe it was nothing..."

"What?"

"After he drove off, I noticed a puddle in the alley." And it hadn't rained for weeks. In fact, as a firefighter, he considered the current weather conditions dangerously dry.

"I didn't notice it earlier," she continued, "so whatever it was must have leaked out of his truck."

Cody tensed, but he held in his curse now. Someone had cut his brake line once, and he had nearly died. But he didn't want Courtney to know how concerned he was. Braden was determined to keep it secret that the stunts weren't accidents. But Cody had been right—he or his boss should have told Owen the truth.

Then the paramedic might have been better prepared for something like this. Would he even know what to do if someone had cut his brake line?

Courtney let out a shaky sigh. "It was probably nothing. Maybe just condensation from his air conditioner…"

Cody doubted anyone had turned on the air conditioner yet. But he didn't argue with her.

"And he might not have picked up the phone because he didn't recognize my number," she said. "I'm sure if you call him from yours, he'll pick up."

Cody expelled a shaky little sigh of his own. "Yeah, you're right. I'll give him a call from mine. Do you want to wait? To see if I get ahold of him?"

She shook her head. "No…" She pointed to the jacket. "I just didn't want him to have an excuse to come back to the store. Give him his coat the next time you see him." She turned and hurried off the porch then to the car parked in the driveway.

And Cody wondered if what she'd said was true. She'd said that a little too forcefully. Did she actually want Owen to go see her again?

When Cody tried his number moments later and got voice mail again, his concern grew. He hoped like hell that he would see Owen again. Alive…

Because he had a strange feeling about what Courtney had found in the alley.

What if someone had cut Owen's brake line, too?

Nothing was broken. No tendons cut. Owen had known it even before the ER doctor had shown him the results of the MRI of his arm. Some stitches and a tetanus shot later, he was heading back out to his truck.

He probably should have asked for the doctor to check out his head as well. There must have been something wrong with it that had compelled him to kiss Courtney Beaumont.

Or maybe that hadn't been the mistake.

Maybe the mistake had been that he'd stopped kissing her...when he should have gone on and on and never stopped. He should have pulled her closer, should have carried her up the stairs to her apartment over her store. But his arm hadn't been in any shape for that—then.

He was better now. He could go back—on the pretext of getting the jacket he'd left behind—but he doubted that she would let him back in now.

Or ever...

He sighed as he opened the door to his truck. Before hopping onto the seat, he pulled his cell phone from his back pocket and glanced down at the screen. He'd turned it off while he'd been in the ER. Maybe he'd leave it off.

All he'd been getting were calls from coworkers worried about him. He was fine. Dirk was the one who hadn't survived.

The one who was gone...

They should save their concern for his widow. Poor Louanne.

Owen hoped she was doing better now. That she'd

had someone to talk to—like he'd talked to Courtney. Despite her resentment of him, she had actually made him feel better. Whatever had happened hadn't been his fault.

It had been an accident.

Or had it?

If he called anyone now, it was going to be his boss. But that conversation could wait until morning. It was late now and so dark that the parking lot lights barely dissipated the blackness. He shivered and pulled the door closed to shut out the cold.

He shoved the key into the ignition and turned on the motor. Since he'd left his jacket behind, he had to turn on the heat. High…

Thinking about Courtney, about that kiss, had his blood pumping hot through his veins again. He really wanted to go back for her.

He shouldn't have tensed when she'd touched his face. But he'd been worried the scar would turn her off—as it had other women. He wasn't the scholar athlete she remembered from school. He wasn't the homecoming king anymore.

He was disfigured. He was the real freak. But she didn't even seem to notice the scar when she looked at him. He might have been better off if she did; then maybe she would pity instead of resent him. Not that he wanted her pity any more than her anger.

No. He didn't want to see Courtney again. Not tonight. Maybe ever…

He had enough going on, enough to worry about, without having to worry about her, too. And she would worry him.

She was so mad. So bitter…

So fierce and independent.

He'd never known anyone quite like her. Maybe that was the reason for the attraction. That and how damn beautiful she was…and sexy.

Yeah, he should have had his head x-rayed, too. Luke Garrison's wife, Willow, had suggested it. She'd been the nurse on the desk when he'd shown up. Now estranged from Luke, Willow thought anyone who worked as a firefighter needed their head examined, along with anyone who fell in love with one.

Owen shook his head, to clear thoughts of Courtney from his mind, and focused on driving out of the lot. As he stopped before pulling onto the road, he felt that squishiness in his brakes he'd noticed when he'd pulled out of the alley behind her store. He used his personal vehicle so rarely that he hadn't had it serviced in a while.

A glance at the sticker on the windshield reminded him he was overdue for an oil change. He probably needed to get new brake pads and have the tires rotated as well. He'd been too distracted lately to think about vehicle maintenance. Or his job…

While he had been distracted that morning, he hadn't caused the accident. Cody hadn't noticed anything wrong with the cable either. So what the hell had happened to make it snap like that? Had it had something to do with that strange smell…

Like burning metal? The brittle little fibers of the cable that Willow had washed out of his wound had looked burned, too.

Had someone tampered with the cable? But why?

He pressed harder on the accelerator as anger coursed through him. If someone had deliberately sabotaged the equipment…

He shuddered as he considered what that would mean—

that Dirk had been murdered. That he could have been killed, too.

His headlamps shone on a warning sign for a curve ahead. He eased his foot from the accelerator and moved it to the brake. But the pedal gave him no resistance. It pressed completely to the floor.

And nothing happened.

The tires didn't squeal. There was no slowing.

The brakes were not just unmaintained. They were gone.

He had no way of stopping. Just like he'd had no way of stopping that cable from snapping that morning. He could only hope that he would survive this accident as he had the last one—because he knew there was no way he was going to avoid crashing.

The truck was going too fast for him to safely maneuver around the sharp curve in the road. He was going to crash. Had someone tampered with his brakes like they'd tampered with the cable?

It was the last thought he had as he gripped the wheel and braced himself for impact.

Courtney should have just gone straight back to the store and her apartment above it. But she knew she wasn't going to sleep.

She would have liked to blame it on the fumes from the stripper. They'd permeated the building, making her apartment smell, too. But she knew the odor wasn't what was keeping her from her bed.

It was Owen.

Not that she wanted him in that bed with her. She just wanted to make sure he was all right. His forearm had looked badly injured. And he'd been through a hell of a lot that day.

But she'd already done her due diligence to help him. She'd told Cody her concerns. He would look out for his friend. He would make sure that Owen was all right.

She could go home.

Home...

She'd never really considered Northern Lakes her home. Her father hadn't either. That was why he'd abandoned her mother and their twin babies. He hadn't wanted to live in a backwater burb in Michigan. And he'd wanted nothing to do with the boardinghouse that had been her mother's heritage and her life.

It was gone now. And so was her mother...

So Northern Lakes should have felt even less like home. But Serena was here. She was the only family Courtney had. And she'd nearly lost her... To the fire that had destroyed the boardinghouse and to her own stupidity.

She never should have let Bradford talk her into filing that lawsuit against Serena to force her to sell the boardinghouse. She hadn't wanted her sister to fall victim to the same early death their mother had. But she hadn't wanted to lose her relationship with Serena either. Bradford Wentworth, esquire, had cared only about the money. Or maybe he'd wanted to make sure that Courtney had no one but him.

She shuddered as she remembered how he'd looked at her. It definitely hadn't been how Cody looked at Serena. Of course, Cody didn't want to control Serena. He just wanted to love her.

How had Owen looked at Courtney? With apology? With regret?

Kissing her had been a mistake.

Looking for him was, too.

She needed to turn around and head back to the shop.

But she drove past the hospital parking lot first, looking for Owen's truck. Had he had his arm treated?

She hoped so. But if she went inside to ask, they wouldn't reveal any information. Legally they couldn't, since she was nothing to Owen. Not his wife or his relative. Not even a friend...

She needed to go back to her place. It was so late. But instead of turning right after the lot, she turned left. She wasn't going to sleep anyway, so she might as well head past some of the lakes for which the town had been named. Not that she would see much in the dark...

But as she maneuvered around the next turn, she saw lights—the rear lights of a pickup truck that had driven off the road. The front of the truck was embedded in one of the steep, brush-filled ditches on the edge of the road. They were generally referred to as suicide ditches because people either died from the impact when their vehicle hit one or they drowned from the water that filled them whenever it rained.

She was careful to pull her car to just the edge of the road beyond the truck before she jumped out. She couldn't see much of the truck beyond those taillights. She couldn't discern the color or the make, but somehow she knew that it was Owen's.

She'd been right to worry about him. That hadn't been condensation from the air conditioner that had leaked into the alley. That had been fluid from his brake line.

Because there weren't any skid marks on the asphalt behind his truck. If he had tried to stop, he hadn't been able. He'd driven right off the road.

Was he okay?

Before she could scramble down the bank toward the

truck, strong arms wrapped around her—jerking her back. She couldn't see who had grabbed her.

Was it Owen?

She doubted it. He would have been lucky to have survived the crash at all.

Was it whoever had caused it?

Because she had a feeling that amount of fluid hadn't leaked accidentally from his brake line…

Someone must have cut it.

Was someone trying to kill Owen James? And had they succeeded?

And was that person now going to try to kill her?

Chapter 8

The minute Owen closed his arms around her, he realized it was Courtney he held. But still, he didn't want to let her go—not even when she struggled against him. The only mistake he'd made earlier had been when he'd walked away from her.

Or had that been a mistake?

Could he trust her?

He'd been lying under his truck, using a flashlight to inspect the brake line, when he'd heard the other vehicle approach. He'd jumped out from beneath his truck to wave down the driver. Then he'd reconsidered when he'd wondered why someone else might be out on the road at that hour...

To make sure his brakes had failed; to make sure he'd crashed. And then he'd wanted to see who that person was before he revealed himself.

Courtney...

Could she have been the one who'd tampered with his brakes—maybe while he'd been inside the hospital? Was she the one who'd drilled the little hole he'd found in the line?

"Let me go!" she yelled in protest as she continued to squirm. Her fingers clawed at his forearms locked around her, and when she hit the bandage, he grunted in pain and she stilled. "Owen?"

He released her then, and she whirled around to face him.

"Are you all right?" she asked, and her gaze skimmed over him from head to toe.

Was she trying to see how successful she'd been?

He shivered at the thought of her trying to kill him, of anyone trying to kill him. It wasn't as if it was the first time, though. During his deployments there had been several attempts on his life, and some had come damn close to being successful.

He touched his fingers to the scar on his cheek. "I already had this," he assured her.

She narrowed her eyes in a glare. She didn't find him nearly as funny as he did.

But joking about it usually put other people at ease over his old injury. It gave them an excuse to stare, so that they didn't feel embarrassed that they had already been staring. Courtney seemed to barely notice the scar, though. She just kept staring into his eyes.

What was she looking for?

Fear?

She would have seen it earlier. He had definitely been scared when he'd realized he had no brakes—no way of slowing down for the upcoming sharp turn. He had managed to throw the shifter into Park and grip the steering wheel, holding the truck steady enough that he only went off into the ditch.

He'd hit the bottom of the ditch hard, though. Hard enough that his head had struck the roof of his pickup and his elbow had jabbed against the armrest on the door. He'd been seeing stars for a moment—before he'd rallied enough to try to get out.

The ditch blocked his doors from opening, so he'd had to crawl out the window. And then to investigate what had caused his brakes to go out, he'd had to crawl underneath the truck—into the water standing in the steep ditch. He shivered as the wind cut through his damp clothes and skin.

"You're freezing," she remarked as she huddled inside her own coat. "I left your jacket with Cody, so he could give it to you at the firehouse." Her teeth nipped at her bottom lip, and she glanced again at the wrecked truck.

With disappointment?

Was she sorry that he had managed to escape relatively unscathed? She was the only person in Northern Lakes that he could think of who might want to harm him. But then, after his hellish day, he could barely think at all. His knees began to shake; maybe because he was starting to shiver or maybe because they were starting to fold beneath him.

"Get in my car," she told him.

To finish him off? He didn't really believe that, didn't really believe that she was a bad person, despite how she'd treated him and how she'd treated her twin. He figured she'd just been in pain and lashing out. But she was also the only one in town who seemed to have anything against him.

He hesitated a long moment, studying her face. He

couldn't understand earlier why she'd been nice to him, since she'd been anything but since her return to Northern Lakes.

Earlier she'd even let him kiss her. Hell, her lips had moved beneath his. She'd kissed him back.

Hungrily.

Passionately.

Just like then, he was wondering what the hell was going on.

Was she really here?

And if she was, why?

Despite her heavy coat, Courtney shivered. The chill that passed through her had nothing to do with the wind and everything to do with the way Owen was staring at her. Suspiciously...

Like he wondered what she was doing there?

He wasn't the only one. She wondered what she was doing there, too.

To remind herself, she told him, "After you left the store, I noticed a puddle in the alley—where you'd been parked. I was worried that you had some kind of leak. But I didn't know how to get ahold of you, so I talked to Cody. He tried calling you to warn you."

He just kept silently staring at her.

"Check your phone," she told him.

He pulled it from the back pocket of his jeans, but no light came on. The only light was from the headlamps of her car. "It's dead..."

She wondered if the battery had died or if it had gotten wet. His jeans were damp and so was his sweatshirt and the bandage on his forearm. He must have slipped in the ditch. "You got your arm treated."

He nodded. "I had my phone off while I was at the hospital."

That explained why he hadn't answered earlier. "Let me bring you back to the hospital," she said as she started toward her car, hoping he would follow her.

He was freezing. He needed to get inside with the heater vents blowing on him to warm his damp clothes and skin.

"You could have a concussion from the crash..."

Which would explain why he kept staring at her so strangely—like this was all her fault. He didn't follow her to her vehicle.

Instead he remained standing behind his truck and asked, "You were so worried you came out looking for me?" And he sounded skeptical.

As if she was incapable of doing something nice...

Maybe his being suspicious of her meant that he was fine. He certainly didn't look as if he was hurt. Just cold. And his skepticism chilled her as well. Did he think she was such a horrible person that she would try to hurt him?

"Forget it," she said, and the disgust she felt for letting herself care turned into sarcasm. She gestured at his truck stuck in the ditch, saying, "I obviously had no reason to worry."

"Why would you worry about me?" he asked. "You've made it clear that you don't like me at all."

She didn't. But her lips were still tingling from his kiss. And she wanted another one. She wanted more than that.

Since returning to Northern Lakes six months ago, she'd been focused on getting the store up and running. So she hadn't dated anyone. Not that anyone had actually asked her out. Owen hadn't asked her out either.

But he'd kissed her. Maybe that was why he'd affected her so much—because it had been so long since she'd been kissed.

"I don't like you," she agreed. "But everybody else in this town is crazy about you, including my sister." And she was trying to mend fences with Serena. Although her sweet twin had forgiven her for the lawsuit, they weren't as close as Courtney wanted them to be, as they should have been. "So get in my car and I'll drive you home before you freeze to death."

Finally, he moved toward her car. But he stopped at the passenger door and looked back at his truck. "I need to call the…"

"Tow company?" she finished for him when he trailed off. "Get in the car and you can use my phone."

He hesitated for another long moment before pulling open the door and crawling into the passenger side. He held out his hands toward the vents and sighed, probably in appreciation of the heat. "It is warm in here."

As she extended her phone across the console to him, she noticed the stains on his fingers. Was it mud or grease? Had he crawled under his truck to check it out?

He shook his head. "I'll call from my house. I have another phone there."

She should have been relieved that he wasn't going to touch her phone with dirty hands. But she had a tight knot in her stomach. "Are you sure I shouldn't drive you to the hospital instead?"

"I'm fine," he said.

But he was lying. She could see the tension in his muscular body. And he'd had a hell of a day. Such a hell of a day that she wasn't going to argue with him at the moment. She just followed the directions he gave her to his house.

It wasn't far from the hospital. He could almost have walked from the crash site, but he probably would have frozen to death in his damp clothes.

"Is this it?" she asked as she pulled into the driveway and her headlamps lit up the porch of a small log cabin.

"Yes," he said. But he didn't reach for the door handle. He didn't act as if he was in any hurry to get inside his house to make that call for a tow truck.

"Then why aren't you getting out?" she asked.

It was getting too hot in her car, and it wasn't just because of the heat blasting from the vents. She debated leaning across him and reaching for the handle herself. But she was already too close to him, with only the console separating his big body from hers. His shoulders were so broad that one of them touched her seat.

"Aren't you going to walk me to my door?" he asked, his deep voice a low rumble in her ear. And now heat coiled inside her.

He'd seemed cautious with her earlier—now he wanted her around? He was probably just baiting her to irritate her—just like he had when they were younger. But he hadn't been joking back then or teasing. He'd just been a jerk.

And his remark didn't warrant a real reply. She snorted instead.

He smiled at that. "Then how about just the kiss goodbye?" he asked, and he leaned over the console.

Her heart started beating harder and faster in anticipation. But she raised her hand to hold him back, and beneath her palm, his heart beat just as hard and fast. She wanted to curl her fingers into his shirt and pull him closer, wanted to press her mouth to his. But she couldn't forget what he'd said to her the last time he'd kissed her. "No," she said. "I don't repeat mistakes."

He flinched like he had when she'd touched his injured forearm. "That's not what I meant."

"I don't care what you meant," she said. "It was true. It was a mistake. And it won't happen again." Using her hand on his chest, she shoved him back. "Good night…"

"Courtney…"

He was bigger than she was. He could have resisted. He could have kissed her anyway—if he'd really wanted. But instead he opened the door and stepped out onto his driveway.

And she felt a flash of disappointment. She should have been relieved, though—that he had respected what she'd said. But she realized now that she hadn't meant what she'd said. She had wanted him to kiss her.

Now it was too late. Or was it?

He bent down and leaned inside the door. He didn't come any closer, not close enough to kiss her. And all he said was "Thanks for rescuing me."

Before she could reply, he closed the door and walked away from her.

All she'd done was give him a ride home. She hadn't really rescued him. He'd crashed his truck into the ditch before she'd found him. He was lucky he hadn't been hurt worse than he already was. But then, he wasn't really lucky at all—not after having two accidents in one day.

But she remembered the pool of fluid in the alley. And she wondered if the last one had actually been an accident or something else…

In the headlamps of her car, he was illuminated as he walked across his porch and unlocked his front door. She hesitated for a long moment before backing out of his driveway, and she had that eerie feeling she'd had earlier—like she was being watched.

But he was focused on unlocking his door. He didn't even glance back at her. So who was watching?

Shivering despite the heat blasting out of the vents, she finally backed out onto the street and drove away.

Damn it! The plan hadn't worked. He'd survived—just as he had the first time. That could not happen again. His luck had to run out. The next plan would have to be more carefully plotted—would have to be foolproof. There could be no way for Owen James to escape again unscathed.

The next accident had to claim his life, or people were bound to get suspicious—would begin to wonder if these accidents weren't actually accidents at all. That could not happen—just as Owen James could not be allowed to live. Because if he survived much longer, he would be certain to figure it out—who Dirk's killer was and who was going to kill him.

Chapter 9

Fury had kept Owen awake the night before—fury and thoughts of Courtney Beaumont. He hadn't really expected her to kiss him good-night, but he'd been disappointed when she hadn't. That disappointment was nothing in comparison to the displeasure he felt for his boss and coworker. It had turned back into fury, which he now felt during the meeting in the conference room on the third floor of the firehouse.

All the Hotshots had been called to it—even the ones who hadn't been working on the firebreak yesterday. He knew they would have come even if Braden hadn't called the meeting, though—because of Dirk's death.

His senseless death due to an accident. Supposedly…

Braden continued to claim that was the case as he stood at the podium at the front of the conference room. But Owen couldn't help but think that the man he'd always respected so much—whom he'd idolized and tried to emulate since grade school—was lying through his damn teeth.

That belief, and his anger, compelled Owen to nearly jump up to say as much. Cody had taken the seat next to his and, as if he'd sensed what Owen might do, gripped his arm—holding him down.

When Owen turned to him, Cody shook his head. "Not now," he whispered in a gruff voice. "Not here…"

Son of a bitch…

So Braden was lying—to all of them.

Why?

Ethan Sommerly turned slightly in his seat and glanced back at the two of them. His bushy beard dominated his face but for his dark eyes, which were squinty with suspicion. "What's going on?"

Cody shook his head. "Nothing…"

Trent Miles sat on the other side of Cody and he leaned across him to look at Owen. His eyes were brown, too, but not dark. They were an eerie light brown. "You sure you're okay?" he asked, and his gaze skimmed over the bandage on Owen's forearm—fortunately, the one Cody was not clutching.

Owen had changed the bandage last night—after it had gotten wet in the ditch water under the truck. But he figured Trent wasn't worried just about his physical condition. Even though Trent had been working his regular job at a firehouse in Detroit, he'd been told, along with all the other Hotshots not at the scene, about Dirk's "accident"—as Braden was calling it. Trent knew Owen had been there.

Owen had seen a lot of horrific things during his deployments as a Marine. And the day before, with the loss of his friend, had brought all those horrible memo-

ries rushing back to him. All that horror, all that senseless loss...

He'd been affected when he'd thought it was just
an accident. Now that he suspected it could have been
something more—he was furious.

But he held on to his anger and just nodded at Trent.
Then he turned his attention back to the meeting. Braden
shared the details for Dirk's funeral. And Owen felt a
tightness in his chest. He dreaded the funeral, dreaded
seeing Dirk's distraught widow again.

Because now he felt even more responsible. Not only
had he been unable to save Dirk, but he might have been
the reason his friend died. If the accident hadn't been
an accident, then Owen must have been the intended
target—since someone had tried again for him, messing
with his brakes after the cable had failed to take his life.

He shuddered.

"You're not okay," Trent said to him as they stood
and the firefighters started gathering around the re-
freshment table after the meeting.

He opened his mouth, but before he could say anything, Trent continued, "And you shouldn't be—not after
what happened..."

"It wasn't your fault," Cody said, just as he had the
night before. He sounded as if he was taking responsibility for it—maybe because he'd been responsible for
inspecting the equipment.

"It wasn't yours either," Owen said. Especially not
if that accident had been meant for him.

Maybe all the little things that had been happening
to the equipment had been targeting him. He looked
around the room for his boss, but the man had slipped
away. Owen tried to do the same, but everybody kept

stopping him to make sure he was okay. By the time he got to Braden's office, the smile had frozen on his face.

He pushed open the door without knocking, and Braden glanced up as he entered. And just like everyone else, his first question was "Are you okay?"

But Owen didn't give him the response he'd given everyone else. He didn't lie. He was sick of the damn lies, and that sickness rushed over him. "Hell, no!" he replied vehemently.

And just as he had upstairs, Cody shushed him.

Owen jumped. He hadn't even noticed the other man following him from the conference room. But Cody must have known where he was going and why. He nudged Owen fully into the small office and closed the door behind them.

"Stop trying to shut me up!" Owen yelled at his coworker. "Or I'm going to start thinking you're the one trying to kill me."

The color drained from Cody's face and he stumbled back against the door as if Owen had struck him. "How could you think that?"

Cody had shown up at his house last night—right after Courtney had dropped him off. He'd called for the tow truck and had Owen's vehicle brought to the firehouse. But shouldn't the police have been called instead?

Owen had been so exhausted at that point that he hadn't argued with Cody. It was only after his friend had left that he'd begun to question Cody's involvement, just as he'd begun to question everything else.

Owen released a ragged sigh. "I don't know what the hell to think right now. And you two lying is making it hard for me to trust you."

Or anyone else…

Those close calls with death were making him paranoid. He'd even been wondering about Courtney, about the way she'd shown up right after his crash. She claimed she'd noticed the fluid in the alley and been concerned. But what if the fluid hadn't leaked out until his truck had been parked in the hospital parking lot?

What if she'd followed him there and tampered with the brake line then?

"We're not lying," Braden said.

Owen couldn't tell if he sounded self-righteous or defensive. And he narrowed his eyes to study his boss's face.

"We're not," Braden insisted. "We don't know anything for certain right now. We have suspicions but no proof."

"What about the hole in my brake line?" he asked. "That's proof that someone tampered with it!"

Braden shook his head. "It's just proof that something pierced it, which could have been an accident. You drive over rough terrain all the time. We all do. There's no way of knowing for certain that a human caused that leak."

His stomach muscles tightened as frustration joined the anger coursing through him. "And the cable...? Something caused it to snap."

Braden lifted his shoulders in a shrug. "We don't know what. It could have been a malfunction."

Owen cursed at the excuses and turned on Cody again. "You inspected it. You know that's not true."

Cody sighed now. "I don't know what happened for sure."

"Well, we need to find out," Owen said. "We need proof."

Braden shook his head.

And Owen cursed again. "I don't believe in coincidence," he said. "I don't believe that those two things both happening yesterday—the cable and the brake line—were just a coincidence. I believe someone's trying to kill me."

"Who would want you dead?" Cody asked.

"Whoever it is, the rest of our team deserves to know that none of this is an accident." Owen moved to the door. If Braden and Cody wouldn't voice their suspicions, he sure as hell would. He didn't want anyone else getting hurt because of him.

Courtney could have killed him. She hadn't slept at all the night before—thanks to Owen James. She'd kept reliving her every encounter with him, especially their kiss. She could not forget that kiss—not that she'd tried all that hard. She actually found herself trying to remember every detail—to remember the exact texture of his lips, the rich taste of his mouth, the warm heat of his skin...

And heat flashed through her with the memory.

"You're working too hard," Tammy Ingles remarked as she shifted from checking out the store to focus on Courtney. "You're all flushed."

Courtney thought Serena had just brought their friend to the store to show her around. Now she wondered if her twin was staging some kind of intervention. "I have a lot of work to do yet to get it ready next month."

"Hire it done," Tammy said. "Then you'd have some hunky construction workers hanging around here that we could ogle."

Courtney laughed. Tammy was an incorrigible flirt. Like Courtney, she hadn't been as popular in high school as Serena had been. But she was making up for it now. She'd lost a lot of weight since high school. Her skin had cleared up, and either her vision had improved or she wore contacts. Her personal transformation was probably the secret to the success of her beauty salon and spa.

"I don't need anyone to ogle," Courtney said, but an image of Owen flashed through her mind. His big body, his golden hair, even the scar that marred the side of his handsome face. She wouldn't mind seeing him with his shirt off. Maybe if she had walked him to his door last night...

"You really are flushed," Serena remarked. "Are you feeling okay?" She reached out and touched Courtney's forehead. She was so much like their mother and grandmother had been—so maternal and caring. Maybe that was why it seemed like she'd forgiven Courtney for not even coming home for their mother's funeral and then filing that lawsuit against her. If their situations had been reversed, Courtney would not have forgiven her—not until she'd proved herself worthy of trust.

That was one of the things she intended to accomplish with her return. But despite her good intentions, she found herself forcing a smile and lying. "I'm fine."

"Cody said you stopped by last night," Serena said. "After I fell asleep." Serena blushed now.

"You should have known better," Tammy said with a twinkle in her hazel eyes. "After what happened yesterday, they were going to need some *private* time."

Serena sighed. "I'm lucky. I got to be with Cody last night. Poor Louanne..."

Courtney sighed, too, as she remembered the inconsolable widow. Would her sister one day experience that same unbearable loss?

"How do you do it?" she wondered aloud.

"That's kind of personal," Tammy teased.

Courtney snorted. "Does your mind always go to the gutter?"

Their friend laughed. "Of course." Tammy had always used humor—to protect herself from bullying when they were kids and to hide her own insecurities and fears.

Was that what Owen had been doing last night when he'd joked about her walking him to his door? Had he really been hiding his fear?

Of her?

That was ridiculous. She pushed aside those thoughts of him to focus on her sister instead.

"How do you handle Cody having this dangerous job?" she asked. "How do you cope with knowing that you could lose him at any time?"

Serena shuddered but shook her head. "I won't," she said. "Nothing's going to happen to him."

Louanne Brown had probably thought that, too. But Courtney bit her tongue, so that comment wouldn't slip out.

Tammy had no such filter. "Dirk died. And it wasn't even during a fire." The twinkle in her eyes turned to a sheen of tears. Despite all of her goofing around, she was very sensitive. Or maybe that was why she goofed around so much—to protect her sensitivity.

Courtney could relate. She'd always acted tough to hide the fact that she wasn't tough enough. She wasn't strong like Serena and their mother and grandmother had been. That was why she hadn't come home for her mother's funeral—because she had known she wouldn't be able to handle it without falling apart. She'd already felt so damn guilty for leaving. Maybe if she'd stayed like Serena, maybe if she'd helped, too, her mother might still be alive. Suddenly needing a hug herself, she sufficed with squeezing Tammy's slender shoulders. "Did you know Dirk?" she asked.

Tammy shook her head. "No. I just feel bad that it happened, and out of the blue like that…"

"Yes," Courtney agreed. "It was such a freak accident." But it hadn't been the only one.

And from the way Serena's brow furrowed, she suspected her twin knew that as well.

"Did Cody tell you about Owen's crash?" she asked.

Serena tensed. "What crash? Is he okay?"

"Yes, is he?" Tammy asked anxiously.

Courtney nodded.

"How do you know about any of this?" Serena asked.

"I came upon his truck in the ditch shortly after he'd gone off the road," she admitted. But she wouldn't confess to the rest—that she'd actually been out looking for him, that she'd been worried. "He was fine."

"He was probably distracted," Tammy said, "after what happened earlier. I heard it was a terrible scene…" As the beauty salon owner, she was the first to hear all the town gossip.

Remembering the blood on his jacket and his arm, Courtney nodded in agreement. But then she also remembered the fluid in the alley.

Had Owen just been distracted?

Or had something malfunctioned on his truck? When she'd seen that puddle, she'd worried that something was wrong. And her concern had been justified.

But it was also stupid. Why the hell should she worry about Owen? He had never worried about her—not about her feelings in high school or even after her mother had died. Maybe she hadn't given him the chance since she'd lashed out the first time she'd seen him about how he'd failed, how he'd let her mother die, and that she should sue him. Maybe because of that threat, he hadn't offered the condolences or the concern that everyone had offered Serena. Of course, Courtney hadn't come home until long after the funeral, but even then, some people had said sorry. Like Tammy...

Tammy blinked away her tears and smiled brightly, too brightly, as if she was forcing it. "Let's focus on happier things—like Serena's wedding. We need to go dress shopping soon."

"No, we don't," Courtney said.

"Nothing's going to happen to Cody!" Serena exclaimed in exasperation. "We *will* be getting married."

"Of course," Courtney quickly agreed, apologetic that she'd upset her sister. Again. "That wasn't what I meant..." And she shouldn't have worried her sister just because she was worried. "I meant that you don't need to find a dress because I'm making you one." Then she realized how presumptuous she'd been, especially when Serena's eyes widened with shock. "But if you would rather pick out something yourself, I totally understand. I should have asked you first..." No wonder Serena had never been close to her; Courtney didn't know how to be a good sister.

Serena's wide eyes filled with tears. "I was going to ask you to make it, but I knew you were so busy with getting the store ready to open that I didn't want to add to your stress. I would be so honored..."

Tears stung Courtney's eyes, but she furiously blinked them back. "Only if you're sure..."

Serena's face lit up. "I'm delighted! Thrilled!"

Tammy clapped her hands together. "A Courtney's Couture original! You are so lucky!"

"I'll make you one, too," Courtney promised.

Tammy snorted. "Like I'm ever getting married…"

"You're more likely to get hitched than I am," Courtney assured her.

Serena chuckled. "You two used to have this same argument in high school."

When they'd been the ugly ducklings…

And while that had changed, other things hadn't. Like this town.

Courtney had been crazy to think she could come home to it, and that anything would have changed. Tammy and Serena were the only ones who talked to her—just like in high school. After last night, after she'd let Owen kiss her and had wanted more…even when he'd so obviously been suspicious of her, she wasn't sure she should stay here. She wasn't certain she could trust her judgment, and she didn't want to wind up in another situation like she had with Bradford, which had been difficult for her to escape.

She wanted to be closer to Serena, but that didn't necessarily mean that they had to live in the same town. While Courtney had committed to opening the store, she didn't have to manage the day-to-day operation of it. She could find a manager for it. In fact, it would probably be more successful if someone—anyone—besides her ran it. Maybe her sister would even agree to manage the store for her. Then Courtney could leave after Serena's wedding. She didn't have to stay in Northern Lakes.

"Stay here!" Braden called as Owen whirled toward the door like he was about to storm out. But Cody blocked his way—fortunately. The last thing he needed was for everybody on his team to be aware of what was going on. "All you have are suspicions, and if you go around spewing those, all you're going to do is upset everyone—needlessly."

"Needlessly?" Owen's body shook with fury as he whirled back around to face Braden. "A man is dead. We all need to know the truth about why that happened."

"I agree," Braden said. And he damn well intended to find out the truth once and for all. "But the rest of the team is already shaken up enough. We don't need to upset them any more."

"We need to find out what the hell happened—to that cable and to my truck!" Owen exclaimed.

Braden shook his head just as he had the last time Owen had made that pronouncement. "Not *we*," he clarified. "You're a firefighter and a paramedic—not a cop."

"So call the cops," Owen said. "Let them go over my truck for evidence."

Braden drew in a breath. He hated to share any more suspicions. But he had no choice. Owen deserved to know. "I don't trust them."

"You don't trust the police?" Then his body relaxed as a ragged sigh shuddered through him. "You don't trust Marty Gingrich."

While Owen had been a few years behind Braden and Marty in school, he had probably witnessed some of their rivalry. Unfortunately, Marty hadn't left that bitterness behind in school. The state trooper had carried it with him into adulthood. He'd even stolen Braden's first wife. Although, in retrospect, he'd done Braden a favor. Instead of trying to find the arsonist terrorizing the town, Marty had tried to blame Braden and his team for the fires. Just how far was the state trooper willing to take that rivalry?

"So that's why we have to investigate this on our own," Owen said.

"Not *we*," Braden repeated. "You need to focus on healing, so you can get back to work. You're on light duty until your stitches come out."

Owen flinched, but he couldn't argue with what the doctor had probably told him as well.

"Take it easy and don't worry about this," Braden urged him. "I've got it handled."

Owen's brow puckered, and his blue eyes narrowed with skepticism.

Braden didn't blame him for being skeptical. They had lost a member of their team, so obviously he didn't have it handled yet.

But he would.

"You're not the only one someone might be holding a grudge against since high school," Owen said, and he laughed bitterly. "In fact, if anyone wants me dead, it's Courtney Beaumont." His face flushed and he looked away from Cody.

Color rose on the other Hotshot's face, too, but he stayed silent—almost as if he was afraid that Owen might be right about his fiancée's sister.

Could Courtney dislike Owen enough to want him dead? Things between them had gotten pretty ugly after the Beaumonts' mother died.

"The things that happened yesterday might have been meant for me," Owen continued, and Braden could see the torment in his face.

"But other stuff has happened," Braden pointed out. "Cody's brakes went out."

"Cody?" Owen turned back toward the other blond man. "But we thought that was the arsonist since he also burned down the boardinghouse."

Braden had been able to sense that fire, but he'd still been too late to stop it from destroying the entire home and nearly taking Cody, Serena and Stanley with it.

"We don't know for sure about the brakes and a few other things that happened to me," Cody reluctantly admitted. "The arsonist wouldn't take responsibility for those incidents."

"Was Courtney back in town then?" Owen asked quietly. Before Cody could answer, he nodded in reply to himself. "Yes, she was back then. She was here."

Until now, Braden hadn't heard about any female suspects besides the two on his team. Thanks to that anonymous note, nearly everyone on the team was suspect. He would prefer to think it was someone else, though.

But then, what the hell had the note meant? Who on his team was not who Braden thought they were?

"Courtney Beaumont hates my guts," Owen said with a heavy sigh of regret. "I don't think she's too fond of Cody's either."

"That's not a reason to make her a suspect," Braden said.

"I'm not sure that I suspect her. But I can't think of anyone else in Northern Lakes who would have it out for me," Owen said.

Cody shook his head. "No. Courtney's the one who told me about something leaking out of your truck."

"To cover her tracks?" Owen suggested. "Maybe that's why she was actually nice to me last night. She found me at the crash site. Was she checking to see if it worked?" He shrugged and sighed again. "I'm probably just being paranoid."

After yesterday, he had every reason to be. So Braden didn't argue with him.

But Cody did. "No, she wouldn't know how to sabotage that winch or what to do to your brake line. It's not Courtney." He was marrying the woman's twin, so he probably felt obligated to defend her.

Braden, not so much. "We'll check her out," he promised. And if not for Cody's sake, he would have hoped she would prove to be the guilty party rather than someone on his team. He didn't want the culprit to be someone he knew and trusted.

Owen breathed a slight sigh of relief. "Good. We need to look into her."

"Not you," Braden told him. "You'll stay away from her."

But Owen shoved past Cody and opened the door.

"Owen!" Braden called after him.

The other man was already stalking down the hall—maybe racing right into danger, if his suspicions about her were right.

"He's not going to stay away from her," Braden murmured with frustration.

Cody shook his head. "No, he's not."

Moments ago, Braden had hoped that Courtney was responsible, so it wasn't one of his team. But the way Owen had raced off changed his mind and made him uneasy.

"I hope he's wrong about her," Braden said. Or Owen was putting himself in even more danger. He waited for Cody to defend her again. But he remained silent, and Braden knew that the man had his doubts about Courtney, too.

Right now, Braden had doubts about almost everyone. At least he had someone coming in from the outside whom his wife, Sam, had recommended. He needed that objective party to be able to assess the situation.

That was why he didn't want Owen trying to investigate. There was no way he could be objective—not now, not after that person had tried to kill him, too. Despite what Braden had told the paramedic, he didn't believe that the brake line on his truck had been accidentally punctured.

Owen was right.

Someone was trying to kill him.

Chapter 10

Although he would be damned if he'd admit it, Braden was right. Owen couldn't go around accusing people or even sharing his suspicions with anyone else. He shouldn't have told Braden and Cody of his doubts about Courtney. Hell, he wasn't even sure why he'd mentioned her except that she'd been constantly on his mind since her return to town. Still, it had been strange that she'd shown up last night when she had. And so, to clear up his doubts about her, he'd driven to her shop to seek her out and find out what he could.

When he neared the open back door of her store, what he heard only raised more doubts in his mind.

"I'm not sure I can stay in Northern Lakes…"

His blood chilled as he recognized Courtney's voice. Why couldn't she stay? Because she was worried about getting caught?

Back in high school, after she'd dyed a lock of her

hair white, everybody had started calling her "skunk" instead of "freak." And mysteriously, all their vehicles had started to smell like skunk—like someone had put skunk spray in their vents. That had been revenge. But it had been petty and harmless. Nobody had been hurt. Even if she hated him enough to want to hurt him, murder was something else. She wouldn't kill him, and she certainly wouldn't have risked killing someone else by accident the way Dirk had died. She had too much going for her with her store and her designs and her life back in New York. A life to which she probably wanted to return.

She stepped into his line of vision as she leaned back against the display case she'd been working on the night before. "I didn't want to talk about this in front of Serena. But now that she's gone, I can tell you that I don't think I can stay here," she murmured again.

"Why not?" A female voice asked the question burning in the back of his throat.

"You know how much I hated living here."

"Yes," the other woman replied. "I was surprised that you decided to move back and open a store. But you did. And you're committed to it now."

"To opening the store," Courtney agreed. "But I don't have to be the one to run it."

"Don't look at me!" the other woman said. "My salon is hopping."

Now he recognized the voice. Tammy Ingles. She owned the popular beauty parlor.

"I barely have time to go out for drinks anymore," Tammy said. "I don't want to take on another business. Now, a boyfriend…"

Courtney shuddered. "I'd rather run the store."

"Bad experience?" Tammy asked.

"Bad experiences," Courtney admitted.

Now Owen had other questions burning in the back of his throat. He wanted to know all about her, about the men who'd disappointed her. And if he was one of them...

Not that they'd gone out in high school. They might have, if he hadn't been such an idiot—if he hadn't cared so much about being cool. He didn't blame her for being angry about how he'd treated her then. He really couldn't imagine her acting on that anger now—even with a petty prank.

But after she'd sued her sister, even Serena and Cody didn't completely trust her. To rule her out as a suspect, he would have to find out exactly what Courtney was capable of now—as an adult. That meant getting close to her, and the thought of that—of getting as close to her as he'd been the night before with his lips on hers—had his pulse pounding hard and fast.

In order to get that close again, though, he was going to have to turn on the charm and apologize for the jerk he used to be. So he had come prepared. He knocked on the door frame of the open back door before stepping through it with a big bouquet of flowers in his hand. Instead of pretending he hadn't been eavesdropping, he decided to face it head-on.

"Unfortunately, I'm probably one of those bad experiences you're talking about," he said as he extended the flowers to her.

She stared at them, her dark eyes wide with horror as if he held a bunch of snakes instead of a bunch of roses. Maybe the roses had been overkill, but she didn't seem like the daisy or carnation type.

"Bad experiences don't come bearing gifts," Tammy

remarked with a little chuckle. Then she turned back to her friend. "You've been holding out on me."

Courtney shook her head. "I don't know what he's talking about…"

"You don't?" he asked, and he feigned shock. "Was it all just my imagination?"

Her face flushed with embarrassment, but she replied, "Must have been."

She might have been able to forget that kiss, but he hadn't. His pride smarted with a little prick that compelled him to slip back into the persona of that arrogant jock he'd once been. And he wanted to tease her like he had back then.

He moved closer. "I have a very vivid imagination, then…"

Tammy cleared her throat. "Well, I know when I'm third wheeling, so I'm going to roll on out of here."

"Tammy!" Courtney called out as her friend hustled out of the store.

Owen heard the panic in her voice, and he raised the flowers a little higher to hide the smile curving his lips. She remembered their kiss, and maybe she was afraid that he was going to kiss her again. And that, just like she had last night, she would kiss him back.

Panic coursed through Courtney as the door closed behind her friend. Her ex-friend. How could Tammy leave her alone with Owen James? She, better even than Serena, knew how Courtney felt about him.

"Traitor," she murmured under her breath.

"You're welcome," Owen replied.

"I didn't thank you," she said.

"That's okay," he said.

"What are these flowers for?" She was trying not

to look at them, even though they were in her face, because they were so beautiful. The petals of those roses, which were red and yellow, looked as soft as velvet. She wanted to touch them. She wanted to bury her nose in them. But she resisted.

"To thank you," he said.

"Thank me?" He didn't seem particularly grateful to her and he hadn't last night either. In fact, he'd been more skeptical and suspicious than anything else.

"I had a really bad day," he said, "and you were really nice to me."

She snorted.

"You were," he insisted. "You talked to me at Dirk's house." His throat moved as if he was choking down his emotions. "And more importantly, you made me talk."

She suspected that was something he rarely did. Despite the town talking endlessly about their hero, nobody seemed to know exactly how he'd gotten the scar on his handsome face. It had happened during a deployment, but that was all anyone knew.

She doubted she could make him talk about that. And after he'd graphically told her how Dirk had died, she didn't want to ask. So she held her silence now.

"You also rescued me from the roadside," he continued. "So these flowers are the least I could do." He thrust them toward her again.

The roses were not the least of anything. They were beautiful, too beautiful not to be enjoyed. With a sigh, she finally took the tissue-wrapped stems from him. "They are not necessary," she told him.

"I know you don't like me," he said. "But you won't take it out on the flowers, will you?"

"No," she assured him. And with another sigh, she headed toward the stairwell at the back of the store.

"They need water." Which she had in the restroom on the main level. But she also needed a vase.

She didn't invite him, but he followed her up the narrow stairwell anyway. The kitchen and living area were one big loftlike room at the top of the steps. With tall windows, lightly varnished, natural wood floors and white cabinetry, it was all very bright and cheerful.

"I hope I have something to put them in," she murmured as she settled them into the sink before she started pulling open cupboard doors. She wasn't quite tall enough to reach the upper cabinets, so Owen stepped in and opened them for her.

But as he did so, he trapped her between the butcher-block counter and his body. His big, warm body...

She felt the heat of it against her back, and her body warmed, too. Maybe overheated...

She shouldn't have let him follow her upstairs.

"I should have sprung for the vase," he said. "I don't see one..."

Those upper cabinets were empty—because she hadn't been able to reach them and because she hadn't brought much stuff with her. She waited for him to step back. But he remained nearly pressed against her for another long moment—in which she held her breath and he drew a deep one, like he was taking in the scent of her hair.

Then finally he stepped back, and she released her breath. Her hands shaking slightly, she pulled a pitcher of lemonade from the fridge. "I can use this," she said.

"I'm surprised you don't have a vase," he said. "Thought you'd be getting flowers from all kinds of guys."

"Not in Northern Lakes," she said. "So I left all my vases in New York."

"You still have a place there?" he asked. And he sounded shocked.

"Yes," she replied. She'd sublet it, so she couldn't move back in until the end of the sublease.

"With all your vases…" he murmured. "And the guy who gives you flowers to fill them?"

She shuddered at the thought of that. "No." Her last boyfriend had given her so many flowers, but Bradford's gifts had always had strings attached. She suspected these flowers did, too. But since it wasn't the flowers' fault, she cleaned out the pitcher and added the preservative packet and fresh water. Then she arranged the flowers.

"Beautiful," he murmured.

She looked up at him. "What are you up to?" she asked.

"I told you I'm thanking you."

"These roses are an extravagant thank-you," she said, "for a two-minute ride home."

"And the talk—"

"Talk now," she said. "And tell me the truth."

His lips curved into a faint grin, and he murmured, "That's ironic…"

"You think I'm lying to you?" she asked, and she tensed with indignation. If anything, she was usually too honest—sometimes brutally so.

"I don't know what to think of you," he said, and his heavily uttered words had a ring of truth to them. "I do, however, know exactly what you think of me."

Now her lips curved into a smile. "Does that bother you—that I don't idolize you like the rest of Northern Lakes? Is that why you brought these?" She gestured to the roses.

"You're right," he said. "They're not just a thank-you."

She'd suspected as much. "Then what are they?"

"An apology," he said, his voice husky with remorse. "A long, long overdue one."

She sucked in a breath, shocked that he'd finally offered and that it rang sincere. The sincerity also shone in his bright blue–eyed stare, which was focused on her face.

"It is long overdue." So much so that she thought she would never receive one. She'd thought that, just like with her mother's death, he was going to maintain that he'd done nothing wrong.

"I was such an idiot back in high school," he said. "I was so damn concerned with looking cool in front of my buddies—"

"And your girlfriend," she interjected. That girl had had everything—looks, grades, money, popularity and the homecoming king—but she'd still acted so jealous and hateful toward Courtney. She'd acted as the ringleader of the circus of kids who used to pick on Courtney.

He reddened now but for the scar that remained a rigid, jagged line of white on his handsome face. He shook his head. "Like I said, I was an idiot back then. A big one. It doesn't matter what Becky or my friends did. I never should've joined in and I'm sorry. I said terrible, hurtful things to you, and I should have apologized to you a long time ago." His repentant gaze met hers.

She narrowed her eyes and studied him. "Why didn't you?" she asked. "If you truly regretted it, why didn't you ever call me up and apologize before now?"

Before that kiss…

"I didn't know how to contact you," he said. "Your sister didn't even know how to contact you."

She flinched as she remembered her self-imposed estrangement from Serena. Just as she'd hated Owen in high school, she'd hated her twin, too. Actually, what she'd really hated was how everybody had always compared her—unfavorably—to her perfect sister. None of that had been Serena's fault, though.

But Owen had been responsible for the things he'd said to her—for the names he'd called her.

"I was still here for two years after you graduated," she said. "You could have apologized then or, better yet, before you left for the Marines…"

He nodded. "I probably would have if I hadn't been pissed at you."

"At me?" Her eyes widened with shock. "Why were you pissed at me?"

"The skunk spray," he said. "You put it in the vents of all our vehicles."

Her brow furrowed. "I don't know what you're talking about."

His eyes narrowed now. "Skunk spray. It had to have been you. After you dyed your hair, we all started calling you…"

"Skunk," she finished for him. "I remember." All too well…

Any other place, she might have had the freedom to express herself. But not here—not in Northern Lakes.

It was too small a town, too conservative. She looked around the store on which she'd been working so hard. It wasn't going to be successful—not here. She should have known better than to try to come back here.

"You didn't do it?" he asked, his eyes narrowed with skepticism. "You didn't put the spray in the vents of our vehicles?"

She shook her head. "Nope. I heard it happened, but I didn't do it." But now she realized why everybody had switched from calling her skunk to Carrie. They'd thought she'd taken revenge on them. She laughed and shook her head.

"But you were so mad," he said.

She nodded. "Yeah, and I told you all what I thought of you to your faces." And she'd been even meaner than they'd been to her. Whenever she'd gotten hurt, she'd always lashed out—at her mother, at Serena…

That was another reason she hadn't come home for her mother's funeral—because of that guilt that consumed her over their estrangement. Just like everyone else in town had seemed to favor Serena, she'd thought her mother had, too. Because she'd offered to help Serena with nursing school but she'd refused to help Courtney with her classes in fashion. She'd been so hurt that she'd cut off contact with both of them, and she would never forgive herself for all those years she'd lost with her mom, because she'd done that. Maybe that was why she was so angry with Owen for not saving her, for not giving Courtney a chance to make it up to her mother.

He winced. "Yeah, I remember…"

A smile tugged at the corners of her mouth, pulling up her lips. "Don't go looking for any flowers from me as an apology."

"There's something else I'd rather have from you," he said, and the intensity of his blue-eyed stare had her pulse racing. Then he leaned forward and brushed his mouth across hers.

And shock gripped her so hard, her heart seemed to stop beating for a moment before resuming at a frantic pace. He'd kissed her before, but it still caught her by surprise. Not the kiss so much as the passion that coursed through her. She'd never felt so much desire from just a kiss. And why this man out of all the men she'd dated over the years?

Why Owen James, who'd hurt her in high school with his cruelty? Who hadn't saved her mother?

Why would she be so attracted to him?

It wasn't just because of his flowers and his apology. She'd felt this passion last night, before he'd come bearing the roses and his mea culpa.

She'd worried about him yesterday, but just like in high school, she didn't believe it was possible that he really cared about her, that he wanted her. Was he up to something? What did he want from her?

His mouth brushed across hers again. Then his lips nipped at hers, and a gasp escaped her. He deepened the kiss, and she tasted his passion.

He wanted her as badly as she wanted him.

And that was bad…

Very bad.

Because she had a feeling that if she let herself give in to her desire, she would be the one who wound up hurt next…

Chapter 11

Owen was dying. His body ached with pain…that had nothing to do with his arm. Another part of his body throbbed, and tension filled him.

What had he done?

What had he said?

Somehow he'd screwed up. Because instead of pulling him into her bedroom, Courtney had pushed him toward the stairs instead. He was probably lucky that she hadn't pushed him *down* the steps.

She could have if she really wanted to hurt him. But hell, turning him away after that hot, passionate kiss had hurt more than bouncing off a few stair treads would have. He now highly doubted that she'd tried to physically harm him. She hadn't even pulled that high school prank out of revenge all those years ago. Why would she try to kill him? It made no sense.

What made sense was that she just wasn't interested

in him or, after the way he'd treated her all those years ago, she didn't trust him. And he couldn't blame her.

He didn't completely trust her either. And he probably shouldn't trust his attraction to her. He'd just lost a good friend and suspected that someone had intended to hurt him instead. He was reeling from that guilt, and maybe he'd focused on Courtney as a way to feel something—anything—besides that guilt. Which was ironic since she'd been piling the guilt on him since her return to Northern Lakes. Now she was the only one who could get his mind off it, because when he was with her, he couldn't think about anything but how much he wanted her.

That was crazy, especially as he'd briefly suspected that she might hate him enough to want him dead. And maybe he'd been right to suspect her. Nobody really knew Courtney Beaumont. He certainly didn't. He'd wanted to get close to her to find out more about her, but once he'd been close to her, he'd suspected her less and had wanted her more. She'd been right to push him away. She obviously couldn't get over her resentment of him as easily as he'd gotten over his suspicions.

Should he trust her when the only thing he'd learned was how much he wanted and needed her? The heat had cooled; the passion had faded…a bit. But that need…

How the hell could he *need* a woman he barely knew? A woman who didn't even intend to stay in Northern Lakes? A woman who had a life back in New York…

She had kissed him back again, though. And she'd touched him. But eventually the hands on his chest had pushed him away from her. Then she'd told him in a throaty voice, "You need to leave. Now."

He'd reached for her again. But she'd stepped back, and her eyes had widened. Seeing the fear in them had left him no choice. He hadn't wanted to scare her... especially now he'd learned of her bad experience with men, and when he now realized fully how much he'd hurt her all those years ago.

Courtney didn't see him as a hero like the majority of the town did, and why should she?

But then, maybe he was wrong about how the town saw him, because when he'd left her apartment and joined his teammates at the bar around the corner, they became silent and uneasy in his presence.

The day before, they'd been supportive and protective of him, but now that they'd gotten over the initial shock and had time to think, to miss Dirk, their attitudes seemed to have changed. He wondered if they were now holding him responsible for Dirk's death, just like Courtney held him responsible for her mother's death.

There was no way he could have saved Dirk. Surely his team realized that. But maybe they thought that he, as the younger Hotshot, should have been wrapping the cable around the tree. Maybe they thought, like he did, that Dirk had died in his place.

He had only one beer, pleaded a headache and left the bar so his coworkers could relax again. It hadn't been entirely a lie. His head pounded, just like that need in his groin. He felt like crap.

If only Courtney hadn't thrown him out...

But she'd been right not to trust him. Had things gone further tonight, he might have just been using her to distract him from what had happened to his friend. Now he needed a distraction from her.

No. He needed some rest. Fortunately, his truck wasn't his only means of transportation. He had a car, too, which he'd driven to work. He drove home and around the back of his cabin to park in the detached garage.

As he closed down the door and headed toward the house, a strange sensation rushed over him. He glanced down and noticed the evidence of other tread marks in the gravel drive. Courtney had dropped him off last night, but she hadn't driven around the back. Cody had, though, when he'd shown up later. But there appeared to be more than just Cody's tracks.

Who else had been to his house? Just coworkers checking on him? Nobody had mentioned stopping by when he'd seen them at the bar. But not all of the twenty-member team—nineteen now—had been there. He flinched as he relived that moment when they'd lost a man.

Had that cable snapping been meant for him?

Maybe Courtney wasn't the only one holding a grudge against him over the past. Or over his failing to save a loved one…

Maybe there was someone else who wanted him dead, someone who was watching him now. He hurried up the back steps and crossed the deck to the sliding door. He'd barely pushed it open when he noticed the mouse lying next to the glass.

Living out where he did, he was used to them getting inside the house. Usually he caught them in live traps and put them back outside. But this one hadn't given him the chance. It had died before Owen could catch it.

His brow furrowed in confusion. But how had it died? Then he smelled it. Gas. Something had been left on. The oven? He hadn't used it that morning. He hadn't turned on anything but the shower and the coffeepot. Maybe the pilot light on the water heater had gone out. That was gas. And it was old.

He pulled the slider open all the way and stepped inside the house. He needed to open more windows to air it out, and he needed to shut off the damn water heater. But he barely made it a few more steps into the living room when the drapes at the slider moved like someone was walking in behind him. Before he could turn around to face them, something struck him. Hard. His vision blurred. His knees gave out, and he dropped to the floor. The smell of gas was thicker down here. While the blow hadn't completely knocked him out, the fumes would.

And worse…

He was going to wind up like that hapless mouse if he didn't get back up, if he didn't get the hell out. But before he could get to his knees, something struck him again. And he lost consciousness.

Braden was too late. A man had died—because he'd thought he could handle the investigation on his own.

"Stop beating yourself up," his brother-in-law said. Patrick "Trick" McRooney looked nothing like his sister. Whereas Braden's wife, Sam, was blonde and petite, Trick was dark-haired and enormous. With his height and his breadth, he nearly filled Braden's small office. "You had no way of knowing this would happen."

Braden shook his head. "I got that note, and the accidents kept happening…"

"Little things," Trick reminded him. "Nobody really even got hurt until the other day."

"And now a man is dead. A woman is a widow—because of one of those little things…because of someone tampering with equipment." He pushed a hand through his hair.

"Looks like it was torched," Trick remarked.

Braden tensed. The word *torched* was not one a fire-fighter liked to hear. "What?"

"Someone took a torch to the cable, nearly melted it down in a spot."

"How? When?"

Trick shrugged. "I don't know. I wasn't here."

But he should have been. Braden should have brought in outside help sooner.

"It wouldn't have taken very long," Trick said. "Could've even happened after Cody inspected it."

"But Dirk was there," Braden said. "And Owen…"

"I need to meet this Owen," Trick said. "Get a handle on him…"

Braden shook his head again. "It's not Owen."

"What?"

"The person in the note—the one who isn't who I think he is," Braden said. "It's not Owen. He grew up here. I know Owen."

"He's a former Marine, right?" Trick asked.

Braden nodded now.

"So's Mack."

"Which Mack? Your dad?" Braden had two in-laws who used Mack as their first name even though it wasn't.

"My dad was Air Force," Trick said. "My brother Mack was a Marine. He didn't come back the same person who left. Hell, we're not even sure half the time that he is back—none of us ever see him."

Braden knew that was true and how much it bothered Sam that she wasn't as close to her oldest brother as she was to the others.

"That's not Owen," Braden said, defending his friend. "*He* came back."

"With a scar."

Braden expelled a breath. "Your sister has filled you in." Of course Sam would have. She was thorough. The best arson investigator with the US Forest Service.

Trick nodded. "She's filled me in but not so much that I won't be able to make my own assessments."

That was Braden's problem. He knew it. He was too close to his team to suspect any of them of sabotage. But it had gone beyond that—it was murder now.

"Since she talked to you," Braden continued, "there was an attempt on Owen's life. Someone tampered with his brakes. That's his truck sitting in the bay."

Trick nodded again, but it was clear that he was still suspicious of the paramedic.

"He could have been killed," Braden said.

"But he wasn't," Trick said. "Either time. I don't know many people who are that lucky."

"Two near misses in one day," Braden said. "That's not lucky." He flinched as he considered how much danger Owen was in. He'd nearly been killed twice. A sudden urgency coursing through him, Braden reached for his phone and punched in Owen's contact.

"Who are you calling?" Trick asked. "Sam?"

"Your suspect," he replied. But Owen's phone went straight to voice mail. Fear gripped Braden that whoever was after Owen had tried again.

And wasn't the third time usually the charm?

Courtney couldn't focus, not with those damn roses smelling up the place. And not with her lips still tingling from Owen's touch. She shouldn't have let him kiss her again, and more importantly, she shouldn't have kissed him back.

Or maybe what she shouldn't have done was push him out the door.

"Why'd you get rid of him so quickly?" Tammy asked as she opened the front door and walked back into the store.

Courtney sighed. "Were you watching?"

Tammy chuckled. "No. I was at the Filling Station when he showed up, looking kind of like you look now."

Courtney lifted a hand to her flushed face and pushed back the hair that had fallen across her cheek. "Like what?"

"Frustrated as hell," Tammy said.

"I am not frustrated," Courtney said, but she ground the words out between clenched teeth—which kind of proved Tammy's point.

Her friend laughed. "Yeah, right. And here I was wondering if you'd already done something for those flowers."

Courtney snorted as she remembered how Owen had tried to pass them off as thank-you flowers. No wonder Tammy thought he'd been thanking her for something.

He'd probably actually been using them to try to get something. But her? Could he really want her? Despite it no longer being high school, she was still an outsider in Northern Lakes.

For being different. Dressing differently and acting differently. For suing her sister. Everybody knew about that, and nobody was as forgiving as Serena had been. Certainly not Cody and his Hotshot friends.

She shook her head. "I don't know what he was up to with those flowers."

And Tammy snorted now. "Yeah, right..."

"No, I don't," she maintained. But she'd felt like he was up to something, which was why she'd told him to leave. That and she'd felt too much, too much desire and passion, and she'd been overwhelmed.

"Do you need me to tell you about the birds and the bees?" Tammy teased.

Courtney laughed. "You did that when we were ten."

And Tammy laughed, too. "So you know what to do about that frustration."

"This is Owen James," Courtney reminded her friend.

Tammy uttered a lustful sigh. "Then hurry up about it."

"He wasn't nice to us in high school," Courtney reminded her.

"He was like everybody else," Tammy said with a dismissive shrug. "Just trying to look cool in front of his friends. You did the same thing."

A smile tugged at Courtney's lips and she replied, "But I *was* cool."

Tammy arched a perfect tawny brow. "Looks like you lost your cool—at least with Owen."

She was never cool with Owen. Not when they were kids and not now. She shouldn't have taken those flowers from him. Her last relationship had taught her that gifts often came with an agenda, with some secret motivation. Anytime Bradford had brought her flowers, he expected her to go where he wanted to go and do what he wanted to do. He'd used presents to try to control her.

She wondered what the hell Owen's secret motivation was.

But she wasn't going to wonder much longer. She was going to find out and throw his flowers back in his face. Tammy cheered her on as she collected the pitcher of roses and headed out.

Her friend probably thought she was going to take her advice about the birds and the bees. But Courtney was only going to get close enough to Owen to hand him back his flowers.

She wasn't going to kiss him again. She wasn't going to assuage the frustration twisting inside her.

She was lucky she didn't get a ticket as she sped

through town and past the hospital to his cabin. His truck wasn't parked in the driveway. It was probably at a repair shop. But another set of tire tracks continued past the front of the house around to the back, so she followed those and parked in front of a detached garage.

The door was down, so she wasn't sure if he was home. Maybe it would be better if he wasn't…since Tammy had put some unfortunate thoughts in her head.

She would just set the flowers on his deck and leave then. That was probably safer anyway.

For her…

And for him…

But when she walked up the steps to the deck, she glanced through the slider and saw him lying on the floor. What the hell had happened?

Had he been hurt worse the day before than he'd admitted? She wouldn't have been surprised. She wrapped her trembling fingers around the handle of the slider, tugged it open and nearly gagged—at the sight of the mouse lying dead just inside it. And at the smell.

That wasn't the scent of dead mouse.

It was gas.

"Owen!" She rushed inside and dropped to the floor beside him. The odor was even stronger, and she coughed and gagged. And the flowers, which she'd brought inside with her, began to wilt over the edges of the pitcher. She tossed them aside and reached for him. Shaking his mammoth shoulders, she called his name. He was too big for her to move alone.

But then she realized she wasn't alone—as she heard the creak of floorboards. Someone else was inside with them. Had the gas knocked Owen unconscious, or had it been an intruder?

She was afraid that it had been this person, and that

they were coming for her next. But she wasn't going down without a fight. She fumbled around, looking for a weapon. That was when she noticed the baseball bat lying on the floor near where Owen lay. It wouldn't be much protection from a gun. But since the intruder must have used this on Owen, they probably didn't have a gun. She wrapped her hands around the bat, ready to swing.

Chapter 12

A wave of nausea crashed over Owen, and he choked and sputtered on it. He wasn't sure what was making him sick—the smell of gas or the pain reverberating throughout his skull. Someone had attacked him. But he wasn't dead yet. He needed to fight.

And he fought…to drag open his eyes. His vision was blurred, so all he could see was a shadow crouched over him. He blinked and could see clearly that it was Courtney, holding a bat. "It was you," he murmured in shock. He really hadn't thought she was capable of violence. What a fool he'd been. "You hit me…"

"Of course not," she replied in a whisper that was somehow still quite indignant. Despite her whispering, her voice reverberated inside his aching head.

He pushed himself up from the floor and nearly passed out—from another wave of pain and nausea. "Then what the hell are you doing here?" He rode out the wave of wooziness before adding, "With a bat."

That must have been what had hit him. Had it shattered his damn skull? Had she?

Her face flushed. "I came to bring back your flowers," she said.

He followed her gaze to where the roses lay wilting on the floor. He hadn't noticed those or the pool of water beneath the tilted pitcher when he'd come into his house. Just the mouse. The very dead mouse...

That was still there. And that bat was still clenched in her hands.

"What the hell happened here?" she asked. "Are you all right?"

"My head hurts," he murmured, lifting his fingers to a bump on the back of it. When he pulled his hand away, blood stained his skin. "Is that why you're whispering?"

At least she was being considerate, which would have been ironic if she was the one who'd shattered his skull. Even though he didn't think she would have been strong enough to swing the bat as hard as it had been swung at him, he still wanted to get it away from her. But he wasn't sure he had enough strength to wrestle her for it yet.

She shook her head. "No. Right after I found you like this, I heard someone in the house. That's why I grabbed the bat from the floor."

There was someone else in the house? He made it fully to his feet now but swayed as a wave of nausea overwhelmed him. His head wasn't pounding just from the blow. Despite the open slider, an odor hung heavily in the air.

The gas...

He started shoving her toward the door. "Get out!

Get the hell out of here!" His shouts nearly finished up the shattering of his skull. But he didn't want her succumbing to the fumes.

"What's wrong with you?" she asked. "You can't think that I hit you. I just got here."

She must have surprised his attacker. But if the person was still there, Courtney was in danger from more than just the fumes. "And now you need to leave," he said.

"What's the gas smell?" she asked.

"Leak," he murmured as he stepped onto the deck with her. He gasped mouthfuls of the fresh air, but it only made him more nauseous. How much noxious gas had he inhaled? How long had he been unconscious?

She reached for the purse dangling from her shoulder, but he caught her hand before she could pull it out.

"What are you getting now?" he asked.

"My cell phone," she said. "We need to call the police."

"Why?"

"You were attacked," she said. Then she glanced fearfully toward the house. "And they could still be inside. I heard someone moving around."

She said that was why she'd picked up the bat. Dare he believe her? He wasn't sure what to believe. And he wasn't sure he wanted the police involved either—not after what Braden had said about Marty Gingrich. While Owen had been a couple of years behind him and Braden in school, he'd still kicked the trooper's ass athletically and academically—just like Braden had. So Marty could have been going after either of them.

Or both of them…

After how defensive Braden had been when the trooper had tried blaming the arsons on them, Marty

knew how much it would hurt the Hotshot superintendent to lose a member of his team. Maybe Marty intended to pick them off one by one. The guy wasn't
quite right with how obsessed he seemed with trying to
beat Braden. First he'd gone after the man's first wife
and then his reputation and now his team…

Owen shook his head. "No need to call the police.
The water heater's got a gas leak. The fumes knocked
me out and I fell on the floor, hitting my head."

"What about the bat?" she asked. "You accused me
of hitting you with it!"

He shrugged. "Because you were standing over me
with it. But I must have hit my head on it when I fell.
I'd left it there," he lied. His sporting equipment was
kept in a closet in the utility room—near the furnace
and water heater.

She narrowed her eyes. "On the floor?"

"I'm a slob," he said.

"But I heard someone…"

"Must have been a mouse," he replied.

She pointed toward the one lying near the slider.
"He's not moving."

And neither was she. But if someone was still inside
the house, he needed to get her the hell out of there. And
he knew what would get rid of her: her prickly pride.

"Can't you take a hint?" he asked. "I don't want you
here. I don't want you at my house. I don't want you."

Her mouth fell open with a hiss of breath, and her
face flushed—not with embarrassment but with indignation. "I don't want you either!" she shouted back. "I
knew you were just playing games like you used to—
looking at me like you liked me, then calling me a freak
or other names…"

He *had* liked her. Too much. He still did. That was why he wanted her to leave.

"That's why I brought your damn flowers back," she said. "I don't want anything from you or to do with you!" And finally she turned and stalked off his deck and back to her car.

He didn't release the breath he was holding until she drove away. To safety...

She was furious, so damn furious that all the flowers in the world wouldn't earn her forgiveness now. That should have been the least of his concerns—after that latest attempt on his life.

But guilt and regret filled him that he'd hurt her. Again.

"I hate him!" Courtney had been ranting the words since she'd left his house, so they slipped out the minute she stepped inside her sister's kitchen.

Serena glanced up from the stove. "I don't need to ask who, do I?"

Since Tammy was at the counter near her, slicing up vegetables, she had undoubtedly filled in Serena about what had happened that day. "Yeah, I hate guys that bring me gorgeous flowers, too." Tammy uttered a self-deprecating laugh. "Oh, that's right. I don't have any guys that bring *me* gorgeous flowers, so I can't say for sure. But I probably would hate them."

As usual, her friend made Courtney smile—even though she was so enraged. "Thanks for the solidarity," she said with a glance at Serena, who was biting her bottom lip—either to hold back a smile or a comment.

"Doesn't look like you took my advice about the birds and bees," Tammy continued. "You seem even more frustrated than you did earlier."

She was, but it wasn't sexual anymore. She was frustrated with the way Owen kept swinging from sweet and sympathetic to suspicious and mean. But then, if someone had hit him over the head with that bat, he was entitled to be suspicious and mean. And what about his brakes? And the accident that had killed Dirk?

Her head began to pound as she remembered all he'd endured in the past day and a half. Or maybe the pounding was from the gas fumes.

She breathed in a deep breath, and all the delicious scents of Serena's cooking. Her stomach rumbled. "I'm just hungry," she told Tammy.

Her friend wiggled her brows and replied, "And I know what you're hungry for. Or should I say who?"

"Whom," Serena automatically corrected her. She was going to make a great mother someday. And it sounded as though she would have a lot of kids to mother. She had shared her and Cody's plan to foster children in the future, once they rebuilt the boardinghouse.

Nobody was better suited for it than Serena. Those kids would be lucky to have her.

Tears stung Courtney's eyes, but she blinked them back. They were probably because of the fumes, too.

"He really got to you," Tammy remarked, and she stepped away from the counter to squeeze Courtney's arm.

Courtney blinked again. "No, it's the onions."

Tammy chuckled at the lie.

"What's with all the cooking?" she asked. This was a lot of food even for Serena, who was used to feeding boarders.

But the boardinghouse was gone now. All that remained was the land, where Serena and Cody would get married this summer—once the scorched ground and woods began to bloom again.

Courtney had to stay at least until then. But after that, she suspected there wasn't anything else that would keep her solely in Northern Lakes. Not once she found someone to run the store. Unlike when she left before, she would come back often to visit, and she would get Tammy and Serena to visit her, too. But she wasn't sure she wanted to live here. She wasn't sure she *trusted* herself to live here, not when it compelled her to do foolish things, like kissing Owen James.

"This food is for the funeral," Serena said.

"The firefighter's funeral?" Courtney asked. "You're catering that?"

Tammy laughed. "Catering for free…"

"It's the right thing to do," Serena replied.

And of course her twin always did the right thing while Courtney always seemed to do the wrong. The wrong men, at least…

At least she hadn't taken Tammy's advice and done Owen. Not that he'd given her the chance. He didn't want her; he'd made that clear.

"Pick up a knife," Serena said. Then her lips curved into a smile. "Since Owen isn't here, I'll trust you with one."

"Chopping up stuff is a pretty good stress reliever," Tammy admitted. "Not as good as sex, but…"

"I'd rather cook," Courtney said as she joined them at the counter. She started cutting up celery on a butcher-block cutting board.

Serena laughed. "That's saying something, since you really hate cooking."

She'd hated anything to do with the boardinghouse. Cooking, cleaning…all the things that had run her mother into an early grave. But she'd hated them even before her mother had died. Running the boardinghouse had never been her dream—she knew she'd have to leave town to do what she really wanted. Become a clothing designer...

She'd had success, her label in several stores. But to open her own shop here in Northern Lakes...

Maybe she'd hoped it would make the townspeople see that they'd been wrong about her. That she wasn't the loser they'd called her in school. She shouldn't have cared what they thought about her, though. Not anymore.

"Is it Owen you're upset about?" Serena asked. "Or that last guy you dated before moving home?"

Courtney shook her head. "Owen."

"I would've picked the last guy," Serena remarked. "To hate..." She knew that Bradford Wentworth was the lawyer who'd talked Courtney into filing the suit against her.

"It's not worth my time thinking about Bradford anymore," she said. "I left him in the past." In New York. Maybe going back there wasn't the best idea. At least, not until he'd moved on to someone else. Of course, Courtney had blocked his number for calls and texts, and his emails, so maybe he had moved on and she just wasn't aware of it.

Now she was the one who needed to move on—from Owen. He wasn't worth her time either. Yet she couldn't stop thinking about all the things that had been happening to him.

"Maybe you'll meet someone new tomorrow," Serena remarked.

"Someone new? What are you talking about?" she asked. She'd already turned down her and Tammy every time they'd tried dragging her along to the new night-club in town.

"At the funeral," Serena said matter-of-factly.

"I'm not going to the funeral," she said. "I didn't even know the guy."

"That doesn't matter," Serena said. "Attending is the right thing to do."

"Why?"

"Because he lost his life trying to protect our town," Tammy answered first, but it was probably what Serena was going to say as well. "And the whole town will turn out to show our appreciation for his sacrifice."

"You're right," Courtney begrudgingly admitted. She'd never felt like part of this town, but then, she hadn't really tried to be part of it either.

"It's also a great place to meet guys," Tammy said with another wiggle of her brows. Apparently, funerals were the new pickup spot.

Courtney didn't want to meet any guys, and there was one she didn't even want to see again. But she knew that he would be there for certain.

She cleanly sliced through a carrot and her breath hissed out. Owen damn well better stay away from her after the way he'd treated her. Or the next funeral he'd be attending would be his own.

All the Hotshots had turned out for the funeral of one of their own. But it should have been for two of their own. How the hell did Owen James keep escaping death?

How did he manage to survive every damn attempt? Was he just that lucky? Was he like a cat with nine lives? From the scar on his face, it was clear that he'd survived something bad during his time as a Marine. That must have used up at least one life.

And the cable, the car crash and the concussion that blow with the baseball bat had to have given him...

All those accidents had to be taking their toll on him, taking away all those extra lives of his.

Eventually his luck would run out. It had to...because Owen James had to die.

Chapter 13

This should have been his funeral. Not Dirk's…

It probably nearly had been his funeral, too. Over the past two days, Owen could have died at least three times. Once with Dirk, once in his truck and then in his own damn home.

If Courtney hadn't shown up when she had…

He was lucky she had decided to throw his flowers back in his face since her arrival must have scared off whoever had attacked him. She was lucky that person hadn't attacked her as well. But clearly, he'd been the intended victim. Why? Because he was a Hotshot? Or because someone specifically wanted him dead?

While he'd briefly wondered if Courtney might have messed with his truck, he didn't believe she'd attacked him with the bat. For one, the flowers hadn't been in the house when he'd walked in, and for two…

He knew she wasn't capable of this violence. She was

too straightforward for these sneak attacks, and she was more sensitive and empathic than he'd realized, too. She was the one who'd comforted him the most after Dirk's death. She wasn't a bad person; he wouldn't have been so damn attracted to her if she was. Sure, she'd done some bad things when she'd skipped her mother's funeral and sued her sister. But Owen had made mistakes, too…so many mistakes.

One of those mistakes might have been the reason for Dirk's death. What had he missed that day?

What had he missed yesterday in his house? Or maybe the better question was whom.

Someone had messed with the water heater. The gas line to it had been twisted loose enough for the gas to leak out. Maybe the intruder had thought it would look like corrosion or normal wear and tear had damaged the line. But Owen had recently cleaned the entire house, so the metal shavings beneath the heater were fresh— probably from someone using vise grips or pliers to twist the line loose.

He shuddered as he thought about the gas smell filling his house. But today wasn't about him…unless he had been the intended target and not Dirk. Then this was *all* about him—it was all his fault.

He suspected he wasn't the only one who blamed him. Since the other day at the bar, most of his team had been keeping their distance from him—except for the new guy, who'd slid into the pew beside him during the church service.

And now he headed for him again, crossing the crowded living room of Louanne's home to join him. "How are you holding up?" Trick McRooney asked.

Owen hadn't slept in two days. Maybe because of what had happened, maybe because of what *hadn't* happened—

with Courtney. She'd messed with him—with his body and with his mind. Because now that he'd ruled her out as a suspect, he had no idea who was after him. That lack of sleep had frayed his patience, and he snapped back at McRooney, "Why the hell do you care?"

The guy was big—even bigger than Owen—so maybe he shouldn't have been so blunt. He already had more than enough bumps and bruises—on his body and his soul.

But Trick stepped back as if Owen was the threat. "Sorry," he said. "I didn't mean to bother you. Now I guess I understand why everybody else has been keeping their distance."

Owen flinched. The guy couldn't have hurt him more if he'd hit him. So it wasn't his imagination. The other team members had started avoiding him. Maybe they'd figured out, from Dirk's death, that it was dangerous to get too close to him.

Then one of the team spoke up from behind Trick. "We're keeping our distance out of respect," Henrietta "Hank" Rollins said. "Something you clearly know nothing about."

Hank was a tall woman, but she wasn't nearly as tall as the newcomer. He eclipsed her—with his height and his breadth. But she clearly wasn't intimidated. She didn't even step back when the guy whirled around to face her.

"I guess where I come from," he said, "I'm used to people actually showing that they give a damn."

Her golden complexion turned darker as her face flushed with embarrassment. "Maybe you should go back to where you came from, then."

"Hank."

The way their boss said her name had her bowing

her head like a little girl being chastised—when in reality she was a fearless firefighter. Her braid, thick and black like Serena's, swung over her shoulder.

"I understand that today is difficult," Braden said, "but let's all play nice."

Difficult didn't begin to describe it. But that had nothing to do with the new guy, except that his addition to the team made their loss even more pronounced. But that was their loss...

Dirk was the one who had lost everything. And from the way his widow sobbed on the couch, Louanne had lost everything as well.

Guilt gripped Owen as he stared at her. It should have been him—not Dirk. He didn't have a wife. His homecoming-queen girlfriend had dumped him when he was in boot camp. And since returning home from the Marines, not many other women had wanted to date him, with his scar and his dangerous profession. He didn't have anyone who cared about him but for his parents and his team. Well, his team *had* cared about him; he wasn't so sure now. None of them would even meet his eyes. But he had that strange sensation that someone was staring at him. He lifted his gaze and met Courtney's.

Maybe he shouldn't have been surprised that she was there, since everybody else in Northern Lakes had come to pay their respects. But Courtney Beaumont had never done what everyone else in Northern Lakes did. She'd never dressed or acted the way everyone else did. Even now, when everyone else was wearing black, she wore a deep burgundy dress in some clingy fabric that made her look more like a supermodel than a fashion designer.

Serena must have dragged her along. Maybe out of penance for missing their own mother's funeral. Why hadn't she come back for that? He wanted to ask her, wanted her to open up to him like he had to her.

But she looked at him like she wanted to drag him—behind her car down a very bumpy road. Was she angry over how he'd spoken to her the day before, or over how he'd spoken to her all those years ago?

Both were unforgivable. But he'd wanted her out of danger yesterday. Now he was the one in danger.

A hand wrapped around his arm, and he found himself being pulled aside. "You okay?" Braden asked him.

"No," he replied—honestly.

Braden lowered his voice to a whisper and asked, "Do you have a concussion? Any aftereffects from inhaling the gas?" While his boss was concerned, he obviously didn't want anyone else knowing about the latest incident.

That was why Owen had told only his boss about what had happened yesterday. Braden had insisted on him going to the hospital to get checked out, and he had. "I've been told I have a hard head." Too many times he'd been told that, but having that hard head had probably saved his life. Many times over. "And my lungs are strong and clear."

"Your conscience should be, too," Braden said, as if he'd read his mind.

Owen shrugged. "You don't know that. You don't know that wasn't supposed to be me in that casket today." And neither did he.

"It still could be you if you're not more careful," Braden warned him.

Owen snorted. "You put me on light duty, remember? I haven't been doing anything dangerous." He hadn't been doing anything at all but trying to stay alive.

Braden looked away from him, and Owen followed

his gaze across the room to Courtney Beaumont. No. He hadn't been doing her. But he couldn't deny that she was damn dangerous. She wasn't a danger to his life, though. She was a danger to his sanity. Just looking at her had tension gripping his body again, had his flesh heating and tingling.

Maybe the Marines hadn't cured him of his desire for danger. What would cure him of his desire for Courtney so he would stop obsessing over her? Having her? Sleeping with her? That was unlikely to happen after the way he'd spoken to her. But he'd only wanted to protect her from whoever was after him. Who was it?

"Just leave the investigating to the experts and concentrate on healing," Braden told him.

"I can't heal if I'm dead," Owen pointed out. Not that he wanted to add to the stress and guilt that bowed Braden's broad shoulders. It was killing the boss that he'd lost a member of his team. Owen had a bad feeling that Dirk wasn't going to be the only one lost and a worse feeling that he'd be next.

"You want him," Tammy said in Courtney's ear as she sidled up next to her.

Courtney glared at her friend. "Yeah, right…"

"You can't stop staring at him," Tammy said.

She wasn't wrong. Courtney had been watching Owen all through the funeral and during the luncheon afterward. He looked like hell and probably felt even worse. Right now he was trying to offer his condolences to the widow, but she jumped up and ran away from him, shrieking like a banshee. Maybe that was how some people grieved, but Courtney thought it was a bit extreme.

Maybe that was because Courtney hadn't really let

herself grieve her mother, though. That was partly why she hadn't returned for the funeral. Seeing her mother in a casket would have forced her to accept that she was really gone. Too young. Too soon. Too senselessly...

Just like this man's death. She felt a pang of guilt for judging Louanne. And for judging Owen.

He'd lost his friend and had nearly lost his own life over the past couple of days. And now the widow had lashed out at him...like Courtney had been lashing out at him. That pang of guilt became a hollow ache of deep remorse.

Tammy sighed and murmured, "Oh, poor Owen. That had to have hurt."

He looked like the woman had slapped him. He stood frozen for a long moment before moving toward the door. None of his team members stopped him.

Didn't they see how much he was hurting? How much he was blaming himself?

Instead of worrying about Owen, they were focused on the widow. Some of them followed her from the room.

"Damn," Tammy remarked, her brows lowered as she scowled. "Maybe the rumors about her and Luke are true..."

"Luke?" Courtney asked.

"One of the guys who rushed out after her," Tammy said. "He and his wife just split up, and everybody's been wondering why."

"Some things never change," Courtney murmured. "Everybody gossips about everyone else." She could only imagine the things that had been said about her.

Tammy nodded. "That's the nature of my business, you know. But it's probably just gossip. Louanne looks way too broken up to have been cheating."

Maybe she was so broken up because she felt guilty. That was probably why Courtney had been so angry with Owen. It was easier to blame him for her mother dying than to blame herself for not sticking around to help with the boardinghouse like Serena had. Maybe if she'd been here, too, their mother wouldn't have worked herself into an early grave.

"Now I need to give people something else to gossip about," Tammy said as she looked around the living room. "The new guy is damn good-looking." She flipped out her compact and checked her teeth for food, then murmured, "Let me find out if he's single…" Then she headed toward him, deserting Courtney.

She couldn't handle the funeral anymore. Despite growing up in Northern Lakes, she didn't know that many people in attendance. Only a handful of the Huron Hotshots were actually stationed in town during the off-season. Most of them were posted at other firehouses or US Forest Service outposts. At least, that was what Serena had told her.

She was surprised now that she remembered that. That she'd paid any attention. She'd been trying to be supportive of her sister even as she worried that getting involved with a firefighter was going to end up hurting Serena.

She couldn't deny that her twin was happy now, as she leaned against her fiancé and Cody kept an arm affectionately—or was it protectively—around her. She'd noticed a new watchfulness in her brother-in-law-to-be.

She'd heard the murmurs from the other team members talking about there being too many accidents lately. Did they know what Owen had been going through? Or were they talking about other incidents?

She would have asked Cody, but she figured he would think it was none of her business. And it wasn't. She shouldn't care. But she couldn't get the image of Owen's face from her mind—couldn't forget how devastated he'd looked when the widow had thrown his sympathy back at him. Something compelled her to head out the door through which he'd disappeared moments ago—compassion for him.

She found him just a short distance down the driveway. He was cursing and kicking at the tires on a car blocked in between some trucks.

"What did it do to you?" she asked.

He tensed and whirled around to face her. His face was flushed, his blue eyes wild.

And that wildness called to her, urging her to do something stupid. "My car is parked farther down the road," she said. And she'd made damn sure it wouldn't get blocked in for just this reason, in case she'd wanted to make a fast escape. "Need a ride?"

His breath shuddered out in a ragged sigh. But the tension didn't ease from him. If anything, he looked worse, as if he was about to break. Or as if he needed that tension and frustration to ease.

She did, too. It was stupid. But she grabbed for his hand and tugged him along with her—to her car. And once she'd parked in the alley behind her shop, she did the same thing, tugging him from the passenger seat, to the back door and then up the stairs to her apartment.

"What are you doing?" he asked—even as she reached for his tie and jerked it loose. Then she moved her hands down the buttons of his shirt, pulling them open. "You hate me."

"I know," she said. And she would probably hate

herself later. But at least she would have relieved the frustration building inside her.

"Then why?" he asked, his brow puckered with confusion. But his eyes were dilated now, and color had returned to his face with the flush of desire.

She shook her head. "I don't know. Maybe I was like everyone else all those years ago and wondered what it would be like to be with the homecoming king, the quarterback, the golden boy of Northern Lakes."

His lips curved into a slight grin. "Bullshit…"

She smiled, too. "Yeah, I hated you then, too."

He chuckled. And the sound lifted her heart. Just moments ago, he'd seemed so frustrated, so defeated.

While she'd never rooted for him like everyone else had, she hadn't wanted him to fail or falter either. And when she'd found him cursing in the driveway, he'd been faltering. And hurting…

She wanted to ease that pain for him, even if it was just for a little while.

As if he'd seen her intention, he tensed and caught her hands in his, stilling them. "This isn't out of pity or something, is it?"

She shrugged. "Do you care?"

A muscle twitched along his cheek. And she knew that he did—that it affected his pride. He didn't want her pity.

"Well, don't worry about it," she assured him. "This isn't about you."

He arched a golden brow. "It's not?" And he pressed her palms against the bare skin she'd exposed on his chest.

She shook her head. "It's about me. I make bad choices," she said. Suing Serena, moving back to Northern Lakes… men. She always made bad choices with men. Maybe she was more like her mother than she'd realized.

"And I'm a bad choice?" he asked.

"The worst," she said. "You don't like me any more than I like you."

"I don't hate you," he said.

She laughed at the ridiculous conversation they were having. "You sweet-talker, you."

His face flushed slightly. "I'm not…"

"So shut up," she advised him, and she covered his mouth with hers. As with all their kisses, the passion was so hot and overwhelming.

Instead of fighting it, this time Courtney savored it—the taste of the desire on his lips, his tongue…his mouth. She kissed him deeply.

He released her hands to move his over other parts of her body. He lifted the skirt of her burgundy dress and ran his hand along her thigh.

She shivered at the sensations racing through her. She throbbed with the need for release. She needed skin against skin. She stepped back—out of his arms—and he groaned in protest.

"Are you just teasing me?" he asked.

She lifted her dress over her head and let it drop to the floor. She wore only a burgundy silk bra and G-string beneath it.

He groaned again. "Showing me what I can't have?"

"Do you want it?" she asked. "Do you want me?"

He must have heard the vulnerability she'd inadvertently let slip into her voice. And he reached out. But instead of touching her body, he touched her face, sliding his fingertips along her jaw. "More than anything… more than anyone. I'm sorry for what I said yesterday at my house. I was just… I was lying. I do want you. I want you so damn much…"

Her breath shuddered out in relief. Maybe she wasn't making as big a mistake as she'd feared.

He leaned down and kissed her again, but there was tenderness now along with the passion. It was nearly her undoing.

Then he undid the clasp of her bra and the silk dropped away from her body. A chill raced through her. She was nearly fully exposed, and only his shirt was unbuttoned. She reached out and pushed his shirt and jacket from his broad shoulders. As they fell away from his body, she gasped.

"You should see the other guy," he murmured.

The scar on his face wasn't the only one. He had a few crisscrossing his chest and shoulders. And now, when the bandage was removed, he'd probably have another one on his arm as well.

"Guy?" she asked.

"IED," he said with a shrug. "There was nothing left of him."

Thinking of the danger he'd faced, the pain he'd endured, had tears stinging her eyes. She hated to think of him that way, hurting, like he'd been hurting back at the funeral.

"No," he said. "You promised me this wasn't pity."

She shook her head. "No. Just a bad choice." A very bad choice, because now she wanted him even more than she had. And she hadn't even had him yet.

She leaned forward and pressed her lips to a scar on his chest. And she could feel his heart beat beneath her mouth. "Not pity," she assured him. "Disgust."

He sucked in a breath.

"That everybody might be right about you after all," she murmured. He really was the town hero. "I'd rather keep thinking that you're a jerk."

"Oh, I am," he assured her. But he was grinning.

And she knew for a fact that real jerks, like Bradford, were never self-aware enough to admit to their failings. Owen might be her failing. She was trembling with the need coursing through her.

He leaned down and kissed her shoulder, then the side of her neck, before moving his lips lower. He kissed her breasts before pulling one of her nipples into his mouth. He lapped his tongue across the sensitive point, and she cried out with pleasure.

His hands moved down her body, over her butt and then between her legs—legs that shook with desire. As if worried she might fall, he lifted and carried her to the bed. Before he joined her on it, he unbuckled his belt and lowered his pants. There were some scars on his thighs, too, and one across his left knee.

But like the one on his cheek, the scars only added to his sexiness. With his sculpted muscles and those scars, he had the body of a warrior—strong and resilient.

And like a warrior, he conquered her—with kisses. Their mouths mated, and she arched up, rubbing her body against his, wanting him inside her—filling that hollowness she'd had for so long. But he took his time with her, kissing her everywhere, touching her everywhere. She writhed against the bed and moaned as pleasure flooded her. She came, but it wasn't enough. She was still achy, still needy.

And so was he. His body so tense that cords stood out on his neck and his temples. He strained with the effort for control. So she kissed and touched him until his control snapped.

He had enough willpower to pull away from her and find a condom, which he rolled over his erection with a shaking hand. Then he parted her legs and joined their bodies. Just as she'd thought, he filled her—and then some. He felt so damn good inside her, moving, thrusting...

She clung to him, arching up to meet his thrusts. They moved together frantically—each desperate for release as the tension built. Finally it broke, her body shuddering with a powerful release.

Then his body shuddered, too, as he came, groaning and uttering her name. She melted into the mattress, satiated and staggered by the force of her release. He didn't collapse on top of her. Instead he climbed out of the bed. But moments later he was back.

She didn't want to open her eyes, didn't want to see if he was gloating. She just wanted him to leave while her body burned with embarrassment over what she'd done, over how she'd almost literally dragged him home with her.

But the mattress dipped as he joined her, rolling her into his arms—against his chest. He held her.

And the enormity of what she'd done hit her. She had made a very bad choice.

"Where the hell did he go?" Braden wondered as he noticed Owen's car parked among the few left in Dirk Brown's long driveway.

"He's not at his house," Trick said as he walked up from the truck he'd just parked. "I just came from there."

Braden bristled. He hated that Trick suspected every damn member of his team. It was like someone calling all his babies ugly. And it made him want to strike his brother-in-law. "Did you find the evidence you were looking for?"

Trick nodded. "Yup."

Treat Yourself with 2 Free Books!

GET UP TO 4 FREE BOOKS & 2 FREE GIFTS WORTH OVER $20

See Inside For Details

Treat Yourself to Free Books and Free Gifts.

Answer 4 fun questions and get rewarded.

▼ **DETACH AND MAIL CARD TODAY!**

	YES	NO
1. I LOVE reading a good book.	○	○
2. I indulge and "treat" myself often.	○	○
3. I love getting FREE things.	○	○
4. Reading is one of my favorite activities.	○	○

TREAT YOURSELF • Pick your 2 Free Books...

Yes! Please send me my Free Books from each series I select and Free Mystery Gifts. I understand that I am under no obligation to buy anything, as explained on the back of this card.

Which do you prefer?

❏ **Harlequin® Romantic Suspense** 240/340 HDL GRCZ
❏ **Harlequin Intrigue® Larger-Print** 199/399 HDL GRCZ
❏ **Try Both** 240/340 & 199/399 HDL GRDD

FIRST NAME   LAST NAME

ADDRESS

APT.#   CITY

STATE/PROV.   ZIP/POSTAL CODE

EMAIL ❏ Please check this box if you would like to receive newsletters and promotional emails from Harlequin Enterprises ULC and its affiliates. You can unsubscribe anytime.

HI/HRS-520-TY22

And Braden sucked in a breath. Owen was the last person he would have suspected. "Oh, no…"

"You were right," Trick said.

And Braden was confused.

"Someone messed with the brake line on his truck and the gas line on his water heater," Trick said. "Owen is in a lot of danger."

"You don't think he did those things himself? You don't suspect him of Dirk's murder anymore?" Braden prodded. He wanted to hear the guy admit he'd been wrong.

Trick shrugged as if it was no big deal. "I was just speculating. And remember, I'm not an investigator like Sam. I'm a Hotshot—just like all of you."

"If you weren't, the rest of the team would never have accepted you," Braden said. That was why Trick was the best man for this job—to infiltrate his team and help Braden figure out who was after them.

But the man laughed. "And you think they're ever going to accept me now?"

"They just have to get over losing Dirk," he said. God knew they all did.

Trick sighed. "They're not going to get over losing him."

That was what Braden was afraid of…and that was why he couldn't lose anyone else. "So, after looking at his brake line and that gas line to his water heater, you agree that Owen is not a suspect?"

Trick nodded. "And if that wasn't enough proof, I managed to distract a nurse long enough that I got a look at his medical records at the hospital, too."

He didn't have to ask how Trick had distracted the nurse. Sam had warned him that her brother was quite the charmer. It didn't look as though he'd charmed Hank earlier, though.

"He couldn't have hit himself in the back of the head like that," Trick said. "And he was lucky that cable didn't take off his arm."

Braden flinched. Owen had certainly downplayed the severity of his injuries. He looked around the driveway. Where the hell could he have gone?

Had the concussion confused him and he'd wandered off? Or had someone taken him?

Urgency coursed through Braden. "We've got to find him."

"He wasn't at his place," Trick repeated. "I just came from there."

"We'll check out the Filling Station, then." Braden headed toward his truck.

"Filling Station?"

"Local bar in town," Braden explained. "I'm not sure where else he might have gone."

"He was checking out a little brunette inside the house," Trick said with a glance toward Dirk's place. Only a few people had stayed behind—probably to make sure Louanne would be okay. She'd been so upset during the funeral and luncheon, especially with Owen.

No wonder he'd left. But his vehicle was still in the driveway.

"What brunette?" Braden asked. But he was afraid that he knew.

"There were two of them in there with identical faces. One had long hair. It was the one with the short hair. She walked out just a little while after he did."

Braden cursed.

"What?"

"She's the one he suspects of being behind these accidents," Braden admitted.

Trick cursed, too. "Then we better hurry up and find him. He could be in serious trouble."

Chapter 14

He was in serious trouble.

Owen stared down at the woman sleeping in his arms, and something tightened in his chest. Maybe it was just panic. Or maybe it was something else—which would be a cause for panic anyway.

Courtney's head lay on his chest. She murmured in her sleep and shifted against him. And that panic increased, as did the pounding of his heart.

He ran his hand down her bare back in a soothing caress. But he needed to soothe himself as well. He'd already decided she wasn't responsible for the things that had happened to him and to Dirk. But that meant he had no reason not to fall for her—and falling for her would put him in nearly as much danger emotionally as he already was physically. Women either wanted nothing to do with him because of his scars, or they were just with him out of pity over what he'd been through.

He hadn't felt like anyone had ever really loved him because nobody had ever really known him. He kept so much locked up inside him about his deployments and his scars. Except with Courtney; somehow she had found the key to making him talk about things that he hadn't talked about with anyone else.

But she was leaving. He'd already overheard her saying that she couldn't stay in Northern Lakes, just like she'd always said in high school. While he loved his hometown, she hadn't been able to wait to leave it. She was a fashion designer, and he was a firefighter. They had nothing in common. And he had nothing to offer her to keep her here. Was she going back to her apartment in New York or a guy she'd left there?

He wanted to ask, but she was asleep. And she probably wouldn't have answered him anyway. He doubted she was over how he'd talked to her the day before. He couldn't believe she'd given him a ride from the funeral, that she'd brought him back to her place. That she'd...

Done so much more to him and with him.

His body hardened thinking about what they'd done, about the pleasure she'd given him. He hadn't felt anything that intense in...

Forever?

He'd had a couple of serious crushes, but he realized now that he'd never been in love, not the kind of love Cody and Serena shared or Braden and Sam. His first serious girlfriend had been his high school sweetheart. Except that she hadn't been that sweet...

She had probably been what Courtney would have called a mean girl. A popular cheerleader who'd looked down her nose at everyone else—including him when he'd dropped out of college to join the Marines.

She'd dumped him then. And since he'd been relieved rather than heartbroken, he'd realized that hadn't really been love. Then there was the younger sister of a guy from his unit. She'd written to him professing her love...until her brother hadn't made it back from their first deployment and Owen had.

Then she'd hated him...just like he'd thought Courtney hated him. But if she really did, why would she have kissed him, undressed him, touched him...driven him out of his mind and body with pleasure?

Tension tightened his groin. He wanted her again. Still...even after that mind-boggling orgasm. She was incredible. Her body, her touch...her kiss...

But instead of sleeping with her, he was supposed to be figuring out who was trying to kill him. Maybe Braden was right. Maybe he had no business looking into these accidents himself. Maybe he should leave it to whomever Braden had found.

His brother-in-law?

No. The guy was a Hotshot without a home. Hell, maybe he was the one behind the accidents, trying to make an opening on Braden's team. Was that what this was about?

The arsonist who had terrorized Northern Lakes had done so because he'd applied for a position and hadn't been hired. So he'd tried to make another position available for himself. Could that be the same case here?

And look who had taken that position...without an interview, probably without even applying for it? He'd known it was his because of nepotism. All Trick McRooney had needed was the opening...

Dirk's death had given him that, so why try to kill Owen, too? Had he seen something that he hadn't realized he'd seen that day at the job site? Had he missed a clue? Or had it been the smell? That burning metal smell...

A chill passed through him as he considered it. He'd gone over and over that day in his mind, and while he'd noticed the smell, he hadn't seen anyone else hanging around who shouldn't have been there. Nothing had seemed amiss, nothing out of place but his own head. He'd been distracted—because he'd been thinking about Courtney.

Since her return to Northern Lakes, she was all he thought about, which was foolish. He knew how little they had in common, how little they had to build upon for a future. They had no future together. And if he was so distracted by her that the killer succeeded next time, he wouldn't have a future at all. Panicked at the thought of someone trying to kill him, he scrambled now—out of the bed and out of danger of falling for Courtney.

Too bad she wasn't the one trying to kill him. Then he wouldn't make the mistake of falling for her. And it would be a mistake that would only cause him pain when she left.

He grabbed up his clothes from the floor and made his way toward the stairs, stopping every time a board creaked beneath his weight. He didn't want to wake her up because he knew that she would just distract him again and he would stay. His being here might have put her in danger like he'd put Dirk in danger. So he did the same thing on the steps, testing each one before descending to the next, quietly moving down until finally he stood on the main level. He was a little woozy from the concussion, so to steady himself while getting dressed, he leaned against that case she'd been working on. As he did, he bumped up against an open toolbox, overflowing with screwdrivers, pliers, vise grips and hammers, and a screwdriver rolled over the side and fell to the floor. He held his breath for a moment, listening for any movement above him, but she must not have heard it. When he dropped the screwdriver back in the box, he noticed a pair of pliers. Something like that had been used to loosen the gas line to his water heater.

Who could have done that? Who wanted him dead?

He had that sudden sensation again—of being watched. The front of the store was all windows that looked onto the street. And it seemed as though Courtney usually left the doors open or at least unlocked. While she'd lived in New York City for a while, she hadn't lost her small-town trusting ways. How had she survived all those years in the big city?

Or maybe she was just fearless. He'd always respected that she'd gone her own way in school instead of trying to fit in by dressing and acting like everyone else. He couldn't wait to see what fashions she brought to their small town. But would the town give her store a chance?

Would they give Courtney a chance? Everybody thought so highly of her twin that they weren't likely to forgive her for hurting Serena. And even if they did, he doubted she would stay. She was too stubborn to change her mind about leaving. Or about him…

She still considered him a jerk. A bad choice.

He couldn't help but think he'd made a bad choice, too—not in sleeping with her but in leaving her sleeping alone. He never should have left her bed—because he had a feeling he would never get invited back into it.

He suddenly realized why he had that feeling he was being watched when he heard the floorboards creak behind him. With a sense of déjà vu, he whirled around to find Courtney standing behind him with a bat in her hands.

Owen James had been difficult to track down. But, fortunately, other people had been looking for him, too. So following them had led to him.

But that made it difficult to act. Staging an accident now would not be easy. There would be too many witnesses. Everybody could see inside the storefront with all its windows looking onto Main Street. There was no way to make his death look accidental now.

It would have to be murder.

But that didn't mean that his murder would ever get solved. It wasn't as if anyone would ever figure out why Owen had to die. So if they didn't figure out the motive, they weren't likely to find the right suspect.

Not that there would be many suspects…

Most of the town loved Owen.

Except for Courtney Beaumont.

Why the hell had she brought him back to her place? What the hell had she been thinking? Or hadn't she been thinking at all?

She was sometimes like that—impulsive, like opening this store in Northern Lakes. Like anyone in this town would appreciate her sense of fashion. They never had before. She would have been smart to go back to New York. Now it was too late.

Bad things were about to happen, and she was right in the middle of it all.

Moments ago, Courtney had awakened alone in bed. She hadn't been surprised that Owen had sneaked out while she'd been sleeping. In fact, she'd been almost relieved that he had, because then she hadn't had to face him again. She hadn't had to face the mistake she'd made in bringing him back to her place.

But had it been a mistake?

It had been so hot, so passionate, so powerful...

She shivered.

Yes, it had definitely been a mistake. One she didn't dare repeat. Her body reacted to that thought, tension building inside her. She wanted him again.

But just physically...

Emotionally she couldn't trust anyone. Men either abandoned her, like her father had, or they smothered her, like her last boyfriend, who'd tried to control every aspect of her life.

Thinking of Bradford chilled her. And that was when she'd heard the noise downstairs. The quickest thing to grab was the dress she'd worn for the funeral, so she pulled that on. Then she reached for the weapon her landlord had given her when she'd asked for a security system for the building.

A baseball bat was security in Northern Lakes. After she slipped quietly down the back stairs, she gripped the bat in both hands and raised it over the shadow looming in the middle of the store.

He lifted his hands, palms up, and implored her, "Don't swing, slugger. It's just me."

Instead of slowing down, her heart rate sped up, and her skin heated up. She'd thought he'd left.

But he was still here.

Why?

"What the hell are you doing?" she asked, and she had yet to lower the bat.

"I didn't think you wanted me to stay the night..."

Heat rushed to her face with embarrassment that she had actually wanted him to stay, to hold her.

And this was why making love with him had been a mistake. She couldn't get used to this, to him being here. Had he just been waiting for her to fall asleep to make his escape, to do his walk of shame for sleeping with the town pariah? He had no vehicle in which to escape.

"Or were you looking for my car keys?" she asked.

"Car keys?" he repeated, and despite the fading light, she could see his brow furrowing. "You think I'm trying to steal your car?"

She shook her head. "Just borrow it," she said, "so you can get out of here."

He stood up then and walked toward her. "What makes you think I want to leave?" he asked, his voice going all deep and sexy.

She shivered and tightened her grip on her bat. "I don't really care what you want," she said, but it was a lie. She cared. She wanted him to want her. Now that they were grown up and she realized he wasn't the jerk he'd been back in high school. He'd been through a lot since then—as a Marine and as a Hotshot.

But maybe she had wanted him back in high school, too, even when he'd been such a jerk to her. She'd been teasing him earlier when she'd said she'd been like everybody else back then, wondering what it would be like to be with the homecoming king. Despite herself and despite how much he'd annoyed her back then, she had wondered.

And now she knew—that her girlhood fantasies hadn't even come close to the staggering reality. But had it been reality? Or just an escape from it?

She wasn't going to actually stay in Northern Lakes.

And despite his stint in the Marine Corps, he was never going to leave.

That had been the problem with her parents, or so her father had claimed when she'd tracked him down after she'd left Northern Lakes. Her mother would have never left the boardinghouse, and her nomadic father hadn't been able to stay in one place. They hadn't been able to make it work, and they'd actually loved each other. So her father had claimed.

Now, she and Owen…

She wasn't sure what he felt for her. And for so long she'd hated and resented him. But as vulnerable as she'd seen him over the past few days, she was having a hard time holding on to that resentment. In seeing how unfairly Louanne Brown had treated him, she'd realized she had probably been unfair to him, too.

He stepped closer to her, so close that she could feel the heat of his body even through his clothes. He'd dressed, too. Obviously he'd intended to sneak out while she was sleeping, so that they wouldn't have to discuss what had happened.

Feeling like such a fool for wanting him to stay, for bringing him here in the first place, she said, "You were right. I really don't want you to stay. In fact, I want you to leave right now." Before she gave in to desire again…

"I'd take the lady at her word," a deep voice commented from behind her.

Before Courtney could whirl around to confront the intruder, Owen reacted. He grabbed the bat from her hands and stepped in front of her, between her and whoever had broken into her store. If the intruder had a gun, he was going to take the bullet for her. He might very well die right in front of her.

Damn it!

He really was the hero the entire town had always thought he was. She was the one who'd been wrong. And she might be about to find out exactly how wrong she'd been.

Chapter 15

Northern Lakes wasn't a place where a person could leave their doors unlocked anymore. After someone tampered with his water heater, Owen should have known that. He should have checked to make sure the back door was locked before he'd gone upstairs with Courtney.

But he'd been so shocked that she'd brought him back to her place that he'd been in a daze...of desire. He'd needed her so badly then that he hadn't thought of anything else, which was crazy with his life in danger as much as it had been over the past few days.

He didn't actually fear the guy who'd walked in without knocking. He'd recognized his voice even before the man had flipped on the lights. Braden wasn't going to hurt either of them.

But Owen was still stunned by his sudden appearance. "What are you doing here?"

"Saving you from getting knocked out again, apparently," Braden replied, and he gestured at the bat Owen had taken from Courtney.

"She wasn't going to hit me," he said. She wasn't behind the attempts on his life.

"Don't be so sure," Courtney murmured from behind him.

He'd never been sure of himself with her. Not when they were teenagers. Not now. Not ever...

"That's why I walked in without knocking," Braden explained—to Courtney. "I wasn't sure what was going on here..."

She moved around him, into the light, and he saw her face had flushed a bright pink. "Nothing," she said—quickly and defensively. "Nothing's going on here."

Had she thought Owen was going to brag about his conquest? He hadn't even done that in high school. He wasn't about to do it now. Not that she had been a conquest—more like a conqueror.

"What are you really doing here?" Owen asked again.

"Looking for you," Braden replied matter-of-factly.

"Has something happened?" Owen asked. Another accident?

Braden looked between them, from one to the other, still obviously suspicious of the scene he'd walked in on. "You'd have to answer that..."

And Owen wasn't going to do that.

His boss must have sensed as much, because he continued, "We all noticed you'd left your car at Dirk's house—with the keys in the ignition." He held up the ring, and the overhead light glinted off the metal.

He'd been a little preoccupied at the time—with the way Louanne had reacted to his condolences, and with Courtney.

"I'm fine," Owen lied. He wasn't fine. After that sexual encounter with her, he was shaken.

But he wasn't scared for his life—just his heart. From the way Braden was staring at her, he clearly had suspicions about her now. If they stayed much longer, Courtney was going to pick up on those suspicions, and then Owen would have to explain that he'd planted those doubts when he'd first wondered if she could be responsible.

"I could use a ride back to my car," Owen said.

"I'm sure Ms. Beaumont wouldn't have made you walk," Braden mused. He seemed to be baiting her.

She took it when she replied, "I'm sure a walk wouldn't hurt him."

Owen could have argued with her. He'd so often gone out on emergency calls to help pedestrians who'd been struck along the road.

"But you seem to think *I* was going to hurt him," she continued, and now she narrowed her eyes in the same way Braden was looking at her—with suspicion.

"You were brandishing a bat when I walked up," Braden reminded her.

Her face reddened again. But then she must have remembered why she'd grabbed the bat. And she held out her hand to Owen.

He handed back the bat, which she took and leaned against the display case. She definitely hadn't been planning to use it on him. As much as she resented him, she still kept reaching out to him when he was down. She'd done that even more than his team had, so she was more like Serena—kinder and more sympathetic—than she seemed to want people to know.

"Goodbye, gentlemen," she said. And although she was

much smaller than both of them, she shifted them—with the sheer force of her coldness—toward the front door.

The minute they stepped outside, she locked it behind them. Owen could see her through the glass, though—even after she shut off the lights. She headed up the stairs to her apartment, and his body ached with desire to follow her back to her bedroom.

"What the hell were you thinking?" Braden asked him. "Why would you go anywhere with her if you suspect—"

"Shh," he interjected. "Not here."

Braden nodded. "Right, you don't want her to overhear and know that she's a suspect."

Owen tensed with indignation. Braden considered her one? While Owen had initially considered her a suspect, he'd quickly ruled her out. But a pang of guilt struck him for thinking her capable of such crimes, just like he'd thought the worst of her in high school, too. He *was* the jerk she thought he was.

Braden touched his arm, and he jumped, startled at the sudden contact as much as the pain over his boss inadvertently touching his wound. "You okay?" his boss asked. "She didn't…"

"I'm fine," Owen assured him. He wasn't fine, though—he was consumed with guilt and desire. He also had that weird feeling again that he was being observed. Yet when he glanced around he didn't see anyone staring at him. He didn't see anything but his car parked on the street and Braden's truck behind it. "How'd you get my car here?" he asked.

And how had his boss been so damn sure that he'd left with Courtney? Someone must have seen them. Maybe that feeling he was being watched wasn't just paranoia.

"Trick," Braden replied.

And he glanced over to see the big man was now sitting in the passenger seat of Braden's truck. Just how well did Braden know his brother-in-law? It wasn't as if he and Sam had been married all that long. Just a couple of months and, hell, Sam wasn't even around that much. Braden's wife was based out of Washington, DC, and was sent all around the country to investigate arson fires.

Theirs wasn't the only long-distance relationship among the Hotshots. Dawson Hess, one of the two assistant superintendents, was married to a reporter who worked in New York City. If Courtney moved back there, a relationship wasn't necessarily out of the question... if she was interested in one with him. If she could forgive him for being such a jerk to her and for not saving her mother.

His heart grew heavy with that burden...and with his acceptance that it was a lot to forgive. Maybe too much...

"Let's talk in the morning," Braden said.

Owen tensed. "Where?" he asked.

"I'll be up in the conference room," Braden replied.

He only held meetings there when there was more than a couple of people attending it. Who the hell else was going to be at this meeting? He had no intention of talking about Courtney, or anything else, in front of the new guy. Most especially not Courtney...

Owen nodded in agreement but added the caveat, "Just you and me."

"No," Braden replied as he opened the door to his pickup truck. "Dawson and Wyatt and Cody will all be there as well."

He waited until the pickup backed out of the alley

before he released a sigh of relief. Good. He'd be meeting with the people he trusted most.

He glanced up at the second story of Courtney's building. A light glowed behind the blinds. She was up there, and he wished like hell that he was with her. He never should have left her bed. Never should have left her...

"I don't trust him," Courtney said as she settled into a chair in Tammy's salon. It hadn't opened for customers yet, so she, Tammy and Serena were the only ones in the place. She could speak freely if she wanted to. She wasn't sure how much she wanted to reveal about the night before, though.

"So you didn't sleep with him?" Tammy asked with a little puff of disappointment.

Heat climbed to Courtney's face, and she glanced down at her fingernails. She needed a manicure badly. But until she was done working on the store, it would be a waste of money and time.

Serena laughed. "You know there's no way she would sleep with Owen."

And the heat got hotter.

Tammy laughed now. "I think there is a way. Too much wine?"

She wished she'd had that excuse. She wasn't even sure what had compelled her to bring him home...except the way he'd looked so stricken when the widow had started screaming at him. She knew the woman had had a horrible loss, but after the way she'd treated a man who was probably mourning nearly as much as she was, Courtney didn't feel much sympathy for her. Of course, she wasn't as empathetic a person as Serena was...except with Owen.

She'd empathized with him. Too much...

"You did?" Serena asked, her dark eyes wide with shock. "I thought you hated him."

"I do," Courtney said. Especially after she'd caught him sneaking out the minute she'd fallen asleep, as if he was ashamed of being with her.

"Then..." Serena trailed off.

Tammy laughed and spoke to Courtney as if her twin wasn't in the room with them. "Your sister is so naive. She doesn't know that sometimes it's hotter that way..."

Courtney had known Tammy a long time. She was probably more naive than Serena was. Her provocative act was just that—an act. Yet she might have been right about this...if Courtney actually felt like she hated Owen anymore. Seeing him struggling with his pain and guilt over the loss of his friend had her regretting how she'd treated him after her mother's death.

Had she been as unreasonable as Dirk Brown's widow?

She dropped to her knees in front of her sister, who was sitting in one of the chairs under the dryers. The dryer was up, and she grabbed Serena's hands and looked her in the eyes. "I want to ask you a serious question."

"Are you proposing?" Serena teased. "Because I'm already engaged."

Courtney laughed but shook her head. Cody, and his irreverent sense of humor, had rubbed off on her sister and maybe on some of his coworkers as well. Owen seemed to have that same sardonic sense of humor.

Serena squeezed her hands. "I'm sorry. What do you want to ask me?"

"Do you think Owen could have done anything differently to save Mom?"

Serena didn't even hesitate before replying with an adamant "No."

"But what if he'd arrived at the boardinghouse faster or had gotten the defibrillator hooked up to her sooner?" she asked. She knew that just seconds might have made a difference between life and death.

"You—apparently, better than anyone—know how fast Owen moves," Serena said with a smile. "You know that he moved as fast as he possibly could." Her face turned earnest now. "You know that he did everything he possibly could to save her. She was already gone when he and Dawson got there. She was dead. They couldn't have brought her back. Nobody could." She cocked her head and studied Courtney's face. "Why have you never blamed Dawson for her dying? Why has it always been just Owen?"

Her face burned, and she tried to pull away from Serena. But her twin was strong and held tightly on to her. "Why, Courtney?"

"Because she's always had a thing for him," Tammy answered for her. "How didn't you know that?"

Serena looked from Tammy back to Courtney. "Because you two were always closer than we were."

And for the first time ever, Courtney heard resentment in Serena's voice. She hadn't resented giving up nursing college to help with the boardinghouse. But she'd resented Courtney's closeness to Tammy?

Tammy must have heard it, too, because she dropped down onto the floor next to Courtney. She slung an arm around her shoulders and bumped her head against Courtney's. "That's because the two of us were the misfits in this town," she told her. "And you weren't…"

"You two weren't misfits." Serena rushed quickly to their defense.

"She dressed like a vampiress, and I looked like a whale," Tammy reminded her. "And you…"

"You were perfect," Courtney said, but for the first time in a long time—maybe ever—she didn't resent that. She didn't resent her sister. "You still are."

Serena's face flushed now. "Am not."

"Are too," Courtney argued. "And I am creating the most perfect wedding dress for you."

The smile returned to Serena's face. "When can I see it?"

"Soon," Courtney promised. She needed to get it finished. "That way if you don't like it, you'll still have time to find something else before the wedding."

Serena squeezed her hands again. "I'll love it."

Tammy shook her head. "Remember how she used to dress? Do you want to look like Dracula on your wedding day?"

Instead of being offended, Courtney laughed. "I promise I made it to your taste. Not mine."

"You'll save the black lace for your own wedding dress?" Tammy teased.

Courtney shuddered. "Not going to be a wedding dress or a wedding for me."

Serena smiled. "Are you sure about that?"

She answered as vehemently as her twin had replied to her question. "Yes!"

Serena's brow puckered. "I hope this isn't because of that sleazy ex-boyfriend of yours."

"The lawyer?" Tammy asked.

Serena shuddered now. "Yes. He emailed me recently."

Courtney tensed. "He did? Why? What did he want?"

"He claimed that he wanted to apologize," Serena

said. "But I could tell he was only doing it so I would tell you that he had."

And she hadn't. "Bradford has an agenda behind his every action," Courtney agreed. Even giving her flowers…

That was why she'd wondered what Owen's agenda had been. Had he just been thanking her and offering a long-overdue apology for the past like he'd claimed?

Somehow she doubted that.

What the hell was actually going on with him?

"What the hell is going on with you?" Braden asked. He still wasn't sure what he'd walked in on the night before between Owen and Courtney.

Owen sighed and shook his head. With dark circles beneath his eyes, he looked like hell—like he hadn't slept for weeks. "I wish I knew…" he murmured.

Both Dawson and Wyatt cast a worried glance at him before turning toward Braden. They were all sitting around the conference table while Owen paced before the windows that looked down onto the main street of Northern Lakes. As exhausted as he appeared, he was also restless.

Or nervous…

"I told you not to try to investigate on your own," Braden said. And that was clearly what he'd been doing. But was it all he'd been doing?

Both Owen and Courtney had been dressed when he'd seen them, but there was an awareness between them that Braden hadn't noticed before…but that he recognized. He and Sam still had that awareness, that intense chemistry…

Braden was a lucky man—personally. Now he needed that luck to extend to his professional life as well. He needed to find whoever was sabotaging their equipment before he lost another team member. Before he lost Owen...

"And why are you so sure Courtney is responsible?" Cody asked, probably in defense of his future sister-in-law.

Owen snorted. "You suspected her, too."

Cody looked down at the conference table, as if trying to hide the suspicion in his eyes. But Braden had seen it.

Owen shook his head and sighed before admitting, "I don't suspect her anymore."

Cody's eyes narrowed as if he was now doubtful of his friend's about-face. Braden was wary, too, especially after he'd found them like he had the night before.

Then he remembered what he and Trick had discussed the night before, and he wondered if Owen was right. He asked him, "What if someone's trying to hurt you because of something else?"

Owen stopped pacing and turned to face him. "What else?"

"Maybe something you heard or saw that morning at the site," Braden said.

Owen shook his head. "I didn't see or hear anything out of the ordinary. I had no clue..." His broad shoulders drooped with the heavy burden of his guilt.

Braden hated that the paramedic was blaming himself for a problem that, as superintendent, Braden should have handled long ago. But the arsons around town had been happening at the same time as the little acts of sabotage to his team, so he'd thought that one person was responsible for everything. Then those little acts had continued after Matt's arrest, supporting his claims of not being responsible for taking out the brakes on Cody's vehicles and other things, like that note…

Braden hadn't been able to figure out who the damn note had been referring to, who wasn't really whom he thought they were…

What the hell did that even mean?

He had no idea. And, apparently, Owen had no idea about what had happened the morning Dirk died. "Go home," he advised him. "Get some sleep…"

Owen must have been as exhausted as he looked, because he didn't argue. He just headed toward the doors without so much as a goodbye to any of them. Just a few minutes after he walked away, Braden wondered if he'd done the right thing. Maybe it was safer to keep Owen where he could see him, where he could protect him.

He jumped up from the conference table, but it was too late to catch Owen on the stairs. So he headed to the windows Owen had been pacing in front of moments ago.

"What's wrong?" Dawson asked. "Did you forget something?"

Cody cursed. "He forgot that we need to keep an eye on Owen."

There were eyes on Owen other than his. One pair was Trick's. While he'd pointed out that he was not an investigator, he was observant enough to have thought of something Braden hadn't. He was also observant enough to watch out for Owen. But his weren't the only pair of eyes on the paramedic.

Whoever wanted him dead had to be watching him, too, to know when to mess with his brake line and then with his gas line. Braden opened the window to call down to Owen, to call him back into the firehouse.

No killer would be able to hurt him if they all watched over him.

Finally the paramedic appeared within sight, striding out the open doors of the garage bays. As he headed across the street to where he'd parked his car, Braden called out, "Owen!"

But Owen didn't glance up. He probably didn't hear Braden over the roar of the engine as a car barreled down the street toward him. It didn't slow down. Instead the engine revved louder, and the tires squealed against the asphalt as it sped up and bore down on him.

"Owen!" Braden shouted.

But he knew there was nothing he could do—no way he could warn Owen in time to save him.

Chapter 16

Could anybody save him...from himself? He shouldn't be here. Owen knew that, yet he found himself at Courtney's store again. As usual, her back door was unlocked. He knocked and called out to her, but after waiting long moments, nobody came toward the door. He pushed it open and looked around the main floor. She'd finished the display case with a whitewash stain that matched the beadboard ceiling and wainscoting.

She was far handier than he'd thought. But then, before she'd left Northern Lakes, she'd probably helped with the boardinghouse Ms. Beaumont had run. She'd hated it, though, just like she'd hated Northern Lakes so much she'd sworn that once she left, she was never coming back.

Why had she? Was she only trying to make amends with her sister? Or to expand her business with the store?

He'd initially thought it had been to make his life miserable, like she probably considered he'd made hers miserable back in high school. Now his need for her was the thing making him miserable, in a different kind of way. He couldn't seem to keep himself from her, especially when something bad happened.

All he'd seen as he left the fire station was a blur of black. Someone had tried to run him down, and he'd jumped behind the postal drop boxes. Fortunately, the driver must not have wanted to risk the metal boxes wrecking the vehicle, because they hadn't swerved onto the sidewalk. The car had continued down the street. Owen hadn't had time to roll over and get the plate before it had disappeared from sight.

And Braden, watching from the third floor, had seen only the roof of the vehicle, not the license plate or the driver. He hadn't even been certain what make and model it was. Once again Owen had had a near miss with no clues leading back to who was after him. Or why...

He hadn't seen or heard anything the morning Dirk died but his friend in agony...and all he'd felt then was guilt and loss. Until Courtney Beaumont—of all people— had eased his pain. The only comfort he'd found from his guilt and his fear was with her. Maybe that was why he'd come here after what had just happened. Or maybe there was another reason he was so drawn to her...

Was she even here?

"Courtney?" he called out again, and he pressed his hand to the hollow ache in his chest. He needed her. Had she already left? Had something happened to her?

The main level was empty but for him. Then he heard a strange, mechanical humming sound above his head.

The ceiling seemed to vibrate with it. He headed for the stairs.

He passed through the tiny kitchen down the hall that led him to her bedroom. But that was empty. The humming sound emanated from the room next to it, and he found her leaning over a table, running a sewing machine—a mound of white lace and silky-looking material pooling around it.

Her head was down and she had earbuds in, which must have been why she hadn't heard him calling out to her.

So he walked closer and touched that mound of material. And she glanced up and then jumped and pulled out her earbuds. "What the hell! Don't sneak up on me like that!"

"You didn't have a bat in your hands, so I figured it was safe," he replied.

"For whom?" she asked as she stared at him.

He snorted. "You're not afraid of me." He doubted there was very much that ever scared her. "You're not afraid of anything. You took off on your own for the big city after high school, just like you always said you were going to do. And you accomplished everything you said you were going to do."

She shrugged as if her success didn't matter to her. But he knew that she must have worked hard to have achieved so much at such a young age; her designs had been picked up by some major retail stores. Serena often bragged about her twin.

He touched the white lace. "This seems a departure for you, though. From all the black lace and leather you used to wear..."

"It's a wedding dress," she said.

His heart jumped with shock. Was she getting married? Was she that serious about someone?

She chuckled. "Don't worry. It's not mine. It's Serena's."

"You're making her wedding dress?"

She nodded.

"That's very generous of you."

She shook her head. "It's the least I can do, after what I put her through."

"She's already forgiven you," he assured her.

Tears glistened for a moment in her dark eyes until she blinked them back, and he realized she hadn't forgiven herself.

That was why he was so drawn to her; they had much more in common than he'd realized. They were the hardest on themselves. But she was hard on him, too. And she was also honest with him.

She stared at him for a long moment, a speculative look in her fathomless dark eyes. Their prolonged eye contact unnerved him, but it must have unnerved her as well, because she shivered. "Maybe I should be afraid of you," she murmured finally.

He shook his head. "Me? I'm harmless."

"You look like hell," she remarked. And she rose from the chair at the sewing table and walked around it to stand in front of him.

"You sweet-talker, you," he said. But he flinched when she lifted her hand to his cheek.

She wasn't reaching for the scar but for the scrape on the other side where his face had hit the sidewalk when he'd leaped out of danger. "Are you okay? What happened?"

He shrugged and grimaced. His shoulder and arm had hit the sidewalk, too. Fortunately, it wasn't his already bandaged arm. Or maybe it would have been better had it been—then he'd only have to wait for one arm to heal to go back to work. He had a feeling that Braden wasn't going to welcome him back to the job until whoever was after him was caught, though.

"What happened?" she asked again.

"I had a run-in with the sidewalk when someone tried running me down earlier."

She gasped. "Oh, my God! Are you okay? No wonder you look like hell!"

He nodded. "I'm just a little banged up. That's nothing new for me."

"Getting banged up?"

"That," he agreed. Then he released a ragged sigh and added, "And someone trying to kill me."

She drew in a breath sharply, and the hand she'd had on his face moved to her mouth, as if she was holding back another cry.

"Did you see who tried running you over?" she asked. "Did anyone get a license plate number?"

He shook his head. "Nope. No clue…"

Then she narrowed her eyes and stared at him. "Do you think it's me? Is that why you've been coming around here? You're trying to figure out if I'm guilty?"

Knowing that she would be furious if he admitted to even his fleeting suspicions about her, he kept his voice light as he teased, "No. I know you're guilty."

She jerked back.

"You're guilty of making me crazy," he said. "I don't know why I'm so drawn to you, but I am. Hell, I always was. Even in high school…"

She snorted now, derisively. Obviously she wasn't ready to believe that yet.

"There's something about you. Even as prickly as

you are with me, you give me comfort when I need it most," he admitted, his voice getting gruff with the emotions rushing through him. "And I need it most... I need you..." He lowered his head to hers and kissed her with everything he felt in that moment.

She pushed him back and gasped again—but this time it was for air. Once she had some, she pulled his head down, her hand on the back of his neck, and kissed him back.

They had so much desire between them. It was powerful, heating his skin and his blood.

Her skin was hot, too, her face flushed. And her hands left streaks of heat as they moved over him. Like the day before, she attacked the buttons of his shirt, opened it and spread her palms across his chest.

How did his scars not turn her off? Yesterday she'd kissed one. Today she ran her fingertips along them. His skin tingled—not from the scars but from her touch. Nobody had ever turned him on like she did.

She sucked his tongue into her mouth and nipped at it, kissing him so hungrily. And her hands moved down his chest to the button on his jeans.

He stepped back then. And now he was panting for breath and fighting for control. He wanted to take her right there—standing up. But he wanted her as ready as he was.

She must have taken his step back as resistance, because she smiled at him. "Don't be scared that I'm trying to trap you into marriage. I swear that wedding dress is Serena's."

He chuckled. "I know."

She was making her sister's wedding dress. She was a far more caring and considerate person than she appeared. More caring and considerate than she wanted

anyone to know. Did she act so tough for her own protection? Because she didn't want anyone to see her
vulnerability? Because she'd been hurt so much in her
past…

He flinched as he realized he was one of those people
who'd hurt her. He reached for her, swinging her up in
his arms. He wanted her so badly. So he carried her the
short distance to her bedroom. To her bed…

The sheets were still tangled from their lovemaking—
had she not gone back to bed after she'd left it? Had she
not been able to sleep like he hadn't?

He'd wanted to be back in this bed—with her. But
he'd known last night that he wouldn't have been welcome to return. He had a pretty good idea that she'd
changed her mind now—from the way she pushed his
shirt from his shoulders and tugged him down with her
as he laid her on those tangled sheets.

He planted his hands on the mattress, so his entire
weight didn't crush her. But she pushed on his shoulders
and rolled him to his side. She straddled him, grind-
ing her hips against the erection straining the fly of
his jeans.

He groaned and clenched her waist. But he didn't lift
her off. Instead he tugged up her lightweight sweater,
pulling it over her head before tossing it onto the floor
with his shirt. Then he undid her bra, which was clasped
between the cups. As it fell away, she shrugged the
straps from her shoulders.

She was so beautiful. Perfect face. Perfect body…

Something other than guilt struck him now, but it
wasn't just a twinge. It gripped his heart, making it
pound frantically.

She leaned down to kiss him, and her breasts brushed

against his chest. And she continued to rub against his groin.

She was driving him crazy. So damn crazy...

Before he lost control, he sat up and lifted her from him. Then he pushed down her pants. She arched against his hand, which he stroked over her mound. She was so hot, so ready for him.

Her fingers fumbled with the button on his jeans, undoing it before she jerked down the zipper. His erection strained against his boxers now. He lifted his hips from the bed and pushed his underwear down with his jeans. But before he tossed them aside, he pulled out a condom. He needed her. Now.

And she needed him just as badly. She arched and rubbed against him on his lap, moaning. He wanted her as crazy as she'd made him, so he leaned down and kissed her mouth, then her chin and her neck before moving his head lower. He closed his mouth over a taut nipple, teasing it with his tongue.

She cried out. But it wasn't with pain. She was panting with pleasure. Then she was pushing him onto his back again as she took the condom from his hand. She ripped the packet open and rolled the condom over him.

He nearly came then—he was so on the edge, the tension in his body nearly unbearable. She straddled him again and guided him inside her. Then she rode him—fast and hard like their beating hearts and their breathing.

Her body tensed, then quivered as she came. His name was a scream from her parted lips. He held on to his control for a little longer, thrusting up again and again until she reached another peak, one so high that she trembled with the power of her orgasm.

Then an orgasm ripped through him, and his body

shook with the power of it, his heart beating so fast that he thought he might die from the pleasure. It would be a hell of a way to go—a lot better than getting run down by a car.

Shaken from the power of the release, Courtney collapsed onto his chest—gasping for air. His chest rose and fell sharply with his own pants and the mad pounding of his heart. Once they could breathe again, he finally moved, rolling her to her side so he could get up and use the restroom. The minute he slipped away, panic assailed Courtney.

It was too much. Too intense. More intense than anything she'd felt before. He affected her as no one else ever had. He got to her—got inside her—and she didn't like it. She didn't like that he'd seen how she felt about Serena, that he'd seen her tears, her guilt, her heart...

She felt too vulnerable. She was too much like her mother, with faulty judgment when it came to men. Bradford could have ruined her life, and she hadn't felt anything for him like she felt for Owen already. And she knew because of that, she was going to get hurt, so hurt that it could be a pain she might not survive. That panic drove her to grab her robe and wrap it around herself—though she could barely tie the sash with how badly her hands were shaking. When she heard the faucet in the bathroom shut off, she grabbed up his clothes from the floor.

The minute he stepped—in all his naked glory— out of the bathroom, she thrust his bundle of clothes at him. "Get dressed."

His brow furrowed as he stared down at her. "Why?"

"So you can leave," she said, forcing her tone to sound patronizing, as if he was an idiot.

He grinned like one and asked again. "Why?"

"Despite what you claim your reasons for coming around here are..." And they'd been so sweet, so much like what she felt for him that her heart ached as she remembered his words, she couldn't accept them. After years of not being as good as Serena and not feeling good enough for anybody, she couldn't accept that he'd started coming around because he actually cared about her. "...I think you have suspicions about me being behind these attacks on you. And I don't want you to have to stay awake all night fearing for your safety." Even though she was the one who would probably lie awake the rest of the night. She wasn't afraid for her safety, though. She was afraid for her heart.

He chuckled. "I'm willing to take my chances."

She wasn't. She'd already taken enough of one having sex with him. But the feelings...

She wasn't going to risk developing those, although she had a suspicion of her own that it might be too late.

"I'll sleep with one eye open," he said, and he sounded as if he was joking.

Maybe he really didn't think she was capable of murder. But if he did—if he had...

She was so sick of everyone thinking the worst of her. That Serena was the good twin and she was the bad one. But for Owen to think it...

She shook her head and insisted, "You have to go." Now. Before she got used to him being in her bed, before she got used to being in his arms.

Finally, with a sigh, he reached for his clothes. She swallowed a sigh of her own—of disappointment—as he stepped into his boxers and pulled them up, over his already forming erection. "You're missing out," he told her.

She couldn't argue with him. She knew exactly what she was giving up—more pleasure. But pleasure with him would come with a price, one she wasn't willing to pay. So she forced herself to snort and reply, "And just what am I missing out on?"

She heard the challenge in her voice and knew what she was doing—daring him to show her exactly what. His body, his lovemaking skills...

But his reply was "Your chance to kill me in my sleep."

"I knew it," she said. "You do suspect me." She pointed toward the doorway. "Get out! Get the hell out!"

"I don't," he said. "I don't..."

"Anymore?" she asked.

He shook his head. "That's not what I was going to say."

"You said enough the other day," she reminded him. "At your house—when you threw me out."

He'd hurt her then, just like he'd hurt her in the past. She couldn't trust him. And she couldn't trust herself around him. Because the minute he'd looked so wounded when the widow had gone after him at the funeral, she'd gone after him—to comfort him. He got to her in a way nobody else ever had, and if he stayed, they would make love again. And again. And then she might begin to think she was actually falling in love with him.

That couldn't happen. This had to stop.

This had to stop. Owen James's luck was about to run out *now*. He'd escaped death too many times.

Maybe that was because those other deaths wouldn't have been as fitting as this one. A lighter flicked on, the flame tipped toward the pile of rags taken from the dumpster in the alley. They'd already smelled like furniture stripper. But a quart of mineral spirits had also been poured over them, saturating them so completely the chemical trailed across the hardwood floor.

The flame grew as it met the fumes from the rags. Then the cloth caught fire, too. A whoosh of air fanned the flames higher as they devoured the rags and began to lick up the sides of the refurbished display case.

Even with the disguise on, it was possible someone on Main Street might be able to see inside the store. Not the guy who'd also been following Owen, though.

He was out. Maybe he'd even drunk enough of the sedative, slipped surreptitiously into his cup of coffee at the diner, that he might never wake up again. But Trick McRooney was a big guy, so it was hard to determine how much it would have taken to kill him. He didn't need to die, though, not like Owen needed to die.

Unless he awoke to see something that he shouldn't. Somebody else might peer inside the store and notice the flames…and the person who'd set the blaze.

This would need to be done fast before a quick escape to the back alley. But not before a board was also nailed across that door to the shop…

Nobody would be getting out the back.

And with the fire in the middle of the store, between the staircase to the apartment and the front doors—there would be no escape for Owen James.

He was finally going to die.

Chapter 17

Braden tried the number again, but it went directly to voice mail. Where the hell was Trick? He was supposed to be keeping an eye on Owen. He cursed.

And Sam murmured and rolled over in bed. Her blond hair was mussed around her beautiful face. "What's going on?"

Something. Part of why Braden had become a firefighter was because he'd always had an uncanny sense about fires, like an instinct for knowing when one was about to start. After losing Dirk, and with Owen in danger, the last damn thing he needed right now was a fire.

His team wasn't even a team anymore. Owen was out until he was completely healed, and nobody had accepted Trick as a new member. Where the hell was Trick?

Sam pushed her hair off her face and sat up. "Braden, what is it?"

"I can't reach your brother," he admitted.

Her blue eyes widened, and she grabbed her cell from the side table. She punched in a number.

"You think he's just avoiding his new boss?" Braden asked. He was only half teasing. He was expecting a lot from Trick—maybe too much. Trick probably was more likely to answer his sister's call than his new boss's.

"If it was Mack, I wouldn't worry, but Trick always answers," she said. She cursed. "It went straight to voice mail."

"So he's not answering for you either," Braden remarked.

"Maybe he's with someone," Sam suggested, "and he can't talk now."

Braden nodded. "That's possible..."

"But you don't think that's the case," she said.

His wife knew him too well for him to try to downplay his concern, even though he didn't want to worry her either. This was her brother.

"I wouldn't have suggested Trick help out if I didn't think he could handle himself," she said. "He's fine."

But was she downplaying her concern now to try to make him feel better?

"It's not just Trick I'm worried about," he admitted.

"Of course. Owen is in danger—"

"That's it!" he exclaimed. "The fire—maybe it's about Owen..."

Sam sucked in a breath. "Oh, no, that's what woke you up." She knew about his sixth sense where fires were concerned. And she fully trusted it and him. She threw back the blankets and jumped out of bed.

Braden jumped up, too. He had to be ready. It was only a matter of time before they got the call...because somewhere in Northern Lakes, a fire had started.

* * *

Owen wanted to stay and not just to have sex again. He wanted to stay to hold Courtney—like he'd held her the night before. But she stood there all tense and…

Scared?

Was she scared of him?

Was she beginning to feel like him—too much?

She wasn't the one who'd been trying to kill him. He knew that. He had probably always known that, but he'd used his initial suspicion as an excuse to get closer to her. And even after making love with her, he wanted to be closer still. But when he stepped nearer, she stepped back.

"You need to leave," she maintained.

"You thought you heard someone in the house," he reminded her. "That's why I threw you out. I didn't want you in danger."

She narrowed her eyes. "You accused me of hitting you with that bat."

"I woke up to you standing over me with it," he reminded her.

"But then you said you'd fallen and hit your head on it."

He groaned. "I lied—"

"Get out!" she shouted. "I never should have brought you back here yesterday."

"Why did you?" he asked like he had then.

She glared at him now—like she used to back in school when he'd called her a freak or skunk. "Because I felt sorry for you."

He flinched as the comment struck him like a slap, and it wasn't just his pride that hurt. Angry with her, and with himself for screwing things up once again with her, he pulled on his jeans and dragged his shirt over his head. Then he dragged in a deep breath, and as he did, he inhaled a whiff of smoke. He was used to his clothes smelling like smoke—if he'd been around a fire. But he hadn't been near one in weeks. The wildfire season hadn't started yet, and there had been no other fires. Until now...

Something was burning. And it was close. Then he heard a rapid pounding sound. It reverberated up from the alley. What the hell was going on?

"Get dressed," he told her.

Her brow furrowed. "This is my place," she said. "And I'm not leaving."

"Yes, you are," he said, urgency coursing through him. He had to find the fire. But first he had to get her out. "Don't you smell the smoke?"

She sniffed, and her dark eyes widened as she nodded. She didn't argue now—just quickly got dressed. But when they rushed out of the bedroom, she didn't head toward the stairs; she turned back toward the other room where she'd been sewing.

"We need to get out of here," he said. "Now!"

But she protested, "Serena's wedding—"

He didn't give a damn about the dress. He cared only about getting her to safety. He swung her up in his arms and headed toward the stairs. The main floor glowed orange.

He'd found the fire. At least it wasn't at the bottom of the stairwell. They could make it to the back door. But when he turned toward it and grabbed the handle, the door didn't budge. He hadn't locked it behind him. It shouldn't be locked now—unless someone had come inside while they'd been upstairs; unless someone had started the fire and trapped them inside the building. That was probably the pounding sound he'd heard—something being hammered across the door. He turned toward the front of the store, which reflected back the flames from the fire burning in the middle of the space—near where she'd been working on the display case.

Courtney screamed and struggled in his arms. "Let me down!"

"I'll get us out," he assured her. But he wasn't sure exactly how...yet.

She wriggled loose from his grasp. But instead of pounding on the door, she headed back up the stairs.

He ran up after her and caught her shoulders. "We have to get out of here."

"Serena's dress," she screamed as she wrestled free of him and headed down the hall.

Smoke clouded the second story now, hanging heavily in the air. "Do you have an extinguisher?" Owen called out to her. But he didn't wait for her to reply; he pulled open the kitchen cabinets, looking for one.

Not that an extinguisher would put out that fire. It was already too big. An accelerant must have been used. But an extinguisher might beat down the flames enough that they could make it to the front door—because he didn't know if he could unblock the back door before the fire overtook them.

"Courtney!" he yelled. It wasn't safe in here—especially not with all the smoke. He headed down the hall where she'd gone. She was bundling that mass of lace and silk into a garment bag. "Courtney! Come on!"

She coughed and sputtered.

"It's just a dress," he said.

But she shook her head.

She had possessions in this place, stuff she'd worked hard on, but the only item she wanted to save was for her sister. He had seriously misjudged her. But not only that, he'd also endangered her.

That fire wasn't meant for her. It was meant for him.

"Come on!" he shouted at her.

She looked at him, tears streaming from her eyes. He didn't know if she was that scared, or if it was just the smoke burning her eyes like it was burning his. He blinked hard, too.

Too desperate to get her to safety to argue with her any longer, he lifted her and that damn dress into his arms. Grasping the extinguisher in one hand, he headed back to the stairwell. It was so thick with smoke now he could barely see the steps. He felt for each with his foot before putting his weight, and hers, on it. He didn't want to drop her—because he could see now that the fire had moved closer to the stairwell. It was moving too fast.

He had to get her out. There was no way he'd beat down the fire enough to get her to the front door. He turned and set her and the dress down onto one of the steps. Then he used the butt of the extinguisher against the back door. He beat at it until the wood splintered and finally the door broke open against whatever had been blocking it.

Then he lifted her and the dress from the stairs and carried her into the alley. "Call for help," he told her, as he thrust his cell phone at her. Then he turned, with the banged-up fire extinguisher, to head back into the store.

She grabbed at his arm. But he barely felt her grasp through the thick bandage wrapped around it. "Where are you going?"

"To put out the fire."

"With that?" she asked, her voice raspy from the smoke. She pulled on his arm. "You can't go back in there. It's too dangerous."

It would be if the fire raged out of control and spread to the adjacent buildings. "Call for help!" he yelled at her. Then he jerked free and headed back inside.

The last thing he heard was her screaming his name.

The fire was beginning to roar now as the flames consumed the building. Courtney screamed for Owen again. Maybe he hadn't heard her, but she suspected he had and was just ignoring her. Her hands shaking, she dropped the garment bag onto the ground and punched 911 into his phone. It might have been faster had she just run down the street to the firehouse. The dispatcher picked up on the second ring, and she gave the address for the fire. Then she clicked off and dialed another number. Serena's.

"Get Cody over to the store," she said. "It's on fire."

"Are you okay?" her sister asked, her voice full of alarm. "Oh, my God, he just got the call for it. It's the store, Cody!" she shouted at her fiancé. "It's the store." Then she turned her attention back to the phone. "Are you okay?"

"I'm fine," Courtney said. But she wouldn't be if Owen didn't come back out. "Owen got me out. But he went back inside." Her voice cracked with emotion. "Tell Cody to hurry!"

"He's already gone," Serena said.

How fast had he moved? She could hear the wail of the fire truck siren. They were coming. Help was coming.

But would they get here in time? Owen was still in there. Smoke billowed out the back door. Could he even see? Had he passed out?

She needed to go in—to try to help him. But as she neared the back door, the smoke billowing out of the building choked her. She coughed and sputtered for breath. Between coughs, she shouted his name. "Owen! Owen!"

He had to come out.

He had to...

But he didn't. She started toward the door again, fighting through the smoke that filled the alley now. Just as she was about to step through the back door, strong hands gripped her—pulling her away from it.

"You can't go in there."

She turned, hoping it was Owen—that he'd gone out the front. For a moment she couldn't tell who it was— with all the equipment on him.

"Cody!" With sudden recognition, she gripped his arms through his heavy yellow jacket. "Owen's in there!"

Without any of his safety equipment. All he had was the banged-up extinguisher. Had it even worked?

"You have to find him!" she implored her sister's fiancé.

Cody cursed. Then he thrust her away from the building. "Get out of the alley," he said. "I'll get Owen."

It was hard for her to trust anyone, but she trusted Cody. He would do his damnedest to find Owen. He was already heading inside, so she grabbed up the garment bag and ran from the alley.

Cody wasn't alone. Other firefighters were on the street at the front of the building. They hooked a big hose to a hydrant and turned it on the broken windows. Had the fire done that or had Owen, trying to get out?

She searched the area for him. But she saw only the guys in their yellow jackets, hats and heavy pants. Owen wore only his jeans and an unbuttoned shirt. He should not have gone back inside. Why the hell had he?

A scream burned the back of her throat, but she held

it there. Cody had gone inside; he would bring Owen out. He had to...

Just moments ago, she'd wanted to get rid of him, but not like this.

Never like this.

Before, she'd been scared of him getting too close, and that she would get too attached. Now she was scared that he might be gone. Forever...

Like in the alley, big hands grabbed her arms, turning her around. Like Cody's, these were in gloves. She stared for a moment into the face beneath the fire hat. Then she recognized the brown eyes, which were full of concern.

"Are you okay?" Braden Zimmer asked her, just like her sister had.

But she knew his concern wasn't just for her. He must have known what she'd told Serena. "Owen's inside."

He nodded. "Cody went after him."

"Did he find him?" That was all she wanted to know. Or had he been overcome from the smoke?

Braden shook his head. "I don't know."

The building wasn't that big; it shouldn't have taken Cody this long to find him. Finally, the radio dangling from the lapel of Braden's yellow jacket crackled as Cody's voice emanated from it. "I found him."

"Is he okay?" Courtney shouted the question before Braden could.

But Cody was still talking. "I'm bringing him out now."

I'm bringing him out. Not that he was coming out on his own. Owen must have needed help getting out. Maybe he wasn't able to even move himself. Maybe he'd passed out. Or worse...

She gasped.

Braden must have been thinking the same thing, because he asked, "Do you need help?"

"Is Dawson here yet? We need a paramedic," Cody responded, his voice either choked from the smoke or, since he'd been wearing a mask, more likely with concern.

Why the hell had Owen gone back inside? The fire had been too big already for him to take down with the extinguisher. It had been too big because of her— because she'd insisted on going back upstairs for the wedding dress.

If only she'd gone outside when they'd first come down the stairs...

Then the fire wouldn't have been so bad. And maybe he could have taken care of it himself. But he still shouldn't have tried. He shouldn't have risked his life for a damn store, and she shouldn't have risked hers for a dress. She could have made another.

It was just a dress.

Owen...

Owen wasn't just anything. He was everything.

She dropped the garment bag and clutched Braden's arm. "Where are they?" she asked. It seemed like hours since Cody's radio call, even though it had probably only been seconds.

Braden shook his head. He looked as worried as she was. He must have realized that they should have been out by now.

Saving Serena's dress had been a waste of time if her sister lost her fiancé. And even though Courtney didn't really have him, she didn't want to lose Owen either.

Where the hell were they?

Chapter 18

"What the hell were you thinking?" Dawson Hess asked as he leaned over Owen in the back of the paramedic van.

Owen pulled the oxygen mask away from his face and replied, "I was thinking I could put out the damn fire before it spread to the other buildings." And he'd hoped to save some of Courtney's hard work. But the display case was a burned-out skeleton of its original structure, and flames had charred all the wainscoting and the floors. He'd been too late, and his heart ached for her loss. His lungs also burned from all the smoke inhalation. He coughed some of it up.

Dawson slid the mask back over his nose and mouth. He inhaled a deep breath and coughed some more.

At least Courtney had saved the dress she was making for her sister. That seemed to have been her main concern.

But then she came around the side of the building and ran toward the paramedic rig parked at the mouth of the alley. She didn't stop until she reached him. Then she just stared at him, her dark eyes wide. "Are you okay?" As if she didn't think he could answer, she turned toward Dawson. "How badly is he hurt?"

His pride was burning the most—that he'd let a fire get set right under his damn nose and hadn't stopped it. Hadn't even been able to put it completely out...

"That concussion he had a couple days ago must have been bad enough that he thought he could put out that fire on his own," Dawson replied. "But other than an addled brain, he's going to be fine."

Owen wasn't sure that Dawson was completely telling her the truth. He didn't feel fine. But that probably had less to do with the smoke inhalation and more to do with how he'd doubted her. How could he have ever—even for a moment—suspected that she was capable of murder? It was clear to him now that her heart was nearly as big as, if not even bigger than, her sweet sister's.

He pulled off the mask to tell her, "I'm sorry...so sorry..."

"Why are you sorry?" she asked. "You did everything you could." She shuddered. "If you weren't there, I wouldn't have been able to get out of the building."

If he hadn't been there, the fire wouldn't have started. He cursed, then coughed.

Before Dawson could reach for the mask, she pulled it back over Owen's mouth and nose. "Take it easy," she told him. "Breathe in some fresh air."

Smoke billowed out of the alley and hung heavily around them. At least he'd contained the fire to her building, and the rest of the crew had arrived just in time, before it had gotten completely out of hand. The store was damaged, but the place wasn't a total loss.

If something had happened to her because of him...

He shuddered now, and he dragged off the mask to say, "You need to get away from here."

She glanced fearfully toward the building near them. "Did it spread?" she asked.

He shook his head. "The smoke... You should stay away from the smoke." He glanced at her empty hands. "Where's the dress?"

She looked down as if she hadn't realized she'd lost it. "I—I don't know..."

It wasn't inside; she'd made certain of that.

"You should find it," Owen said. "For Serena." He knew how much it meant for her to make that dress for her sister.

She shook her head, as if she didn't intend to leave him. She turned back to Dawson. "Is he really okay? He didn't get burned?"

Dawson had stuck an oxygen sensor on Owen's finger when Cody had first helped him from the building into the van. He glanced at the monitor. "He's going to be fine," he assured her. "His levels are going up. Blood pressure is good, too."

That surprised Owen. His heart had been beating overtime since he'd first shown up at her place—from making love with her to nearly losing her in the fire.

He pulled aside the mask to tell her himself. "I'm fine. You don't need to worry about me."

She nodded, then stepped back from the van. "I'll—I'll find Serena's dress."

Cody and Braden passed her on the street. They walked toward Owen as she walked away.

"You damn fool," his boss admonished him.

"He kept it from spreading to other structures," Cody said, defending Owen to their boss. Inside, Cody had been the one calling him a few choice names.

"What the hell happened?" Braden asked.

Thinking of what had happened had Owen's blood pressure and his temperature rising again with fury. He began to cough and had to put the mask over his face again, so he couldn't answer.

Cody gave his assessment instead. "Courtney's been working on the floors and walls and some furniture in there. Looked like the rags with the stripper on them caught fire near the display case."

Owen shook his head, then pulled the mask away. "No. The rags were gone when I got here tonight. She'd put them in the dumpster days ago. Everything was done…" And now she would have to start all over again. His stomach lurched, not from the smoke but with guilt and regret for so many things where Courtney was concerned.

"Then how the hell did the fire start?" Cody asked.

"Just like everything else that's happened the past few days," Owen said. "It wasn't an accident."

"I told you to stay away from her," Braden said. "You shouldn't have been trying to investigate her on your own. You're not a detective. Any evidence you collected wouldn't have been admissible in court anyway. And you were putting yourself in danger."

"What?" Courtney ducked out from between Braden and Cody. Their big bodies had hidden her approach.

"I—I…" he stammered and began to cough again— so much that he had to gulp in more oxygen.

She turned away from him as if she couldn't even look at him and focused on Braden. Of course, he was the one who'd been running his mouth.

Owen silently cursed him beneath the oxygen mask.

"What evidence are you talking about?" she demanded to know. She looked from Braden to Cody, who lowered his head. "Oh, my God, you thought it, too. I guessed that Owen suspected I had something to do with those accidents..." The color drained from her face as her eyes grew wider yet. "But they weren't accidents..." She looked back at the smoke billowing from the alley and her building. "This wasn't an accident either..." She shuddered. "Someone tried to kill us..."

No. Someone had tried to kill *him*. He wanted to tell her that—wanted to explain that while he'd initially doubted her, he'd been wrong. And he was sorry. So damn sorry...

But she turned away from him when another woman ran up—one who had the same face Courtney had. "Are you okay?" Serena asked as she pulled her sister into her arms.

Courtney clung to her twin. She wasn't okay—because of him. She was shaken and scared.

This was all his fault.

When he tried to stand up, tried to walk toward her, his legs wobbled a bit. Dawson grabbed his shoulder. "Take it easy."

He breathed deep of the oxygen. Yet it wasn't what he really needed. He needed Courtney. But he had a feeling he'd lost her as completely as if he'd lost her in the fire.

Courtney felt like such a fool, though she shouldn't have been surprised. She'd already noticed that Owen seemed suspicious of her, and he'd admitted that someone had been trying to hurt him, had run him over. But her? He'd really thought it had been her? He hadn't just been joking...

She'd known, when he'd brought her those flowers, that he had an agenda, but she'd let him get close anyway. Maybe she'd had a crush on him all those years ago, and finally being with him had allowed her to live out some old fantasy.

But it had been just a fantasy. Nothing about him— or the way he'd treated her—had been real. He'd only been getting close to her so that he could find evidence against her.

"What's the matter?" Serena asked as she gripped Courtney's shoulders and stared into her face under the illumination of the streetlamps. "Did you get burned?"

More than she knew...

But she dragged in a breath and shook her head. The action tickled her throat, and she coughed.

"Smoke inhalation," Serena said. "Dawson needs to look at you." She tried steering Courtney back toward the ambulance, but Courtney planted her feet and refused to budge.

"I'm fine," she insisted. Physically. Emotionally was another story. Why had she let him get to her? Why couldn't it have just been sex like Tammy had suggested?

Because Courtney and Tammy, despite all her brazen talk, didn't do just sex. No matter how tough Courtney wanted the rest of the world to believe she was, she was vulnerable and emotional. That was why she got so mad and held such grudges—because things affected her deeply.

Making love with Owen had affected her deeply. And he'd only been using her...

Tears stung her already irritated eyes, then began to slide down her cheeks. She hoped her sister would think it was just the smoke causing her eyes to water, like it had earlier.

But Serena sucked in a breath as if shocked. She hadn't often seen Courtney cry, even when they were little kids. "Don't worry about the store," she said. She must have thought that was what had upset Courtney. "Everybody in Northern Lakes will help you get it ready to open. It'll just be a little later than you planned."

"I'm not worried about the store," she said. In fact, the fire gave her the best excuse to not even open it at all. She would go home to New York now and back to concentrating only on designing. She'd been happy doing that, successful. She didn't need a store.

She didn't need Northern Lakes.

And she certainly didn't need Owen.

When Owen tried standing up from the back of the paramedic van, Braden caught his shoulders and held him down. "You're not going anywhere."

Not without a damn armed guard at his side.

Braden had nearly lost him too many times.

Owen shook his head. He was peering around Braden toward where the Beaumont sisters stood on the street.

Braden felt a pang of regret that she'd overheard him. He hadn't meant to hurt her feelings, but he wasn't entirely sure that she was innocent either. "She could have set that fire tonight," he maintained.

And what about Trick?

He'd found him in his vehicle when the engines had rolled up. Trick had been parked down the street within sight of the store. But he hadn't seen the fire start—because someone must have drugged his coffee, knocking him out.

When he'd come around, Trick had felt guilty and

worried that he'd fallen asleep. But Braden had a suspicion that something had been slipped into the coffee Trick had taken in a to-go cup from the diner earlier. Could that have been Courtney as well?

Maybe she'd noticed Trick following Owen and had wanted to make sure there were no witnesses to what she'd planned for him.

"There's no way she could have started that fire," Owen protested. "She was never out of my sight since I got here."

Braden narrowed his eyes and studied Owen's face. "Never?"

Owen's face, already red from the heat of the fire, turned a shade darker. "Just for a few minutes. Not long enough to retrieve the rags from the dumpster and set the fire before I noticed she'd left the room."

"She couldn't have done it," Cody said.

Braden wasn't surprised that he would defend his sister-in-law-to-be—especially within sight of his wife, who held her sister close now.

"She's worked too hard on that store, getting it ready, to do any damage to it herself," Cody added.

Owen nodded in agreement. "She might hate me." He snorted derisively at himself. "She most certainly hates me now. But she loved that store." His shoulders slumped with a new burden of guilt.

Clearly, he'd already felt responsible for Dirk's death. Now he blamed himself for this fire.

Braden had to agree with their assessment. As much as he wanted someone to blame for everything that had happened, he knew it wasn't Courtney Beaumont. But he needed to find out who the hell it was before someone else got hurt. He didn't give a damn about the store.

It could be rebuilt; people could not. He had nearly lost another team member tonight.

Hell, he could have lost two. For a moment earlier, when Trick didn't immediately awaken, Braden had thought that he might have. And when Cody hadn't come out the front door with Owen, he'd worried that neither of them might make it out.

"So if it's not Courtney, who the hell is it?" he wondered aloud.

Who the hell is so determined to kill Owen? And why...

Just because he was a Huron Hotshot? Was this not about Owen personally at all? Was he just being targeted because of *what* he was—not who he was?

Braden had to find out. He had to stop this killer from claiming another member of his team, from taking the life of another friend.

He felt a twinge of regret about Courtney again. But if it had been her, they would have been able to stop her. Without knowing who was after them, they weren't able to see the next attempt coming.

And Braden knew that there would be another attempt.

Chapter 19

She hated him. Owen felt her contempt the minute he stepped into the Filling Station. She sat in a booth at the back—with her sister, Cody and Tammy Ingles.

He wasn't alone either.

He hadn't been alone since the fire. Braden had made certain of that. Everywhere Owen went, he had a shadow following him. Like Dawson or Wyatt or Cody or Trick McRooney...

Owen couldn't help but wonder if having Trick protect him was a little like having the fox guard the henhouse. If Dirk hadn't died, there wouldn't have been a place for Trick on the team.

Hell, there *still* wasn't a place for him.

Owen wasn't even sure if there was a place for *him* right now. It had been a few days since the fire in the store, but Braden still wouldn't let him resume his duties, which made for long, boring days with too much time for Owen to think.

He'd screwed up. He never should have suspected Courtney even for a second, and knowing he was in danger, he never should have gotten anywhere close to her. Because in doing so, he'd put her in danger, too.

On the way to the Filling Station, he and Dawson had passed the boarded-up storefront of her building. She hadn't started repairs yet. He wondered if she would.

Or had she decided to give up on Northern Lakes again, like she had as a teenager?

He wanted to ask. He wanted to talk to her. But he knew the better thing for her—the safer thing for her—was for him to stay far away.

With the way she was looking at him, her brown eyes even darker with fury, it was probably safer for him, too. Because while she hadn't wanted him dead before, she probably did now—after figuring out that he had initially suspected her.

"I don't think it was a good idea for you to come here," Dawson remarked as the dark-haired man slid into the booth across from Owen.

Owen sighed. "I'm sick of lying low."

"Lying low has kept you alive these past few days," Dawson pointed out. "There have been no new attempts on your life."

"I've had no life for anyone to make an attempt on," he grumbled. Tension filled him and it wasn't because of the danger he was in—it was because of Courtney. Because he needed to be with her again...

But he'd shattered her trust. He'd hurt her. Again.

And he doubted she would let him close enough to hurt her again. Not that he wanted to hurt her. He wanted to make up for hurting her. He wanted to kiss away her pain. To hold her...

"There's a big difference between being bored and being dead," Dawson admonished him.

He knew that. He'd lost too many people during his deployments—and more recently, Dirk—to ever take life for granted. He knew all too well how quickly it could change, with an explosion, with a fire. Maybe that was why he hadn't tried to have a serious relationship in so long, because every time he'd started to care about someone, she'd left him. He'd known that Courtney was going to leave soon, but he'd let himself start to care about her, too. He sighed. "I know. I know..."

Dawson was a quiet guy. He didn't understand the need for conversation, for companionship. Even though Dawson was married now, he and his wife spent a lot of time apart, with her career as a news anchor having brought her to New York City. Until he'd started seeing Courtney, Owen hadn't seen the need for conversation and companionship either. He'd liked his alone time.

Now he hated it. Not that he'd ever really been alone. Wyatt, Dawson and Cody had stayed inside his house with him during their babysitting shifts. Trick was the only one who'd stayed outside in the US Forest Service truck. He must have realized that Owen didn't really trust him.

Hell, after all the attempts on his life, he would be crazy to really trust anyone. But, after being caught in that fire with her, he trusted Courtney completely. It was ironic that the only person he trusted now hated him the most.

Every time he looked toward the booth in the back, she was glaring at him. But he couldn't stop looking. She was so damn beautiful. He missed seeing her face.

Most of all, he missed being with her, touching her, kissing her...

His body ached with a tension that only she could release for him. He needed her.

But he couldn't be selfish again. He couldn't keep putting her or anyone else in danger. Most especially not her...

She'd already given him one second chance, after the jerk he'd been to her in high school. He doubted that she would give him another, after his suspicions and after he'd cost her the store she'd been working so hard to open. He sighed. "You're right. We should go."

But before either could move from the booth, a waitress set two mugs in front of them. "Courtesy of the man at the bar," she told them.

Owen turned to see Luke Garrison sitting on a stool nearby, nursing the last of his own drink. The man had been spending a lot of time at the Filling Station since his wife had left him. Although Owen didn't know from personal experience, from his team members he'd learned that being a Hotshot was hard on a marriage. Either the marriage ended or the Hotshot left the job to save the marriage.

That was why Owen had determined long ago to stay single. Some of his team members had recently taken the risk, though, and seemed to be doing well. If he'd found the right person, he might have been compelled to take the risk, too. But he'd never found the right person—the person who would see beyond his physical and emotional scars.

He glanced over at Courtney again. Had she really slept with him just out of pity? She didn't look too sympathetic right now.

Dawson was looking at Luke as he asked, "How do you think he's doing?"

"Not good," Owen said.

"Neither is Willow," Dawson remarked. Luke's soon-to-be ex-wife worked as a nurse at the hospital, so he and Dawson—as paramedics—often saw her. "I wonder what the hell happened between them."

The rumor mill had been going strong, with the usual excuses, ever since Luke had moved out of his house. Another woman. Another man.

Owen had no idea, and he wasn't the type to pry for information. He did, however, wave Luke over to thank him for the beer. He slid farther along the seat of the booth to make room for him.

But Luke shook his head. "I was just on my way out," he said as he pushed his overly long black hair back from his forehead. "Think I've been spending too much time in this place."

That was another rumor running around the mill of Northern Lakes—that his drinking had ended his marriage. But Owen knew Luke hadn't started spending time here until after his wife had thrown him out. They had once seemed so happy. Apparently, appearances could be damn deceiving.

So maybe Courtney's appearance of hating him wasn't real. Maybe she would give him another chance if he asked for one. Or begged for one.

Luke was the one who needed to be begging for that—especially now—with his wife. Before it was too late. Before he missed too much.

"How are you doing?" Owen asked him.

The other man shrugged.

"Do something about it," Dawson, who usually didn't say much, advised him. "Fight for her."

Luke shook his head. "It's too late…" And without another word, he headed toward the door.

"It is too late…" Owen murmured.

"He should still fight," Dawson said.

Owen nodded in agreement. "I was thinking about me…"

Dawson followed his gaze toward the booth where Courtney sat with her sister and Cody. Tammy had taken Luke's empty stool at the bar. "She might forgive you," Dawson said.

Hope burgeoned in Owen's aching heart.

"But it would be selfish on your part to ask for her forgiveness now," his friend continued.

And Owen knew he was right. He couldn't put her in danger again. "We have to find out whoever the hell is after me," he said.

Before it was too late for Owen, too. Before Courtney left Northern Lakes for good.

"I'm leaving," Courtney said.

"I'm done," Serena said as she pushed her half-full glass toward the center of the table. "I'll leave with you."

"No," Courtney said. "I'm not talking about the bar." Although, she intended to leave here, too. It was too hard sitting with him just a few yards away. It was too hard to feel him staring at her and not react. Her pulse quickened; her skin tingled. She wanted him even as she hated him.

He must hate her, too—how else could he have thought so little of her? How could he have thought she was a killer? That she would have hurt him or his friend?

"Are you talking about our house?" Serena asked. "I know it's a little crowded with Stanley and Annie."

Courtney shook her head. The sweet kid had tried to give up his bedroom to her, but she'd insisted on taking the couch. She knew, as a foster kid, he hadn't had a whole lot in his life that was his. And he'd never really had a home until Cody had brought him to live with him in Northern Lakes. So Courtney had not been about to take his room from him, especially when she was the one who was not going to stay. Northern Lakes was not her home—no matter how sweet and supportive everyone had been about the fire at the store.

Everyone but Owen.

He'd said nothing to her. Not a word since she'd learned the truth behind his reason for finally being nice to her. She'd been such a fool. That was why she couldn't stay here. Even if the rest of the town accepted her now, it didn't matter. She still felt like that outcast she'd been in high school—because of him.

"I'm talking about Northern Lakes," Courtney said. "I'm leaving."

Serena gasped. "But you have the store opening."

She shook her head. "That's not going to happen. Not now."

"Tammy's right now coordinating the Hotshots at the bar to help you repair the fire damage," Cody said. "They've all offered to help you fix it back up."

The fire had damaged more than the store. Her heart had been damaged, and it could not be repaired. She suspected Cody knew that. He'd been there when she'd overheard Braden's comments, and he hadn't really rushed to her defense. Apparently, he'd shared Owen's suspicions about her.

That hurt, but it was probably her own fault, for how she'd treated her sister. Apparently, there was some damage that could not be undone, some trust that could never be rebuilt. While Serena was sweet and forgiving, her fiancé was not. Or maybe he loved Serena too much to forgive anyone who'd hurt her.

Courtney was happy they'd found each other. And because Serena had him, she didn't need her twin back in her life—at least, not on a daily basis. They could be close from a distance. "The store was a bad idea," she said. "Moving back here was a bad idea."

"Because of Owen?" Cody asked. "Don't hold his doubts against him. He's been through hell the past week. He was right there when Dirk died."

She flinched, remembering the story he'd told her, about how it had happened. "I wasn't there. I had nothing to do with that or with anything else that happened to Owen." And it hurt, so much, for him to think that she had.

He'd thought so little of her in high school. Apparently, he thought even less of her now.

"You shared those doubts of his," she accused Cody. "You should be happy I'm leaving. You must hate having me under your roof!"

Serena's mouth fell open with shock. Courtney had kept all this to herself for the past few days, had just let Serena think she was upset about the store. She hadn't told her, or anyone else, about Owen's suspicions. It had hurt too much. She wasn't always the nicest person, but she was not a killer.

"I'm sorry," Cody said.

While she appreciated that he didn't lie to her, it hurt to have confirmation that he'd thought the worst of her, too.

"What are you talking about?" Serena asked, her brow furrowing with confusion.

"The only reason Owen was trying to get close to

me was to prove that I'd been trying to kill him," she explained, and she glanced across to find him staring at her again. She couldn't stand it anymore. She jumped up from the booth. Now that Tammy had left, she was on the end, so it was easy to slip out. "I better leave now, so I don't scare him."

Cody reached out and caught her arm. "He doesn't believe that anymore."

"Anymore," she scoffed.

"He hasn't for a while, and he feels really bad that he ever suspected you, even for a moment," Cody continued. "And so do I."

She shrugged off his hand. "Don't worry about it," she said. "And tell Owen not to worry either. He'll be safe since I'll be leaving Northern Lakes very soon."

If only that was true...

She wasn't the one who'd tried to hurt him. That person was still out there and would probably try again. Pain pressed hard on her heart at that horrible thought. She needed to leave the bar now. Despite Serena calling her name, she rushed toward the door. She loved her sister, but Serena couldn't say anything to make her feel better right now. Nobody could.

Cody almost hoped Serena would run after her sister. She was obviously torn, looking from him to the door. But maybe she'd decided to give Courtney time to cool off, because she stayed sitting. Although, she slid farther around the corner booth until she faced him fully.

"What have you been keeping from me?" his fiancée asked.

"It wasn't my choice," he said. "Braden doesn't want anyone to know." And, fortunately, the bar was so loud that it wasn't likely anyone overheard what Courtney had said.

"What?" she asked. "That everyone thinks my sister is a murderer? What the hell reason would she have for killing Dirk Brown? I don't think she's ever even met him."

"Not Dirk," Cody said. "Owen."

"You think she would try to kill Owen?"

"I—I…" He had had his doubts, and Serena knew him too well to miss that. "I'm sorry," he said, just as he had to Courtney. "Owen suspected her first. She's the only one he can think of who has a grudge against him."

Serena sighed. "I know he and a lot of other kids weren't very nice to her in high school. But even though she thought he was a jerk back then, I think she had a little bit of a crush on him, too."

"That's not how she's acted," Cody reminded her. "She blames him for your mother's death."

"She blames everyone and everything for that," Serena said. "Because she's hurting. Owen hurt her in high school with how he used to treat her." She shook her head. "And he's hurt her even more now."

But as they watched, Owen headed toward the door—following Courtney out. Now Cody was worried about both of them. It wasn't safe for anyone to be around Owen right now, not with his life in danger like it was. Whoever was trying to kill him could have killed Courtney, too, in that fire. As it was, she'd lost her store and whatever feelings she'd started having for Owen.

Was she about to lose more?

Chapter 20

Owen hadn't been able to hear what had been said at the corner booth. But he'd been able to see how upset Courtney was and how Cody had tried to stop her. Still, she'd raced out anyway.

Seeing her like that, in obvious distress, compelled him to follow her. Whatever her reason for being upset, it was his fault.

The damage to her store. The damage to her relationship with her future brother-in-law. The damage to her ego. Or had he hurt even more than that?

Had he hurt her heart?

He ached with regret for all the harm he'd caused her. The best thing he could do for her was to stay away. But instead of slowing as he pushed open the door to exit the Filling Station, he sped up. He was supposed to stay inside until Dawson got back from the restroom.

The door swung shut behind him as he hurried off

down the sidewalk. The bar was on a corner, so he wasn't sure which way she'd gone. To the right or to the left?

He looked to the right first, but she wasn't there. The sidewalk was empty. So he rushed off to the left. And there was she was...not far from the boarded-up front of her store. She stopped in front of it, and her shoulders shook as if she was crying.

His heart wrenched, as if somebody was physically pulling it out of his chest. He closed the distance between them and put his arms around her, holding her close.

She gripped his shoulders. "Let me go!"

"It's me," he said, hoping he hadn't frightened her in addition to everything else he'd done to her.

"I know," she said.

She must have seen him follow her. Or maybe she'd recognized his touch just like he would have recognized hers. He always physically reacted to her closeness, and he wanted nothing more than to hold her as close as they could get to each other. But she wouldn't let him...

He'd ruined everything they could have had—with his suspicions and with the way he'd treated her. "I'm sorry," he said. "So sorry. I never meant to hurt you now or back then. I am the idiot you've always thought I was."

She stiffened even more in his embrace before jerking loose from his hold. "You didn't think you could hurt me," she said. "You didn't think I had any feelings or conscience or..." Her voice cracked.

"I wasn't thinking at all," he admitted. And not just because he'd been in shock since the accident that had claimed Dirk's life. He couldn't think around her—all he could do was feel, so much attraction and desire and need. Even now, with as angry as she was with him, his body ached for hers.

"If I'd been thinking," he continued, "I would have realized I was just looking for an excuse to get close to you, to be near you."

She shook her head. "Don't!" she yelled at him. "Don't turn on your charm for me. I will never trust you again."

His stomach dropped as he accepted that she was probably telling the truth. And if she couldn't bring herself to trust him again, then she could never fall for him—like he'd begun to fall for her.

"I'm sorry," he said, and he wasn't just sorry that he'd hurt her. He was sorry that he'd hurt them and whatever chance they might have had for a relationship.

She shook her head. "I can't believe I felt sorry for you," she said.

He flinched. He hated pity. Since he'd come back to Northern Lakes with the scars, he'd had entirely too much of it.

"I thought the widow and your team weren't being nice to you, weren't supporting you through your loss..." Her voice cracked again.

And his heart cracked as well. She had reached out to him when barely anyone else had, and he'd returned her sympathy with suspicion.

"I'm sorry," he said again. It was all he could say.

She shook her head. "I'm sorry," she said. "I'm sorry I keep making bad choices." Her bottom lip quivered as if she was about to cry.

His heart ached even more, hurting so much he nearly clutched his chest. He hated seeing her like this—in so much pain—because of him.

"First I let that idiot I was dating talk me into suing

Serena so she would have to sell the boardinghouse," she murmured. "I only wanted her to stop killing herself like Mom did…"

"I thought you blamed me for that," he reminded her. "I thought you hated me for her dying."

"I hated myself for leaving her," she said. "I hated that I wasn't here when it happened. I hated that I took off and didn't help her like Serena did. That I was selfish and resentful and petty…"

She didn't blame him anymore. He should have felt lighter with some of that guilt he'd been carrying lifted from him. But he could see that she was carrying that guilt herself.

Tears pooled in her eyes, but she blinked furiously, seemingly trying to fight them back. "I've made so many mistakes," she murmured. "But you might have been one of the biggest…"

He couldn't accept that, couldn't accept that what they'd had, what they'd done, had been a mistake. But she wasn't the only one who'd said so. Other people had pointed out that his being near her had put her in danger, had cost her the store and nearly her life.

He knew that to keep her safe he should walk away. Hell, run away, so that she was nowhere near him—nowhere near the danger that had been plaguing him the past week.

It would have been one of the worst weeks of his life—losing Dirk, the accidents—if not for her. And because she'd done so much for him, he needed to do this for her. He needed to let her go.

So he turned around and began to walk away.

Courtney should have been relieved that he was going to leave her alone. That damn lawyer she'd dated hadn't let her go as easily. He'd tried to use his powers of persuasion and his legal arguments to convince her to give him another chance and another and another.

Owen wasn't even asking for a second one.

He was just letting her go. And all that proved to her was that he'd never really wanted her. He'd only wanted to prove her guilt.

And in doing that, he'd proved his. He was guilty of lying and taking advantage of her—of being a creep instead of the hero the rest of the town had always thought he was. When she'd said she would never trust him again, she hadn't been sure if she'd been telling the truth—until now. Now she knew that there was no way she could.

Fury bubbled up inside of her, and she let it loose. "You son of a bitch!" she cursed him. "You may have fooled this whole damn town, but you never fooled me."

She was lying. She was no smarter than anyone else; Owen had fooled her, too. He'd fooled her into thinking that he had been genuinely attracted to her. Instead he'd just been tricking her, so he could find evidence against her—according to his boss.

She continued, "You're not the golden-haired hero everyone thinks you are."

His hair was golden, though, and it shimmered under the streetlamps. He was so damn good-looking that it wasn't fair. Maybe that was why fate had given him that scar—to even the odds. It had only made him more handsome.

It really wasn't fair.

But life had rarely been fair to Courtney. She should have been used to it—should have been used to being on her own. She'd always felt safer that way. Because anytime she had ever let anyone close, they'd hurt her.

Just like Owen had…

He was hurting her now—because he wasn't arguing with her. He just kept walking. He wouldn't even turn around to face her.

A scream of frustration burned the back of her throat, and while she held that inside, she couldn't stop herself from following him. "What?" she taunted him. "Are you still afraid of me? Still think I'm the one trying to kill you?"

He stopped then, his entire body tense, but he only turned his head slightly to look back at her over one of his broad shoulders. "I probably wouldn't blame you if you were…"

She snorted. "How like you—to be so magnanimous," she scoffed. "So understanding…"

"I understand I hurt you," he said.

And that infuriated her more. "You didn't hurt me!" She was lying again—to protect her pride and her heart. "I would have had to care about you in order for you to hurt me, and I didn't care." Her voice sounded hollow and brittle even to her ears. But she continued, "It was just sex. That's all it was."

Sex like she'd never experienced before—with passion and pleasure of an intensity she'd never known, would have never thought existed. Until she'd felt it. With him…

Why had it had to be with him?

He turned fully toward her then, and his blue eyes narrowed. He studied her face, which the streetlamp overhead had probably illuminated like a spotlight. She stepped back, but the light seemed to follow her.

Or maybe that was the headlamps of a car. She faintly heard the rumble of an engine, but she ignored it. She was totally focused on him, just as he was totally focused on her.

"If it was just sex," he said, and a muscle twitched along his rigidly clenched jaw, "then why are you so mad at me?"

She released a breath but no words. She had no explanation.

He took a step toward her. "It was more than sex, Courtney," he said.

But then he turned away from her again, the car catching his attention as it started down the street. Its engine revved again, and its tires squealed as it headed straight toward them. Owen reached out, trying to shove her down.

And Courtney released the scream that had been burning the back of her throat. But it wasn't from anger anymore. It was from terror.

Owen hadn't escaped this time. The car had definitely hit something, and bodies had flown across the sidewalk. The driver had wanted to stop, had wanted to check to make damn certain he was dead this time. But somebody was running from the bar toward the scene.

The driver sped away, careening off the sidewalk and onto the street. The windows were tinted so dark nobody could see inside the vehicle—to see who was really driving it.

Nobody would know who had done this—who had killed Owen James and maybe Courtney Beaumont as well. It would be unfortunate if Courtney died. But it was her own fault for getting close to Owen James.

She'd professed to hate him. But if that was the case,

why had she been spending so much time with him? That had been a mistake—a mistake that had cost her the store she'd been opening and now, maybe, her life.

Chapter 21

Owen couldn't stop shaking, and it wasn't because the car had struck him. It was because Courtney had struck the concrete—so hard that she'd been knocked out.

And she hadn't regained consciousness yet.

"You need an MRI," Dawson told him. "You could have broken bones or another concussion."

He shook his head and continued to pace the ER waiting room. "I'm fine."

"You're not," Dawson said. "You're bleeding."

He looked at his hands, but the blood on them wasn't his. It was hers. Her head had been bleeding. What if her skull had cracked open? Or what if it hadn't? What if she had a subdural hematoma, with the swelling putting too much pressure on her brain?

"Owen, you need to be treated."

He shook his head again and began to resume his pacing. But Dawson caught him by the arm, and he flinched. His shoulder had already been bruised from when he'd struck the ground the first time that car had tried running him down.

"Did you see it?" he asked his teammate. "Did you get the plate number?"

Dawson shook his head. "No. I was just coming out of the bar when I saw the car jump the curb and plow into the two of you." He shuddered. "I thought you were dead."

Owen was fine, but he was worried about Courtney. She'd been so still—so lifeless—lying beneath him. He'd thought he'd done the right thing to protect her, jumping between her and the vehicle barreling toward them. But the car bumper had done less damage to him than the concrete had done to her.

He hadn't hit his head.

"Your leg is bleeding," Dawson continued. "It could be broken."

"I can stand," he pointed out. Hell, he could pace, and he needed to, with all the nervous energy coursing through him. And the anger.

He was nearly as angry with himself as he was with the driver of that car. He'd known he should have stayed away from Courtney—that his mere presence put her in danger. But when he'd seen her run out, so upset, he hadn't been able to stop himself from following her, from trying to comfort her...

He cursed. "This is all my fault."

"Yes, it is!" a female voice agreed.

He stopped pacing, and his heart lifted for a moment. The voice was so much like Courtney's, but it wasn't Courtney.

Serena had jumped up from where she'd been sitting with Cody in the waiting room. Angry, she sounded so much like her twin. "This *is* your fault!" she accused. "You kept putting her in danger. Over and over again..."

He couldn't argue with her. She was right.

"He didn't know that." Cody tried to defend Owen even as he wrapped his arm around his fiancée's shoulders.

She shrugged it off, as if she was angry with him, too. Maybe she was. "He didn't know someone was trying to kill him? He didn't know?"

He answered for himself, not wanting Cody to get in any more trouble with Serena. "Not at first." He'd thought the cable snapping had been an accident. But the brake line and the gas to the water heater...

And then the car...twice.

"I'm sorry, Serena," he said.

"You should be!" she said. "She felt sorry for you—for how everyone was treating you after Dirk's death, and she was being so nice to you. And you were never nice to her..."

He flinched.

"You don't deserve her forgiveness," Serena said. "You don't deserve her!"

He didn't. And Courtney wasn't likely to ever give him another chance. He'd screwed up too badly. "I'm sorry" was all he could murmur.

There was the sound of a voice clearing, and he turned to see that Luke's wife had joined them in the waiting room. "The doctor said I could come out and inform you..." The blond-haired nurse glanced around the room as if looking for someone else. Maybe her husband, or estranged husband...

But it was Owen and Serena who rushed forward.

"How is she?" Serena anxiously asked.

"Has she regained consciousness?" Owen asked. The

longer she was out, the more damage might have been done and the more damage could be done.

Willow smiled at him. "She's awake now. And she's asking for you."

Serena touched her chest. "Me?"

The nurse shook her head. "For Owen. She wants to make sure you're okay." Her gaze ran over him. "You don't look okay, though. You really need to let us check you out."

Probably. His leg and arm ached. But he figured they were just scraped and bruised. He could move everything without too much pain. "I'm fine."

"And my sister?" Serena asked. "How is she?"

The nurse smiled again. "She has a concussion, but she's going to be okay."

"Can I see her?" Serena asked.

"I'm only supposed to let one person back at a time right now…" She looked away from Serena to Owen and reminded him, "And you're who she wants to see."

He shook his head. His presence would only upset her more—or put her in danger. He had to stay away from Courtney because he cared too much about her to let anything happen to her again. "You go, Serena," he said.

She started forward, then stopped and turned back to him. "I'm sorry," she said. "I know you're not a bad guy, Owen. You're not like the last person Courtney dated. But you're just as bad for her as he was."

He flinched again.

"Maybe worse," she said. "Because at least he didn't nearly get her killed."

He closed his eyes as pain and regret overwhelmed him. When he opened them, she was gone—to see her sister. He ached to see Courtney, too, to make sure she was really all right.

"I'm sorry," Cody said. "Serena is just really scared. She lost Courtney for quite a few years when they rarely talked to each other. She doesn't want to lose her again."

Neither did he.

But Courtney had never really been his to begin with...

And now she never would be. The only way he could make up for suspecting her, for putting her in danger and costing her the store, was to find out who was really responsible for Dirk's death and his and Courtney's injuries.

He nodded and assured Cody, "I understand."

Then he turned toward Dawson, his assigned guard, who was obviously struggling with guilt over losing him at the bar. He hated to do this to him again. But he needed to think, and he couldn't do that with a shadow. "I think you're right," he lied. "I'm going to go back and get an MRI."

Dawson blew out a ragged sigh. "Good, good. I'll go with you."

"You can't go with me into Radiology," he said. "I'll be fine. I'll be right here—in the hospital." And he headed through the door the nurse must have taken Serena through to see her sister.

He wanted to see Courtney. But he didn't dare take the chance. He only had so much time to escape out the back of the ER before Dawson realized that Owen had ditched him again.

But as he pushed through a back door to the employee parking area, a pang of fear struck his heart. It was dangerous going out alone. Somebody was determined to kill him. But he had a better chance of surviving on his own than when he had to worry about someone else—somebody with him getting hurt, like Courtney had.

No. It was better—for everyone—that he go off alone. He just hoped that he could figure out who was after him before that person found him again.

Courtney's pulse quickened as she heard the footsteps approaching. She pushed herself against the pillows until she was sitting up on the bed. But when it wasn't Owen who stepped around the curtain, her shoulders sagged with disappointment.

Hadn't he wanted to come?

Hadn't he wanted to see her?

Or was he unable?

She looked at the nurse who stood beside her sister. "Is Owen hurt worse than you told me he was?" She closed her eyes, and her last lucid moments—before waking up in the ER—flashed through her mind. The car barreling toward them and Owen jumping between it and her, using his body as a shield. The car had to have hit him. And with as fast as it had been going...

The young woman shook her head. "He was pacing around the waiting room worrying about you, so he seems fine."

Then why hadn't he come back to see her?

"Where is he?" she asked.

Serena stepped closer, took Courtney's hand in hers and squeezed it. "Don't worry about Owen," she said.

And the sharpness in her usually serene voice caught Courtney's attention. She turned toward her twin, whose face was flushed.

"It's his fault you got hurt," she said, her voice rising with anger. "It's his fault you lost the store. It's his fault you want to leave Northern Lakes. Just forget about him!"

Courtney flinched at the volume of her sister's voice, and her head pounded. The nurse had given her something for the pain of the concussion and the stitches the doctor had had to put in on the back of her head. The drug either hadn't fully taken effect yet or hadn't taken away all her pain. She still had a dull throbbing in her skull. But like Serena's voice, it was sharper now.

"Shh, you need to be quiet," the nurse admonished Serena. "She has a concussion."

"I'm sorry!" Serena exclaimed, and her face flushed an even brighter shade of red. Then she lowered her voice to a whisper and said, "I'm sorry…"

The nurse nodded in acceptance of the apology and stepped out of the curtained area.

"I'm sorry," Serena said again. "I've just been so worried. When we followed Dawson out of the Filling Station and we saw you…" She shuddered. "I thought you were dead. I thought Owen had gotten you killed."

"It's not him," Courtney said. "He's not the one who drove that car over the curb and at us. He's the one who saved me from it. Just like he saved me from the fire."

Serena pointed at her head. "You're hurt. He didn't save you. And if you hadn't been with him, no car would have tried to run you over. Somebody was trying to kill him. Not you."

"That's not his fault," Courtney said. "You've known Owen a long time. You know how everyone feels about him…"

Everyone but her. Until recently, she was the only one who'd held a grudge against him, who'd accused him of not doing enough to save her mother. Maybe Dirk Brown's widow felt the same way now. Or maybe

Louanne had only been lashing out at the funeral because of her own pain and guilt—like Courtney had been.

Serena shrugged. "Maybe you were the one who was right about him all along. Maybe everyone else was wrong."

Courtney drew in a deep breath. This was probably going to hurt nearly as much as the car running her down, but she had to admit it. "I was wrong. Owen's done nothing to deserve what's happening to him. It doesn't make any sense."

"You're the one who's done nothing wrong," Serena said. "Except getting too close to him. And that was his fault. Even though Cody swears Owen only suspected you for a moment, he had no right to think you were capable of such violence."

Courtney released the breath she'd drawn in a ragged sigh. "I'm not. But I have made mistakes. I'm the only one who has said bad things about him, who hasn't treated him like the hero he is." And he *was* her hero. He'd saved her life more than once. "Where is he?" she asked anxiously. A twinge of pain struck her heart. She hated to think of him hurt and alone—like how he'd been at the widow's house.

Serena shrugged. "Probably still in the waiting room."

If he was waiting, maybe he cared about her. Maybe he cared about her as much as she cared about him. "Get him, please." She had to see him, had to make sure he was all right.

But even if he was okay now, he probably wouldn't stay that way. He was in too much danger. Someone was very determined to kill him, and if they weren't caught, eventually that person was going to succeed.

* * *

"He's gone?" Braden exclaimed. "What do you mean—he's gone?"

Dawson's face was pale with worry and guilt. "He said he was going to get checked out."

Instead he'd checked himself out—of the hospital— without letting anyone know where he was going. Where the hell could he have gone?

"What was he thinking?" Braden wondered aloud. "Why does he keep giving this damn maniac another chance to take him out?"

"Maniac?" a female voice asked.

He whirled around to find that Serena had joined them in the waiting room.

"I hope you're not talking about my sister," she said, her dark eyes sharp with anger.

He wasn't surprised that she knew about his and Owen's suspicions. Courtney must have told her what she'd overheard after the fire. "I'm sorry," he said. "Is your sister all right?"

Serena nodded. "They're releasing her. We just have to monitor her the next few days due to the severity of her concussion." She glared at him. "Surely now you know you were all wrong about her."

"Yes," Braden agreed. "She was just one possible suspect." There had been others. Trooper Martin Gingrich, for one. But Braden hadn't had any more luck finding evidence to implicate his old nemesis than Owen had his.

"All these accidents started happening around the time that Courtney came back to town," Cody added in their defense.

Serena suddenly tensed and whirled on her fiancé. "You didn't tell me that."

"At the bar," he said. "I was trying to explain why we suspected her."

"And as you were explaining, someone was trying to run down her and Owen outside."

Cody grimaced. "I'm sorry."

Everything was falling apart. His team. The relationships of his team members. Braden had to find out who the hell was responsible. Now.

Before anyone or anything else was harmed.

Serena looked hurt, probably because Cody had kept Braden's secrets for him. Then her mouth fell open, and she looked stunned.

"What is it?" Cody asked her, his voice gruff with concern. "What's the matter?"

"I know who it is," Serena said.

She had Braden's full attention now. "Who?"

"Courtney's ex," she said. "He's the lawyer who talked her into suing me over the boardinghouse."

Braden hadn't realized someone had talked Courtney into doing that. "Why did he do that?"

Serena shrugged. "Maybe for money, maybe just because he was trying to isolate her. He was creepy. Controlling. And even though she blocked his calls and texts, he tried getting to her through me."

"He did?" Cody asked. He took a protective step closer to his fiancée.

She shuddered. "I just thought he had such an over-inflated ego that it was hard for him to accept that anyone wouldn't want him."

But what if it was more…?

What if he'd been stalking Courtney?

"But why go after Owen?" Braden wondered.

"She did blame him for a while for Mom dying from

her heart attack," Serena said. "Maybe he thought hurting Owen would regain Courtney's favor."

"But she could have died in the fire," Braden said. "And the car nearly ran her over, too."

"If he's here in Northern Lakes, then he's been watching her," Serena pointed out. "Maybe he was enraged when he realized how close she's gotten to Owen."

If someone had been watching Courtney, they would have seen Owen hanging around. He'd been at her place, until later in the night, at least a couple of times. And one of those times, her place had been set ablaze.

That did seem like the act of a vengeful lover.

"We have to find Owen," Braden said with renewed urgency. He was out there alone, with no idea who was after him. Maybe it was already too late to save him.

Chapter 22

This was it...

Where it had happened. Where Dirk had died and where Owen could have as well.

Had that cable been meant to take out him?

Or had it all just been an accident?

Night had slipped away from Owen, dawn chasing the darkness from the woods. The site had been abandoned. Owen wasn't the only one who hadn't been working on the firebreak since Dirk's death. A yellow tape cordoned off the area, not allowing anyone inside, but he'd stepped easily over it—when he'd first arrived at the site.

Now, after having a look around, he struggled to lift his leg over it to walk back to the road. He was sore, every muscle aching. He definitely felt the effects of the vehicle striking him now.

How was Courtney? Was she sore, too? He wanted

to go see her. To make sure she was really going to be all right. But she wouldn't be, if she was near him, until the killer was put behind bars.

So before he could see Courtney, there was someone else he needed to see first. Owen had a feeling that he might have figured it out as he stood here, replaying through his mind every minute of that morning, every smell, every word. There had probably been so many attempts on his life so he wouldn't have time to figure it out. So he would be too preoccupied trying to stay alive to understand what had really happened.

He'd looked at the tree trunk again. That damn beast of a tree that had pinned Dirk to the ground. If they had been able to cut it up, they wouldn't have needed the cable to move it. But someone had sunk spikes deep into the trunk. No wonder it had chewed up so many chain saws.

Losing equipment was nothing in comparison to losing a life. To losing one of their own...

Poor Dirk.

Owen had been blaming himself because he'd been distracted that morning. But Dirk hadn't been himself either. He'd been unshaven and disheveled. He'd looked like he hadn't slept in days. Something had been bothering him—something he hadn't been willing to share with Owen.

But Owen knew whom he might have shared with... whom he might have told his concerns to...

Owen had to talk to that person now.

The only person he really wanted to talk to was Courtney. She'd regained consciousness. That was the important thing. And of course the hospital, and her sister, would keep a watchful eye on her.

Everyone would make sure that she stayed healthy

and safe. And to do the same, Owen had to stay away from her—until the person responsible for putting her in danger was put away…for life.

The painkillers must have worn off, because the dull throbbing was a sharp ache now, gripping Courtney's head. Maybe that wasn't entirely due to the concussion but rather what Serena was telling her.

"You think Bradford is behind the attempts on Owen's life?" she asked.

Now she understood why Cody had been so watchful when he'd driven them home. He'd kept looking in his rearview mirror as if he expected someone might be trying to follow them. But the only vehicle behind them had been Braden's truck. He and Dawson and the new Hotshot firefighter had followed them home. Why weren't they with Owen instead of her?

He was the one in danger.

But not from Bradford.

"That doesn't make sense," she told her sister.

"It does," Serena insisted. "He was obsessed with you, controlling, manipulative…"

"Yes," she wholeheartedly agreed. "That's why I dumped him."

"But a man like that—with an ego like his—doesn't take no for an answer," Serena said.

"You've watched too many of those crime news shows," Courtney said. "You think it's always the boyfriend or the spouse now."

She tensed with a sudden realization.

Serena settled onto the bed next to her. Stanley's bed. If she hadn't been so damn nauseous from the concussion, she would have refused to take it from him. But he'd insisted.

"Is it your head?" her sister asked with concern. "Is it hurting more?"

It wasn't hurting less. But the pain was the least of her concerns. "I'm fine. Where's Owen?"

Serena tensed now and closed her eyes.

"What?"

Serena shook her head. "Nobody knows."

"So why is everybody here?" Courtney asked. She was in Stanley's room, at his insistence, but she could hear all the male voices rumbling in the living room. "They should be out looking for him. He's the one in danger."

"If it's Bradford, though, Owen will be safer away from you," Serena pointed out.

Courtney nearly smiled at the irony of her sister's about-face. Earlier she'd been blaming Owen for putting her in danger. Now she believed the reverse was true. But Courtney knew—neither of them were at fault.

"Owen won't be safe until she's behind bars," she said.

"She?" Serena asked. Her brow furrowed as she stared at Courtney, maybe trying to gauge how much brain damage the concussion had done.

In order to get Serena and the others to listen, Courtney would have to lead her twin to the same conclusion she'd just drawn. "How come you didn't ask me what happened when you came to see me in the ER?"

Serena's eyes narrowed further as she studied Courtney's face. "Because I saw the car speeding away. I saw you guys on the sidewalk."

"But if you hadn't been there," Courtney continued, "if you just came to see me in the ER and you didn't know…what would have been your first question?"

"Are you okay?" Serena asked.

Courtney didn't know if she'd meant that as her first question or if she was asking that now because she thought her twin had lost her mind. "But once you knew that I was…or wasn't…okay. Then wouldn't you want to know what happened?"

"Of course," Serena replied. "I would want to know."

"Who didn't ask that?" Courtney prodded her.

Serena shook her head. "Everybody in the waiting room knew what had happened to you and Owen. Dawson was ahead of us and he must have told Braden."

"No. I'm not talking about last night." Courtney shook her head and nearly passed out at the wave of pain crashing through her skull. She gasped and leaned back against the pillows.

"You need to rest," Serena said, her voice cracking with concern. "This is too much for you."

The concern was too much. She grasped her sister's arm. "Get the others. Tell them it's her."

"Who?" Serena asked.

"Dirk's widow," Courtney said. She instinctively hadn't liked the woman and her overdramatic display of grief. But Courtney doubted she'd been overacting out of guilt—she'd been overacting to *cover up* her guilt.

"What?" Serena exclaimed. She stared at Courtney with something akin to fear.

She was definitely afraid that Courtney had brain damage. Courtney uttered a groan of frustration.

"I'm going to call the doctor," Serena said. "You're not doing well."

"You're not paying attention," Courtney said. And it could cost Owen his life. He would never suspect her, just as nobody else had. Unless he'd realized what Courtney just realized.

"I'm trying," Serena insisted. "But you're not making any sense."

"She never asked," Courtney reminded her. "She never asked what happened to him."

Serena gasped.

"Owen told her that her husband had died, and she never asked how," Courtney continued. "It wasn't like he'd gone out to battle an out-of-control wildfire. He'd left her that morning to work in the woods. Why didn't she ask what happened?"

Serena shook her head. But her eyes were wide now. She was beginning to understand.

"Because she already knew," Courtney said. "She'd set it up. She murdered her husband. And she must be trying to kill Owen because there was some clue at the scene. Or Dirk said something…" Her blood chilled as she remembered what it was, what Owen had told her. "Her name…"

Serena nodded now. "Dirk said her name. I thought it was sweet…"

"He was identifying his killer," Courtney insisted. "He had to be." The poor man had known—when it happened—who was responsible.

"Cody!" Serena yelled. And her fiancé pushed open the door as if he'd been standing outside it. "Courtney thinks she knows who's responsible."

"The lawyer," Cody said. "Dawson's wife is in New York. She's checking to see—"

"He's there," Courtney said. There was no way Bradford would leave New York—not even for her. His career meant more to him than anyone or anything else. "You need to know where Owen is and warn him that Dirk Brown's wife is the killer."

Cody stared at her like Serena had—like she'd lost her mind with the concussion.

But her sister backed her up. "I think she's right. I was there when Owen told her. And she never asked what happened to him."

Cody understood immediately and called out for his boss.

The pounding in Courtney's head increased, making her wince. But she didn't blame it on the concussion. She blamed it on her fear for Owen. She hoped they found him before it was too late.

Before the woman finally succeeded at killing him…

He'd survived again.

Louanne Brown knew it because he was walking up to her front door. What the hell was he doing here?

Had he finally figured it out—just as she'd feared he would? Or was he just here to check on her? To make sure she wasn't blaming him?

He was so used to the town's adoration that it was probably killing him that they'd turned on him. She smiled with satisfaction. At least she'd succeeded at that, crying to everyone everywhere that Dirk had died—that the Hotshot paramedic hadn't saved her poor husband. That she couldn't believe Owen hadn't noticed the faulty equipment…

She'd made him look guilty. But it hadn't been enough. She had to kill him, too, so he wouldn't realize what Dirk had really been telling him that day. His last word had been her name for a reason.

Because she had killed him…

And now she needed to kill again.

The doorbell rang. But before she headed to it, she

stopped at the bureau in the foyer and pulled out a gun. What could she make this look like?

It wouldn't pass as an accident.

Self-defense?

A suicide?

That would be good. Owen killed himself to make amends for Dirk's death. Out of guilt over it...

Everyone had seen how guilty he'd felt about Dirk dying. That was why it had been so easy to make him look responsible. That was why it would be easy to convince people he'd killed himself.

And if anyone brought up the car trying to hit him...

That would be explained when they found it parked in the Filling Station lot with blood on the front bumper. It was Luke Garrison's car, and everybody knew how much he'd been drinking since his wife had left him. They'd think he'd just been driving drunk.

She smiled as she opened the door, holding the gun behind it. "Hello, Owen..."

She'd hoped to catch him off guard, but it was clear from the look on his face that he knew. He wasn't looking at her with guilt or sympathy like he had the day he'd come to deliver the news of Dirk's death.

He was looking at her with suspicion and recrimination. But he had no proof. Just a man's dying words and maybe evidence that the cable had been torched, but no way to prove who'd torched it. And soon, he would have no life.

She pointed the gun at him. "Come on in," she said as she stepped back.

He stared down the barrel, and all the color drained from his handsome face.

"What did you think I was going to do?" she asked. "Give you a tearful confession? Let you take me to jail?

Why do you think I've been trying to kill you all this time? So you wouldn't figure it out."

"Too late," he said. "But I'm not the only one onto you…"

She laughed. "You've played cards in my house too many times with Dirk and the others. Just like all of them, I can tell when you're bluffing."

He'd come alone. So nobody else knew. And once he was dead, nobody would ever know. She moved her finger to the trigger.

Chapter 23

Braden pressed harder on the accelerator, pushing the truck to go faster. He couldn't be too late now—not when he'd finally learned the truth.

Instead of investigating Courtney, they should have had her lead the investigation. She'd figured it out. Once she'd told them about Louanne's reaction to the news of her husband's death, it had been easy to find the motive.

Wyatt's wife, a local life insurance agent, had checked with some underwriters and found a large policy Louanne had recently taken out on her husband. Fiona wouldn't insure firefighters, especially Hotshots, because she and the company she represented considered them too great a risk.

Other companies offered policies but with exorbitant premiums. Louanne had paid only a couple of months of that premium for the policy she'd purchased, with an accident rider that would double her payout now.

Dirk had had to die *accidentally*.

Maybe that was why she'd initially tried to kill Owen the same way. It hadn't worked as easily as it had with Dirk. So she'd used a car instead to finish him off.

Whose car, though? Had someone else been involved in her moneymaking plot?

Braden would worry about that later. Right now he had to get to her—before she got to Owen. But when he slowed to turn into her driveway, he saw Owen's car parked there.

He was already there.

Was he just checking up on her? Or had he figured it out like Courtney had?

It didn't matter; either way he was in danger. Louanne must have thought he'd seen something or that Dirk had told him something.

And maybe he had when, with his dying breath, he'd uttered her name. He'd known that his wife had killed him, and maybe he'd been trying to warn Owen.

Owen pointed at the gun. "You're not going to shoot me."

She could have pulled that trigger a few times over already, but she just stood there with her finger on it. He couldn't grab it—because he had no doubt she would shoot him if he tried.

And even if he didn't try, he had no doubt that she intended to shoot him rather than let him leave. She'd tried to kill him too many times already to have a change of heart.

Did she have a heart?

Courtney hadn't been comfortable with her grieving-widow act, and now Owen knew why. It had been just an act.

"You're no good at bluffing, Owen," she reminded him.

As she'd reminded him of all the times he'd been in this house, playing cards with the guys, watching games... He had never noticed any real emotion between the married couple. His parents hadn't been especially demonstrative either, so he hadn't thought anything of it at the time. But a couple of the other guys had shivered.

Louanne was cold. So why all the fake tears? To hide her guilt...

Hopefully someone else had figured it out, so that he hadn't come here to confront a killer without any backup.

What the hell had he been thinking?

He hadn't been. He'd intended just to check her garage for the car. But only a truck had been inside—along with an assortment of tools. Dirk had been a handy guy, with his own set of torches and welders and power tools.

Louanne must be handy, too, to know how to use that torch, to have meddled with the cable, and then later with Owen's truck and water heater.

"Why?" he asked. It was that question that had drawn him to her door, despite the fact that he hadn't initially intended to confront her. He'd wanted to know so badly what could compel someone to do what she had done.

She shrugged. "I don't know," she said. "You just have this inherent honesty about you that makes it impossible for you to pull off a lie."

"Not me," he said, shaking his head. "You—why did you do it?"

"Does it matter?" she asked, smirking. "You're going to die. Dirk can explain it to you in the afterlife, if he didn't before he died."

"Is that why you've been trying to kill me—because you think Dirk told me something?"

"He did," she insisted. "He said my name. And when you showed up here, telling me that, you had some of the fibers from the torched part of the cable stuck in your coat. You had the evidence that it wasn't an accident, and if I was going to collect double on that insurance policy, his death had to be ruled an accident."

"Insurance policy..." Owen murmured with sudden understanding. "You did all this for money?"

She shrugged, and that smirk twisted her mouth again. "There might have been other reasons..."

"But even if it was proved that it wasn't an accident, there isn't enough evidence to get you arrested, let alone convicted of his murder. So why go after me?"

She rolled her eyes. "If you figured out it wasn't an accident, there would be a police investigation that could have gotten people looking into things, like the fact that he was going to meet with a divorce lawyer this week and the life insurance policy and the affair..."

Owen narrowed his eyes and studied her face. "Affair? With who?" Had it been her or Dirk who'd had the affair? He usually ignored the town gossip, but he wished he'd listened now.

"I've already wasted enough time on you," she said. And she raised the gun toward his head. "It's past time to end this and put you out of my misery."

"You will go to prison for this," he warned her. "For my murder."

"Suicide," she said with a smile. "You're going to kill yourself."

He snorted. "And you think anybody's going to be stupid enough to buy that?"

"They bought Dirk's accident," she reminded him.

"You didn't stage that as well as you thought," he told her. "Braden and Cody—they know that someone messed with the cable."

She shook her head. "Nobody reported it to the police. Nobody official thinks it was anything but an accident," she insisted.

"Even if you get away with that," he said. "You won't get away with this. It's too sloppy. Nobody's going to believe that I came to your house to kill myself."

Her brows puckered together. "You've been feeling so guilty about Dirk. Everybody knows that."

"And everybody knows that I wouldn't put the poor grieving widow through any more pain. I would not kill myself in front of her." For once, he could use this whole "town hero" image to his advantage.

She pursed her lips now, as if mulling over what he'd said. And he knew she realized he was right.

"That damn good-guy reputation of yours," she murmured. "I've been working on tarnishing it this past week, but it wouldn't have worked at all if not for Courtney Beaumont paving the way for me. I can't believe she was stupid enough to get involved with you."

He wasn't sure why Courtney had either—because he wasn't always a good guy. At least, he hadn't been to Courtney. He had to survive this, so he could beg her forgiveness for the past and the present. Not that he expected her to give him another chance…

But he at least wanted to make sure that she didn't hate him. "If you're going to sell this whole suicide thing," he continued, "you're going to have to bring me to my house."

And hopefully someone would be there, looking for him. Braden had to be furious with him that he'd slipped away from Dawson again. Poor Dawson—he'd wind up blaming himself, just like Owen had blamed himself for Dirk's death.

But it hadn't been his fault. And it wouldn't be Dawson's either—because Owen was the one who'd gone off on his own. And then he'd come here…

"No," Louanne said, shaking her head. Her red hair tumbled around her shoulders. "Not your place…"

She was smart; that was how she'd nearly gotten away with the perfect crime. Hell, maybe she still would. He was the only one who knew the truth. And if she killed him, that might never be known.

He had to figure out some way to get that damn gun away from her. But he didn't dare reach for it, not with her finger resting on the trigger. He was certain to get shot if he tried anything.

"I know!" she exclaimed. "We'll go back to where Dirk died. You'll kill yourself there."

"With your gun?" he questioned. "You don't think that'll raise suspicions?"

Louanne glanced down at the Glock and chuckled. "It's not my gun."

"It's not mine." Owen had had enough of weapons during his years as a Marine. After seeing firsthand, and trying to repair, the damage the weapons had done, he'd wanted nothing to do with them again.

She shrugged. "People will just think you borrowed it." She shoved the barrel at him. "Now get moving…"

But when he neared the door, it was apparent that they were no longer alone. A dark shadow loomed behind the glass.

She cursed.

"Louanne," Braden called out. "We know the truth."

Owen would have breathed a sigh of relief. But he didn't believe it was over yet.

Louanne Brown wasn't going down without a fight.

"Duck!" he yelled, just as she pointed her gun toward the glass and fired at Braden. "Get down!"

The gunshots reverberated inside Courtney's head like the pain from her concussion. She cried out in fear. Had that bitch killed Owen?

His car was in the driveway, parked in front of Braden's truck. She'd insisted on Cody and Serena bringing her along. She'd threatened to drive herself if they wouldn't drive her.

When she reached for the door handle, Serena caught her arm and held her inside Cody's truck. "You can't go out there!"

"She's not going to shoot me," Courtney said.

"She's already tried to kill you," Serena reminded her. "She doesn't care who she hurts."

Which meant that she'd probably already hurt Owen. The man had endured so much in his life—with the Marines and then with Dirk's death.

He didn't deserve this.

"Check on him!" she yelled at Cody.

But when he reached for the door handle, Serena stopped him, too. "We need to wait for the police. Braden should have waited, too."

His truck was empty. He'd gone up to the house.

Maybe the widow had been shooting at him.

More shots rang out.

If she hadn't hit him before, she probably had just now. And Owen...

He'd already been inside the house with her—for who knew how long. She'd had plenty of time to kill him already.

Tears coursed down her face as pain spread throughout her chest. She felt like she'd taken one of those bullets straight to her heart, like it had pierced it—leaving her bleeding from the inside out.

While she'd never wanted to admit it, she had had a crush on Owen back in high school. She'd thought she'd outgrown her fascination with him long ago.

But this past week, when she'd witnessed his pain and his guilt, that crush had started coming back. Then he'd turned on the charm and they'd made love, and he'd made her feel things she'd never felt before.

She'd fallen for him.

She loved Owen James. And now she would never have the chance to tell him.

Chapter 24

"Why are you so damn hard to kill?" Louanne murmured as she stared up at Owen. He was leaning over her, trying to stop her bleeding. "Are you freaking invincible or something?"

"Or something," he remarked.

In this case he'd just been stronger than she was. When she'd shot at Braden, Owen had grabbed the gun. She'd kept firing as he'd wrested it away from her. Somehow she'd been hit, and he'd escaped unscathed.

Blood bubbled out of the wound in her abdomen. She was bleeding out internally. A bullet must have hit an artery. She would never make it to the hospital.

"It only took one try to kill Dirk," she murmured. "But then, he was never a lucky man."

No. He hadn't been—because he'd married someone as mercenary as she was.

"So when you put the spikes in the tree, it was just so

we'd have to use the logging truck and the winch?" he asked her, wanting all the details now. The spikes in that tree had been the reason for the cable in the first place.

She stared up at him, her eyes wide. "Spikes?" She shook her head in denial, but then her mouth fell open, blood trailing from it, and she gurgled out her last breath.

She kept staring at him. But he couldn't help her now. She was dead. Just as he reached down to close her lids, the door burst open behind him.

"Are you all right?" Braden asked.

Owen nodded. "What about you?"

Had he warned his boss in time?

She'd fired right through the glass.

Braden nodded, and shards of glass fell to the floor from his hair. "Yeah, you saved my life."

If only he'd been able to save Dirk's...

But he'd had no idea the other man was in danger. He had a feeling that Dirk had known, though—that he'd suspected she was up to something. That was probably why he'd looked so damn exhausted—too many nights of sleeping with at least one eye open to watch her.

Braden looked down at the widow's bloodied body. "Oh, my God..."

Owen sighed. "I fought her for the gun."

"In self-defense," Braden said. "And in defense of me. She could have killed us both."

She'd certainly wanted to.

"I know," he said. But he hated to lose a life—any life.

"It wasn't your fault," Braden insisted. "None of this was."

Hurting Courtney. That had been his fault, and he

didn't expect her to ever forgive him for it. Hell, he would never forgive himself for that.

He blew out a ragged breath. "I should have listened to you," he admitted. "I shouldn't have tried to investigate any of this on my own." Not only had he hurt Courtney, but he'd also almost gotten himself killed. "I'm damn lucky you showed up when you did."

If she hadn't fired that gun at Braden, he wasn't sure he would have ever had the chance to get it away from her.

Owen narrowed his eyes and studied his boss's face. "Why did you show up when you did?" Had the guy put a GPS on him or something?

"Courtney figured it out," Braden said.

He shouldn't have been surprised. Some of the comments she'd made about the widow were why he'd figured it out as well.

"You're alive," a voice murmured.

They both turned to where Cody stood in the doorway. He glanced down at Louanne lying on the floor. "Courtney was right."

Braden nodded. "Yes, she was. If she hadn't figured it out…"

"I owe her my life," Owen said. Because if Braden hadn't shown up when he had and distracted Louanne, he was pretty sure he was the one who would have taken a bullet.

"She's in the truck," Cody said. "If you want to thank her."

He glanced down at his bloodstained clothes. Some of the blood was Louanne's. Some of it was his. He had scrapes and bruises from the car hitting him. He didn't want to see Courtney like this. Didn't want to upset her any more than she'd already been upset…

He shook his head. "You should bring her home," he suggested. "Make sure she gets some rest." She'd been through so much because of him. She'd lost her store, all her hard work, and he knew he'd hurt at least her pride, maybe more, with his suspicions about her. Had she begun to care about him like he cared about her?

Hell, he more than cared about her. He loved her. But she was going to leave him just like the other people he'd cared about...

As sirens wailed and police cars pulled into the driveway, Owen knew he would get no rest for a while. There were going to be a lot of questions to answer.

He wasn't sure how helpful he would be when the only thing on his mind was Courtney. Would she stay in Northern Lakes...if he asked her to? Or was it too selfish of him to ask her to stay in a town she'd always hated?

"It's not her," Braden murmured as he stared down at the street from the windows of the conference room on the third floor.

"Of course it is. *Was*," Trick corrected himself. "She confessed to killing her husband."

Braden nodded.

"So I can leave," Trick said. "You don't need me here." And he obviously already had one foot out the door, with his duffel bag slung over his shoulder.

"She torched that cable to set in motion the 'accident' that killed her husband," Braden agreed. "But she didn't put the spikes in the tree. Owen asked her about that right before she died." Those spikes—which had made moving the tree in pieces impossible and had doomed Dirk just as surely as the cable had—were a separate act. Someone else had placed them there...

That had come out during the questioning with the irritated state police trooper. But then, Marty Gingrich was usually irritated with anything to do with the Hotshots. He could have still been the one responsible for those spikes, because he'd shrugged off the comment like Louanne had been lying.

Why confess to the killing and lie about the spikes? It didn't make sense. And the other incidents with equipment and Cody's brakes had happened before Louanne had even taken out that policy.

So it probably had more to do with that damn note...

Someone on his team wasn't who Braden thought they were. Dirk Brown had been exactly who Braden had thought he was—a hardworking, honest man who'd done nothing wrong but marry the wrong woman. Braden had done that once himself.

He'd gotten lucky the second time—with Trick's sister. "I need you to stay," he said. "I need you to help me figure this out before someone else gets hurt."

"Even if whoever is staging these little accidents isn't responsible for Dirk's death," Trick said, "they're not necessarily a killer."

"Yet," Braden agreed. "But it's only a matter of time before someone gets seriously hurt or worse. We have to stop them."

Trick nodded. "Okay, I'll stay."

Was Braden doing the right thing? As Trick had warned him, he was not an investigator. So was Braden only putting his brother-in-law in danger?

Courtney stood in the middle of the store, amazed at the transformation. Only a couple of weeks had passed since the fire, but it was as if it had never happened.

The wainscoting was painted creamy white again,

the wallpaper above it replaced with the exact same paisley pattern. There was even a display case that looked eerily similar to the one that had been destroyed.

Northern Lakes had done this for her. Not the town but the wonderful people who comprised it. Tammy had organized the work bees, and along with some contractors the insurance had paid for, all the Hotshots had worked on the repairs. Or so Courtney had been told. She hadn't come to the store as it was happening. She hadn't wanted to see Owen, because it was clear he hadn't wanted to see her.

His only interest in her must have been as a suspect—because now that he'd figured out who'd really been trying to kill him, he'd stayed away from her.

She should have been relieved, but her heart ached as much as her head had from the concussion.

She was healed now. No more headaches or nausea. And the stitches, under her hair in the back, were gone, too.

Just like the store, she looked as though nothing had happened. But she didn't feel the same—about anyone or anything.

She couldn't leave Northern Lakes—not now, not after everything the community had done for her. She had to stay, and not just for Serena. She had to stay for everyone—to show her appreciation.

And she *wanted* to stay, too…for Owen.

She loved him.

Yet it was just like high school and he didn't return her feelings. At least this time he wasn't dating the head cheerleader, so she might have a chance.

If she dared to take it…

But she'd risked her heart on him once and discovered he'd only been using her. She wasn't sure she could trust him enough to risk her heart again. She wasn't sure if she could trust him at all.

Something clattered overhead. And she jumped, startled. She'd thought everyone was gone, that all the work was complete. That was why she'd returned, to move back into her apartment above the store.

But someone was up there. She heard the heavy footfalls overhead. Had someone broken in?

It was Northern Lakes. She would have thought it was safe if someone hadn't tried burning down the store and running her over.

That person was dead now.

Louanne Brown couldn't hurt her or Owen anymore.

Maybe Tammy was upstairs, opening a bottle of wine to celebrate her return. Hopefully Serena would join them, too.

Courtney loved having her friend and her sister back in her life. Because she'd always been so busy with her career, she hadn't realized how lonely she'd been until she came home. And Northern Lakes was home.

She wasn't leaving ever again.

She headed for the stairwell, hauling up the overnight bag she'd wound up using for several overnights at her sister's. Stanley was probably thrilled to have his bed back.

And she couldn't wait to sleep in her own room tonight. Her only regret was that she would be sleeping in it alone.

No Owen.

But when she cleared the top of the stairs, there he was—standing in her kitchen. She'd been right about the open bottle of wine, and he was the one pouring it into glasses. In the middle of her small kitchen table sat a huge bouquet of roses.

As happy as she was to see Owen alive and looking so damn well, she couldn't run over to him. She couldn't just forgive him for the pain he'd caused her. "What are you doing here?" she asked stiffly.

And why hadn't he come sooner? Why hadn't he come to her hospital bed or the truck that day? Or stopped by Cody and Serena's house any of the days since? Why hadn't he cared enough to check on her?

Her eyes burned, tearing up, but she couldn't blame it on the smoke this time. Not even a hint of it was left in the air. These were tears of frustration. For so many years, she'd wanted his attention—had wanted him to care about her.

But it was never going to happen. The rest of the town had changed their opinion of her, yet she felt she would never be worthy of the town hero.

And she needed to finally accept that. To finally let go of her old schoolgirl fantasy.

"Courtney," he began.

But she held up a hand to stop his words.

"No..." She shook her head. "I don't care why you're here. I just want you gone."

"Courtney," he said again, his voice gruff with emotion, and he moved closer to her.

She used her hand to hold him back. She didn't dare let him touch her, or she would lose what little of her pride she had left.

"I just want you to leave," she reiterated. "Get out of here." Before she lost it and begged him to stay, begged him to care about her. To love her.

Chapter 25

Owen's heart ached more with each tear that slid down her face. "I am so sorry," he told her. "I don't know how to make it up to you for doubting you. I don't know how to ever earn your trust again."

She blinked then, as if trying to clear the tears from her eyes. But of course, she was proud. If she ever cried in public, it was probably rarely. And she wouldn't want him to think she was crying over him—not after how he'd treated her.

"I was such an idiot," he continued. "I was so damn stupid…" He didn't really know what else to say, how to remedy everything that had happened. He'd been a fool to think that a bottle of wine and another bouquet of roses would earn him another chance with her.

"Are you expecting me to argue with you?" she asked.

He shook his head. "Of course not. You're the one person who has always seen me for who I am."

She uttered a sigh then, a ragged-sounding one. "I don't know... I think I saw what I wanted to see...when we were teenagers and now."

"What do you want to see?" he asked. Because he would try to be whatever she wanted him to be.

"The worst," she said. "So then I wouldn't be disappointed that you were never interested in me."

He snorted.

And her face flushed.

"I was interested in you," he said. "That's why I always stared at you."

"You stared because you thought I was a freak."

"I stared because I thought you were beautiful and brave," he said. "You didn't care what people thought of you. And I admired that. I admired you... I still do."

She shook her head, and he didn't know if she was unwilling to trust him or if she didn't believe how wonderful she was.

So he continued, "You are so strong and determined. You've accomplished everything you said you would. You're a famous designer. Then you came back here, to this town you always hated, to rebuild your relationship with your sister, despite the town never accepting you, despite how they saw you after the lawsuit. That takes guts. That takes incredible courage. And love. You love your sister so much you were willing to do anything to save your relationship—even come back here. You're incredible. And even though I knew you hated me, I was drawn to you, drawn to your beauty, drawn to your drive..."

Her eyes widened with what appeared to be shock. And hope?

He had to convince her that he was telling the truth. "I think that's why I claimed to suspect you were the one behind the accidents," he said, "because I was looking for an excuse to get close to you."

She snorted now. "Suspecting someone of trying to kill you is not a good excuse to get close to them. Haven't you ever seen *Basic Instinct*?" she asked, and now there was a twinkle in her dark eyes.

She was teasing him.

He'd never loved her more.

But he knew that he could—if she gave him the chance. "What a way to go," he said with a lustful sigh.

And she laughed.

He stepped a little closer, and the hand she'd held up to ward him off settled against his chest. She didn't push him away. Instead her fingers fisted in the material of his shirt.

"I want to hate you," she said.

"I know."

"I want to think the worst of you," she continued.

"I know that, too." And he understood why. She was trying to protect herself, and his heart ached that she felt the need to protect herself from him.

"I don't deserve a second chance, but I'm here," he said. And now he dropped to his knees on the hardwood floor. Fortunately, the gashes on his legs from the car bumper had mostly healed, so he felt only a twinge of pain. "And I'm begging you for one."

"Why?" she asked him. "Why do you want one? Just for sex?"

He shook his head. "Not that I would withhold if you wanted that..."

Her lips curved into a bigger smile. And he knew

she wanted it. He had hope—hope that he could eventually convince her to give this a real try.

"Do you want that?" he asked her, and he stood up again.

Her dark eyes brightened, and he recognized the gleam of desire in them. "I want you," she admitted.

It was a start. That was all she'd offered him before— just sex. He would work to turn it into something more— into the same love he felt for her.

He stepped closer, leaned down and stayed that way for several moments, just savoring the closeness, the warmth of her body, of her breath against his lips. Only an inch separated their mouths; he could already taste her. But he held back...until she slid her hand to the nape of his neck and pulled his head down to hers.

Their mouths met, mated, with hungry kisses. It felt like it had been forever since he'd touched her last. His hands shook a little as he skimmed them down her back to her hips. She arched against him and moaned as his erection rubbed against her belly. He wanted her so badly—needed her so badly.

Yet he forced himself to pull back, and now his whole body shook. With tension, with desire, with his need for her. "Are you sure?" he asked.

He knew that he'd hurt her. Not just her pride but her heart, and that hurt him.

"I want you," she repeated.

It wasn't enough. But it was more than he probably deserved. So he lifted her up and carried her the short distance to her bedroom.

He'd managed to convince Tammy to let him work on this room alone. He'd painted and papered and purchased the new sheets and blankets. Everything was soft and silky...like her hair, like her skin...

He didn't lay her on the bed. Instead he let her body slide down his, groaning at her closeness, at her heat. He needed to bury himself inside her. But for him, this wasn't just about sex, and he wanted her to know that.

Before he could say anything, she tore at his clothes, pulling his shirt over his head before she unbuttoned and unzipped his jeans. He groaned again as she freed his erection and ran her hand up and down the length of it. And his knees shook so much they nearly gave way beneath him.

He caught her wrist and stilled her hand. "Slow down…"

"I thought this was what you wanted," she said, and her breath was coming fast, her eyes dilated with desire for him.

"This isn't the reason I want you to give me another chance," he told her.

"It's not?"

He shook his head. "No. I want another chance because I love you. And I'm going to use this chance to show you that I can earn your trust again and maybe, one day, your love."

Despite the fact that she was wearing all her clothes, a sweater and a long skirt, she shivered. He reached out to wrap his arms around her, to hold her close.

She planted her palms against his chest again. His heart leaped beneath her touch. And she smiled, as if she'd felt it. Then she looked up at him through her thick black lashes, and he could see the doubt in her eyes.

The doubt he'd put there because of the doubts he'd had about her.

"I'm sorry," he said. "I'm sorry I was such an idiot."

Her lips curved into a smile. "I'm glad you were."

"You are?"

"Yes, because now you don't seem so perfect any-more…like everybody thought you were."

"Everybody but you," he reminded her. "But then, I was an ass to you. I was hardly perfect then, and any-body who thought I was changed their mind once this happened." He moved one of his hands from her back to the scar on his cheek.

She pushed his fingers aside and ran hers along the ridge of his scar. "This makes you perfect, shows your courage and your commitment."

He shivered now, but he wasn't cold. His flesh was burning up with need for her. "I am committed," he said, "to you, Courtney. To us…if you'll give me an-other chance…" He drew in a deep breath, bracing him-self for her reaction.

After what he'd done, he couldn't expect another chance. He could only hope…

Courtney felt like she had when that car had jumped the curb and mowed them down on the sidewalk. She felt like she'd been knocked off her feet and barreled over.

"Why?" she asked.

His brows furrowed together and then he smiled. "Because I love you."

"Why?" she asked again. "That's what I want to know. Why do you love *me*?" She knew why she loved him—for the same reasons the town adored him. "Why me?"

And his brow furrowed even more, as if he didn't understand what she was asking.

"I'm not Serena," she said. "Everybody loves Se-rena. She's sweet and caring and generous. I'm none of those things."

"You're all of those things," he said. "You just hide your sensitivity because you're afraid of being vulnerable and of getting hurt. But you're the one who hurts yourself the most. You blame yourself for things that you have no control over, like your mother dying..."

She gasped with a sudden surge of guilt.

He shook his head. "It wouldn't have mattered if you'd stayed here, if you'd helped her with the boardinghouse. She had an undiagnosed heart condition. She could have died in her sleep. It wasn't your fault."

And for the first time since it had happened, Courtney fully accepted that, fully believed it, and she let the guilt go.

But she didn't feel relief. She felt fear; it coursed through her with the realization of how well he knew her, that he saw what no one else but her sister and Tammy saw in her.

"You are so caring that when I was at one of my lowest points, you reached out to me when no one else did," he said. "Even though you hated me."

"I never hated you," she said.

"You didn't like me very much," he said.

She sighed. "I didn't then."

"But that's changed?" he asked, and his blue eyes brightened with hope. "You like me now?"

"You saved my life a couple of times," she reminded him, and he'd put himself in danger to protect her.

He stepped closer. "You just *like* me?"

Her chest ached with the mad pounding of her heart, with the love inside it trying to burst out. But for her to say the words...

For her to give that much trust to him, it was so hard. Yet all the things he'd said...

Tears stung her eyes, and she blinked them back. "If only I really believed how you feel about me..."

"Why is it so hard to believe that I love you?" He touched her cheek now, then slid his fingertips along her jaw. "You're beautiful and smart and funny. You make me laugh. You challenge me. You infuriate me."

"Sounds like love," she mused. And to her, it did. He really loved her, and that love buoyed her heart, filling and lifting it like helium in a balloon. "I love you for all those same reasons. I love your humor. And I love how you insist on taking responsibility even for the things you shouldn't. And I love how much you care about people and how hard you try to help everyone."

"And my body?" he asked. "Do you love that?" He sounded as if he was teasing.

But she wondered. "I love your body," she said. And she leaned forward to press her lips against his chest and then his shoulder. "I love your face..."

"Scars and all?" he asked.

And she heard the same vulnerability she'd felt with him. "I love you, scars and all," she assured him. And she rose up on tiptoe to press her lips to the scar on his cheek.

His breath shuddered out in a ragged sigh. Then he turned his head, and his lips met hers. He kissed her hungrily.

She was hungry, too—for his kiss, for his touch.

He pulled off her clothes just as quickly as she'd discarded his. Her sweater dropped to the floor. Her skirt pooled around her feet. And her bra and panties disappeared into the mound of discarded clothes.

His jeans dropped, along with his boxers, until nothing separated skin from skin.

He lifted her again and put her on the bed. The sheets

were silky beneath her bare back. "Mmm...nice... Remind me to thank Tammy."

"I picked these out," he said, his voice gruff with passion.

"You are perfect," she said with a sigh of pleasure. But it was nothing compared to the pleasure he brought her moments later.

He made love to her with his hands and his mouth and his tongue. She squirmed and shifted against those sheets as euphoria flowed through her. As she came, she cried out his name. But it wasn't enough; she needed him inside her, filling the hollow ache she'd had for so long.

He tore open a condom packet, and she rolled it on him. He gritted his teeth and he groaned. "I need you so badly."

He eased inside her, and a long sigh escaped his lips. "I'm home," he murmured.

That was how it felt to her, too.

Like they weren't two people anymore, like they were one—an entity, and that entity was home. She arched up, meeting his thrusts, clinging to him.

The tension built inside her again, twisting tighter and tighter until she cried out with a powerful release, her body shuddering in ecstasy.

He tensed and then joined her, his body shaking as he uttered her name with such awe, with such wonder. Then he lifted himself from the bed and slipped away.

She suddenly felt cold and alone and wondered if she'd just dreamed what had happened. It wasn't possible. Was it? Did Owen James really just proclaim his love to her?

In moments he was back. He wound his arm around her and pulled her tightly against his side. And he stared down at her with such a caring look on his handsome face, with such love glowing in the depths of his blue eyes, that she could not doubt how he felt about her.

He genuinely loved her.

And she loved him.

"You're not going to kick me out tonight?" he asked.

"No," she said as she settled against his chest. "I'm never going to kick you out."

He released a shuddery sigh of relief. "That's good," he said. "I wouldn't go anyways. But it's good to know you want me to stay." He leaned down and kissed her. "Because there's no place I would rather be…than with you."

"You'll have to go sometimes," she said. "You know… like when there's a fire or an emergency…"

He nodded. "True. I have been cleared to return to work now."

The wound on his arm had turned into another scar. She shivered as she stared down at it.

"Are you okay with that?" he asked. "With my job? I know it's dangerous."

She'd once thought her sister crazy for falling for a firefighter, but she realized now that there were far greater perils than fire.

"You were in the most danger when you weren't even working," she reminded him. "Since you survived all those attempts on your life, I trust you to survive fires and emergencies and whatever else comes our way."

"I trust *us* to survive," he agreed. But his brow creased, as if something was still bothering him.

"What is it?" she asked.

He shrugged. "Just a feeling…"

"About?"

"That something's still going on," he said. "Something with the team..."

"Maybe it's just because it's changed," she said. "With Dirk gone and Trick replacing him."

"Maybe," he agreed. Then he sighed again and leaned down and pressed his lips to hers. "It doesn't matter. Nothing matters but that you love me."

"I do," she said.

And he grinned. "I like the sound of those words on your lips..."

She had a feeling that she would be saying them someday soon—because a love like theirs was strong enough to survive anything. It was going to last. They were going to last.

* * * * *

If you loved Hotshot Hero Under Fire,
*be sure to read the first four books in
Lisa Childs's Hotshot Heroes series!*

Available from Harlequin Blaze

Red Hot
Hot Attraction
Hot Seduction
Hot Pursuit

*And watch for the next book in this
steamy and suspenseful series!
Coming soon from Harlequin Romantic Suspense.*

"You think this is a joke? I wonder how many pieces of you I can cut away before you stop laughing."

On the counter lay a scalpel. Darcy picked it up. The handle was still stained with Gretchen's lifeblood. Chloe went cold as she realized that she'd pushed too hard for information.

Knife in hand, Darcy slowly, slowly approached the bed. Chloe pressed her back into the pillow, trying in vain to get distance from the killer and the knife. It did no good. Darcy pressed Chloe's shackled hand onto the railing and drew the blade across her palm. The metal was cold against her skin. She tried to jerk her hand away, but it was no use.

Darcy drove the blade into Chloe's flesh.

The cut burned, and for a moment, her vision filled with red. Then a seam opened in her hand. Blood began to weep from the wound. She balled her hand into a fist as her palm throbbed, and anger flooded her veins.

Chloe might've been handcuffed to a bed, but that didn't mean that she couldn't fight back.

"Damn you straight to hell," she growled.

With her free hand, Chloe pushed Darcy's chin back. At the same moment, she lifted her feet, kicking the killer in the chest. Darcy stumbled back before tumbling to the ground. Had Chloe been free, she would have had the advantage.

But shackled to the bed? Chloe had done nothing more than enrage a dangerous person.

Standing, Darcy brushed a loose strand of hair from her face. She smiled, then scoffed before echoing Chloe's words. "Damn me to hell? Hell doesn't frighten me, Chloe. Nothing does—especially not you."

Don't miss
The Agent's Deadly Liaison *by Jennifer D. Bokal,*
available July 2022 wherever
Harlequin Romantic Suspense books and
ebooks are sold.

Harlequin.com

HRSEXP0522

Love Harlequin romance?

DISCOVER.
Be the first to find out about promotions, news and exclusive content!

f Facebook.com/HarlequinBooks

𝕏 Twitter.com/HarlequinBooks

◎ Instagram.com/HarlequinBooks

𝓟 Pinterest.com/HarlequinBooks

You Tube YouTube.com/HarlequinBooks

ReaderService.com

EXPLORE.
Sign up for the Harlequin e-newsletter and download a free book from any series at
TryHarlequin.com

CONNECT.
Join our Harlequin community to share your thoughts and connect with other romance readers!
Facebook.com/groups/HarlequinConnection

HARLEQUIN